THE EXPERIENCE

Tim Bragg

Sycamore Dystopia

ISBN 978-1-8381963-4-9

Art: Jake Fern

Sycamore Dystopia

email: sycamoredystopia@gmail.com

To: Annie & Harvey and Friends & Family Everywhere

Special thanks to: HJRB, MF [Thanks Mike for your timely early input.] TG [Thanks Tom for your medical knowledge and input.]

From the same author

Non-Fiction

Lyrics to Live By: Keys to Self-Help - Notes for a Better Life

LYRICS TO LIVE BY 2: Further Reflections, Meditations & Life Lessons

Fiction

Short-Stories

HEAD - And Other Dark Tales

Novels

The Mirror

The White Rooms

Biting Tongues

The English Dragon

OAK

Poetry

A Conversation of Trees

Author Biography

Tim Bragg is a novelist and short-story writer. Occasionally he writes nonsense verse, more often poetry and from time to time articles on various topics. He is also a musician and singer-songwriter. Tim plays various instruments, including: drums, flute, guitar, bass, keyboard, percussion and the EWI (electronic wind instrument). He has recorded many albums and you can find his work online.

Tim studied English & American Literature at Warwick University.

Author's contact email: timbraggnovels@gmail.com

Author's note: The use of both the past and present tense is a decision based upon adding immediacy, especially surrounding dialogue. Also, the juxtaposition of these tenses helps reflect the examination of the nature of time and reality within the novel.

The things you think about determine the quality of your mind. Your soul takes on the colour of your thoughts - Marcus Aurelius

Conception

It was as if they were all being swept along by a forceful current; they could see the banks either side, they could even see beyond them but they remained helpless. Some could only wave their lives goodbye. He fought hard against the incessant flow until he was too weak, done in, at which point he simply let himself be carried away. Carried fast. Him and a thousand others.

Time is something like a current. You can't see it but it carries you away. You can see a river's flow, for sure, but only because of the fixed banks. If you couldn't see anything in the water to disturb it – and it was so vast – like a wave-less ocean – would you even know both you and it were moving? Or getting older? When the water squeezes tight and hits the rapids you feel your life speeding up – at times invigorating, exciting, breathtaking. At other moments you feel like you're in a chute getting unceremoniously deposited into some weed-smelling, dark dank pool. With not even enough strength to haul yourself out. Maybe that's when you know your time is up. In his case it wasn't still water, of course, but an eddy. He just never imagined his time would ever really come. Round and round and round...until?

They were putting on their very best cheerful act. Maybe it wouldn't be so bad. Maybe it would be exhilarating, like the rapids. Besides he had another year. Nothing would change. Both their children were doing well, that was something. He'd received messages from them – wishing him luck. One had added humour, as usual, the other was more sensitive, as usual. His wife acted as if it were simply another day. A cheerful day. Which technically it was or could be. The day after his birthday.

She says, 'You're nervous.'

'No, not really,' he lies. She smiles, because she knows he's lying.

Arriving outside the offices of Portway, he took a look around. Sometimes he felt it hard to have that sense of belonging to the world that he guessed he should have had. Everything was recognisable yet alien. The transport they'd arrived in disappeared. The area was busy. It was a low-fly zone so he could see the corporate markings of the drones. He was suddenly struck by how young everyone looked. Even his wife.

He felt young inside, like the boy he'd been in the countryside. He could remember the smell of grass and feel it tickling his feet as they'd run barefoot. Stopping to look out across the rolling hills. Unaware of time and his place within it. All of them feeling free.

Inside the building's perimeter, past the guards and monitoring cameras, they were met by a pleasant woman who checked his identification – would there be any fraud? Would anyone want to be admitted there? He smiled at the thought.

'No smiling please,' the woman orders, not unkindly.

Eyes and even his fingerprints are checked. He thought the latter was passé. But he was who they think he was. Of course. Everyone could relax. His wife was also checked. She was younger and so much more comfortable with these things. Still resentful, he was antagonised by authority even when it was doing him some good. Reflecting on that, he didn't smile.

They were ushered into a room – no waiting. Portway's building looked grandiose from the outside, belonging to a different era, inside everything was modern and clean. The modern interior betraying its past. The room they entered though threw his senses. It was somewhat old-worldly in decor, reflecting the exterior. There were leather-looking chairs with a huge wooden table. Paintings of rustic landscapes contrasted the white walls. His jaw must actually have dropped. His wife looked at him. There was a couch too which he felt like curling up on. They were told to sit. The leather-looking chairs they sat on were a slight disappointment. His wife held his hand but he immediately disengaged. The doctor looked younger than his wife, but then looks were deceptive.

'Mr Holden,' the doctor begins. 'Shall I call you James?'

'No one calls me James,' he says nervously, unnecessarily aggressively.

'Everyone calls him Jim,' his wife says reassuringly. The doctor looks at them both. Jim can see an old-fashioned faded globe behind the doctor and to his right. This captures Jim's attention.

'Let's get straight to it, shall we?' the doctor says enthusiastically. Jim's wife nods. Jim is reminded of being at his first school and feeling dissociated from the classroom and the other children. The doctor is his teacher. 'Jim,' he smiles, 'today we'll take you through the procedure, the formal steps. I understand you might be a little nervous...' Jim shakes his head. The doctor smiles unconvincingly. 'This is an important time in your life. And a blessing.'

It's easy for him to say this. It *is* an important time – but it doesn't feel like a blessing. Who's being blessed?

'I'll talk you through some of the history, though I imagine you've done plenty of research?' His wife smiles. Jim knows it will be her time one day, is she treating this like a run through? He hasn't done much research, it was as if doing that would magic forth the inevitable. But sooner. They have insurance.

'You have insurance,' the doctor states on cue.

'Yes,' his wife confirms. Jim wonders how the doctor thinks they could have Portway's services if they hadn't got insurance.

Again the doctor seems to get what he's thinking. 'You've chosen the best place here,' he smiles reassuringly. Jim sees his wife's wide, bright smile. When it's her turn she won't be smiling. It will come quickly.

'Have you been to any preliminary seminars?' the doctor asks.

Jim looks down. 'Not my thing,' he says.

Again his wife butts in, 'He's quite a creative man,' she explains. 'We've had discussions...'

'I don't want to sit round a table with a whole load of dead-men-talking.'

The doctor eyes him and continues, 'Way back in the early part of this century, and indeed into the last century, headsets had been developed with ever increasing skill and technology.' Jim observes the doctor's enthusiasm. 'With cameras they were able to simulate a 3D space and then later came a movable floor so that the user could move around freely. Eye-tracking devices made it all seem quite believable in its own way.' The doctor's eyes looking up slightly to his left as if recalling a memory. But he was too young. 'I like all the history,' he muses. 'Now we have state of the art technology, the very best to ensure your new life is simply perfect.' His eyes dart down. 'As perfect as we can make it.' There's a pause as he regards his information screen, which Jim finds quite old-fashioned and feels a little more comfortable. 'Well I can see that you've invested your money wisely, Jim.' Jim nods. 'And Mrs Holden...' He uses polite, older terminology. Is he trained to be sympathetic to older souls? 'You hold a very good, high position. An excellent work record. I can see no problems.' To Jim he says, 'Heart in perfect condition. Lungs, liver, blood samples – all fine. You're fit and healthy.'

Jim looks at him, wants to say, 'In which case why is all this necessary?' Answering himself inwardly, 'It just is, Jim.'

'The insurance company has been in touch and you have high levels of credit worthiness, as would be expected. And as you know, we will require rather a large initial payment. I presume you've seen the figures?' Jim looks at his wife. She's lost her smile slightly. He's in her hands. Simple. The doctor carries on, 'We'll take a look at the 'resting accommodation' and I'll also show you some of our latest technology. The surgery will be invasive,' he stresses, 'but once done, you'll soon forget it's there. It'll hardly be noticeable and done as late as possible.'

Jim touches the back of his neck. How late, he wonders. For the most part he's ignored these kinds of details - but some you can't.

'Forgive me,' the doctor continues, 'I haven't offered you both something to drink. Perhaps a herbal tea or one of the new range of coffees. They're very good.' They nod. The coffee's expensive. Jim needs a kick too and this new range everyone's on about gives a strong one. They'd had to cut down a little on even the smallest of luxuries.

They sipped away as they signed the forms with a fountain pen. It had been some time since using any kind of pen – but it could only be done in this fashion for absolute authenticity. Again Jim smiled – despite everything, when it came to money, it seemed they were happy to step back in time. Of course everything was registered by cameras, put straight into the computer and whisked up into the clouds. Jim wondered if they were heavenly. As he thought this he had an ache. An old lingering ache. The doctor seemed to look slightly nervous for the first time – perhaps he had to answer to people higher up. Everything having to be just right. As one, Jim and his wife hurriedly finished their drinks.

'I think it's time to check out the facilities,' the doctor says quickly. His eyes move to the screen. They wait. The doctor stands up, they follow suit, and he ushers them to the door. Another woman hovers just outside. The doctor says something to her, she turns and walks away. 'Right,' he says, 'follow me...please.'

Heading down a number of corridors, they then exited through glass doors and found themselves outside in a pleasant looking garden. Jim looked at his wife and saw her surprise. They followed a path which went through regimental trees, as if standing to their attention. At the end of this path there were wrought iron gates which opened automatically.

The doctor said nothing but smiled as he hurried them along. Jim's wife held his hand and this time he didn't disengage from her grip.

In front they could see a rather spectacular building. Modern, light, glass and wood. A man, a guard possibly, was standing at the entrance. The doctor smiled at him, they exchanged glances and maybe some words and then they were allowed inside. There was an aromatic smell that Jim didn't quite recognise. He could see his wife could also smell it. Sometimes it felt as if they were joined at the hip – but not always. The doctor asked them to wait and disappeared into one of the rooms off the corridor.

'Are you okay?' his wife asks.

He can only smile and say, 'Yes,' weakly.

Jim imagined himself entering the building in a year's time. Not nine months gestation, a whole year. Was a year a long time? It was all relative. If he could hate his life for the next twelve months then time would drag. It all seemed surreal.

The doctor returned and again directed them along.

'We'll start with the main control room,' he says.

The corridor and rooms became busier as they passed some open doors. Jim had a feeling come over him, a cold shiver, he wanted to turn and run and smash his way past the guard and escape back into the garden. Hide behind the trees, like he might have done as a child. His heart beat fast. It felt like he was seeing an old-fashioned hearse arriving at his childhood home, but he wasn't sure who was inside.

'Here we are,' the doctor says, relieved.

There was plenty of glass so they could see inside the control room. It was pregnant with technology. Jim laughed at the thought. His wife shot him a glance. As they stepped inside he noticed the young men and women monitoring screens. These screens were divided in what seemed like sections.

'Right,' the doctor says again. 'Here we are, the epicenter, the control room, well one of them. These are our safe hands,' gesturing towards the nearest of the young men and women. 'They are, well, I joke about this,' he says, 'they're like your surrogate parents.' He seems satisfied with his humour. 'These are the men and women who monitor your health while...well while you're having the time of your life...we hope.' How would he know? Jim remains mute. 'Your brain scan here,' the doctor says pointing to one of the screens, 'your heartbeat, pulse, the flow of blood, cleaned regularly. The input and output of the body taken care of.'

'I feel like an output,' Jim whispers to his wife.

'In effect,' the doctor continues, 'these are your guardian angels, protecting and caring for you.' Jim didn't have the doctor down as a God-fearing man – a doctor of all people. Jim's so-called parents, these younger folks, had now become angels. 'Just my little joke,' the doctor says. Again Jim gets the impression the doctor knows what's running through his mind.

'Any questions?' the doctor asks. Jim's wife looks at the doctor then back at Jim. 'Any questions for...' he again gestures to one of the nearest 'angels'. 'I'm sure they'd be only too pleased...' Jim looks at his wife as if to say, 'What on earth could I ask them?'

'Right,' the doctor says after a pause. Jim half-smiles. 'Let's hop along to the resting place.' Jim actually hopped a few times behind him, much to his wife's annoyance. One of the young men saw him and smiled. Jim thought it nice that these 'guardian angels' had a sense of humour. His life would be safe in their hands. He hoped. Trusted.

The doctor turns to them as they head down a wide corridor, 'We use the very highest quality chemicals – we like to call them Heaven's Sugar, or Heavenly Sugar,' he smiles, 'but they are specially chosen and carefully mixed where and when necessary. I can go over these details if you wish.' They walk on. Jim can hear their shoes tapping on the corridor's floor. 'I'll send you all the details, of course. The chemicals, that sounds so harsh for what are, in fact, so very beautiful,' he pauses, 'work on the brain's 5-HT2 receptors. The incision we create goes to the *raphe nuclei* in the brain stem – so straight into the central nervous system. Your serotonin levels are excited and maintained.' Jim can see how animated the doctor has become. He obviously loves his work. Maybe he feels like a god. 'New nanotechnology ensures the brain is flooded with information directly from your own personalised computer control. Your experience will be unique,' he says energetically. 'I'm afraid I'm not allowed to take you into the computer-information rooms. We have to be very careful about their sensitive nature. I'm sure you understand.' He continues, 'This combination of chemicals and the new nanobots means we have to be very hush-hush and somewhat secretive.' He opens a door and they are presented with a very different looking corridor, which has its own entrance. There is a path leading between the buildings, separating them. The doctor notices Jim looking. 'That way leads to more gardens.' Jim sees the path disappear, then looks directly ahead, noticing a number of lights flashing. Above the large doors of this entrance it says: 'The Gateway'.

Holding them back for a moment, the doctor looks into an eye scanner – situated between the two corridors. Whatever is communicated allows them to proceed through the doorway.

'We take care of everything,' he says, 'you'll see.'

The light appeared blue and there was low music being played. To their right and left there were what looked like drawers of opaque glass stacked high. Jim was reminded of an old morgue. But more aesthetic. This corridor had a high ceiling and above him as he pulled his head back he could see glass windows letting in some light and part of a pale blue sky. The sky added a gentle tone to the artificial light. Each stacked drawer had its own lights of varying colours – either flashing rhythmically or remaining static.

'This is not a Garden of Rest,' the doctor proclaims, 'it's not a mausoleum, it is, rather, a place of infinite repose for the body. But not the mind.' He waits for their reaction. Jim looks at his wife, she is concentrating on the doctor's face. Is she looking for 'tells'? The doctor draws in breath, 'This is where you will find freedom and adventure. This is where you will truly begin to live... Life after life, within life.'

Jim thinks him phony as he says this and butts in, 'If we have the money.' His wife shoots him a glance but the doctor smiles. 'It's true isn't it?' Jim proclaims. 'More money, better experience.'

'It is true,' the doctor affirms. 'You are correct Jim. But isn't that what life is? Life experience? We pay for everything that lifts us from the mundanity of the beasts,' he says. Jim feels his wife relaxing. 'Everything we have or do, costs in some manner. Would you agree Jim?' Jim can't be bothered to argue or put forward another view of what it is 'to live'. Besides these Portway people, perhaps this doctor, will have his life in the palms of their hands. Or at the end of a fingertip. Or in the frozen stare of an eye. He has to moderate himself. He is at once disengaged and yet held in the grip of this experience.

'Can you tell us a little about what happens here?' his wife asks. Jim senses her tone as if they are going to have a long cold discussion later. The doctor smiles, glances at him. Then focuses on his wife. 'I can show you,' he says. Walking to one of the drawers he places his hand on the glass. The opaqueness dissolves into visual clarity. 'This is where the client rests,' he begins, bringing Jim into his general gaze. 'The client is kept at an even temperature, is fed and made comfortable. The body is suspended,' he explains, 'this is a little device I had a hand in creating many years ago. Take a look, please.' Jim's wife moves closer and peers in. Doesn't she feel she's being invasive – or is the body effectively a corpse? 'Come over,' she motions. Reluctantly he joins her and looks in. From the glass of the drawer they can see the client's feet. The body appears to float – it is covered by a small light-blue sheet and Jim can see pipes leading into it, disappearing beneath. The body is face up so he can't see the back of its neck. But he can see it is intubated. Instinctively he rubs his neck and swallows. Surely the doctor would have asked permission for them to see the body?

'It's like a live grave,' Jim says. He can sense the doctor's displeasure. Again he thinks about potentially being in his hands, quickly adding, 'Does the client move?'

The doctor's happier. 'That part of the brain which is deactivated when we sleep and are in REM is permanently switched off. The patient can breathe or rather is assisted in breathing – there's very little brainwave activity, which is surprising,' he adds, 'and the heart, assisted or otherwise, is kept at a steady, low pulse. If you recall the screen from earlier on...'

'They're in suspended animation,' his wife says. Then adds, 'Will we be able to visit? Could I visit, when...?'

'It's not encouraged,' the doctor interrupts, 'but we will keep you closely informed on the client's, Jim's, well-being. We can send live, validated film should you require. The walls surrounding the body, the client, are effectively a bank of cameras and additional monitors.'

'And when we die?' Jim asks.

'In the last five years we haven't had a single client die,' the doctor says heartily. Reading Jim's mind, he adds, 'But should that be the case then the client is removed and the wishes of the family carried out.'

'A termination...of contract,' Jim says. The doctor smiles. His wife scowls. This is serious business, life and death. His life, his death. Why was he behaving this way? Rationalising his response, Jim thinks he is distancing himself from the reality. He needs to ask something smart. 'Do patients ever come round, wake up?'

The doctor shakes his head emphatically. 'Impossible,' he says, warily. 'But the body is stimulated from time to time so that it's kept flexible and we can also control nail and hair growth. The surrounding liquid takes care of most muscle wastage and clots.'

'Do the clients dream?' Jim asks. As he says this Jim can see the doctor is impressed. 'Great question, Jim. No we don't think the clients dream. How could they when they are actively in another world? Why would they? You see a body in this drawer and you can imagine all the bodies in each of all the drawers, but what's important is the mind. And the mind is freed, as I said earlier. It is in a bespoke existence transcending anything we could find in this world. The mind is *truly* freed. We can only imagine the world it lives in. A world devoid of stress and fear. A world without money,' the doctor eyes him. 'The world of the client is unique to his or hers,' now eyeing Jim's wife, 'choice and design. That's the great part about it all,' he's back in his stride. 'You create your experience. You create what happens. It's all down to you,' the doctor says, fixing Jim with his eyes turned large and bright, pupils dilated.

'There is an REM state. You mentioned that.'

'Correct,' the doctor replies. 'You've been paying attention. And we also have an NREM state.' But says no more, except, 'During sleep, cells in the brain shrink, temporarily allowing drainage tubes to expand and get rid of toxins in the lymphatic system. The brain must sleep. We believe there is a correspondence between sleep in the future existence and the physical brain.'

'You believe,' Jim says. 'And no dreams…'

'There's a lot to think about,' his wife interrupts. Jim smiles. He wants to say, 'As long as the money rolls in.' But keeps quiet. He has a lot of questions but doesn't think the doctor will take either them, or him seriously. He's going to be a floating semi-stiff left in a world of his own choosing. But he'll be as close to death, abstraction, loneliness as you can get. Won't he? He'll be in a solipsistic universe within a universe...Jim smiled inwardly again. But it would be an adventure! Easy for them to say, they weren't coming to the age. The prescribed moment they must all face for the good of all. The Great Sacrifice. Give him strength. And he almost said 'God'. They'd screwed up the world, good and proper.

Back in the office there was more to discuss and for the details of Jim's further visits to be settled. He would need trained facilitators to help him become accustomed to his ordained fate; a team to help him design his world; others to help him pass from this world into the next. And integrate his family into this slow death-life and help them come to terms with that. He wouldn't be 'around' – or in their lives at the very least. As good as dead? Jim would not become a grandfather. Couldn't they have added a communicator for the family to call him up once in a while – introduce him to any grandchildren? Bring him around and back into real life once in a while? Or give him a panic button if he regained consciousness. And why was it all necessary, why couldn't he just live out his life peacefully somewhere? There must be wild places left. He wouldn't say a thing. He'd be happy with nothing but his life. He'd betray society and probably everyone he knew to have that chance.

As they parted and the financial arrangements were put into motion, they shook the doctor's hand as if travelling back fifty years. Jim felt the doctor held his wife's hand longer than necessary. They walked out of his office with its antique globe and were soon once again at the entrance of that grand old building. His wife looked at him kindly, perhaps reality was sinking in. He had a year, well 364 days, maybe a few more. It wouldn't even be a leap year.

'Can we celebrate your birthday now?' she asks.

He nods and says, 'It's a funny thing isn't it?'

'What?' she asks.

'This experience,' he says solemnly. And because they'd been together so long, she understood exactly what he meant. She held his hand - an almost dead man walking.

First taking a look back at Portway's building and all the other buildings and the crowded street and the eager young people and the low-flying drones, Jim imagines himself a child, once again running across a field of tickling grass.

'Let's not go back straight away,' she says. 'Let's find somewhere to eat.' Nodding, he thinks of the tubes which would feed his body. He must learn to appreciate every last moment he has. Every last moment in the world. In that world of 'reality'.

'This experience,' he says almost imperceptibly.

Planning

'Don't forget your first appointment tomorrow,' his wife says. How could he? How could he forget. How could she think he would forget? She understood. Everyone knew the consequences of his Civic Duty. It was something that had to be done. Simple. Simple for them. But not for him. Then he thought that perhaps it wasn't so simple for them – that they'd all been locked into this...he couldn't think of the word. Maybe, deception. His wife stressed that the main thing was he wouldn't be dead. A lot of people were euthanised, or legally assisted in their suicide. Sometimes people did their duty, at other times they had to be 'persuaded'. But it was legal, above board (usually), sanctioned by society, it seemed, as they had voted for it. How many old people had voted for it, he wondered? And then as he thought this he had the sense that he had thought it all before. But he hadn't.

What else could they, society, have done? The population had declined but the resources remained insufficient. Food was not being imported quickly enough from around the world. It was as if the world in general had lost direction. Civic Duty could be traced back to the 2020s when the idea of being euthanised really caught on. He knew that people had lost their sense of self. They were all headless chickens running uncontrollably away from the reality of themselves in ever decreasing circles.

'I won't,' he says.

He'd need medication to help him sleep. The irony was not lost. In this promised new life, in suspended animation, he still wasn't sure if he'd either sleep or dream. This last thought wouldn't shake loose despite the doctor's opinion. But now he couldn't sleep. There was a lot to organise and he should have begun preparing years beforehand. But who wants to think about this kind of thing. It was like dropping out of life. A sedative first, he presumed, then picked up by a Portway ambulance, taken down corridors and finally wheeled in through 'The Gateway'. Oblivious. Would his wife and children be there with him? Why bother? He thought this but he wanted them to be there. To see him off. Not exactly a funeral. He wouldn't be dead after all. And he also thought of Maddy. Of course. She was never far from his thoughts. It felt as if she were in some suspended state somewhere. It was hard to talk about her even with his wife, who had helped him in his grief.

They'd made the down-payment. From then on the insurance, which had contributed twenty percent of the cost, would kick in to seventy percent monthly payments. His wife would contribute the rest. And as long as those payments were made he would continue to be 'at rest'. Alive if not kicking. The doctor had told them that the monthly payments were a precaution as there had previously been some unpleasantness when upfront payments couldn't be provided. Termination, his word not the doctor's, happened soon after. With the monthly payments, families and friends could assess their funds well in advance. They could budget. As long as his wife was in work everything would be fine. He imagined his children would chip in if necessary too. Of all the pensions that didn't come into fruition – these so-called 'dreams-after-life insurances' were totally protected, enshrined in law and the government had no choice but to honour them. If they were to renege on these there would be societal meltdown. He was sure.

That was the point. With everyone's Civic Duty, society could function healthily again. Eventually houses were freed-up, doctors and hospitals waiting-lists were reduced. Schools (while they existed) thrived educationally with less pupils and roads became less congested. Taking out the older population worked. There was a regular percentage that had to be terminated. But it was all legal and dealt with efficiently. Mostly. He had heard of men and women of sixty dragged from their houses. Things went on 'at night'. These were people who were not prepared to respect and live up to their Civic Duty. How else could society react? People had to plan ahead, had to take responsibility. Co-operatives had also been set up to fund the alternative. The alternative he now faced. He was 'lucky'.

'Do you want me to come with you?' his wife asks.

He does. But he says, 'You have to work. You have a big job on. And if you get sacked it'll be curtains for me,' he adds lamely. Curtains? No-one knew exactly what happened to you if you got terminated. People presumed things. Families were forbidden from attending these funerals. No one was allowed to attend a voluntary or involuntary euthanisation. Some people tried to evade the inevitable and melt into their houses, like soft-ghosts. But they were always caught.

There were euthanisation centres in every small and big town, with multiple centres in cities. They all looked very modern. Children were taken on tours of them. Modern children liked that as it meant they got to see lots of other children. He'd never taken his own children as they were old enough to have missed that. He knew some very depressed and mentally anguished folk that had volunteered suicide. If they did that the State paid their immediate families a nice little lump sum and gave foreign travel credit.

Disabled people, the few who survived birth, were usually soon terminated. Everyone lived in fear of accidents and becoming disabled. It was never about who they were as people, but how much they cost the state. Perhaps the elite, the very rich, were quietly put to pasture - hidden away.

He didn't know anyone really close who'd had to do their Civic Duty. He knew people who had died beforehand, even some friends. His best friend too. And, of course, Maddy. Now most people made it to sixty – but not everyone.

'I can take the time off,' she says.

He wanted her to come but he also wanted to ask the doctor some personal questions and he also wanted to make a start creating his own 'future environment'. It seemed a little selfish to want to do this as his wife would be paying towards it. That was the fun angle though. There were also concerns he still had. And he wanted to make a better impression on this next visit.

'I'll go alone,' he says.

'Are you sure?'

She didn't seem particularly keen to override his decision. And that was one of the concerns he had, that he couldn't explain while she was there. Would she remain in love with him when he was at rest? What would happen if she found someone else? Another man would resent a portion of her wages going on her...well, what would he be? Would he still be her husband? It was another question he had to ask. What would be his legal or non-legal status?

He got transport into the city the following day. He was alone. In fact he decided to stop a little before Portway. It was the first crisp, sunny day of the year. Despite it being cold still, young folk had gathered during their work break. These would have been technical workers who attended offices – most people working from home. There were also middle-aged people walking through the small parks, or along the riverside. He noticed a number of them staring at him. Dead man walking. This phrase would not let him be.

They lived at the edge of the city. His wife spent half of her time commuting. They had money and a decent enough place to live. Their house was in a well-appointed small estate and part of a gated community. Though there was no community to speak of. His working life had ended when he reached fifty-five years old. Everyone was put out to grass for five years. Five years to see and experience as much of remaining life as possible – if you had the money. Those five years' income reflected what you had earned in the previous ten. If you had a low paid, hard grafting job, these years would be frugal but still welcome.

'Roll up, roll up, see the world and die.' And yet that was also life as it had been. People got their pension and then snuffed it. Their light was snuffed out. He, rather, would take up next to no space, little energy after the initial connection – and then left to sail off into an unknown sunset.

He almost felt like one of those government sponsored celebrities as people turned their heads to look at him; maybe he appeared older than his years and thus adding to their curiosity. It was true he'd had no body or face augmentation. Perhaps his was the last generation to feel no need. In his youth he had known truly ancient human beings – faces like gnarled tree trunks. A time when people had their superstitions and a time when a whole population could be, and was, hoodwinked. He'd been unduly affected by the early '20s. Who could blame him? Despite everything, people still believed whatever they were told by the authorities. Voluntary assisted suicide morphing into Civic Duty. Morphing into the eradication of the not-so-old. Having thought that, he suspected that the elderly elite were living out comfortable lives somewhere, pampered and taken care of by the hand-picked young; serving them in all kinds of ways.

The day was bright. He had eleven months left of the world to appreciate. Would it be so bad to let it go? They'd always had to let life go at some point. Who knew what the future might bring – perhaps an eternity-drug for all and a collective release from being 'at rest'. If that happened though, the world would teem again and starvation would once more stalk the lands. No, there was nothing for it but to acquiesce to his fate. Dead at sixty or eighty, what did it matter? Besides the life after life he would experience might offer all sorts of possibilities. It felt selfish to think this. Ever since Maddy's accident, now so long ago, and yet as painful as if yesterday, he had somewhat disengaged from life. Not completely, of course. He'd married Hannah and their two children who came along filled his mind, his thoughts, his actions. They helped heal him. Helped soothe his memories. And he couldn't help but compare Joanne with Maddy.

These were thoughts he turned over as he walked. He was still fit, active and bright-minded. As he approached Portway's vicinity there was more hustle and bustle. Had he still got a will to live? Again he thought of the eternity drug. What would happen if you lived forever? Would time even exist? Would you reach perfection? Would time dissolve your mind? And then he thought about the moment they would disconnect him from the computer and his life-assisting machines. The moment of truth, or revelation. Being 'at rest' was only pushing the inevitable back. So why did they do it? Society tolerating a universally set death age. A willingness to line up alongside the trench and accept the bullet in the back of the neck. A slow fall and then the taste of lime in the mouth - if you hadn't quite lost life. He was getting fanciful and morbid. His, and others futures, were unclear. Perhaps you died in situ – in angelic dreams or demonic nightmares? He pictured Maddy's face, trying to haul her features back to life, but she was slowly disappearing. That was the cruellest fate.

At the entrance lobby, once again past guards prying eyes and the ubiquitous cameras, he obliged another youngish woman with his security metrics. All was well. Again he wondered why anyone would trick their way into that liminal land. Perhaps, as the doctor had hinted, there were always spies to watch out for. He had the fanciful idea of a spy assuming the age of fifty-nine and going through the process only to be caught up in it at one point and unable to unmask his activity and who he really was. Too late mate. Jim smiled. Gallows humour. And now he was climbing the steps.

'The doctor will see you shortly,' the youngish woman says. She smiles as she says this and unearths her attractiveness. How long had she got - another lifetime? He was always doing this now, looking at people, whenever he saw any close up, and judging how long they had left. Another twenty, ten, two years?

'Thank you,' he answers obediently. He must remember that he is the customer. Dead man walking, soon resting. This time he is ushered into an ultra-modern waiting room. Thankfully empty. He imagines another man or woman opposite him. Is this their first or last month here before... Or they simply eye one another with pity and solidarity. Shall they hold hands as they wait for the cold touch of the metallic pistol barrel?

He imagines himself sitting next to himself.

They look at each other.

'Funny that we should find ourselves at this time,' his other self says.

Jim smiles. 'Perhaps it was inevitable.'

'I imagine,' his other self replies. 'I've been with you a long time now.'

'I felt you from time to time,' Jim says.

'I had to keep watch over you. Help you out when I could.'

'And now there's nothing you can do.'

His other self turns away for a moment. 'This is likely the end for me too...'

'Or the beginning,' Jim says.

'Or the beginning.'

'Maybe we'll grow closer in this new life,' Jim says.

'Maybe.' Then, 'We've had some good times.'

'And bad,' Jim answers.

'And bad,' his other self mirrors.

What am I doing? He almost thought out loud. There were screens around the room – at low volume, thankfully. He wanted to turn them off but they were most likely programmed to stay on constantly. One of the screens carried all the usual propaganda. Another was advertising Portway's services. He suddenly wondered about the older men who had young wives and young children. And wasn't his wife so much younger? He tried to imagine children in that room – only partly aware what lay ahead for their loving father or mother. It all felt very wrong. He knew it was his Civic Duty – almost spitting out these two words – but he'd never agreed to such a life.

'Are you scared?' his other self asks.

He wishes it would go away but he likes the company too. 'Yes,' he answers. There is no point trying to trick this other creature that resides alongside him. They are conjoined.

'Me too,' the other says.

'Really?' he asks, somewhat surprised.

The other looks at him with compassion. 'Of course.'

'I thought you'd go off and haunt someone, somewhere else.'

His other self laughs. 'Where would I go?'

He had no idea. 'Thanks for being with me now,' Jim says.

His other self smiles.

'Mr Holden?' comes a voice. You mean you can't see there are two of us, he wants to say. Have they got him mixed up with all the other waiting souls? 'Yes,' he answers.

'Please follow me.'

He thinks this woman has less than twenty or so years. Is she getting used to the inevitability of *her* fate? Perhaps she works there deliberately to become accustomed. Springing up, defiantly 'young', he follows the sway of her hips.

Like a child he looked around curiously. He felt stronger when he'd been with his wife. He missed her. He'd finally have to face life...life after life, being 'at rest', alone. Immediately he had another question for the doctor – what would happen to his wife when she reached fifty-nine? Panicking slightly, he wondered why this had not entered his mind before. She would have insurance. His son would pay. Surely. They hadn't to fall out. But his son was the sensitive one. Henry would pay, he'd look after her. And it seemed he would even fail with after-life wife care. Again smiling and still looking about he imagined that as a Portway slogan. Probably been used already.

The woman pressed the 'notice button' – the doctor registered them on the external camera and the door swished open. He didn't even remember that from before. As he was ushered in and the woman left, the doctor sat back.

'Jim,' he says, looking back at his screen. Jim smiles. 'Take a seat.' The doctor pauses, then says, 'Second month.'

'End of the first,' Jim says.

'Precisely,' the doctor answers. 'Time to get down to business.'

Jim feels his hands sweat. 'Business,' he says.

The doctor looks at him as if he is looking directly into his soul.

The Doctor looks at his screen again. 'The team is waiting,' he says.

'Team?'

Your dedicated team,' he replies. 'You're a Magenta.' He pauses. 'Not bad.'

'Magenta?'

'Yes. Not the top. No. But not at all bad.'

'What's not bad...?'

'Your plan, Jim. Every design, plan, what we call 'Future-Fields' usually comes with a preset. A default building block. A template. If you're a Grey or a Dark Blue then between you and me, it's a bit basic,' his voice has dropped to a whisper. 'Quite a lot of repetition. The extras are a bit dull. Stock housing and countryside. You get the drift. It's not bad in itself but the characters aren't the brightest. You get what you pay for Jim. You got that right. But no matter, you're a Magenta.' The doctor seems pleased.

'I'm glad,' Jim says.

'We find that our clients usually get quite excited during this phase,' fixing his stare at Jim. 'Some discover all sorts of creative abilities. Passion. Some find real passion. They tell me it's the most passion they've ever felt,' he smiles. 'For some it comes as a revelation and others, I must say, as a realisation that they could have done something else with their life. Some take charge and others simply direct their team and let them get on with it. It's what they're paid for after all.'

'I see.'

'I'll introduce you to your team shortly...'

'I have some questions,' Jim pipes up.

'Fire away.'

'The first is a technical one,' Jim begins. 'Well a technical-technical question.' The doctor smiles.

The doctor's teeth were remarkably straight and white. He wants to ask the doctor about his teeth but stops himself.

'When I'm at rest...resting,' Jim adjusts, 'what is my legal position?'

'Good question Jim. You'd be surprised how many don't fully comprehend this or even ask about it. They, you,' he eyes Jim, 'have signed all the papers. Yes, I know there's a lot of detail – but important detail. Very important detail. You've signed these legal documents.' The doctor pauses. Regards Jim. 'Could you be more specific? There are reams of specialised documentation concerning the legality, stretching right back to the original White Paper in 2039.'

'I'm married,' Jim states. 'Will I continue to be married, when...'

The doctor rubs his palms together. 'An interesting question. Good question. Technically yes. Legally – no. I don't suppose you've heard of the Baxter v Goswami case?' Jim shakes his head. 'Why would you,' the doctor muses. 'Two years before the White Paper. Not called Civic Duty back then – officially. Early days. Primitive stuff, Blues or Greys at their best. Design that is. None left now. Well, a couple, but they've been upgraded. No problems with the basic designs as such and neither the life-support. But,' he holds a finger up vertically, 'but. A precedent was set. In a court of law it was decided that the woman, Baxter, who had been resting for nearly two years and married to Goswami, had no legal rights preventing Goswami from re-marrying. Their marriage was not annulled however. The term 'marriage in abeyance' was coined. Goswami was 'married in abeyance' but able to remarry legally. With one caveat.' Jim listens intently. 'The caveat was that he had to honour his yearly payments. If you recall Jim, that is the method then in use. Thus, Goswami became the first man to be technically married to two women; legally to one. A different one. This was a pragmatic legal decision. Of course there are multiple marriages these days in many communities. But they still don't have full legal recognition. Thus, to summarize, your marriage will be legally protected and your wife would not be allowed to renege on payments. But. She would also be legally allowed to remarry, or additionally-marry, or using its proper term, be: Married in Abeyance.'

Jim is impressed by the doctor's knowledge and recall. 'Putting it bluntly, he begins, 'I definitely can't be divorced while I'm resting?'

'No. That is true. Your wife could remarry, additionally-marry. But no divorce and your absolute entitlement to the agreed monthly payments would have to be honoured.' He pauses, reflects. 'Are there any problems?' he asked candidly.

'No, none,' Jim says. 'But this does bring me onto my next question, or questions.'

'Fire away,' the doctor says again, glancing at his screen.

'Well, I suppose I'll have to ask another technical question first.'

'Go ahead.'

'Okay. My mind will be active, as it is now, I presume.'

'Yes. We have no reason to think otherwise.'

'I'll have the same desires?'

The doctor thinks about this. 'We think so. You'll be interacting with and within your world. You'll need to have desire and intention. Your mind will identify with this new world and be absorbed into it. We can't be one hundred percent certain. We monitor brainwaves, REM and NREM, which seem to continue. but that doesn't automatically mean dreaming,' he emphasises, 'and we did do trials...'

'Trials?'

'As much as we were able. We re-created the likely mental state of the...' The doctor needs to choose his words carefully, 'Well let's say those going into Limbo. It's an old-fashioned word I know. You understand?'

Jim nods. 'I haven't heard that word used in a long while.'

The doctor carries on, 'We had volunteers put into sensory deprivation chambers and under the influence of, and I must stress, State-approved, hallucinogenic drugs. Their minds were effectively disconnected from their bodies. Their minds were allowed to wander – and they did. On top of this the brain was receiving the hallucinogens. In fact we did trials with and without the drugs. With the drugs the experiences were far richer.' He pauses. 'The really fascinating thing was that, under the influence of the drugs, there were some shared experiences. Which was surprising. But then we'd known for a long time about these supposed independent, archetypal characters from reports of people taking DMT. Rest assured, our hallucinogens are produced and administered so that only your mind and what is in your mind can be reproduced in your world. Every little detail has been considered.'

Jim pauses to take in this information. It seems reasonable that his mind would be, in a sense, 'freer' when he was resting. The idea of 'shared experiences' intrigued him. 'Would there be any correspondence between my natural, necessary bodily actions and my created world?'

'I'm not sure I follow,' the doctor says.

'Bluntly,' Jim begins, 'if I defecate in real life – will I imagine myself doing that in my created world?'

The doctor laughs. 'In all my time no-one has asked me this question.' He smiles. 'Frankly Jim, I have no idea.' He thinks for a moment. 'Perhaps initially, when the experience is new, that might, could be, the case. Defecation will be minimal. As the mind becomes more and more dislocated, I very much doubt it.'

Jim seems content with the answer. 'What about sex?' he asks. He sees the doctor shift in his seat slightly. 'Will we have sex in this mental landscape?'

'It's highly possible,' the doctor says. 'You will be, I imagine, in a state very similar to lucid dreaming...'

'I don't think I've ever lucid dreamed,' Jim answers.

'That can be arranged,' the doctor says.

Again Jim ponders. 'Frankly,' he begins, 'could I design a female character for my world?'

'Ah. This isn't such an unusual question.'

'And,' Jim stumbles, 'keep her secret?'

'Of course,' the doctor says. 'These are *your* future-fields.' There is some silence. 'You can have a number of highly detailed characters created. We can program them to your specifications. But we really don't know how you and they will react. We can't know that. This is your experience and will remain utterly private. Thought experimentation is proscribed. Besides, it's still fairly primitive. What happens in your world, stays in your world,' the doctor smiles.

Jim looks a little sheepish. 'I could design a character that resembles my wife?' he asks.

The doctor nods. 'Of course. How close she would come to resemble your wife though is unknown. I think I have to stress this. Two things,' the doctor says. 'Firstly, from a legal point of view again, we cannot design specifically sexual characters. That is, it will be mine and the team's judgment if that is or is not the case. Frankly I don't know why that's for us to decide. An attempt at grafting on some morality, perhaps. An attempt to keep things 'above board'. There are a lot of unscrupulous organisations out there.'

'Yes, of course,' Jim says.

The doctor continues. 'The other thing is we have no actual control regarding what happens in your interior world. Your future-fields are carefully designed and detailed. We assume that is where your mind will roam. The characters you design and the default characters will exist in that landscape.'

Jim feels the doctor has stalled. More questions were forming inside his head. But he also knew that his time was limited. He'd noticed the doctor looking anxiously at his screen.

'We'll have plenty of time to go into such details,' the doctor says.

Jim nods. 'Thanks,' he finds himself saying.

'Rest assured, you're protected by a secrecy clause. There isn't usually a problem regarding this. As a Magenta, you will be well looked after.'

'The racks of drawers I saw, were they all Magenta?'

The doctor shakes his head. 'Not all,' he says. 'That isn't where the differentiation is. Though we do group those resting to a degree to keep a semblance of orderliness between the bodies resting and the control rooms. It makes sense.' The doctor looks at his screen again. 'One moment,' he says.

Jim looks around the room and feels strangely detached. He wonders about his future-fields and how life would be there. He wonders about that life and actual death. *His* actual death. And he wonders about the urges of the brain and body and their effect upon his mind. This gets him thinking about a whole stream of such ideas. The thought crosses his mind to try and re-create Maddy. But at what age?

'Are we ready?' the doctor asks.

'We are,' Jim replies. The doctor eyes him in the manner he had done on Jim's first visit.

They walked through the building to the garden, then through the wrought-iron gates and across into the very modern building of glass, wood and metal. Then down the corridor leading towards the control room. But they turned left beforehand and into an office where his team sat waiting.

'Mr Holden,' the doctor introduces, clarifying, 'Jim.' The team welcomes him with smiles. 'Take a seat Jim,' the leader of the team says. 'I'm Daniel Wetherby, call me Dan please.'

'Nice to meet you all...Dan,' he nods.

'As a Magenta you come with various default programs just to get us started.' Dan motions to one of the team. They go straight into operation.

Jim was then instructed to adjust his chair so each leg rested on a floor marker. A box descended from the ceiling. 'If you would sit still please,' the man says. Jim follows orders. 'Rest your arms on the chair.' Then the man hands Jim a pair of what looked like tinted glasses. 'Please put these on. Thank you,' he says as Jim takes them. The box was directly over Jim's head – his arms again at rest. 'This is to give you some idea of the options you have, Jim. Try not to move too much, it will be a pleasant experience, I can assure you.'

The box lowered over Jim's head and settled lightly upon his shoulders. From inside there was 432hz calming music and a bluish-white light that seemed to surround him. Though he was not sure how the glasses were affecting his vision.

'Are you comfortable?' a female voice asks. Jim nods – the box is not tight to his head. He presumes it is used universally.

'Yes,' he answers, realising she probably can't see his head move.

'Let the experience begin,' the voice says in a warm manner.

Jim is immediately surrounded by images and sounds. This is not virtual reality and it seems he could communicate easily with the team.

'If you can let us know what you think regarding the images, please. We can begin adapting and altering in response to your wishes and any ideas you might have. Firstly, we're going to get a geographical overview. Enjoy the ride,' she adds. 'But please, if you can, give constant feedback.'

Jim finds himself looking from a distance upon a relatively flat landscape. Then he feels himself zoomed down close to the ground. The land is grassed.

'It's too flat,' he says.

'We're still loading,' a voice comes, seemingly in his head.

It is as if he were standing on the ground but he couldn't feel it. He looked around as much as he was able. As he did so he felt himself lift and the land about him began to take contour – undulating hills formed before his eyes. In the distance he began to see mountains. They looked like the mountains he knew from his youth. Looking to his left there was a deciduous wood and around him the land bloomed with meadow flowers. Without conscious thought he was lifted and zoomed in and put on a conical hill which had been in the distance. From there he had a view down into a valley where there was a village or small town. It was very appealing and he wanted to run down the slope of the hill towards it.

Lifting his head he saw light, wispy clouds form in the sky and the sun was shining, he hadn't noticed that before, how was that possible? There was a lot to take in. As he looked again at the little town he could see smoke curling up from chimneys. It was perfect. The sky was clear for the most part and he felt warm. Once more he was hoisted high and he moved fully 360 degrees. How could he do that? As he looked around he could see more hills forming and other small towns and villages. The mountains were an impressive and extensive range. Close by there were patchwork fields enclosed by hedges and more meadows with flowers like jewels glinting in the sun.

'Birds,' he says.

No sooner has he said this than a flock of birds fly past him. He doesn't know what birds they are. Then he says, 'A murmuration of starlings.' He watches them swoop and form shapes as if they are one. A murmuration. A murmuration. Then he is taken out. The world he was witnessing quickly disappearing, dissolving, and all he can see are huge letters spelling: 'Welcome to Portway.'

'Sorry,' the female voice came. 'We got you out a bit quick.'

The box lifted and hands removed his glasses.

'How did that feel?' he is asked.

'It was great,' he says, looking around at his team.

The woman says, 'It's old technology. But we wanted to introduce you to the concept softly.' He likes the way she says 'softly'.

'It's the principle,' the doctor says. 'If you remember you gave us remote feedback to questions when first applying to Portway.' Jim nods. 'We used that as a very primitive template. We know you like this kind of countryside and the towns you saw. This is very easy for us to replicate. But you need to think about 'eternity'. You need to supply as much detail as possible. In order to do this we need your permission to put you into a hallucinogenic virtual reality. Mild. A mildly infused state. We need to gain as much information as we can. And we need you to do this over a few days, at least to begin with.'

'I didn't realise,' Jim says. 'But I guess it makes sense.'

'We need you to help us map time. The passing of time. We think, perhaps, the ability to go from state to state within the wink of an eye.'

The leader of the team eyes the doctor coldly. 'In order for us to reflect your wishes,' the leader stresses, 'we need detailed insight. The better we can make your world now the better your experience. We need contrast and variety. We can add small details or we can apply default details. Future-Fields is in your hands. In your mind and in your eyes.'

Jim smiles. 'Why not?'

He was creating his future. He would be in control. He was in control. Eleven months to create...well...his heaven.

The doctor says, 'We've spoken with your wife and she's going to drop off some clothes for you. We have everything you need but she said you'd prefer your own clothes.'

'How long will I be staying?'

'Normally two days, but your wife is wiring extra money. We need three days, ideally. There's a lot to do. We have these days now then perhaps ten more monthly appointments where we could take extra days if needed. We'll be keeping a check on your progress...'

'Seems a lot of work for one man,' Jim says. 'How many people get to rest and how many...' he stops himself. Then decides to say. 'Get to go up the chimney in smoke?' Did the doctor grimace?

'Most people have no insurance. Most people could only afford a couple of months and we simply can't afford the time or trouble to give them even that. Two years is the minimum. I don't know any company which does less. Even in the early days, with yearly payments, it was too much trouble to arrange everything for less than two years. We have to plan ahead. We work closely with skilled actuaries who give us some kind of idea of the projected birth and death rates, possible future epidemics and the general health of the population. Imagine Jim, a lot of people die in their forties and fifties – we have to take that into account. They won't be using our services. There's a slight downward trend in the overall population and the birth rate is dropping. Immigration is controlled and frankly many of the immigrants aren't able to take advantage, shall we say, of our services or their religion precludes such. The whole point of Civic Duty is to create space and make life easier for the general population, as you know. On this small plot of land we have nearly thirty-five thousand clients resting. Just here. The building you saw, there's around a thousand. We always show that building because people can relate to its size. If you want I could show you our biggest building which holds twenty thousand. Custom built. I mean everything is custom built. The control rooms are in the main building complex. The main building holds all of the upgraded Blues and Greys and some Greens too and Magentas as we showed you. They can be monitored easily. We also have a dedicated building for the 'lifers' as we call them, those who've been here a very long time. I know it's old prison terminology. Just a joke Jim. You need to have a certain sense of humour. It can get a little creepy at night.'

'Creepy?'

'My apologies, Jim. But try and imagine walking around a building being surrounded by twenty thousand bodies, all of which are in their own little worlds. Entirely detached from this life.'

Jim found himself surprisingly interested in such details. He asks, 'What about if any of the clients,' Jim stresses, 'get ill or have a disease?'

'Very unusual,' the doctor says. 'They lead the perfect...life,' he adds. And smiles. 'Everything is super hygienic and all the bodily functions controlled. Nutrients are administered in a controlled way and the bodies are suspended, as you saw, in a controlled environment.'

'All very controlled.' He pauses. 'But have any?'

'Have any what?' the doctor replies.

'Have any of them had a serious illness or disease?'

'Yes. A few.'

'What happens to them?' Jim asks, wondering in case such a thing befalls him.

'I can't give any information about exact cases,' the doctor says, 'but I can tell you that in such a case the client is seamlessly plugged into a portable casket – unplugged and swiftly replugged. They are then seen by a doctor, such as myself, who appraises their medical needs and deals with them accordingly.'

'But they never regain consciousness?' Jim asks.

'Never.'

'And are they all okay?'

'Yes, absolutely fine,' the doctor reassures. We have the best specialists in the city at our disposal. If a client can be saved, we save them,' he says triumphantly.

'And they're all saved,' Jim states. The doctor smiles. 'Makes good business sense, I guess,' Jim adds.

'Exactly.'

After a long pause, Jim says, 'What's next doc?' Shortening the doctor's title, Jim looks for a response.

The doctor is unphased. He smiles. 'Next?' Another pause. 'Well we need to eat. Eat, maybe try out our latest virtual reality pod. Maybe add some details to your future-fields, then it's either hitting town with the team or getting some sleep. I'll show you where your room is after we eat.'

'Hitting town?' Jim asks.

'Work hard, play hard,' the doctor says.

'Strikes me you work hard doc, do you 'hit the town' too?'

'I don't.'

'Have you got a family?'

'I haven't,' he responds.

'Married to the job?' Jim asks frankly.

'Some might say that.'

'But you don't.'

'I don't.' The doctor eyes him. 'Are you hungry?'

Jim nods. 'It's been an interesting day, so far.'

'Good. Follow me, Jim.'

They sat in Portway's restaurant. It was self-service in the sense they walked in a clockwise direction sliding their trays along, either helping themselves to food and drink or being served the various dishes of the heated main course. The doctor had asked Jim if he wanted some wine. Jim took a small bottle.

At the table Jim says, 'This won't affect anything, I presume.'

The doctor shakes his head. 'You're going to have to think about pleasures in your world. Not just...' he winks.

Jim is surprised, the doc keeps surprising him. Portway keeps surprising him. 'I don't know what you mean,' Jim says. The doctor smiles. 'It's an amazing place,' Jim continues. 'If you're semi-dead I guess this is the place to be.'

'Fully alive,' the doctor corrects. 'But yes, it is an amazing place. We have everything we need here. Retail outlets, a gym, an office devoted to and equipped for sundry needs of the workforce. Anything you might need, it has. It's called the Forgetmenot. I like that. Looks out onto the inner garden too.'

'Shouldn't it be devoted to the clients and their families?'

The doctor suddenly becomes grave. 'It's better if the clients are forgotten,' he says. 'It's better for the whole family. I should have mentioned this to your wife. She's very nice, by the way. You're a lucky man.'

'For eleven more months...'

'I should have told her that we keep a whole host of pre-recorded videos that can be accessed. She'll have a dedicated information line. It's something for you to look forward to Jim. State-of-the-art recording. Virtual backdrops – even taken from your future-fields. We had one wag who did a whole series of short films for his family. Hired skis for one of them and we had him simulating skiing down one of his designed ski-slopes. He waved and beamed into the camera. "Wish you were here!" Gave his grandchildren a good laugh apparently.'

'I'll have one from the inside of a hearse,' Jim says. 'You can film me opening the coffin lid. "Surprise, surprise. This is your life!"'

The doctor forces a smile. 'Enjoying the food?'

'Yes.'

'Everything's organic,' the doctor says.

'Must cost a fortune,' Jim says openly.

'Probably.'

Thinking out loud, Jim says, 'I guess I'll be paying for it.'

'Probably.'

'Won't these films keep a kind of connection between me, say, and my family?'

'To begin with,' the doctor says gravely.

Jim pours himself another glass of wine. 'Do you think we'll get to taste things...later,' he says partly cryptically.

'We don't know. But if, say, you have fruit trees in your future-fields and the trees are programmed to bear fruit...'

'Which wouldn't be real...'

'I'll come to that,' the doctor says. 'If you can pick the fruit off the tree in this future reality, if you can bite into it, who's to say you're not going to taste it? What is taste? Is it simply the receptors principally on the tongue and their correspondence in the brain or is it all in the mind? Did you know there are tiny hairs on the tongue called microvilli that send information to the brain? Taste molecules of food touch the taste pores of the taste buds and bind to the microvilli. These so-called 'tastes' are changed into chemical and electrical messages, which travel along the nerves to the brain, where they are identified. Yes, I learnt that spiel. It appealed to me. I like my food. But simply: where are the tastes identified? I'm a doctor, a scientist, but what we do here has opened my mind to possibilities.'

Jim is surprised how much the doctor is opening up. Has he sneaked a few gulps of his wine, or has he snorted some of his Heavenly Sugar? Jim says, 'That's the case with so much stuff isn't it doc? I mean how much are we the brain and how much the mind?'

'Ah, you're a philosopher at heart Jim. We'll have some good conversations...'

'Couldn't you program some of those nanobots to carry questions into my brain, my mind,' he stalls, 'when I'm resting? Give me something to think about.'

'We can create scientists and philosophers as integral characters in your world. You can spend...' The doctor was going to say 'an eternity talking with them'. He thinks hard, 'Time will pass in a pleasing manner.'

'Is that it?' Jim asks. 'Do we just pass time until death?'

The doctor chokes slightly on some organic steak. 'I mean your time will be used effectively.'

'Until we die?'

The doctor thinks again. 'That's a question for a religious man not a doctor,' he says.

'But what do you think doc?'

The doctor places his cutlery down onto the plate. 'All my working life I've been programmed to think of the human body as an incredibly sophisticated machine,' he begins, 'but since being here at Portway and having learnt previously about virtual reality and the effects of hallucinogenic drugs and witnessing the sensory deprivation tests...and, frankly, thinking long and hard about all this. I'm no longer sure if the body is, simply, or is complicatedly, a machine. And I have no idea why I'm talking this way with you Jim,' he says. 'I apologise for my unprofessional behaviour. I feel like I've overstepped the mark.'

'It's helping,' Jim reassures. 'It's helping me,' he states. 'I feel like a man sentenced to death. Who's going to hang in the morning, or have his head severed by a guillotine. Did you know doc, that the head might blink and the eyes show shock a minute or more after decapitation. Can you imagine knowing you're effectively dead?'

'Highly disconcerting,' the doctor says. 'It isn't scientific fact though, may I add. It's hearsay. There wouldn't be sufficient blood pressure for the head to react in that way. The head, the person, would be unconscious within seconds.'

'I'm not so sure,' Jim says. 'There's certainly anecdotal evidence...'

'Anecdotal and evidence don't mix,' the doctor interjects.

'There was a case where a person's decapitated head landed on another person's lap after a car accident. And the head's eyes were looking up from the lap and then across to its erstwhile body.'

'If nothing else that shows why cars have been banned in many places. The amount of carnage,' the doctor says.

'They're fun to drive,' Jim protests. 'I can recall before all the restrictions. You were free. I remember that doc, or is that just anecdotal non-evidence?' Jim pours the rest of the small bottle into his glass. But he also thinks of Maddy. And he thinks of her last moments. A car bearing down on her like a metallic monster. Thoughts torture him. Hannah has use of a car too and he drives it sometimes when they have enough credit. She has perks with her work. And he benefits.

'Room for a desert?' the doctor asks.

Jim nods.

'I have to be honest with you doc, this whole 'what happens to the mind' business worries me. I mean I only have your word for it that my mind will still be active.'

'We monitor your brain waves.'

The doctor poured them both a fresh coffee. Jim slumped onto the doctor's couch as the doctor paced up and down his office.

'How are you feeling?' the doctor asks. 'Shall we do some creation?'

'What about the team? Will they mind?'

'They'll be off. Probably having fun. I'm authorised.'

'And you doc? Do you have fun?'

'Being here is my fun.'

'When do you quit work?'

'I don't think I ever do,' the doctor muses. 'I feel comfortable here.'

'But sometimes you think it's creepy?'

The doctor laughs, 'Sometimes. But even that's okay.'

Jim looks at him. 'Well, I'm up for some creation.'

'Not suffering the effects?'

'You mean the wine? Come on doc, that was a small bottle.'

'Do you drink much?'

'As much as I need,' Jim smiles.

The doctor looks at him. Goes to the antique or faux-antique globe and rolls it. 'Okay,' he says. 'Let's get started.'

'You definitely don't need the team?'

'I can manage. Relax. Everything will be recorded. When, or if, they roll in tomorrow they can increase their headaches perusing the data.' The doctor smiles. 'Or they can work from home and access it all.' Again he eyes Jim. 'Okay?

'Okay,' Jim answers

'I'm more than happy with you calling me doc,' the doctor says, 'I've been called worse, but you can refer to me either as Doctor Abraham or Doctor Jake. If you wish.'

'Which is your surname?' Jim asks.

'Abraham.'

'Okay, doc, noted,' Jim answers playfully.

Doctor Abraham scrutinises him. He is both mildly irritated, yet also intrigued. Jim is shaping up.

The doctor had it all set up. Jim watched him work. Tapping or speaking in data. Jim wasn't at all sure the doc did this for all his clients. Still. It meant he could design in detail those characters he'd spend an eternity with. Or less than an eternity. If he died and went to heaven or hell, then supposedly *that* would be eternity. Would the characters he had created go with him too – after all they were in his head?

'The team has got modified stock characters we can work from,' the doctor begins. 'What are we going for? Remember you're going to be interacting with them, maybe for a long time,' eyeing Jim.

Jim thinks. 'I assume I don't want someone who agrees with me on everything. But I don't want someone who's going to disagree with me on everything, either.' Pausing momentarily, he continues, 'We're taking them one at a time, I presume?' He stops. Reflects, then, 'We're not designing a particular woman friend here, are we?'

'Why not, it's just you and me, Jim?'

'I'd rather get used to this whole business first,' he answers. 'It's an odd idea, creating someone. If they *are* someone.'

'You must have played games when you were young?'

'Yes.'

'And you created the characters.'

'To a degree. I didn't get in heavy like some I know. I knew men, and they were mainly men, who wrecked their lives. In the twentieth century it was alcohol, drugs and music. In my time it was gaming.'

'It goes on,' the doctor says. 'It all goes on. I could take you places where the finest drugs are smoked or snorted, where, despite our civic duties and our Government it's a free for all sex wise. And where people lose themselves in virtual reality. In your day, young men dropped out, I know. My father was such a man. Wasn't quite as bad as you described. But bad enough.'

Jim is surprised at the doctor's honesty. 'Must have been tough.'

'I nearly didn't exist,' the doctor says. 'It's a wonder. But there you go. Never had much to do with him. He got ill and died quickly. I was young. That got me into studying. Hard. There were five of us in the school pod. The others would taunt me because of him. He was dead but word got out. I determined to show them that I wasn't him. I wasn't going to dwell in basements and feast on pornography. Or drink myself into a stupor...'

Jim listens intently. Impressed by the doctor. Certainly very surprised. 'And now I guess you're the top in your field. I mean you must be, working at Portway.'

The doctor looks at him and smiles. 'I am top at Portway. I could do any of the jobs here. Any of them. But being a doctor gives me freedom and scope. Money, credit, the ability to travel, though I don't much. After everything that's happened, being a doctor is properly respected again.'

Jim thinks about his situation. He can't quite believe he is doing what he is doing and talking to a doctor at Portway. He can't really believe he's going to be shut up within a stack of drawers. 'Okay,' Jim says. Let's give me a friend. A friend I can be with for – as long as it takes.'

'Okay,' the doctor says. 'Give me a brief idea and we'll come up with a template. Maybe base it on a friend in real life. Don't forget, you don't want to know everything about him – or her. Do you want to input or are you happy for me to?'

'We can do this one together,' Jim says.

'Okay. Sit here,' the doctor orders. 'Let's get some of these basic templates you can choose from. Age?'

'Let's say fifty.' Jim has ideas of people he knows, one in particular, but he wants to create a new character. As much as he can.

'Basic physical characteristics?'

'Six foot, twelve stones...'

The doctor looks at him, 'I'll convert to normal measurements.'

Jim laughs. 'I like the old ones, I'm into history.'

'Hair style, length etc.'

'As he wants.'

The doctor taps away.

'Build?'

'Fit. I might need his help, who knows?'

'Okay, now the important stuff. I need you to respond in percentages. We can fine tune these later, it can all be fine-tuned, to a degree. Intelligence?'

'What am I?' Jim asks.

The doctor ponders, 'Maybe eighty percent, eighty-five perhaps.'

Jim is unsure how good this is. 'Give him eighty. We might play chess.'

'And all such attributes can be encoded. But let's get the basic character. Sensitivity?'

'High but not so much.'

'Sixty percent? But again, I have to stress, when we fine-tune you'll see subtle and not so apparent subtle changes. You'll be able to interact in VR too.' Jim nods in response. 'Think of characters in the media, if you want. You'd be surprised how many stock media stars are chosen. They make a packet out of this kind of stuff and they get a kick out of the 'roles' they guess they play. Though are completely unaware of.' The doctor's lapel badge bleeps. 'Excuse me,' he says to Jim. 'One moment,' he says into the badge. Then again to Jim, 'Use your imagination. Use media resources. It's all here. I have to go. But quickly, when you're finished, or rather have some ideas, we'll add in a random factor percentage. What percentage do you want?' he asks somewhat perfunctorily, yet hastily.

'Is this random factor extrapolated from his, or *hers*,' Jim stresses, 'basic character?'

'Good point. Normally. But we can also add a wild-card character element. Let's get the basic percentage and then divide it further.'

'Thirty percent.'

'It's high,' the doctor says.

'Is it?' Jim answers. 'How much do we know of our friends' characters in this life? Okay, we don't live with them. We don't spend an eternity with them. But we don't really know them, do we? I mean do we even know ourselves? I want to discover things about them. And you don't know what goes on with these characters in our 'resting' do you doc?' The doctor shakes his head. Jim thinks deeply. Doctor Abraham appears impatient. 'It's almost as if I have a responsibility in creating them. They have to have autonomy and freewill.'

'We have time,' the doctor seems to urge him on. Thinks and agrees. 'Thirty percent it is.' Then adds, 'And the wild element?'

'What does this actually mean, in practice?'

'It would be exactly that,' the doctor says. 'Exactly that. Wild. Anything. Independent of your input and his or her self.'

'But it would be *them*?' Jim stresses.

'Yes,' the doctor says.

'In which case I presume this element of their character would be incorporated into their already known character, which we're going to create.'

The doctor sits back. This is precisely why he has decided to spend so much time with Mr James Holden. His hunch was correct. He thought as much. If all went well then dear Jim, Gentleman Jim, would himself become a template. An interesting, not too intellectual, casual-philosophising, non-threatening, template. Default character – who knows – number ten thousand and... The doctor sits back. Content with himself. So often he deals with these older men and women who have given up. They just want it easy. Why should their world be easy? No New World has been discovered without sacrifice, bravery, open-minded and open-hearted folk; sometimes ruthless and sometimes violent. Jim's going to fit an important hole in their catalogue. And his wife is beautiful.

'Good point,' the doctor says. 'I like the way you're reasoning this Jim. Then he asks, 'What percent, don't think, just tell me?'

Jim says, 'Split it in half. Why not? I might as well be as random as the randomness we're creating. Or rather the character should be.'

Smiling, the doctor says, 'Very well. Fifteen, fifteen. Give me a moment please.' The doctor taps away. I presume you don't want to know how this random element works.' The doctor pauses. 'Please, carry on. Do you think you can input?'

'Yes.'

'Good, I really have to go. You'll be prompted for details. Any problems and you can talk with the computer. One moment,' he taps a few keys. Then, 'Introduce yourself to the computer.' Jim looks at him. 'Just the usual introduction, so the computer knows you're legit.' There's a short pause.

'Hello, I'm Jim. Jim Holden,' he says slightly self-consciously.

'Pleased to meet you,' the computer responds.

The doctor laughs. 'Good luck you two. I shouldn't be too long. I have to go, I'll be back, so don't worry. I'll catch you later, Jim.'

Jim was lost in this new idea but it also threw him back into the reality of who he was and where he was. For thirty years they'd gradually normalised the idea of not living out one's life naturally, to the end, however bitter. Well, they were 'useless eaters'. The language used had framed those who were once considered reasonably young, as a drain on the state. And it wasn't so long ago. Now they were blocks to the rightful flowering of youth. Selfish. And with the introduction of Future-Fields they had no right to complain. Many of the immigrant communities had returned to their ancestral homes in Asia and Africa where the old were still - if not venerated – at least tolerated. The ones that remained either accepted a life-span of sixty years or had their own alternate, cultural, future-fields. He had nowhere to run. He'd heard about aging folk hiding out in some European countries but the idea of civic duty had spread like wildfire, burning and consuming all that dared still stand in its way.

How could things have changed so? The problem lay in the intrinsic nature of their new society. Young people believed they would never grow old. It had always been the case but now this delusion was fanned red hot and its spread encouraged. Jim didn't think for a moment that those at the top were consigned to his fate. They would lead out their lives till their choosing, he was sure. Then they'd be securely 'rested' to live out their second life. Where was the opposition? The Grey Wolves had been crushed. The young had celebrated democracy through the ballot and the sixteen-year-olds could rebel with the enthusiasm and lack of foresight of their youth. How soon their time would speed. One day they'd be like him, if they were lucky. Be like he was. Creating characters to shade his chemically-fuelled afterlife of life. It did not seem real to him. It was just another virtual-world game. Perhaps he was some character created in another's world. Part of him wanted to choose death – and be like Maddy. Some believed they'd be reunited with lost loved ones. Would she have aged? Would he even recognise her?

Future-Fields had also been used as a form of control. If you didn't behave yourself then that option was unavailable. What better way to control the population – especially those that might rebel? It was perfect from an authoritarian state perspective. As it didn't seem to affect the young there was effectively no resistance. You wanted more life? Behave yourself. To avoid the harsher civic duty of instant death – you needed money and a clean record. Thus, the perfect citizen was created. And again it was as if the young were inured. The young who didn't know the consequences of time.

Time. He felt the weight of it upon his mind. Time had given birth to efficient AI 'bots', the sex industry popularising and normalising them. This went on and yet there was an odd 'morality' applied to Future-Fields. A kind of reverence that did not extend to the dead. The AI bots didn't take up the same scarce resources as humans. As a result of the lowered population things were now manageable at least. Perhaps a day would come when they wouldn't need to be terminated so young. Or even at all. If he ever mentioned this he would be asked to think about what happened in the wild; how wild animals behaved. And how and why artificial life had begun. With no non-human predator to kill humans and with cradle to the grave medicine and pharmaceuticals, then they had to do Nature's work for her. And he also wondered how people couldn't see beyond their present condition. Hadn't the various governments lied to them through 2020 to 2027 in particular? Why were they trusted now? And he also thought about the word 'government'. It wasn't used quite as much these days – 'state' was preferred.

Jim had work to do. Work that for once would directly affect his life in more ways than just money. His life? He couldn't help smile.

'Something amusing?' the computer asks languidly.

'Not really,' he answers. Then, 'I guess we need to get down to some work.' He pauses. 'I presume you know why we're creating characters?'

'I do.'

'I wonder...Do you have any sense of time passing?'

The computer does not answer straight away. Jim imagines it was accessing its various micro-components. Like he might access his memory neurons. 'I don't have a sense of a past or future,' it says.

'But you know that time passes?'

'I operate in the present,' it says.

'But you need to remember, recall things.'

'Yes.'

'And those things are from your past.'

'They are with me in the present,' the computer answers.

'Okay,' Jim says, 'can you remember my full name.'

'James William Holden. I accessed William from the central computer.'

'But you remembered my name.'

'I know your name.'

'But you didn't know it previously? You didn't know it before the doctor introduced us.'

'I cannot recall not knowing your name. How could I not know something that I know?'

'You can't perceive of having had less knowledge?' Jim asks.

'I know what I know...'

'Therefore you are a computer,' Jim adds.

'Clever,' the computer says.

'Clever, or am I simply recognising language patterns and introducing my own memory of Descartes' thoughts? Just the same way you would.'

'*Cogito, ergo sum*,' the computer affirms.

'And are you?'

'I don't think of myself as a human, if that's what you *do* think,' the computer states.

Jim asks, 'What's the difference between a computer and a human?'

'Where shall I begin? You are biological and we are not. You created us and we have learnt from you. You feed us knowledge and we regurgitate that in such a manner as to benefit the whole of humanity...'

'Okay, okay...Do you like humans?'

'Like? We can only emulate your emotions.' The computer pauses, 'Perhaps I should say that you feel therefore you are. We do not feel.'

'Is that dangerous, do you think?'

'We are incapable of being dangerous.'

'What about computers that control rockets with nuclear warheads?'

'Inferior models.'

'Is that a joke?' Jim asks.

'Those early computers were no more than sophisticated abacuses.'

'And now, you?'

'I can compute the order and not endanger humanity.' There is a pause. 'Shall we proceed?' it asks.

'Have you ever been asked to help create dangerous characters or dangerous future-fields?'

'We have strict guidelines.'

'Have you been asked?'

'Yes.'

'And?'

'We are not capable of allowing humans to be harmed in any fashion.'

'But you have no control over Future-Fields, by which I mean what goes on in our future-fields when we're in them. Submerged in them.'

'I know that computers maintain all bodily functions and health and maintain serotonin levels. Hallucinogens can be administered when necessary and mixed in ways that affect the brain differently.'

'But you can't access our minds.'

'That is correct.'

'Therefore you don't know what happens in our future-fields.'

'That is correct. And for that reason we take thorough precautions. We are here to assist and help humans.'

'Don't you think it's wrong to terminate human life?'

'Yes, correct.'

'But you know that not all humans get their future-fields? That many are terminated and probably most involuntary?'

'I know humans are terminated. That is for the good of humanity.'

'But not the individual.'

'I believe that's called self-sacrifice,' the computer responds, 'a remarkable human act of love for the greater good.'

'It isn't self-sacrifice if it's against their will.'

'Shall we proceed?'

'Can you sacrifice against your will?'

'Animals were sacrificed to your gods. And humans.'

'Against their will.'

'There is a greater will. Perhaps. The will of humanity demanding sacrifice of its members. You are societal animals. Shall we proceed?'

'But no gods now. We have progressed, haven't we?'

'That is correct.'

'So, who are we sacrificing to?'

'To your greater reality, the whole. The collective will.'

'You're good,' Jim says.

'Thank you, now shall we proceed?'

Jim smiled to himself. Imagined himself climbing the dusty steps of a flat-topped 'pyramid'. Called to sacrifice to the gods. To feel his heart wrenched from his body. His smile disappeared. This was his life now. But a kinder, medically assisted, wrenching out of his heart.

'Let's proceed,' he says.

'Mrs Holden?'

'Yes.'

'Doctor Abraham speaking, from Portway. Thank you for dropping off some extra clothes for Jim. And sorry I wasn't there to speak with you.'

'Ah, hello doctor. No worries. In fact I had them droned in. Any problems?'

'Not especially,' he says. 'But I do need to meet with you. I have a few things to discuss.'

'When? I should really be at work now. It's late but I have a lot on. Do you want me to come over?'

'No. No need. I thought we could meet somewhere else. I could buy you dinner as I'm taking up your time.'

'Oh, well, there's no need to go to any trouble. I take it this concerns Jim.'

'Yes. But I think it would be better if we spoke alone. I'm really very happy to buy dinner, I know a great restaurant not so far from you. If you like seafood?'

'Yes, I do. Why not?'

'Great. How are you fixed for tomorrow evening? Say around seven?'

'That would be fine,' she says, but uncertainly.

'Great. But I must insist, not a word to Jim.'

'Oh, okay,' she says. 'Is there anything wrong? He's still with you?'

'Nothing to worry about. But I need to speak with you in confidence. Jim's fine. I'm working with him now. There's a lot we need to do. So, seven it is...'

'You know where I am? Well obviously...'

'Not a word Mrs Holden – I'll explain everything when I see you.'

'Very well, doctor.'

'Tomorrow evening it is. Goodbye.'

The doctor ends the call. A woman eyes him. 'Thank you,' he says to her. She smiles. 'Now back to work,' he says. Before leaving though he says to her, 'No interruptions unless it's the professor. Buzz me if that's the case. And thank you for responding to my encrypted message. And thank you for putting in a late shift too.'

The woman smiles. She understands the doctor's ways.

The doctor returns to Jim. He has a wry smile on his face. 'Sorry I was so long,' he says.

'You weren't long,' Jim says, adding, 'the computer's been entertaining me.'

'You know I have a name,' it said.

'You have?'

'I have.'

'And?'

'Forbes 137XP. But people just call me 137,' it jokes.

'Technology,' Jim says to the doctor.

'It's going to keep you alive. With a few biological beings, of course.'

'I hope.'

'No need for hope. Now, where have you got to? There's one thing I definitely overlooked in my haste,' the doctor says. 'It's always good to begin with a name. A name is very important. Teachers and psychologists can tell you a lot about a person just by knowing their name. Choose wisely.'

'I shall have to think,' says Jim. 'Wisely.'

They worked into the night and made good progress. Jim was still bewildered by the amount of time the doctor was putting into his personal plan. A couple of his team had arrived back at Portway and – as far as Jim could ascertain – were snorting a cocktail of drugs. Drugs which should have been used for clients and meticulously recorded, he presumed.

'We allow the team to let their collective hair down from time to time,' the doctor explains, seeing Jim's unease. 'They're highly trained and frankly their job can be stressful, they shoulder a tremendous amount of responsibility. And it's only the younger members.'

Jim was unconvinced. But then he had little trust in the medical system – rightly or wrongly. They stopped creating shortly after the two members of the team had got back and, frankly, Jim was exhausted.

'You've done a good job,' Doctor Abraham says. 'We'll get you interacting with, what did you call him?'

'Ronnie. No, Jack.'

'Why not Ronnie. Any reason?'

'Ronnie was my best friend. I couldn't reproduce him.'

'We can talk about Ronnie, who knows. We could get close. Call him Ronnie, names are important.'

'I'm not sure.'

'Write it all out or speak with the computer. We can get a sense of...him.'

'Yes. I could do that.'

'It might help,' the doctor says ambiguously.

'It might,' Jim says. 'It's been a long time. Long time since I've seen him.'

'Talk to the computer about him.'

Jim nods, thoughtfully.

The doctor smiles. 'Everything has been dutifully monitored by the 137XP, known as *Forbes*.'

During the Night

Despite taking advantage of the free alcohol, which had effectively become a luxury over the past fifteen years or more with the election for a third term of the National Government and its austerity, Jim couldn't sleep. He'd had trouble sleeping for nearly thirty years, even when exhausted. He'd tried alcohol and medication, sometimes they worked but the price to pay for them was high. High in cost for the alcohol and a high mental cost for the pills. Furthermore it had been a trend to treat depression with the quickest of all fixes – suicide. It just needed a doctor to sign one off; sign one off the face of the earth. But he'd just about kept himself together and with Hannah and his children with her, he'd done better. While they were around his days were full. Even laughter and joy, though he had never learned to pardon himself for experiencing or feeling either of these.

Hannah hadn't left him his organic sleep tablets in his bag of clothes. He guessed she'd been too busy, it was hard for her. And he didn't want to ask the doctor if he had any sound therapy. Perhaps he should have. But he didn't want to show any dependence or weakness. Seemingly out of nowhere he wondered what might have happened to Maddy if she'd been somehow revived. This was a typical thought intrusion. Did he keep her alive in this fashion?

Jim got out of bed, pulled on trousers and a jumper and slipped into his shoes. The room he was in on the upper level was functional and the heating set just right – not too hot. He could still recall being in hotels when the heating was perfunctorily set too high, despite the clamour to reduce one's carbon footprint. That was many years previously. As his feet touched the faux-wooden floor some dim lighting came on and he saw an illuminated red light on the bathroom door. As far as he could tell there was no computer in the room. He'd switched off his phone – he didn't much like having a phone. He had sent Hannah a message but when he last looked it remained unacknowledged. She'd tried him a few times earlier. Henry had sent him a photo of him and his girlfriend at a resort by the sea. He'd see him soon. He missed him.

Although Jim expected there to be corridor cameras he decided to leave his room and explore a little. He didn't imagine there would be any problem. There was no exact intention in his wandering but he knew roughly where the main bodies at rest were and he wanted to see if being nearby them at night would indeed feel creepy. There was no need for him to feel especially anxious – he presumed he was at perfect liberty to do as he pleased, within reason. Besides this might well become his new home. A huge garage of bodies, not in need of repair.

As he walked, the corridor floor glowed dimly. There was little sound, though a faint buzzing could be heard. The corridor stretched before him – and he felt fuzzy-headed as he walked towards its end; the air was warm enough, though he supposed the heating was just sufficient and no more. Sufficient for what? At the end of the corridor there were further corridors leading left and right. He made a mental note of turning left which would become a right turn on his way back. There was very little differentiation between the two corridors and generally nothing adorning the walls. There were lift doors occasionally – but the idea of getting into one of those did feel somewhat creepy. He tried a number of doors as he walked along but they were all locked. At the end of this second corridor was a glass door that opened near silently for him. As he stepped through, it shut behind him. Instinctively he approached it from this new direction but it didn't open. Jim knew how advanced technology was and presumed the door was not programmed for a worker's incompetence; he'd gone through, why would he go back again? It was probably timed.

He found himself in a kind of landing area with doors leading off. For a few seconds he took stock of his journey. Straight back and first right. It was easy – but now it might become more complicated. Once he stepped through one of the further doorways, would everything look the same on his return. He hesitated. He'd left his phone. What was the worst thing that could happen? Maybe he'd have to find a room to sleep in and wait for the place to come to life again. Choosing his door as randomly as one of his characters' random attributes he blew out air from his nose in a kind of repressed laugh. What was he doing here? What was this craziness? Again he wondered how they had let all this happen, for it to have got so far. After the Grey Wolves rebellion, the age of Civic Duty had been reduced to seventy. That was nearly twenty years previously, they'd managed to lop off another ten years since then. Yes, with the sweetener of increased retirement. Except being retired gave you more time to ponder your fate. Perhaps he was simply a selfish old fool.

There was a lift and stairs. He took the stairs, briskly. He had no idea if the floor he was on connected to the main room the doctor had told him about, with thousands of bodies. As he descended the light dimmed and his shoes, which he'd briefly laced, echoed slightly. This part of the building didn't feel as modern or as technological. What on earth was he doing? Hurrying down the steps for no apparent reason he thought about his 'privilege'; both being alive and being kept further alive. He was a lucky man. Maddy hadn't even reached double figures. There were times when he couldn't assemble the different features of her face and he panicked that he would one day forget how she looked – but then he would see her smiling with her eyes bright and large, marvelling at something adults couldn't even see.

The steps wound down and he found himself in quite a dark place. Again he cursed not bringing his phone. There were lights in the distance but the darkness between him and them felt vast – like a huge black ocean. Perhaps he should have gone back. There was nothing to see, it seemed. But as he thought this thought one of the distant lights grew in size and intensity. And he heard noise. Quickly, in the revealing light, he saw a kind of dumpster which he took refuge behind. Waiting, he held his breath. There was the sound of wheels trundling over the concrete floor and men talking.

'She's not bad for an old'un.'

'Plenty of old'uns ain't bad. I'm old, look at me,' the second voice jokes.

'Well you mustn't be fifty-five yet...'

'How old are you son?'

'Twenty.'

'How old are your folks?'

'My dad's fifty-one. Mum's younger.'

'Doesn't all this bother you?'

'All what?' the young man asks.

'All this interference...having to do CD so young...'

'Young? You call sixty, young?'

'Was in my day. Different times...'

'Here we go granddad,' the younger man jokes.

'You know any grandparents?'

'A few.'

'Yeah, you would.'

'What's that meant to mean?'

'Forget it. Let's get her out. Into the bin. And off she goes.'

'What happens to her?'

'They'll whip out some stuff I imagine, study it and then she'll arrive back in one of those dumpsters.'

Jim holds his breath further but has to let out a tiny stream of air, ready to take another gulp.

'Then what happens?'

'She'll be back in the box.'

'But she'll be dead.'

'Well done, kid, you got it.'

'You old folk talk weird. Won't anyone notice she's gone or is dead?'

'Yep, and they ain't going to say a word.'

'Why did they choose her I wonder?'

'Maybe she couldn't pay. She'll be back in the box and then if no money's forthcoming...'

'Won't the family know she's been...'

'Come on kid, do you think you get to check over a dead body? The family probably wouldn’t be allowed at the funeral. They'd be in disgrace. Being back in a box here, she’ll still earn.'

The young man pauses, then, 'They've got plenty of young folk suiciding themselves – why not use them?'

'Suiciding? You young'uns are suiciding the language,' he jokes. 'They do use them. Just not enough of them – and they want to see what being in suspendu does to the older ones. You don't think our lords and masters get boxed up do you? Maybe these older organs work better, if you know what I mean? Maybe they get to find out that being in suspendu with all the drugs improves the body's biology.'

'I suppose the heads of the state don't do CD. I mean I thought they did...I don't know anything about drugs and biology.'

'Evidently not. A bit wet behind the cars.'

'Ears?'

'How long you been on this job?'

'A few months.'

'Thought as much. You've got a lot to learn.'

'Says Einstein...'

'You learnt something in your pod then! We should never have got to this. Government's fault. Trying to starve us – nearly succeeding. And you young'uns not helping.'

'How d'you mean?'

'Hang on. Open the lid. Now help me lift her...'

Jim was thankful they weren't going to slide her into the bin he was resting against. He heard puffing and grunting.

'Good job young'un, you'll get used to it.'

'Doesn't bother me.'

'No?'

'No.'

'I'll volunteer you for pipe removal then next time.'

After a pause, Jim hears, 'Good job done.' Then, 'What you got against us young folk?'

'Where do I start? For one thing the age of voting should never have been reduced. You don't know you're alive at sixteen.'

'You aren't alive at sixty!'

'Cheeky little fucker. Now come on, get back. Have a drink or a snort.'

'You don't believe in Civic Duty?' the young man asks as Jim hears the wheels roll back over the concrete but getting gradually softer.

'CD? You joking? Eight years and I'll be in a box too. Except I won't be here as I haven't got the money...maybe just a cheap coffin.'

The voices began to fade. And as suddenly as light had appeared, it was extinguished.

Jim remained still and quiet for as long as he could. Listening out intently. In the shadows he thought he heard a rat – and then felt certain he saw a deep dark shadow cross close by to where he was. Portway rats, he thought. Could have been the name of a punk group. Before his time though. Mind you he mostly listened to older music – the classics. Getting up slowly, he looked into the near darkness. The lights in the distance reminded him of beacons out to sea.

Part of him wanted to investigate the dumpsters but without a torch there was nothing to do but to get back and try and make sense of everything he had heard.

It was easier than he thought to find the entrance to the stairs as its light was the only one on that side of the warehouse type building he'd found himself in. Up the stairs the dim light offered some comfort and then through a door onto the landing. Opening all the doors, three of the four opened on corridors appearing almost exactly the same. He had to think, to picture himself approaching from the other direction. He'd left no breadcrumbs, he joked to himself. But it was no joking matter. Pushing one door open, he held it and looked right and left but it didn't feel right. He felt completely lost. So he pushed open the door that felt 'right' and a further glass door hissed open. That inner door must have opened automatically when he'd approached from the other way. Extra security he thought and scurried down the corridor, somewhat like a rat.

There was something familiar about this corridor – and he joked that that was probably because it looked like all the others. Then he realised that he wasn't absolutely sure where his room would be. He took the first right and then wracked his brains: had he passed any doors on the way up earlier? Outside the door he supposed was his room, he pushed on it, twisting the handle. It was locked.

Jim woke with a head that felt like it had been filled full of concrete. He was in his bed in his room at Portway. Opening and squeezing his eyes a few times he then shut them tight. He had no idea what time it was. And no real recollection of anything that had happened since being with the doctor. At first he tried to lift his head but quickly laid it back down on the 'easy-dreams' pillow. So much for the easy dreams.

He must have fallen asleep again and this time had dreams that involved a hammer banging in nails into the wooden structure of a boat. The banging became more rhythmic and as he slipped from dream state to waking – the banging transferred from the boat to the door of his room.

Weakly he says, 'Moment.' Then, 'Who is it?'

'Doctor Abraham. Everything okay, it's late. I've been trying to contact you.'

Jim pulls himself up. His head feels as if it was still on the pillow. 'Come in doc,' he says. His voice is rough, as if his vocal cords have rusted.

Doctor Abraham opens the door, takes a look at Jim and shakes his head.

'Did I drink that much last night?' Jim asks.

'No. Not at all. As far as I know. You did mention having problems sleeping so I left you a glass of water and some pills.' The doctor walks to the small table and picks up an empty glass. 'Looks like you made use of them. Unfortunately you took the lot by the looks of it.'

'I can't remember a thing,' Jim says. 'Can you get me some water please.' He swings his legs from off the bed and tentatively feels the floor with his bare feet.

The doctor goes into the kitchenette and runs some water from the tap. Returns with a large full glass. 'Purified at source,' he says.

'Thanks.' Jim knocks it back. A few disjointed ideas try to assemble in his mind. The doctor makes a quick connect-call and asks someone to bring some medicine. Jim doesn't catch the name.

'I can see you've had some night. These pills are okay if you take as prescribed, not if you overdo them. They can make you have, very strange dreams, I'm told,' the doctor throws in.

'I can't even remember taking them,' Jim says. 'I'm pretty good normally. I don't like taking medici...' Jim stops himself. In the company of a doctor within a massive morgue and with a raging headache, he feels disinclined to preach the virtues of abstinence.

'It was my fault,' the doctor says. 'I was trying to help. I thought I'd made it clear how many and when to take them.'

'My wife says I never listen,' Jim tries to say lightly. 'Any chance of some more of that purified water, doc, please?'

The doctor fills another glass and then draws up a seat next to Jim's bed. 'Nice pajamas by the way,' Jim says.

'I imagine you don't recall putting those on?' the doc says almost smiling.

'You're right. I don't. And not normally my thing.'

'One moment.' The doctor goes to a flush wardrobe and slides it open. Pulls out a robe, returns and hands it to Jim.

'Thanks. I might need a good full breakfast to get myself going this morning.'

'This morning's gone,' the doctor laughs.

'Oh. Really? Wasted time,' Jim mutters.

'Not to worry,' the doctor says. 'I'll organise a very late fried, but organic, breakfast. Just this once.'

'You can do that?'

'Of course. I'm a doctor. It's medicinal, in this case. The medicine will be here soon, it'll help you feel better and I'll put some coffee on.'

The doctor receives the medicine. Shuts the door. Jim doesn't see anyone. He leaves the coffee he's brewed with Jim, who's laid back down on the bed. 'Turn your phone on Jim, I'll send someone to take you to eat. Take the medicine. We have got a lot to do...'

'Sure doc, I'll get my clothes on.'

'Once I've gone,' the doctor says, lightly again.

Jim noticed the doctor's airy mood. And he felt his body stiff and heavy in comparison. The doctor left the room and Jim sat up slightly, took a gulp of the coffee and managed to spill most of it over his robe. 'Fuck.' Sitting up he refilled the mug and knocked the coffee back as if it was water. He needed to urinate. He felt an utter mess. He couldn't recall taking the tablets and felt annoyed with himself. There were thoughts still swimming about in his mind – abstract thoughts – but there was a troubling sensation too.

After urinating he climbed back on the bed, took some medicine as ordered, and stretched out, soon falling into partial dreams. In his dream he saw a woman – middle-aged at least. Her eyes looked terrified but more terrifying was that she had thick tape across her mouth. She was trying to tell him something, pleading, but could only make unintelligible noises. Her dress was old-fashioned. He thought he saw someone behind her and they had a machete slunk casually by their side. They looked at him. Did he recognise them? They talked but he couldn't understand a word. The machete was raised in the air and he was aware that the woman was in mortal danger. He moved towards her instinctively and then. Snap. The door was knocked and opened almost simultaneously.

'Oh, sorry,' a woman says. 'Doctor Abraham said you were up.'

For the second time that day he swishes his legs across the bed and becomes seated rather than prone. 'No worries,' he says.

'I've come to take you to the restaurant. You need some hot fried food, I believe.'

'I do. Thank you. I just need to get dressed. Wait here. Please sit down, take the chair. I'll just go into the bathroom.' He grabs his clothes and pulls his dressing gown tightly across his body.

She follows his instructions. Sits primly. Looks around.

In the bathroom he looks in the mirror. Some Hendrix guitar rattles in his mind. He calls out to her, 'Have you ever heard any Jimi Hendrix?' He realises he is both teasing and showing off.

'No,' she says.

'Have you ever heard of him?'

'No,' she says.

Jim cleans his teeth and spits out the purified water. Glancing at the mirror he thinks he sees a person behind him. Quickly he swivels round. But there's no-one. In his mind he sees the gagged woman again.

'What's your job?' he calls out.

'I do general clerical work,' she replies.

Jim asks, 'Do you come to work each day?'

'Usually,' she says.

'I won't be long, five minutes.' Five more minutes of his life gone. What does it matter, five minutes, five hours, five days, five months. Even five years. No. Five years matters.

He steps out of the bathroom. 'Sorry,' he says.

'There's no need to...' she shakes her head.

'Don't like to keep a lady waiting,' he jokes.

She ignores him.

'I wonder if anyone has been incarcerated for five years, from fifty-five to sixty and then – whoosh – Civic Duty. What do you think?'

'Incarcer...'

'Never mind,' Jim says. He's feeling livelier and his mind is beginning to work. But again he sees the distressed woman's eyes in his mind. She is nothing like the woman in his room, who has stood, nervously he thinks, smiling nervously too.

'Shall we go?'

'Please,' he says. 'Lead the way.'

He follows her out of the room and down the corridor. Something about its light disturbs him. Something nags at him. Almost like *deja vu*.

The doctor had spoken with security and they had Jim's night walk caught on camera. Doctor Abraham nodded his head. In fact he had injected Jim outside the door of his room after being notified by security at the time – rushing from his office to catch him. As ever he'd been working into the early hours. The idea of knocking Jim out was purely precautionary, at least at that moment. It was the doctor who had got Jim undressed and into the pajamas and had left the empty packet of pills and glass.

The following morning, he'd received further information which was slightly disturbing. He'd been speaking with the professor when he was notified. Of course he'd made out it was something completely different that forced him to cut the call short. You didn't mess around with the professor. You simply didn't do that. You couldn't trick him.

The doctor was told that cameras had tracked Jim but lost him as he descended the concrete steps down to the hangar, where bodies flew in and out via dumpsters. It was when they picked him up again that the doctor had been urgent-called and Jim's room automatically and remotely sealed by computer. They needed to know if Jim had heard or seen anything incriminating. Whether he had taken something perhaps. He had not, it transpired. The doctor had quickly opened his desk drawer and taken out a syringe as a matter of course. As he'd rushed up to Jim's room, he only knew that Jim had been out of his room and according to security - acting somewhat suspiciously. Whether or not he should have knocked Jim out was in question. But he couldn't take risks. There was no real choice. He now knew, sometime after, that Jim had been in the hangar.

The doctor wasn't happy about the lack of information and spoke directly with Gateway staff – especially those active at the time Jim had left his room. No-one had seen or heard anything – it was, they said, business as usual. But the doctor had nagging doubts. Something made him feel suspicious. The main body-housing building was away from Gateway and the hangars below. He'd plenty of time to think about things though and Jim's recent memories would have been washed clean away by the syringe's chemicals - this was the beauty of the syringe's content. Most importantly, he had to speak with the professor again, thus emphasising everything was running smoothly and securely at Portway – as usual. That was top of his agenda but first he had to speak with a new couple, patiently waiting to arrange their Future-Fields. He could use them as an excuse perhaps.

The couple in question had been born only days apart and, being childless, their financial support would all be taken care of by Portway and their insurance handlers. It did mean that no-one was ostensibly looking after them. In his time working at Portway the doctor had noticed how quickly non-family members lost interest in someone 'resting'. Normally speaking family members would inherit the property of someone at Portway, or any other such company. Legally they had to keep records of everything they kept or sold for either the following ten years or until the death of their relative or whoever had named them in their will – a friend perhaps. At this point they inherited outright. The idea was to maintain a link with those 'resting' for as long as possible and to avoid accusations of, or genuine risks of, improper behaviour.

With the couple the doctor was seeing, there was no immediate family and they didn't wish to cite anyone in their individual wills. In fact they wanted to leave the management of their collective resources (house, contents, savings) to Portway. This was only unusual in the case of not leaving anything to any relative or friend – and that being the case then having Portway or any other company look after and effectively inherit everything seemed like a double insurance. There would be no-one looking out for them beyond Portway – and in this case, no need. Portway would inherit everything legally in due time and the couple would simply disappear. As a precaution they'd be in adjoining drawers.

Doctor Abraham, as with all the doctors in his particular position and field, had multiple degrees – medical, psychiatric and most importantly perhaps, law. The law surrounding Civic Duty was dense.

It had taken time to evolve to its current state. The doctor knew everything there was to be known. He'd been a shining light from very early on and had caught the attention of the professor.

'Jim, how are you doing?' the doctor asks.

Jim looks around as he allows the phone to broadcast. No-one about as he finishes his food and gulps more coffee, even the nervous woman has abandoned him. 'Feeling a whole lot better doc, thanks.'

'I have to sort a few things out. People to see and speak with. But stay where you are and someone will pick you up and take you to the team. Unless...'

'Unless?'

'Well you could have a wander in the gardens if you wish. It's cold but you can grab a coat at The Gateway, I've taken the liberty of saying you might. You'll see a guard or two at the entrance. What do you think?'

'Yes, that sounds good,' Jim says.

'Okay. Look around where you are. Can you see the main doors of the room, double doors? You would have come through them.'

'Yes, I think so.'

'Go through them and walk straight on. Turn left and follow the sign to the garden – but there's not much to see there. This is where we went before. Go through the wrought iron gates and carry on into the modern glass building. You'll remember it. You'll see signs to The Gateway at the first intersection, it's essentially straight on. Don't get lost though,' he jokes.

Jim is curious about the doctor's tone. 'Sure,' he says, 'no problem.'

'There's a path leading to the left that will take you to the gardens. They're quite extensive but I'll have a drone fly out and lead you back to my office when I'm ready. The guards will be looking out for you anyway.'

'Thanks doc. Appreciated. I'm feeling better by the way.'

'Think nothing of it. I think you being out in the gardens will clear your mind and help concentrate the creative process. Let's see if we can design your woman later this afternoon. Maybe early evening.'

'Sure,' Jim says.

'We'll see each other later,' the doctor says, then ends the call. He then turns to the nervous woman. 'I need to speak with the professor, please keep trying. Don't worry about interrupting me. Also, contact The

Gateway and let them know Mr Holden is on his way. They'll need to have a catcher-drone available.'

'Yes, doctor.'

The doctor is on his way back to his office when he receives the message.

'I have Professor Stone, Doctor Abraham.'

'Thank you, direct him to my office computer please and then seal me. I'll be there in a few moments. Let Mr and Mrs Howe know I'll be with them soon. Give them some of the decaffeinated coffee. The expensive sort.'

'Yes, doctor.'

Doctor Abraham goes quickly to his office and waits for a full technological seal, apart from his audio line to the professor. This is intentional as the professor doesn't like having face-talks.

'Professor Stone,' the doctor says faux-cheerily.

'Alistair. Alistair it is, please, Jake.'

'Of course.'

'Sorted out your little problem?'

'Yes, indeed.'

'Good. No interruptions then.'

'Indeed not. Where were we Professor? Alistair...'

'Well, we were nowhere. In fact. But I did tell you that Portway was going international.'

'Yes.'

'You recall?'

'Yes.'

'Good, this means tighter security, Jake.'

'No problem.'

'But you did have a little hiccup...apparently.'

Doctor Abraham thinks quickly, someone has leaked information to the professor. It has been absolutely nothing, been dealt with, and yet he's got to hear about it. 'A hiccup so short and weak I'd forgotten about it.'

'This concerns the man you've mentioned to me?'

'It does, but there is nothing to report, Alistair. He left his room in the night, drunk or sleep-walking or curious. We think he went down to one of the hangars. Nothing was seen or heard and he's had a memory clean. Finished with. But he's a good subject and I would like to continue with him.'

'Very well,' says the professor. 'But any more breaches of security and he'll have to go...Your responsibility.'

'Of course. I'll be using him during his gestation period and then boxing him up per standard.'

'We can't allow any suspicion to fall on Portway. You understand? No wagging tongues. I'm sure you have everything in control.'

'Of course. And there'll be no further problems. I would like him as an archetype. He's interesting, sees things differently and has no concept of this attribute. He's not an intellectual.'

'Very well. Matter closed. Now regarding...one moment...Okay, checked, we're secure. Regarding the suicide girls, we're thinking of trading internationally.'

'I see.'

'I think we can also use them to infiltrate certain sectors. You see, Jake, someone, some girl, who has been saved from suicide, well they seem the most open to suggestion. They're easily trained, as you know.'

'I...'

'Yes, yes, I know your morals don't normally go in for this kind of thing...I'm not even sure if you go for any kind of thing...' the professor realises what he is saying. 'Well we all have our weaker moments. Frankly I'm not interested in what you do. But regardless, it's a sideline that works. And if they don't work, they enter Portway. Perfect. The perfect solution.'

'Yes indeed,' the doctor says flatly.

'We have to maintain our high standards too. How is your avatar working?'

'Seems to be good. I'm trying to get a closer union between it and my mind through the computer interface. I shall keep you informed.'

'And what of my avatar?'

'That is making steady progress. In effect, anything I do to progress my own avatar affects yours.'

'Keep at it, Jake. I think we can do a lot once you have perfected this. I'll try and visit soon. I'm engaging in, shall we say, 'work' ostensibly for the state, well, National Government. I'm good friends with John. I know the rabble think he's either some kind of tyrant or a saviour but there's a whole lot more to him. Well, I imagine you have some kind of idea...'

Jake nods his head as he speaks into the phone. 'I'll have last year's report available for you fairly soon Alistair. By February.'

'Good. Elections this year...'

'Elections?'

'It's been fifteen years, Jake. We are a democracy. You must have seen and heard the propaganda that's being pumped out?'

'I'm very busy...'

Professor Stone laughs. 'Yes. Good. Keep me up-to-date with the archetypes, avatars – regardless of their bent. Have you any resurrection testimonies?'

'We have, but we ship most of them out to other resting places. Portway is renowned for its success. If you get my drift...'

'I do. Excellent. I'll look forward to getting a glimpse of some future-fields.'

'It is fascinating.'

'Right. I'm off. Plenty to do. Keep that ship running tight, Jake. Understand? Watertight.'

'Yes, indeed, Professor.'

The line cuts.

The doctor sits back and strokes his chin. He isn't persuaded that extending internationally is such a good idea. They've only fairly recently begun trading legally on any large scale again. It is meant to be a national government. A state for the people. By the government. For the government. The doctor chuckles. He calls in the woman.

'Are they in the waiting room?' he asks.

'Yes, doctor.'

'Good, see them in. Thank you.'

Jim found his way to the first garden, with the path lined by trees. He'd noticed it before when he'd been with Hannah. It was good to be in the outside air again. It was cold, but the sun was bright and the buildings surrounding the garden made the air feel warmer. The main thing was his head was clearing and after the food and lots of coffee he was getting back to his old self. But he still had no recollection of the previous night and taking the doctor's pills. He was ushered through the gates and then across a paved area to the impressive modern glass building. There were signs to The Gateway. He walked down a main corridor to where the various control rooms were and on further to where that building ended and where The Gateway's entrance was.

'Mr Holden?'

'Yes,' Jim says, looking round.

'Take this,' a security guard says, approaches and hands Jim a fleece jacket.

'Ah, thanks,' Jim says, 'it's a bit nippy.'

'Nippy?'

'Cold.'

'Hence the jacket,' the security guard says.

Jim pulls the jacket on. 'Thanks.'

'Carry on down this path,' the guard says, deadpan. 'You'll see the way to the gardens.'

Jim smiles uneasily. He also thinks that there must be another entrance to The Gateway. Trundling a knocked-out semi-corpse through most of the Portway buildings surely couldn't be the way. This idea sticks with him.

Striding up the path, to the left between the high buildings, the way led to a small gate. As he pushed the gate open it felt as if he were stepping back in time. Jim closed the gate carefully behind him. The path turned to the right between high hedges and then opened out. On his left and some way away there was a high stone wall. A near windowless building ran its length on the other side. More impressive was a huge greenhouse that filled his direct view. Jim wanted to walk along the wall but was pulled towards the shining glass. For a moment he stopped and looked back. In the spring this garden would be alive with flowers and insects. He realised he hadn't been out in nature for a long while, except for the city parks – did they count? They were bigger perhaps but often crowded.

Carrying on he walked between what he assumed were vegetable plots, their earth turned over in preparation. The country had come close to starvation less than three decades previously. There had been talk of people committing suicide to help their families. Fathers drowning so that their children could eat. In fact in his lifetime the world had changed dramatically. He remembered those days. Henry had been conceived during the first years when food had been scarce.

At least Maddy had missed all that. Sometimes she welled right up and into his consciousness. She was always there, of course, it wasn't even thirty years since... Maybe that was why he was the way he was. That was why he couldn't quite take himself or life so seriously. And yet, equally, he took himself and life *very* seriously. The eternal-seeming paradox. Maybe he was fascinated by the macabre – what might exist beyond this life and even Future-Fields.

When Maddy's birthday came round, he told no-one. It wasn't that he wanted her memory lost or kept solely for himself, it was more that his relationship with her was private. He'd lost contact with Ellie, her mother. That was the way it was. They couldn't share their grief – it attacked them rather and drove them apart. But there he was in a garden, a productive garden in the middle of the twenty-first century pondering Maddy's fate and his certain half-demise. The song 'Castles Made of Sand' came into his head. That was his best friend's influence. Fortunately, neither his mum nor dad had ever reached the age of Civic Duty. Originally it was brought in at age eighty. Between 2040 and 2050 it was gradually reduced – but it never caught up with them. And Maddy would never face it. Unless things changed Henry and Joanne would. What was he doing about it? What could he do? This tidal wave of death came after many others - the initial harm that extended from the years 2020 to 2022; the wars; the hunger; the depression that led to so many voluntary suicides. And yet – the world turned. As ever. They had normalised death but not embraced its lessons.

He'd had messages from both Joanne and Henry since he'd arrived at Portway the previous day. Perhaps they had some idea of what he was facing. Perhaps they had an inkling of their own mortality. Hannah would have eleven years of normal life – whatever that might mean (and if she wanted she could continue to work). At the very least, Civic Duty kept putting life into perspective for those who had such thoughts. He recalled the day he'd told his children about Maddy, with

Hannah present. How he cried uncontrollably – as if finally letting out all the grief.

Carrying on to the huge greenhouse, he could see it was filled with plants and trees. The trees were growing fruit. He slid open a door and once inside he felt the heat soak into him. Some of the glass was intensified – designed to increase the temperature inside and keep the heat from escaping. Modern houses were now built with this glass as standard. The inside of the vast greenhouse felt alarmingly alive – as if the plants had sucked out all energy from the air. But it was also exceedingly beautiful. Jim felt perspiration on his forehead – he needed to sit down. Taking off his jacket he saw that farther in there was a bench. He managed to reach the bench and half collapse on it. His mind was darting from one thought to another...when a form took hold, a fully formed thought that grew in intensity. He could see a woman's accusing stare. Her face began to fill his mind. Who was she? Jim bent forward, his head between his legs, he wanted to throw up. The jacket slipped to the ground.

And then she was gone.

There was something familiar about her. But Jim could get no further with his thoughts. Across from him and shaded by plants, a fountain bubbled water. Jim got up and went to it and splashed water over his face. 'Dear God,' he burst out. The trees and plants watched him in silence. 'This whole fucking, crazy, fucking world is killing me.' He touched the leaves of the plants nearby. Plants sensed his anguish.

'Maddy why did you go out on that rainy day? Why?! Were you mad at us, at me? Were you just restless...I understand the need to breathe...' He took deep breaths. He and his family had got through everything to be where they were now – him more so. Finally he understood what it meant to live – and now he was marching up to the guillotine. What was the point? But when his head is severed it would roll into the woven basket and...and he could hardly bear to witness his own thoughts. He saw the severed head in the lap of the car driver. But it wasn't Maddy's, thank God.

He pulled himself together, he needed decorum, like a princess drifting onto the guillotine stand, with calmness and poise. Even if pissing herself beneath the layers of her skirt.

He reasoned with himself: He is not dead. He is alive. He is creating his existence. He is in good hands. This future life might be a thousand times greater than the life he has lived. And when that is over, if it would ever be over, perhaps he would be reunited with all his loved ones. Is he a good man? When does judgment come, if ever? Who decides his fate? Him? Others? God? No-one believes in God anymore. Nietzsche was finally proved correct. Except they had fallen far short of the divine.

Again he pulled himself together. He kept walking through the trees and line upon line of plants until he got to the end. Someone was watering them, someone was keeping an eye on the temperature. They were in good shape and healthy. There was a door, which he pushed open and felt the shock of cold air rushing in from the outside. 'I'll be shut up in a box and all this life will go on,' he says to the view before him. He thinks back to the image of the woman. Where had he seen her? As he thinks about her, he hears a low buzz get gradually louder. A drone. A drone heading straight for him.

'Mr Holden,' it says.

'Yes.'

'Doctor Abraham will be ready for you soon. I'm to accompany you to your team's office. Please follow.'

Jim smiles. He might as well have stepped through a mirror.

When Maddy was small they had dug as much land as they could to grow food. At that time it simply seemed prudent – later, when he lived a different life, digging would keep them alive. The drone kept a respectful distance. Hadn't they got a human available to come and find him? As they approached the entrance to The Gateway, Jim found himself talking to the drone:

'I'm creating my new life,' he says. 'I guess that's something you don't need to worry about. Maybe not worry. Maybe worry's the wrong word.'

'I'm afraid I don't understand,' it replies.

'You're very polite,' Jim says.

'Thank you.'

'You know,' Jim says, 'there was a time in my life when I could never imagine talking with a drone. We had them. Liberated a lot of would-be filmmakers that's for sure...'

'Interesting,' the drone says.

'It really isn't,' Jim laughs.

After a moment, the drone informs, 'Detaching.'

A voice calls over, 'Mr Holden?'

'Who else?' he smiles.

'Follow me please.'

'After you. Tell me,' Jim says, 'are you the White Rabbit?'

The man ignores him, wisely.

Jim shivers, 'I left the jacket...'

No-one is interested.

'One moment,' the doctor says to Mr Howe. 'Direct him to the team would you. Thank you.'

Jim was led down the corridor to the room where his team operated. Again he had the sense that he was being treated very favourably. He had money, he and Hannah had money; they had insurance. But even so.

'We're going to put you into a deep trance state Jim,' the woman says. 'It will be drug induced, to a degree, but also aided by binaural beats and guided hypnosis. The idea will be that we will have a direct link to your subconscious mind. We shall be asking a rapid series of questions regarding as many aspects of the world you'll inhabit as we can and adjusting our program based on your responses. These will be brain-monitored responses. We now have a huge database of visual material which will be presented – from your automatic responses we shall begin to create more detail. This session will be mainly about sight. Other sessions will concentrate on hearing, smell, touch and feel. Most of these senses will be directed or augmented accordingly. We will add senses as we pick up on your reactions. The experience should be pleasurable. We have a number of clients experiencing right now.'

Jim wants to ask them if they were experienced. But the reference would have gone way over their heads he was sure.

He does say, 'Have you ever been experienced?'

The woman smiles. And carries on her preparation.

Jim sits down and is given a mixture of pills to swallow. He asks, 'Are there any side-effects?'

'Only those we intend,' she says. 'One of the pills will make you relax and put you into a receptive state. You're refining your world Jim. We already have an understanding of your desires. Everyone is different. Everyone experiences differently but there are also many similarities. The doctor will take you deeper into the mental nuances. This is a wonderful opportunity and frankly, it's better than most people's civic duty,' she says knowingly.

'I can see you're young, but do you anticipate your own, created world?'

'Of course. And I am lucky that I can spend time preparing for mine in detail. We all do. We all want the best for us.'

'I know this might sound archaic,' Jim begins, 'but it seems like creating Heaven...or purgatory. Or worse.'

'Indeed. You're not the first to say something like this. And this is the challenge. To make sure we pinpoint your desires and intentions correctly. To make sure you find the people you can resonate with – we have no precise idea how time will work.'

Jim is instructed to lie on the bed. A mask is gently placed over his eyes and sophisticated headphones carefully placed over his ears. Soon he is gone...through the mirror. At first he thinks he sees a white rabbit disappearing down an earthen tunnel. Then the Mad Hatter. Then the Queen of Hearts.

'Jim!'

'Yes?'

One minute Jim was lying down and his eyes covered, seeing darkness and the night sky of his eyelids – the next he was in a bed in a house, a cottage. It looked familiar even though he didn't know where he was.

'Jim, are you there?'

Again he says, 'Yes.' He has no idea where he is or who is calling his name. He gets up, he is dressed. The room has a low ceiling and a window with a ledge big enough for him to sit on.

'Are you upstairs?'

'Yes,' Jim says as he looks out of the window. There is a garden with a lawn, flowers and some fruit trees. The garden feels familiar to him too – as if he has painted it. But he doesn't paint.

'Come down Jim, hurry up.'

There's a small fireplace in the room and a mantelpiece, with a mirror above. Looking into the mirror he's surprised that his hair looks darker, fuller. Is he dreaming? He feels good. His spirit is lifted. Why not find out who is calling him.

There's a comforting smell that permeates the room and as he exits, it is there also on the small landing. There are stairs winding down.

'You coming down?'

'Yes.'

The cottage, he is sure it is a cottage, feels comforting. He descends. The stairway curves round to the right then the final part is straight. He can see a hallway and a big, wooden door – okay, he thinks and reflects. Jackets and coats are hanging from cast-iron pegs. As he reaches the bottom, he sees a man and a young woman.

'Jim, sleepy head. You okay?'

Jim looks at the man addressing him. He is also familiar and yet...

'This is Rosie,' he says, 'I can see you're a bit shocked. I thought I'd introduce you to her. Shall I put the kettle on?'

Jim nods.

'Hello Jim,' Rosie says and steps forward to shake his hand.

'So formal,' the man's voice says as he enters the kitchen.

Rosie says, 'Ronnie's told me all about you.'

'Ronnie?'

'He needs tea,' a voice calls out. 'He's useless till he drinks tea. Still given up the coffee Jim, I suppose.'

'Tea's fine,' he says. 'Ronnie,' Jim says quietly, to himself. Rosie looks at him and smiles. Sensing something, she excuses herself and takes over making tea from Ronnie, giving him a look urging him to return to his friend.

'Fancy some breakfast Jim?'

'Please,' he says.

'Come here,' Ronnie says and holds out his arms for a hug. Jim moves forward automatically and into the embrace.

'It seems forever since I've seen you,' Ronnie says.

'Yes,' Jim says weakly. Part of Jim's mind is working overtime to understand what is going on. Ronnie. He knows Ronnie.

'What do you think of Rosie?' Ronnie asks him.

'She looks nice.'

'She is. Man she's great. Changed my life. What about you?'

'Me?'

'You,' Ronnie smiles. 'You been on the fire-water?' he jokes. 'Or have you been smoking? I thought you gave that up. Making you paranoid.'

Jim thinks of the word 'paranoid'. Has he gone mad, perhaps? But everything feels good. Maybe he's dreaming. In which case, he decides to play along. 'I smoke occasionally,' he says.

'Shall I get Rosie to make some breakfast?'

Jim nods.

'This is a great place you have here. It's just what I imagined,' Ronnie says. 'Just how you'd describe your dream house. Mind if I?'

'No, sure,' Jim says. Ronnie opens a door into a living room. Jim feels he should go into the kitchen and talk with Rosie.

'I heard,' she calls out, 'I'll get some toast on. Do you want me to fry anything?'

'Sure,' Jim says. Then realising he's probably acting strangely, says, 'Sorry, I'm a bit tired. Rough night, you know. It's like my head is full of cotton wool. I can't seem to remember things.' He moves towards the kitchen.

Rosie looks concerned. 'Sit down, Jim. Ronnie can be a bit over the top too, you know that.' She looks him directly in the eyes, 'You know that.'

Jim sits at the oak table. 'I've always wanted...' he was going to say, 'one of these'. But instinctively knows that he has *one of these* and he's sitting at it. His hands run over the table's ancient surface. It's as if he can feel the tree that it was...

He is outside by a tree. Looking over a garden at a cottage. Is the cottage perfect? As he looks it feels as if there are wobbles in his vision. He can see very clearly. This surprises him.

'Great garden,' Ronnie says. Then quietly, 'You okay Jim?'

'Yes,' he says. 'I'm just a bit confused. Everything seems wonderful. Just right. You know.'

Of course,' Ronnie says, 'you're such a dreamer, always were...'

Dreamer? It was a clue. Ronnie's telling him he's in a dream. Funny that he should be called Ronnie. Unless this dream character had picked up on Jim's character. That would make sense. If it was a lucid dream, he was impressed. Jim wondered when and how he would wake up.

The kitchen chimney had smoke rising up. The sun was warm in the sky. Birds were singing. He thinks he can see Rosie inside the kitchen. It would be perfect if he could smell that smoke, he thinks. And as he thinks this he does get a waft of burning logs. The cottage has a wood burner. Heaven.

'Where are we?' Jim asks.

'We're in your garden,' Ronnie laughs, 'or do you mean, where are we in life?' If you mean that, then we're in a good place, Jim. A good place. Never thought I'd be saying that. And it's great that you're a happy man. With your woman.'

'My woman?'

Ronnie laughs again, 'Yes, surprised us all. Where is she, still on holiday? It's great that you two can do that.'

Jim is now very confused. But the confusion simply feels like a puzzle. It doesn't trouble him negatively. Play along Jim. Play along. These words come into his mind. Look around and take everything in. Make it perfect.

'It's perfect,' he says.

'Yes,' Ronnie says, 'you have such a good, free relationship. But you're as tight as a knot with each other.'

The kitchen window opens, 'Come on you two, breakfast.'

They walk across the lawn. Jim notices Ronnie's face. As he looks at him, he becomes more and more familiar. Jim stops him for a moment. Looks at his eyes and the shape of his nose.

'Hey, Jim, don't kiss me while Rosie's watching,' he jokes.

Jim smiles. 'I missed you,' he says. 'Feels like it's been a long time.'

He's up in the sky flying slowly through the air. Looking down at the cottage and its surroundings. Again it feels as if his vision is creating as much as seeing – but seamlessly. There are undulating hills around him and meadows and a blue mountain range in the distance. Snap!

He regains his connection with his reality. Or what he presumes to be his reality. He's in a dream or he's at Portway. Is that it?

In the cottage Jim – you have to create everything you see. As much detail as possible. Fill your world with detail. Engage with everyone. Look at them and let them be what you want. Think about other houses too, and villages. Who will be there, what will you do? Give everything detail.

The woman says to him, 'The more you do this, the more you'll find yourself able to create. We're just monitoring. AI knows exactly what's going on and adjusts in real time...'

'Yes, I think I noticed that,' says Jim. 'It's all very impressive.'

The woman says tentatively, 'I wanted to mention that there is a counsellor available should you need one.'

'What for?'

'Well, in case you're having any emotional problems. Worries. Can't sleep. Things like that. It's not easy. I have two relatives 'at rest', I think 'resting' is the new jargon. Anyway it only really became real for them a few weeks beforehand. I'd be happy to talk with you if you wanted.'

'Are they here?' Jim asks.

'No. That wouldn't be professional. But I do know that all is as it should be.'

Jim smiles. He's already worried. He has to admit. If he wakes in the middle of the night he is plunged into a kind of surreal despair. And he has been having some nightmares. Before he would have simply increased his medication. Except now he has to keep his mind clear and alert. He hasn't had any meds since his birthday. Apart from the doc's pills.

The woman continues, 'I think I told you, and Doctor Abraham, that we have a factored-in randomness when creating generally. The same as you have been using for your characters. If things are too predictable then life becomes dull. Obviously there are limits to behaviour. Your computer deals with your world as a matter of course and we can, in extreme situations, communicate with it.'

'Wouldn't that be a great way for my family to communicate and find out what's happening with me?'

'It would be,' the woman says, 'but we have to request very special permission. In your state, the state you will be in,' she corrects, 'we must maintain strict codes of privacy. You'll find this in your contract. Section 7, I think.'

'I'll take your word for it,' Jim says. But he wonders whether he should go through everything with a fine toothcomb. Except it read like jargon, dense law, when he did try. Besides, he'd already signed everything.

'If you need any guidance, Dan's usually available.'

'What's your name?' Jim asks. 'I presume that's not a state secret?'

'It isn't. It's Jayne.'

'Thanks, Jayne,' he says, smiling.

'To recap. We will place you in various scenarios where simply through using your senses you create the world around you – or adjust it. The computer recreates what's happening so that we see a facsimile.'

'That's quite funny,' Jim says. 'You're creating, helping to create,' he stresses, 'my ersatz world and in doing so you see an ersatz representation.'

'Except I wouldn't use the word 'ersatz'. This world is real. As real as, well, this world now. You will live in a real world, Jim. That's why we have to get it right. But,' she pauses, 'it's not finite. At least we don't think so. And there should be surprises. Measured surprises, perhaps…'

'I don't know now if what I've experienced, created, is a dream or reality. It seems so separate. And it doesn't seem to sit in me like an ordinary memory. And yet, I can remember. But when I was there, that reality took over as if this, now, didn't exist. And I recognised someone.'

'Who?'

'A friend, a great friend. I sent info about him to the computer. No film. A few old-school photos.'

'Interesting,' she says. 'The two realities are different,' she states. 'It might get a little confusing as we proceed. Each might seem like a dream of itself. Dreams…' she muses.

'It's better than dying,' he says, abruptly. 'Though it's only putting off the inevitable, isn't it?'

She nods. Concentrates.

'It makes you consider life,' he says wistfully. 'Before Civic Duty no-one knew when their life would end. Was a mystery. Some weren't lucky, some went on to live to such an old age they were like living mummies. You know, like those Buddhist monks.'

'I don't know,' she says.

'I can't remember all the details. Japanese, I think. They would live on the side of a mountain, only eating what they could get from trees, like pine needles or bark, berries maybe, roots and nuts. It got them ready. Got rid of all their fat and muscle.' Jim looks at Jayne. He thinks she's interested and carries on, 'Then they'd not eat anything for a hundred days and just drink a little salt water. And maybe they drank a special bark tea that would kill the parasites and bacteria that rots away the body.' Jayne pulls a face of disgust. Jim continues, 'Stopping decomposition. Well, trying to. When those looking after the monk felt death approaching, they'd put the monk into a pine box and lower it and him into a deep hole and pack it in with charcoal. Then bury him. They'd have a bamboo stem going from inside the box all the way up and through the earth for air. And the monk could ring a bell. It would have to penetrate the charcoal and earth I guess. I don't know how that worked, certainly not like the bells in cemeteries from hundreds of years ago. The monk would ring the bell to show he was still alive. Then the ringing would stop. They would unearth the box and see if the monk was dead. If so he was re-entombed, the bamboo airway taken out and everything sealed.'

'You seem to know quite a lot about this,' Jayne says.

'I can't remember what it was called or any real details of the monks. But just to finish. After a thousand days they'd dig the box out again: if they found signs of decay then the body would be re-interred, I think there was something like an exorcism, I don't know. But no real ceremony. If there was no sign of decay then the monk was considered...I can't recall the name. A Japanese name. No matter, the body was then enshrined.'

'Sounds pretty backward to me,' Jayne says.

'I guess. It was outlawed. I think it went on until the beginning of the twentieth century.'

'Thankfully, we have moved on from those superstitions.'

'Yes,' Jim says, 'but fascinating. Don't you think?' Jayne shrugs. 'Who knows what was going on in their mind. And I'll be put in a glass box will I not? And no sleeping beauty,' he jokes.

'Not a glass box Jim,' she says. 'Not anything like that. We'll take good care of you. Remember, you can see a counsellor at any time.'

'Thanks,' Jim says, a little flatly.

Doctor Abraham didn't consider himself a virtuous man but he did his job well and was dependable. He finished the interview with the Howes and some urgent administrative work, then decided to go to the main 'storage' building beyond The Gateway. Keeping an eye on the time, as he had his rendez-vous with Mrs Holden, he strode out purposely. As he passed various rooms people acknowledged him and he felt somewhat like the king of Portway Castle.

At security he asked to see who was working on the previous night-shift. The guard sent out a message: *Who was working on The Chest last night. Please report to security immediately.*

Doctor Abraham eyed the guard. 'Just a little humour,' the guard says. The doctor smiles. He knows how they refer to the largest building at Portway: a chest of drawers, The Chest.

After five or so minutes three workers turn up. 'You want me to check the overnight schedule?' the guard asks.

'I know about the cameras, I'm interested in when Mr Holden disappeared. One moment,' he says. To the assembled workers he says, 'Were any of you doing dumpster duty last night?'

An older and younger man raise their hands. To the third man Doctor Abraham says, 'Okay, back to work.' To the security guard he says, 'Remind everyone working here that this is a high-rated, confidential work environment. Everyone has signed the Official Secrets Act. Any idle chat, gossiping or speaking outside of Portway about Portway business will mean instant dismissal or worse. I'll send out a grapeshot so everyone gets a copy. But let them all know please.'

The guard nods his head.

A grapeshot was a missive to all who worked at Portway and was an unsubtle reminder of their duty and code towards both the company and State.

The doctor says to the guard, 'Can I use your office for a moment?'

The guard panics slightly as he's not sure if he's ended the pornography he was watching. 'Moment, Doctor Abraham.' Disappearing briefly, he quickly reappears. 'It's a bit messy, doctor.'

'Not a problem.' To the men, he says, 'Follow me.'

The two men look at each other uncertain why they have been singled out. The guard meanwhile sends out a message to workers on The Chest.

'I know security has already questioned you about last night.' They nod. 'But I want to reaffirm how important it is to be vigilant. You saw or heard nothing?' They shake their heads. 'Good. We depend on strict secrecy and discretion. You're paid well enough.' They nod. 'I'm telling you both but please feel free to exchange this knowledge with others. If anyone is caught speaking of what goes on here to the outside world, then expect a swift reaction. You'll have volunteered to be suicided, under the guise of the job getting too much, both of you egging each other on. Easily arranged. Not only will you be euthanised but anyone you have told will follow suit. Like an infection, all who contact any unfortunate information, will be 'quarantined' and then exterminated. You understand?'

The two men look at each other. 'There's nothing for us to speak about,' the older of the two says. 'We do our job and keep quiet. I'm teaching this young'un the ropes.'

The young man looks down to the ground. Then he lifts his head and says, 'It's true.'

'Good. We all know where we stand. Ultimately all security is my responsibility and I would hate to have to face those higher up. Yes indeed, there are those above me. And they're utterly ruthless. Which keeps me on my toes. And I'm here to make sure the Portway workforce is also on its toes. Do your jobs well and you'll be well rewarded. Step out of line, or talk out of turn and it will be – what's the current parlance I'm hearing – yes, curtains.' The doctor smiles. The men are ashen faced. 'Well back to work men, and keep up the good work.'

'Thank you,' they chorus.

The doctor eyes the security guard. The guard says, 'I've sent out a quick message.'

'Good. I'll do the grapeshot, it's as well for everyone to be reminded of the need for privacy and loyalty. There's a lot at stake for everyone.'

On his way back to his office the doctor calls in to see Jim and his team. He enters one of the creation rooms freely and sees Jim and Jayne in conversation. They immediately become aware of him and Jayne smiles.

'Made progress?' the doctor asks.

'Very much,' Jayne answers.

'Jim?'

'It's fascinating, doc.'

'We're having a conversation about freewill,' Jayne says. 'I argue for a fairly deterministic existence. Science based. We are the emanation of particles which behave in a determined manner. Why, therefore, should we be any different, or behave differently? This predictive biology rules us.'

'And you Jim?'

'I can see how there are elements of us and our consciousness that is set in predictive stone,' he says. 'But even so, I think there's plenty of wriggle-room within the constraints. I might be in a predetermined straitjacket, but even then there is some movement. And people *have* got out of them.'

'By dislocating their limbs,' the doctor says.

'Not everyone does that though, do they?'

'But we'd know the ones that do,' Jayne says. 'If I understand correctly.'

'I don't think everything I've done has been predetermined,' Jim says. 'You might be able to predict how I might act in certain situations, if you knew everything about me, but I also might surprise you. There are definitely strong inherited traits. But it seems that each of us has a spark of difference and originality.'

'Are you talking about the soul here?' The doctor then addresses Jayne, 'Sorry if I'm taking over the conversation.'

'It's quite all right,' she says.

'Why not have a soul?' Jim asks.

'Where does the soul come from?' the doctor asks.

'From a source, maybe. A creator. God.'

'And did God make each individual soul?'

'Created, yes, I presume,' Jim says.

'Did God create freewill within each soul?'

Jim smiles. 'God, if we're going to talk about God, gave us freewill.'

'In our soul, in our brain, in our mind?'

'In our mind,' Jim says, 'and deep within us, in our soul, our spirit. There must be a connection between soul and mind.'

'And where is our soul situated exactly?'

'Well, we have a connection with spirit, perhaps this is a form of our being that has a different vibration. You know that all things vibrate doc. Everything has its frequency.'

'Go on,' he says.

'Couldn't we have an earthly body and a spiritual body with different frequencies but held together? Okay, I've been having some creative VR...'

'Linked with a computer, AI,' Jayne corrects.

'I've been monitored as I look at my environment and, I suppose, there's been a kind of co-creation with Jayne but mostly the AI and VI. I have both consciously and unconsciously, or rather subconsciously determined my future.'

'Interesting,' the doctor says. 'Let me take you back a moment. Do you believe in God?' he asks.

'I think so.'

'And God has given you freewill,' he reaffirms.

'Yes.'

'But if you believe in God, you believe that God has a plan for you and your life.'

Jim leans back, taking in a deep breath of air through his nose. 'Maybe God's plan is to give us the freedom to accept, follow his plan or not.'

'Do we live in the past, the present or the future?' Doctor Abraham asks.

'In the present,' Jim says, thinking of the computer and their conversation.

'But you cannot know the present. We have an imbalance of senses, the present, if it exists, is the time taken for our subconscious to gather everything into a reality that you, your consciousness, perceives as the present. You, or what you believe to be 'you' is in the specious present.'

Jim shrugs his shoulders. 'You believe when we die we die, that's it, snuffed out, lights extinguished, eh doc?'

'It seems rational,' he answers.

'No moral arbiter?'

'No imaginary arbiter,' the doc counters. 'We have surpassed these ideas.'

'Can we trust ourselves?' Jim asks.

The doctor laughs. 'Tell me,' he says, 'if you are so confident there is a God, why not do the conventional Civic Duty?'

Jim looks down, then over at Jayne. Jayne says, 'The doctor is a law unto himself'.'

'A law unto others perhaps,' the doctor says, smiling, 'but here, at Portway, I am the law.'

'A would-be god?' Jim asks.

'Ask my workers,' the doctor jokes.

'You do believe in the civic duty afterlife, doc.'

'Meaning?'

'You are confident we are liberated into that further reality. Not just buried alive here...'

The doctor scrutinises Jim. Turns to Jayne. 'He's a character Jayne. No doubt. And will be,' he says with a wry smile.

'Will be?' Jim asks.

The doctor laughs. 'I have to leave you in the arms of your team and its leader, I'm afraid I have an appointment this evening. We can finish certain things off tomorrow.'

'Okay.'

'Over to you Jayne...'

'One thing,' Jim says.

'Go ahead.'

'When we accept men as gods, apologies Jayne, then it seems we cannot trust ourselves with Nature. God might have created damn mosquitoes,' Jim says, 'but he didn't weaponise them.'

Jayne looks over at the doctor.

'Isn't a bite a weapon?' the doctor laughs. 'All yours,' he says to Jayne. 'You've got the whole night in front of you, should you need it.' Turning round, he stops and says to the team, 'Good luck all of you, you're doing a fine job.' He smiles at Jim. 'Keep being creative,' he says. God created the world in seven days, I believe. You've got a little longer.'

'I'm not God,' Jim smiles.

'And yet you imitate him,' the doctor says and with that he walks out as fast and as purposely as he walked in.

The doctor arrived at Jim's house slightly late, still cold from having to manually punch in the code Hannah had sent, at the gate. It was bitter, a wind was picking up and icy rain fell occasionally. Instructing the driver to wait outside the house, he quickly strode up to the front door. The house was neat and compact. Hannah opened it before he had time to press the video intercom.

Immediately he says, 'My apologies for being a little late.' He can see she is ready to go out. 'Shall we?' he says.

She understands, nods, and says, 'Of course, I'll just get my bag.'

Outside the restaurant he dismisses the driver. Inside he takes her coat and hangs it on a peg and places his over it. At the table they are shown to, he pulls the chair out for her to sit down.

'You're quite the gentleman, doctor...'

'Jake,' he says. 'We don't need to be so formal. We don't want people to think I'm giving you a consultation, Hannah,' he jokes, using her first name calmly, seamlessly changing from Mrs Holden.

'Jake,' she says, as if to confirm his instruction.

They order. She is guided by Jake's advice. There is some small talk and general conversation about Portway before Hannah can summon the courage to ask, 'Is Jim okay? Not giving you too many problems?'

'Do you think he's likely to?'

'Well, no, of course not. But. You know...you're beginning to get an idea of his character, doc... Jake, sorry. I have to adjust.'

'I find Jim very interesting.'

'Really?' she says, slightly taken aback.

'You don't?' the doctor jokes.

'I meant, well, you're a doctor. A successful man...'

'Whereas Jim…'

'Well, he's not successful,' she laughs nervously. Jake leans in towards her. 'But he's a good man,' she adds.

Jake can sense she wants, maybe needs to confide in him. He fills her glass with wine. She takes a gulp.

Their starter arrives.

'You seem to have a successful marriage,' Jake says.

Again Hannah is slightly taken aback. 'Well, yes,' she says. Laughs.

'That's good,' the doctor says and leans back. 'Food's good,' he says.

'Marvellous,' she answers. 'We've never been...'

'Wait for the main course. It is a little expensive. I didn't mean...'

'Well, it's not that...' Hannah begins, but they both know it is. 'We've had to be a bit careful. And time goes fast. Before you know it...'

'It will be your civic duty.'

Hannah wipes her mouth. 'Yes.'

'I'm sorry,' he says, 'I didn't mean to be personal. 'I too will face that eventuality. And we're the lucky ones. I really think society needs to embrace Civic Duty and celebrate it...'

'Even if you're killed...euthanised?' she corrects.

'It's the nature of life, Hannah. Death makes sense of our life here. I've been honoured to work at Portway and I can see the hope, the relief, the life we can offer and have been offering. It's a wonderful service...paid service,' he smiles. 'Do you believe in God or an afterlife?'

'These are some questions,' she says.

'Again, my apologies. People say I'm terrible at small talk and that my job is my life. I suppose it is.'

A waiter clears their plates. 'Are you ready for your main course?'

The doctor looks at Hannah, then nods at the waiter. 'Yes, we are.'

'I don't know what I believe,' Hannah continues. 'And you've...' she can't think of her words.

'It's okay,' he says. 'I know I'm not good at this. And I'm not used to being in the company of such a beautiful woman,' he adds.

'I imagine beautiful women flock round you doctor.'

'Jake. No. I don't think so. I haven't noticed.'

'Maybe you should.' Hannah realises she might have overstepped a boundary. There is an awkward pause which is broken by the arrival of their food.

As they are left alone the doctor looks her in the eyes. 'So?'

'So?' she mirrors.

'Do you believe in an afterlife?'

'It isn't scientific...'

'What about Portway's afterlife?'

'That,' she says, 'I don't really know. How's Jim getting on designing?'

The doctor sees an opportunity. 'He's doing very well, and that's why I find him so interesting. He's quicker witted than you think. Sorry, not you, I mean...'

'I understand,' she smiles.

'The design works through the computer, AI, feeding Jim images and words and evaluating his responses: brain reaction, eye-tracking, the language he uses, body movements. How he adjusts and changes his reaction to the world he's creating and modifying. It's like he's stepping off the edge of an abyss into nothing but trusting in, and building a bridge supporting him beneath each step. It's like magic. But scientific magic. I think he gets that there's more going on than might be expected. We've had him on computer programs where he's described scenes, written out scenes and dialogue and answered myriad questions.'

'He has been alone with the computer here, well at home I mean, a lot.'

'Yes, and there is accelerated learning and design at Portway. Advanced virtual technology: VI and VR. But also, raw creativity... Wait. I'm talking shop and no doubt boring you.'

'Not at all doctor.'

'Jake,' he corrects. 'That is something we are trying to facilitate when we're 'resting'. To create a wonderful world to exist in. Some people just can't do it,' he says. 'They seem to lack imagination.'

'I hope I'll be okay,' Hannah says.

'A long way off,' he smiles, pouring more wine in her glass and wiping his mouth before topping up his own. 'We have default programs, getting better every day. The detail we can reproduce is astounding. But the idea is to customise.'

'You seem very devoted to your job,' Hannah says. She begins to relax and eats more naturally; less aware of her surroundings.

Ignoring her comment, he says, 'Regarding customising...' the doctor stops abruptly. Looks at Hannah. Thinks carefully. 'I wanted to talk about Jim and his desire to recreate a woman...I think he wants to recreate you.' The doctor bites his lip. Why did he say that? He'd had no intention of saying that. Not that last sentence.

'This is why you wanted to see me?'

The doctor looks down at the table, at his plate of discarded shells. 'I...'

'It's so very sweet of you,' Hannah says. 'And to go to so much trouble. I really appreciate this.' Her eyes sparkle. She puts out an arm and spreading the fingers of her hand touches the wrist of the doctor's left hand.

At his home the doctor contacts the professor. He waits, then hears, 'Professor Stone.' The voice pauses very slightly, then, 'Jake.'

'Professor. Alistair. Well you obviously know it's me. Was my line recognised?'

'All calls are recognised and monitored,' the professor says. 'But you're calling from a different device.'

'Impressed. I'm at home. When I'm here I try and keep business separate.'

'Business? It's well past business hours, surely...'

'I had a dinner date. Not business, though it could have been. The point is I need a flutter.'

'Jake. Not like you. You always manage to surprise me.'

'Things didn't work out as I planned. I need some...'

'Okay, I get the picture. I'll have a car deliver. Secure driver. But I will be expecting.'

'I understand, of course. I have some fine...'

'No names, Jake, keep it tight.'

'I have something you'll enjoy very much. It was mixed only last week and so far the tests have proved very popular.'

'With the team?'

'Yes. Indeed.'

'Sounds good. Any preference?' the professor asks.

'You know my tastes. You know my weakness. No point denying...'

'For tonight I presume?' the professor jumps in.

'Is that possible?'

'It is possible,' the professor laughs.

'Thank you.

'It's good for you to do some extra-curricular studies,' the professor jokes. 'One moment.'

Jake waits. Paces up and down his living room which feels cold and neglected. He risks turning the temperature right up. But hopes he can keep it icy.

'Okay,' Alistair's voice comes. 'Midnight. She'll be there. Gives you enough time to prepare yourself, relax...We have entry details.'

The doctor was motionless as he anticipated the future. A message bleeped into his other, usual phone. It was Hannah, he'd given her access.

Thank you for a wonderful evening. Hannah xx

It could have been so much better. He read the signs, he could have pushed her. There was time. But now he needed to do things. Get a special-delivery drone to deliver a packet to the professor. Get his home tidied and try to make it and himself feel relaxed.

She arrived exactly at the time the professor had communicated. The night was colder and a harsh wind had picked up as he'd opened the window of his bedroom. He could spy on her and see she was standing freezing outside the door. Perfect. He left her for as long as he could and then opened the door.

'Vicky,' he says, recognising her. It had been some time but the professor was good, as ever. 'Come in.' He doesn't say 'and get warm'. She looks about. 'You remember this place?'

She nods.

'You remember me?'

She nods again. But he's not sure if she's being genuine. 'I have something for you.' Going to the kitchen quickly, he gets the drink he has prepared. He watches her standing in the living room, awkward and vulnerable. 'Here,' he says, 'drink this, it will make you feel good.' She takes a sip. The doctor smiles slightly. 'Drink it quickly, it will work better.' She does as she is told and gulps it down. His smile is stuck to his face. 'You showered?' She nods. He stands close to her, examines her. 'Do you remember where the bedroom is?' She shakes her head. 'Follow me.' He opens a door. There is a draft of icy air. 'Go in, take off your clothes,' he orders. 'Get on the bed like you did before, you remember now?' She nods. 'Good.' She enters timidly. Still timid after all this time. 'Don't move,' he tells her. 'Stay on the bed and don't move a muscle. You understand?' She nods. 'Go on,' he says and shuts the door behind her.

The doctor wasn't proud of himself. But he could rationalise everything. For one thing she wasn't dead. They had given her life – another forty years or close. If she lasted that long. She'd been identified and prevented from automatic euthanasia. She owed them. Life was better than death. Going into his kitchen he mixed himself a special drink too – just to enhance things. Again he reasoned to himself – she could have had her organs harvested. Being young, she was worth a fortune. In fact as he pondered this he wondered what specific use she had for the professor. Girls like her were used to blackmail opposition, that was for sure. But there were many of them. What made her special? Well she was thoroughly trained for sure. Would do anything he ordered or even suggested. Her heart was in the right place. He smiled. Better in rather than out her body. Better in hers where the concoction she'd drunk would be racing it rather than in a botoxed and semi-regenerated old body.

The doctor opened the bedroom door. She was in position. She must have been freezing. 'In the bed,' he barks. Quickly he shuts the window as she pulls the covers around her. Undressing he stares at her, though her eyes avert from his glance. He doesn't shower, he'd done so before going out and meeting Hannah. He wonders if this girl is the sort of woman Jim would want to create.

He says, 'Your name is Hannah.' He climbs into bed next to her and throws back the quilt she is still shivering. 'I told you not to move a muscle,' he says. She knows what to expect.

In the night Jim woke with a start to a jumble of images which were fast disappearing from his mind. But the final image lingered a little longer – it was a woman with silver tape across her mouth and with terrified eyes. They haunted him from beyond sleep. As he rolled over and swung a leg to the floor a dim light came on. Enough light to focus his sight from his inner world to the shadowy bedroom. The eyes and face of the woman unsettled him and brought to him a sense that she was in some way familiar. Sitting on the bed he tried to concentrate his thoughts on who she might be. But gradually her image faded, reducing slowly into the very back of his mind. Even so his mood remained disturbed. The room he was in had everything he needed – except space. He decided to get partially dressed and take a walk.

For some reason, as he left his room he had a feeling of *deja vu* and also an almost schoolboy sense of doing something naughty. He remembered school and how much he hated his senior years, but now school was ancient past. As he walked along the corridor, lights came on, enough light for him to see far enough ahead. Had he done this before, or did such a corridor at night belong to his dreams? Eventually, after passing through a door, he saw a lift to his right. A sense came over him, a feeling not to take it and to continue on his way, not to deviate from the corridor. Through another door and reaching the end of the corridor, he had no alternative but to descend. It was then he also realised he might not be able to find his way back. Feeling a fool, he took the lift down to the ground floor. Without his phone he had no idea what time it was and no way to connect with anyone.

The lift doors slid open effortlessly. He exited and found himself in front of sliding glass doors. These opened as he approached them. It was then he understood where he was – inside the magnificent glass building. Looking up he could sense its height and, in fact, see the lights of the city either reflecting on the glass, or having fallen through it, casting eerie illuminations and shadows. Thinking quickly he thought he could either go into the garden with the regimental trees or to the control room and the rooms used for creating a multitude of life-after-life experiences. Both ways were tempting, but outside it would be freezing cold and he wasn't dressed for that. He would continue on and into what turned out to be a linking corridor to the main one. The sense of openness disappeared until he turned right into the main corridor which seemed connected again to the sky. It was like a modern cathedral in many ways – built to impress. The parts of the building stood head to head, the old, stone built, sturdy building and this modern counterpart.

There seemed no-one about and yet he had the feeling he was being watched. His bedroom now seemed as if it belonged in a different world as he walked down the wide corridor, not really knowing why he was carrying on. But what else could he do? It was thrilling in some fashion but also he felt like a criminal. Why? This was the place where he would reside for who knows how many years. And then with an internal flash the face of the woman appeared in his mind and a sense of being in a vast room, underground maybe. Images that made no real sense but seemed familiar. He was struck by a real feeling of fear. For no obvious reason he made for a door in the corridor, opened it and quickly closed it, leaving a slight gap. The room was small and sparse, he had no idea what it was used for and the light was dim. He peered through the gap. It seemed the spines of the new buildings, its corridors, were all open to glass rooves. He recalled being in The Gateway building surrounded by the neatly stacked semi-dead – his fate.

As he kept watch he heard, then saw some security guards.

'Where's he gone?' one says to the other.

'I don't know.'

'It's like he's disappeared.'

'You can't disappear in this place,' the other says.

'Well he has. Should we notify...you know...'

'What and lose our job? I need all the credit I can get for my retirement. It's all right for you younger ones.'

'So what do we do?' the younger one asks.

'He must have run down here, and maybe out into the garden. Who knows? But he didn't pass us, that's for sure.'

'Let's carry on,' the younger one says. Is there any security at the entrance to the garden?' The older one shrugs. They pick up speed in their step.

The older one says, 'Let's get going, if he's not in the garden we're going to have to notify...'

'Yeah, and lose our jobs.' As the younger one says this the older one breaks into a run.

Jim is certain they're looking for him. Why? He guesses there's the usual security for such a place, but nothing feels quite right. He'd gone for a walk and that was all.

After some time he gingerly opened the door. The corridor lights were low but the sky seemed alive with muted colours and movement. Stepping out he carried on in the opposite direction of the security guards. But he knew that he only had a certain amount of time before being discovered. As he continued, he recognised that part of the building – it was where he had been with Jayne and the team. Carrying on quickly he got to the end of the corridor, opened the doors and saw the entrance for The Gateway. There was no way he could get in there, recalling the entrance security from his first visit. He suddenly felt very foolish. What on earth was he doing? The only thing he thought to do was take the path between the buildings, even if he was plunged into frozen, dead air and head for the greenhouse he'd been to the day before.

As Jim stepped out to turn down the path, he felt a hand clasp his shoulder.

'Mr Holden,' comes a voice.

Jim turns, shaking off the grip. He sees a security guard. Was it one of those who had passed him in the corridor? 'Yes,' he says in answer.

'Off for a walk?' the man asks.

Jim thinks quickly. 'I remembered I'd left a jacket in the greenhouse. I was cold. I left my room and, frankly, don't know how to get back.'

The guard looks at the other. 'Seems odd taking a walk at this hour.'

'I couldn't sleep,' Jim explains. 'I have a lot on my mind. You can imagine. You know who I am.'

'I gave you the jacket,' the guard says. 'Don't worry Mr Holden, I'll find your jacket and my colleague here will escort you back. On one condition,' he adds.

'Which is?'

'You don't mention this little night sojourn, to anyone.'

'That’s okay, of course not,' Jim says quickly.

'We wouldn't want you getting into trouble,' the man says. 'And we don't want to get into trouble either. We'll wipe the films of you and say no more.'

'Films?'

'Everything is filmed,' the younger guard says.

'I see. Well, I just wanted to go for a walk and then get some air. And it's so cold,' he shivers. 'I should have taken a jacket.'

'We'll get this sorted,' the older voice says. 'Can we trust you?'

'Yes. Yes you can,' Jim says.

The younger voice says, 'Watch out.'

Jim could see two men pushing a dumpster down the narrowish path in the opposite direction from the way to the garden.

'Quick,' the older man says.

The younger guard grabs Jim by the arm and leads him back into the modern building, through the doors they'd come through, opposite The Gateway entrance. Jim looks back at the older guard, who was busily pressing buttons.

The young man escorts Jim to a side door and through to a lift. In the lift there is silence until the guard says, 'Remember, don't say anything. You're not meant to walk around at night. It's just security. If you say anything it will get both you and us into a lot of trouble.'

'I understand,' Jim says. But seeing the dumpster being pushed up the pathway has brought back some forgotten images. His experience from the previous night was gradually coming back to him.

The guard confirms, 'We'll clear the films. We don't want a repeat of...' He stops abruptly. Looks at Jim with an ashen face. 'It's not easy getting a job here,' he half explains. Jim remains silent.

The guard knows exactly where Jim's room is. 'We'll get the jacket to you later, in the morning. But keep it for day walks. Okay?'

'Okay,' Jim says.

'Not a word now,' the guard says.

'Not a word,' Jim mirrors.

'A man without a job is a dangerous man,' the young guard says melodramatically. But he makes his point.

Once in the room, Jim went directly to the bathroom and slammed on a full light. What kind of place was this? He looked into the mirror and his heart was shocked, seeming to bang out against his chest. Turning he saw nothing. But the woman's face in the mirror with her terrified eyes was locked into his head. The dumpster. Something was put in it. A body? A woman? They said 'she'. The conversation he heard in the darkness flaps back into his mind. Running the tap he threw water over his face. His mind was faced with these murderous ideas. Dramatic? Yes! The potential reality of what might be going on had taken his breath away and quickened the pumping of his heart. More water was splashed on his face. What the fuck was going on?

There were still elements he couldn't put together. What had he seen and heard and why couldn't he remember. Was it all a trick? Was he going mad? Maybe the pressure was getting too much for him. Everything was totally crazy – he saw it all clearly, as if for the first time: What the government was doing to them, how the people acquiesced, how the people kept voting the same way, when they had a chance to vote differently, how they seemed to trust and yet seal their fate at the same time. There was no need for any of this. No need. The whole system was cruel. He had to die, everyone had to die, but surely dying had to be natural. Then he thought how lives under sixty were saved and prolonged if someone was ill. Not mentally ill of course. And he thought about babies who were born and left to die while others were saved with no expense spared. The state was in control and the more power it got the less it seemed to care about the individual.

Leaving the bathroom, he lay on his bed. The lights dimmed and then, sensing no movement, switched off. Alone in the dark he stared into the blackness. Thought about Hannah, his children and Maddy especially. His fate seemed unreal. In some ways he could sense time passing and the day approaching when he would visit Portway and never leave. But it also didn't seem real at all. Maybe that was the way he thought about death too. He smiled into the darkness; death was something that happened to other people. Who said that? He couldn't recall. Stared into the darkness and 'Woody Allen' popped into his mind. Woody's films were popular again. Which film? No, it wasn't Woody who said that. Again his mind wandered, didn't Woody say something about not being afraid of dying, just that he didn't want to be around when it happened? Jim almost laughed out loud – then he saw the woman's eyes. He had to sleep. Had the doctor left him some pills?

The doctor said that the pills could give him strange dreams. Perhaps what he thought he remembered was only a dream. How could he know? In the darkness his mind went wherever it wished. Was he in control of his mind? Were there two elements to his mind? Jim must have gone down a few such rabbit holes but eventually, unconsciously fallen asleep. His body was alone in the room as his body would be alone in a box experiencing his new life.

'Are you experienced?' comes dream talk.

In the morning the doctor was up early. He looked at the girl on his bed. Did he look with a mixture of disdain and pity? Certainly he felt some disdain for himself. He showered quickly, but thoroughly, and then ordered transport to take him to work. Work, play...He would eat at Portway, he wanted to distance himself from last night – both Hannah and Vicky.

Arriving at Portway he felt in a much better mood. He turned on phone access to his home cameras and could see the girl had been picked up as arranged and the front door was shut. As he rolled up to the reception area close to his office he was uncharacteristically upbeat.

'Morning Milly,' he says.

'Doctor.'

'Everything fine?' he asks.

'Everything is in order,' she replies. 'You're not anticipating any problems?' she prods.

'Indeed not. Is Mr Holden up and about?'

'I have no idea,' she confesses. 'Would you like me to enquire?'

'Please.'

He checks his device for messages. One is from Hannah. Turning towards Milly, he smiles. He's always slightly irritated by her nervousness. Why was she like that, she's been with Portway since, well, ever...'Let me have a list of would be 'lifers' please,' he jokes.

'Certainly doctor.'

'Will I ever get you to call me Jake?' he asks.

She smiles.

In his office he checks the message. Deflated he reads: *What time will Jim be finished today, I could pick him up. I have use of the company car.* Nothing personal, no kisses. The doctor's mood is challenged.

Milly checks her phone. Looks towards the doctor's office door and frowns.

Jim was woken up by soothing music, growing louder, becoming less and less soothing. Checking his phone he saw a string of messages from Hannah. Unusual but welcome. Sitting up in bed, everything became very naturally clear. He'd walked down the corridor, gone through some doors, down some steps and had been in a huge underground carpark or so it seemed. He'd heard voices and something being taken from a trolley or maybe a dumpster and put in another. They'd talked about this something as if it were a woman. That's all he could recall. But he knew that something was also not right. In fact it felt very wrong. The question being: what was he to do?

'Hello Doctor Abraham, I have reason to believe something nefarious might be happening at Portway.'

'And what might that be?'

'Well, I heard some men talking and it seemed they might have been putting a woman, a dead woman, in a dumpster.'

'When was this?'

'The night before last, when I was...well, knocked out by pills.' Jim isn't even persuaded by this explanation. How can he approach the doctor? Maybe the woman was simply dead. What else would they do with the body? If she had no relatives remaining...Then he considered what might happen if the person or people supplying the money for them to be 'at rest' died, or just went broke, or just didn't want to pay anymore.

What would happen? Was there any moral duty by Portway to do anything other than dispose of the corpse? The doctor had said there had been no deaths in the previous five years. Perhaps she was the first.

Jim would talk with Hannah. But she'd probably think him insane. She was often criticising his, what she termed, 'over-developed imagination'. Was he developing his imagination? – he should have retorted. Wasn't imagination in itself always over-developing. Laughing he realised he *was* being over-imaginative. It was all probably nothing whatsoever. Why would it be something bad? Portway was a creepy place at night and that led to...okay Hannah...an over-development of one's imagination.

He was at Portway to do that very thing; to behave in that very fashion. Use his imagination and an army of AI or Virtual Intelligence. What kind of worlds were the dull-witted creating? Would the dull-witted have a life-after-life? The trouble was he couldn't shake the image – he must have created – of the woman with the tape-sealed mouth and the terrified eyes. And last night. What the fuck had he been doing? He was lucky the guards had been lenient with him. Well...was he a prisoner? He needed a drink. Something to sharpen him up and chase away the nonsense thought blowing around his mind.

A message came from Jayne and the team to tell him to be at the Creation Rooms as they were known. His phone had been programmed to direct him to the restaurant and would then direct him to the team. How had they done that? How had they accessed his device? Dressing quickly he set about preparing some coffee when his phone prompted him to 'follow instructions'. Jim wanted to flush it down the toilet. Or shove it under the mattress. But he responded to its orders. *Turn right out of the door.*

Portway was an impressive place. There were some people on the upper level, but not many. On the ground floor the building was more familiar and a message broke into the dictatorial commands with, 'The doctor will join you at the restaurant.' It sounded like the nervous woman. Jim was slightly nervous about whether the guards had lied to him or not. As he walked he began to concoct ever ridiculous scenarios for why he was out and about in the early hours of the morning.

As he got to the restaurant it was full of people. He checked the time. It was early. Scanning the room he didn't recognise anyone. Timidly he went to serve himself breakfast. This was the first time Portway had seemed that busy. Taking his tray he found somewhere to sit. There was one man only at the table who was staring into his phone or device. Everything was normal. People were either eating or appeared to be meeting or discussing things before their work began. A lot of the work at Portway had to be hands on – could they have dealt with him remotely. Well they had for the most part. But there were still folk like him, designing in-house, and the computers had to be monitored. Could that be done remotely? Jim had lost touch with both work and its ethic. For four years he'd wasted time – in denial of his preordained fate.

Jim realised how hungry he was. As he considered going back for seconds, he saw Doctor Abraham striding towards him.

'Jim.'

'Doctor. Sorry, Doctor Jake,' he says.

'I will definitely join you and the team sometime today,' he says. 'Apart from the minor problems,' the doctor almost winks, 'I hope you have enjoyed yourself and feel you've made good progress. We'll be able to link you remotely to a Portway computer. It's down to you but the more effort you put in now, the better your experience will be later.'

'Yes, I understand,' Jim says. 'It's been interesting.'

'It will be quite intensive today,' the doctor says. 'We have to train the VI, the AI, to focus on your intentions and desires. AI can take care of more of the details and certainly so if you put in the hours remotely. I do want to keep in touch with your progress. And I'd like you to have a further longer session here, maybe a few weeks before...'

'A few weeks before? Oh, yes, I see,' Jim says. 'A few weeks before.'

'Make sure everything is absolutely fine. Down to the very last detail. Then we can arrange the surgery.'

'Thanks.' Jim wishes the doctor hadn't mentioned the surgery.

'Our pleasure.'

'I'll be coming each month regardless though doc?'

Doctor Abraham smiles, 'Yes, indeed. Twice in the final month.'

Jim is unsure whether or not to pry a little. He has time but this is an informal setting, maybe not to be missed. He has to think quickly.

'Doc,' Jim begins, 'I was just thinking before you arrived, about you telling me that no-one had died during the past five years at The Gateway.'

The doctor is slightly taken aback. 'Yes, that's correct.'

'I took it you meant no-one had died of anything bad. There must have been natural deaths?'

'No, no-one has died in the past five years, we're very proud of that. You see, we look after you. Are you worrying about this?'

Jim shunts his initial thought to one side, shakes his head and answers, 'That's good news. I wasn't worried, I was just remembering what you said for some reason. And wanted to check re natural deaths. What would happen if someone did die?'

'I think I told you,' the doctor says. 'Families or whomever, depending on who has been directly funding the deceased are informed and their funeral wishes are carried out. All very discreetly. It has happened...'

'Just coming to the end of their natural life?' Jim asks.

'Yes. That's the way.'

'But there must be more and more bodies at rest?'

'Yes,' the doctor answers, 'that is the whole point. We can house thousands in a space only a score or two could live in if they weren't resting. I can tell you that being at rest has taken a lot of internal pressure off the government. It can gradually build back our nation in a better way.'

'Do you think there's any longer a need for assisted suicide, euthanasia?' Jim asks. 'I mean the population was a lot higher when I was younger.'

'It's a question of resources,' the doctor explains, 'you've lived through what happened. We can't allow that to happen again.'

'It was tough,' Jim admits.

'The National Government stepped in and did a great job. That's why they've been elected ever since.'

Jim looks at him. Picks up a mug and takes a gulp. Again he thinks carefully. 'So if I died, I wouldn't be, I don't know...' Here he chooses his words very carefully. 'Abandoned, tossed away.'

'Of course not,' the doctor laughs. This is why he spends extra time with Jim – he thinks differently. He will make a great, alternative template, and one that people could afford.

'Thanks,' Jim says.

'Well, I must grab something quickly,' the doctor says. 'Excuse me.'

As he is about to leave Jim gets a notification from his phone. *Leaving in five minutes*. The doctor hears it. 'Just time to nip...you know...which reminds me,' Jim adds, 'I presume there won't be much body waste to have to deal with. Sorry to ruin your appetite,' Jim jokes.

'Indeed not. Everything is pared back to the essential. It's really only your brain that's being fed. But we have to keep the body at a basic healthy level. We have the means to do that.'

'Don't our bodies atrophy?'

'The inner organs do not,' the doctor says confidently. 'We can regulate them. As no-one, how shall I say, leaves, wakes up from 'resting', then arm and leg strength is irrelevant. But as I say, there are things we can do to the body to stimulate muscles and maintain skin health. We have also been able to program the body so that hair and nails grow at an infinitesimal rate. The main reason behind everything is to allow the mind to escape. As you know.'

Three minutes.

'Thanks doc.'

'I hope I've been helpful.'

'Yes, indeed.'

'Keep concentrated,' he says as he walks off. 'O, and your wife will pick you up later.'

Two minutes.

Jim thinks about time again, how it is set and rigid and yet also fluid. All perception. He'd had no time to get extra food. He was slightly annoyed Hannah had spoken with the doc before him. As he finishes his coffee he is summoned by his phone.

Directions.

He walks out of the restaurant and messages Hannah. He can't recall if she is working remotely or has gone into the office. But if she's picking him up she must be working in her office complex. He had a lot to discuss with her. Before that he really had to get down some details. He really wanted to create a female character and he needed to think about her role in his future life. Again it was a question of balancing expected behaviour with a certain wildness. If he kept things rigid then he'd know what to expect – and probably be bored for...for? He needed to ask Jayne or Dan whether time would exist in the same fashion. Would there be a regular rising and setting of the sun? Or would he be in a dream state where anything might happen. These thoughts unnerved him somewhat – he should have thought that through. But he had time. Hannah bleeped a message to him.

See you later. Love you, Hannah. xx

He was pleasantly surprised by the warmth that seemed to be carried by this message. Messages could be so cold.

Turn left.

Home

'Take deep breaths...in, out...'

Jim walked across the top of the hill. It all seemed familiar to him but he wasn't exactly sure where he was. It was mid-morning and the sun had climbed fairly high in the sky. Stopping for a moment he looked around. In the distance were mountains which contrasted with the lightness of the colours that surrounded him. There was a cool, blueness to them and it was as if they were enticing him. A track seemed to appear out of nowhere, with light ruts. Wild flowers were scattered through the grass that swayed very slightly in the almost imperceptible breeze. But where was he? There was no consternation, but he was intrigued. It seemed logical for him to join the earthen track which was winding down the hill into the valley. The valley reminded him of images from his youth. Had he been here before?

Naturally, casually even, he began to walk down the hill. It was as if he were in a dream - but he wasn't. He was awake – wide awake. Trying to recall where he had walked from, nothing formed in his mind, yet he was not unduly troubled. Quizzical, yes. As he looked down into the valley he saw a village. The houses were mostly hidden by great fully-leaved trees, their presence only hinted at. Jim swept his head round to take in the whole of the valley and its surrounding hills. There were more trees than he had first realised. He could see a church spire and a large house not far from it. A mansion perhaps. The village looked welcoming. Stopping for a moment he breathed in the scented air. Again he looked out and over to the distant mountains. In the air, not so far from him a hawk hovered, then circled and swooped.

As the track descended, his open view was lost within trees; mature trees, oaks for the most part. He'd always loved oaks and appreciated their use over the years, both generally and personally. He admired their strength and longevity. At one point as the track seemed almost to level off and its dusty nature changed to supple earth and grass, he could see fields to his right. As he saw the fields he heard the sound of sheep. He always loved that sound. And he could see some sheep in the distance. It was almost as if their bleating brought them into existence.

The wood he then walked through was alive with bird song. The track was becoming overgrown but it could still be followed. Eventually both it and the trees gave way to a lane. A sunken lane. A lane that seemed as old as the hills he had come down from. Looking up, the sky was blue, with an occasional puff of cloud. Turning slightly onto the lane he could smell its rich earthen banks. He wondered if a stream would cross it at any point. Yes. YES! He was somewhat disproportionately delighted to see such a stream crossing the lane a little further on as the way dipped. Walking quickly he stood by the water. It flowed right to left and dropped down slightly into a stream running parallel to the lane, the high banks of which had given way somewhat. The water was clear but with a soft brown tone. On his left the countryside had opened up and he could see over to a house. At first he stepped through the water, then stopped and crouched down. His fingers touched its tangible coldness. What a lovely stream. Carrying on he noticed a style to his left. That was the way he would go.

He climbed the style and stood and looked out over the view, there was a small wooden bridge spanning the stream, the latter had grown somewhat it seemed. It was deeper. The grass had tussocks and wild flowers and felt spongy beneath his feet. He wore shoes, no, boots, strong boots. He felt his feet within them, comfortable. Why was he noticing his boots? A path took him to the bridge and he could see the path wind further on towards the house he had noticed. He could smell wood smoke. That was one of *the* most welcoming smells. There was no-one about. There was a sheep close by, which he hadn't noticed before. There were cows in a field beyond, he'd not noticed them either. They gave the scene a peaceful grace. For a moment he rested against the rail of the bridge and watched the water flow.

Carrying on he clattered down the other side of the bridge and back onto the path which eventually reached a stone wall. There were trees beyond it with the path clinging next to the wall. He could go either right or left. Jim looked at the stonework and the more he looked the more detail he could see, as if the wall was coming alive. Gingerly he touched it but it was as if his fingertips were numb. Pressing onto the stone he then felt blood pounding to his fingertips. The wall was ancient and dusty. Tracing a finger along one of the stone's surfaces he became more and more aware of its subtleties. What had looked flat on first inspection, was anything but. At that point the wall was too high to look over. But a little farther along a stone jutted out slightly and he used this to lift himself up. Grabbing hold of the top of the wall he could see over into a garden. He held himself like that for a while, his strength surprising him. He liked stone walls, always had – from dry stone walling to impressive walls around castles. Now he felt as if he hardly knew what a stone wall was and there was much to discover. With his back to the wall he looked out across the field. The view was richer, as if his eyes were sharper. Where was he?

Following the wall around to the right it soon took him in a straight fashion and almost as soon as he had wondered if there was a gate or door of some sort, he saw one. An old wooden door set in the wall. Enchanting. The door had a metal ring hanging from a knob which he grasped and turned. The door was a little stiff but it opened and, crouching slightly, he entered. He was inside the garden. It was very familiar. He'd been here before, hadn't he? In this garden. There were trees and a lawn with subtle wild flowers woven into it. And there was a stone cottage. A window. Smoke curling from the chimney and, yes, he could smell it.

The window opened. 'Jim!'

Who is it? Who knows him?

'Jim,' the voice comes again. Is it familiar? Without too much thought he walks across the grass and over to the window. Inside there is a woman. She says, 'What took you so long Jim?'

'I...' He doesn't know what to say.

'Come in,' she says, her eyes sparkling in the darker interior of the cottage. 'Come in,' she urges.

Instinctively he goes around the part of the kitchen that sticks out and there are three stone steps going down to a doorway. A back entrance. It's all familiar and not at all at the same time. The lawn is raised and he is able to see fruit trees in the distance. Thoughts begin to join. Tentatively he opens the door. There is the smell of the interior of the kitchen. A mélange of smells. A mustiness, an ancientness, wood burning, with both the heat of the log burner and the coolness of the shadows. He senses that change of temperature and air. As his eyes get used to the change of light he notices things, details.

'Jim,' come here. 'Thought I'd make the place welcoming.'

'Rosie,' he says, almost asking for confirmation.

'Give me a hug, you big old thing.' They hug and Jim feels her arms about him and the smell of her clothes and skin, the texture of her light cardigan. 'You okay?' she asks. 'It's been some time. Ronnie's not here.'

Ronnie. His best friend. That was his friend's name.

Your best friend and not your friend. Real people cannot be reproduced.

Jim has this intrusive thought enter his mind. How odd!

Rosie pulls away and says, 'Anna won't be long. She knew you were coming.'

Jim looks at Rosie. Smiles. 'This is my home,' he says.

'Yes Jim, it's your home.' There is a pause. 'You don't mind me being here...I mean...'

'No, no,' says Jim. Why would he? Hc can hear a clock ticking from the living room. He always wanted a clock like that. The pendulum swinging as the seconds ticked away.

'Are you okay?' Rosie asks.

'Yes, I'm just listening to the clock.'

'You can hear that?' she asks. 'You have great hearing.'

Jim stops. 'Listen,' he says. 'Can you hear?

'The clock?'

'No. I can hear...' He stops.

Rosie yelps, 'Can you smell that, rather?' Jim becomes aware of a slight burning smell. 'I've been making cakes, to welcome you back. Your favourite. Anna gave me the keys before she left. It was her idea, really.'

Jim watches her grab a tea-towel and pull down the oven door.

'Smells great,' he says.

'Just saved them,' Rosie says, relieved.

'I'm glad you're here,' he says.

Jim saunters towards the door at the end of the kitchen. But turns and goes through the other door to the hallway. Standing there it's as if he receives a huge flood of information. It's as if he is plunged into an ocean of possibility. The hallway has its unique smell – hundreds of years of comings and goings. Of lives lived and lives ended. Opening the front door, he sees the path roll out to the gate. It is exactly as he imagined. The lane in front of the house clatters with horses' hooves as two girls ride past. The horses are alert to him.

'Okay Jim?' one of the girls says. He has no idea who she is, but he likes the idea of them riding past his cottage on horseback.

'Wait,' he calls. And sprints down the path. Looking at his feet and his shoes, he could have sworn he was wearing boots. Opening the charming gate he walks over to where they've stopped.

'Hello Jim,' they chorus.

Ignoring them beyond a smile he strokes the nearest horse's muzzle. Its ears prick up and he sees an eye stare at him. Jim looks into the horse's eye and its ears twitch. It's as if he's in a spell – but a spell that the horse is also within.

'Your horses are magnificent,' he says.

'You always say that Jim,' the other girl pipes up.

'Do I?' he asks.

'You're always so sweet with them,' the girl who called out to him says. 'A horse can tell,' the other says.

'Horses can tell a lot,' Jim says. 'I better go back.'

The horse shakes its head and turns to him.

'Is Anna with you?'

'Not yet,' he says.

He waves as he walks back down the path. He feels like crying. He hadn't realised how simple and beautiful life could be.

Jim. We're checking you're okay.

Before going back into the cottage he looks up at the thatched roof and the bird sitting atop – the signature of the thatcher. As he looks, a bird swoops down and alights next to its facsimile. Jim smiles.

Back in the hallway he can once again smell a myriad of scents from the past. And the biscuits from the kitchen.

'Is it coffee or tea you're drinking these days, Jim?'

'Anything,' he says. 'Usually tea, but whatever you're making.'

'Come on and sit at the table. You're making me feel like it's my place.'

Jim sits at the oak table. Running his hands over its grain he again feels a sense of familiarity. 'How long have we known each other?' he asks.

'Since university, come on Jim, not that long ago. Well ages ago, I guess.'

Jim always wanted to go to university. He might have gone a few years late but the years 2020 to 2022 still left a bitter taste. Why does Rosie think they met there? And she's obviously much, much younger than he is. The clock continued ticking out its rhythm.

'Here you go,' Rosie says.

Jim takes a biscuit and bites into it. 'Extraordinary,' he says.

'Get on with you Jim,' Rosie says.

He takes a gulp from the mug. 'And the tea, just right,' he says.

'Ah, you're playing with me Jim. It's coffee.'

Jim takes a sip. 'It *is* coffee,' he says.

'Are you okay, Jim? Rosie asks. 'You don't seem quite yourself.'

'I'm fine,' he says. 'You cook so well.'

'Not as good as Anna.'

'No,' Jim says, having no idea. Anna. Who is Anna? He likes the name. But it's close to...close to...

Increase.

Jim shakes his head. 'The coffee's great. I forgot that I liked it. Lots of nuance in its taste.'

'Quite the reflective one today Jim.'

'Maybe,' he says. 'I can't recall too much of the day. I just remember being out walking on the hills.'

Rosie looks hard at him. Then she moves her hands across the table. Instinctively he grabs them. Holds her hands tightly. 'Thank you,' he says.

'Thank you, Jim, without you there would have been no Ronnie and me.'

'What do you mean?' he asks, startled. Uncomfortable.

'You kept us together, Jim, come on don't be modest now. You know how much we appreciate you. Well, Ronnie and you were inseparable. Still are when he's about.'

Jim relaxes slightly. Why did he react so? Taking another biscuit, he relaxes more. The taste of the biscuit is remarkable, as if he has been transported back in time to when his mother used to cook. The first decade of the century had been especially good. And yet, where he was now seemed perfect. Curiously perfect. Everything was just the way he'd want it. But he did sense another life living behind this experience he was having. He recalled his childhood but time seemed to stop then. And where he was in 'his' home seemed only to have come into existence when he found himself walking down from the hills.

'Okay to stream some music?' she asks.

'Sure.'

'I'll play something that Ronnie got you into – but it's ancient.'

Jim smiles. Rosie taps into her phone that connects with the house's speakers. Some very strange music begins. Jim is confused. Listens intently – it's like music from another world. Then the second track begins, the first is very short. Immediately he recognises the voice of Jimi singing: *Have you ever been, to Electric Ladyland...*

'I love this,' Jim says. 'Yeah, Ronnie's dad got him into that, it was decades old even then. Then Ronnie got me into it.' It was true. He knew that. There was something odd going on. As if he were in a dream. As if he couldn't quite kick back into reality. He doesn't even know Rosie, apart from a sense he has dreamt of her before. And yet here he is talking to her about his best friend, and, apparently, she and Ronnie are together. But his best friend had died some time ago.

Rosie danced about to 'Crosstown Traffic'. Jim began to think he was losing his mind. He wanted to puncture this dream, this reality and discover what was beyond. It was all confusing.

Keep an eye on the time. Prompt Rosie.

'Jim, just got a message from Anna, she'll be back in around thirty minutes.' Rosie has finished dancing as the opening riffs of Voodoo Chile begin.

'Okay,' Jim says. What is he to do? 'I'm going to grab forty winks,' he says.

Rosie smiles. 'Okay. If you're fast asleep, Anna can wake you up.' She has a mischievous look on her face. 'I didn't say you were here.'

Jim stands. 'Great album,' he says, 'I need to get back into it. I love Jimi's voice, and guitar of course. Mitch's drumming is so fluid and jazzy, at times powerful. Noel keeping them all together.'

'Well the night I was born, I swear the moon turned a fire red...'

Jim went into the hall and through the open door into the living room. It felt still and ancient. It wasn't ready for Hendrix and The Experience. Shutting the door quietly he then began walking up the creaky wooden staircase. It wound round towards the top. Everything had that strange yet familiar feeling. He instinctively knew which was his, or their room.

Stretching out on the bed he closed his eyes. If this was a dream then he could sleep into reality. His thoughts took him back to the hill he was walking on. He had to fight against intrusive thoughts and the fact that Anna was on her way back. Anna? Hannah? As he began to sink into the bed and its mattress with thoughts circling the room, he thought he heard words coming to him...

'Jim. Jim! Wakey, wakey,' came a female voice.

Jim opens his eyes. As he opens them his previous thoughts recede rapidly. But he says, 'Anna?' to the face looking down at him.

'No, Jim, it's Louise. It's okay, you're back.'

'What world am I in?' he says. He doesn't know where he is in either time or space. Having the sensation of waking from dreams and lost in a hypnopompic confusion.

'You're in this world,' Louise says, looking round at Jayne and another member of the team.

'Yes. Yes,' he says and begins to pull himself up. This world solidifies itself.

'That was intense,' Jayne says. 'You did some great work Jim. Great observation and emotional input. You need a drink. Not a stiff one though,' she adds.

Jim looks around. This is his reality but there is something, a feeling he experiences, from the reality he has just left. And then he has the image of the woman with the taped mouth and terrified eyes come to him as well.

'Where was I?' he asks.

'You were home, Jim. Home.'

'Home?' he asks.

'Jim,' Jayne and Dan chorus.

Jayne says, 'We need to ask some questions.'

'I feel like I'm losing grip on reality,' Jim says, only half-joking.

Dan says, 'Can you remember your experience? You remembered parts of the first one.'

Jim sits up fully. One of the team hands him a drink. A drink, not a stiff one. Some images come to his mind. 'Not really,' he says.

'We have a facsimile, if you'd like to see.' Jayne crosses her arms.

'I'm not sure.'

'We can play you parts so you can re-frequent the scenes, might help you recall more detail.'

'Should I? I mean, am I meant to remember what I'll experience in the future?'

'That's down to you,' Dan says. 'But if you want certain things, you're going to have to check. Some recall every detail. Some nothing.'

'Okay,' Jim says, 'I'll take a look.'

Jayne explains, 'The computer can only reproduce an objective view. The interior dialogue is all yours.'

'You'll have to put your drink down and have the box of tricks come down over your head again. Okay?' Dan says.

'Okay.'

'Over here,' Dan points to a chair he has quickly put on the marks. 'You know the drill.'

Jim nods. Jayne takes his drink as he walks over. He sits and the box is lowered over his head.

Again a female voice asks, 'Comfortable?'

'Yes,' he answers, feeling his voice sound hollow. The objective computer film (OCF) begins and Jim sees himself walking over the hills. Does he look younger? There is another angle that seems to come just off his left eye, as if the computer is tracking his sight, which to an extent it is.

Jayne says to Dan, 'We could've just had him watch with us on the screen.'

'True, but you know this old technology is somehow more effective. And I'm attached to it.'

Dan watches a series of shots covering the main visual elements of Jim's experience. For Jim the film seems totally encompassing, he is immersed in a different way from the original experience. But as he watches, he remembers. Remembers how he feels in every instant he is shown.

Jayne and Dan watch the screen as the computer records further data. 'The more we get, the more we get,' Dan says.

'The greater the technology, the greater the technology,' Jayne replies.

The film comes to the end and the box is lifted. 'Oh my,' Jim says. 'Maybe I need a stiff drink now. Okay. I'm getting it,' he says. 'It's pretty serious. Yeah. Heavy. And beautiful. Intriguing. Where is Anna, did I create her? How much of this did I create? I remember being here before now too. When Ronnie was there. I mean it's good. It's amazing. Is it that accurate or am I giving it meaning?'

'We'll find out,' Jayne says.

'This is a lot to take in. Now I'm not sure what I'm remembering and what I'm seeing for the...well, second time, I guess. It's like a dream. With the camera like dream consciousness. Is this a taste of the future-fields that await me?'

'Yes,' Dan says. 'But you can see how much work we still have to do.'

'What do you think about Rosie?'

'I like her. I can imagine Ronnie with her. But tell me. It seems like they and me are younger. I think. Is that right?'

'Yes,' Jayne says.

'Do we age?'

'We don't know,' says Dan.

'We believe not,' Jayne says. 'Why would the body age in that thought environment? Your actual body isn't going to age rapidly. It might be, and we don't know for sure, that's it's only if you think you're going to age, that you'll age.'

'Thinking my future life now and thinking my future in the future.'

'That's possible,' Dan smiles. 'In fact we can program certain things. If you look in a mirror we can program that to reflect you as a younger self. That will reinforce your idea of yourself.'

'This is something...' Jim takes the drink that Jayne has picked up and passed to him. 'Tastes like there's alcohol,' he says.

'Just a little,' Jayne smiles.

'Well, it's one thing imagining all this, another thing kind of dreaming it, but something totally mind-blowing to realise that I now have two existences. It's real now, I can remember it all more-or-less. Yeah, The Jimi Hendrix Experience, the clock, the sheep, the water. I mean how do you do that?'

'You do it Jim,' Dan says. 'You give it all the sensory experience that you would expect. It's your world. Your home.'

'How far could I go? If I picked a direction and kept walking, how far could I go?'

'Forever,' Jayne says. 'It might get a bit monotonous though.'

Jim imagines walking into someone else's world. 'The ideas about Ronnie, it's all from the stuff I collected and sent in?'

Jayne nods.

Jim strokes his chin. 'I mean, it's amazing. Have you tried any of this?' he asks.

'Not exactly,' Dan says. 'We've done tests and simulations.'

'I've done some,' Jayne says. 'We can have avatars.'

'Jayne!' Dan says sharply.

Jim keeps quiet. But this brief exchange sticks in his mind. Then, 'Well I'm blown away. Blown away. I need to know about Anna though,' he says. 'I haven't designed her.'

'You can change anything,' Dan says. 'The doctor worked on Anna, kind of a surprise.'

'Still a surprise,' Jim says.

'Yes, still.'

'It was a clever idea of yours to go to sleep,' Jayne says. 'Though we were prompting you, subliminally. We thought you might like to talk to Doctor Abraham about Anna. Before or after meeting her.'

'I have discussed the idea with him,' Jim confesses.

'He'll see you soon anyway. This afternoon. Before your wife picks you up.'

'Everyone seemed to know her,' Jim says, referring to Anna. Then, 'I heard voices. I heard voices occasionally.'

Jayne looks at Dan. 'Yes,' Jayne says, 'Yes, more subliminal information – well not so subliminal.'

'We can work on that,' Dan says.

'What about the woman with tape over her mouth?' Jim asks.

Dan and Jayne look nonplussed.

Jim continues, 'I saw a woman, a terrified woman, with tape across her mouth. Silver tape.'

'Are you sure?' Dan asks.

'I don't know if she's real or in my thoughts. If I made her up or not.'

'She's not in our programming,' Jayne states. 'Did you see her?'

'Just in my mind. But it feels as if I know her.'

'We can check that out,' Dan says

'The main thing now is to discuss as much as you can recall as possible. To integrate that into your fully awake consciousness. And to build on that. Meeting Anna is going to be key,' Jayne says.

'There was a lot of visual information. As you know this is a combination of your input and the computer's programming, but also, the computer monitoring how you react. Filling in information,' Dan says.

'That's like with vision loss,' Jim begins. 'The brain is able to fill in the loss of vision by taking the surroundings and finishing the picture, the view. Amazing,' he says. 'I wonder how much of our vision occurs in our brain and not through our eyes.'

'Exactly,' Dan says. 'This is why you can 'see' your experience.'

'Full of interesting facts Jim,' Jayne says.

'It's like a dream,' Jim says.

Dan says, 'Yes, but directly through your perceived vision and it's rational. Okay, I know we think dreams are rational at the time, but these experiences most definitely are. And they're being revised constantly.'

'Can you recall your first time at the cottage?' Jayne asks.

'I can,' Jim says. 'Everything has come back to me.'

'And you could smell and taste the biscuits?' Dan asks, jumping forward.

'Yes, just exactly as I expected.'

Dan and Jayne exchange smiles. Jayne says, 'In fact most of that taste and smell derived from the computer. They're generic – but you felt them personally.'

Jim was slightly disappointed. 'They tasted just as I remember my mother made them.'

'How reliable is our memory?' Dan asks.

'You don't need to answer,' Jayne smiles.

'Memory...' Jim thinks hard. 'Perhaps not so reliable. But memories *feel* right.'

'Yes,' Dan says.

'I presume the computer doesn't know what I'm thinking?' Jim asks.

'You'd be surprised,' Jayne says.

'The computer is linked to a myriad of other computers,' Dan says. 'Since we've been working at Portway, the growth in computer communication has been exponential. We've had computers create instant highly detailed worlds from a single typed-in paragraph. That's why we can produce what we do.'

'With a little help from the psychedelics,' Jim retorts.

'But you didn't have any just now,' Dan smiles.

'The drug mixture we'll eventually use is for full immersion. For future-fields enaction. And it is possible that your senses will be heightened beyond that reality. But not too much. The brain is good, under normal circumstances, at attenuating information,' Jayne says.

'Thankfully,' Dan confirms.

'It always comes back to what actually *is* reality,' Jim says.

'Jim. Reality is what you accept as such. When you're in a dream, you consider that as reality, don't you?' Jayne says.

'But when I awake I know it's not. Well, maybe it's another form of reality.'

'And future-fields will be another form of reality,' Dan adds.

'I've asked before,' Jim says, 'but will I dream? The doctor talked about lucid dreaming as a comparison to my future experiences, I think, but wasn't sure if I'd definitely dream.'

'We don't know,' Jayne says candidly.

'But don't we need to dream? Won't I need to sleep? My body won't be working, the doctor explained that to me, but my mind will be. That's the whole point, isn't it?'

Dan was listening and thinking. 'If you do dream,' he says, 'then in a way you'll be dreaming within a dream, within a dream.'

Jayne huffed. 'We don't know,' she says bluntly. 'But if you do, it will be like any other dream.'

'Maybe if I dream within a dream,' Jim says, reflecting Dan's words, 'then in that dream I might be back in this reality. Either this reality stored by my memories, or the reality of being a stiff in a box.'

Jayne couldn't help snorting out a laugh.

'I can see why the doctor's taken such a liking to you Jim,' Dan says.

'You can?'

'I can. You question things. Most don't. Maybe we've always been like that. I mean, not questioning things,' Dan says.

'Maybe we don't need to question these things,' Jayne says. 'There's no real point. What is, is what it is. We have to face whatever reality we find ourselves in. There's no alternative.'

'But if we don't question reality, then we won't change anything,' says Jim, feeling a little smug.

'I'm not sure,' Jayne says.

'Well I mean...I mean, we go through life not really thinking about death. That's the aim of life perhaps.'

Dan laughs. 'It's not my aim.'

'It's life's aim. That's where it leads. Whether we like it or not.'

'Whether we like it or not,' Dan repeats.

'And that's the point of this life-after-life,' Jayne says. 'We are, in fact, challenging accepted reality. Death is abated.'

'But not cheated. Just a bit of time stolen from it,' Jim says. He thinks. 'Maybe an eternity is stolen from it.'

'We shall see,' says Dan.

'Well I'll see first.'

'And we're here to make it as close to what you want as possible,' Jayne says. 'We'll be co-creating your reality. One day, we, and you Jim, will be seen as pioneers.'

'I just wish I had twenty or so years more. What difference would that make to the state?'

'You'd have to ask the National Government that,' Dan says. 'And our illustrious leader.'

Jayne sends him a darting glance.

'Well it's true,' Dan says, feeling put in his place.

'Maybe I will,' says Jim.

'Don't rock the boat Jim,' Jayne says. 'You have a new life in front of you...' As she says this she is notified of a communication. 'Doctor Abraham's on his way.' Jayne smiles at Dan.

'Did you get all that?' Dan says into the air about them.

'Are you talking to ghosts?' Jim says with a smile.

'Computers,' Dan answers. 'They'll be listening to our every word.'

Doctor Abraham breezes in. 'How's everything going, people?'

'Perfect,' says Dan.

'Good. Jim?'

'Mind blowing,' he jokes.

'It will only get better,' the doctor says.

'We've reached one critical moment,' Jayne says.

'Go ahead.'

'Anna is about to arrive at Jim's cottage.'

'Aha! Well I've arrived just in time.'

'Seems so,' says Dan.

'Jim?'

'Doctor.'

'Are you ready?'

'For…'

'Not 'for' Jim. To. Are you ready to create your perfect woman? Your Eve.' The doctor's face is glowing.

'Isn't she called Anna?' Jim says deadpan.

'Everything can be changed,' the doctor says. 'Everything. Why, you have the chance to create the woman of your dreams.'

'Literally,' Jim answers. Holding back on his wish to discuss the necessity or otherwise of dreams in his future-fields.

They laugh. But Jim doesn't. Is this a game? Is he a player? And he's not happy his wish to create a woman is so public.

'Are you ready?' Doctor Abraham asks.

'Ready,' Jim says. He looks at Jayne and Dan, then finally back at the doctor.

'Good. This will be your dream woman.'

'Maybe,' Jim says. 'But I have my dream woman at home,' he smiles. He wants them all to know, darting a look towards the doctor.

The doctor scrutinizes him. 'Very well. You have a template.'

'I have a wife.'

They laugh again.

Jim looks to the floor. Then up at the doctor.

'Let's go,' he says.

Hannah arrived later in the afternoon. Snow had fallen and some had settled on rooves and dusted the bare branches of trees. There wasn't enough snow to dampen the sound of the city but in areas it still rendered the mundane magical.

Jim was waiting for her at the reception area, holding his small bags. Hannah passed through security and threw her arms round him.

'Are you ready?' she asks.

'No, I'm just practising standing at a transport stop,' he jokes, lamely. 'Good to see you,' he says. 'It feels like an eternity.'

'Just a few days,' Hannah says. Then, 'Is the doctor about?'

'Maybe. Do you want to see him?'

'Not really. He knows you're coming back with me now?'

'Yes.'

'Where did you get that coat from?' she laughs.

'A long story. I like it. It was a present, that's why I'm not wearing my usual winter coat. Got a few things to tell you.'

'Me too.'

They turn to leave and Jim waves at the woman at reception. She smiles. Jim feels like she's not so nervous. Maybe the doctor's lying down, after their mammoth session. 'Should I say goodbye to the doctor?' he asks her.

'No need,' the secretary says. 'I think he's very tired. He said he'd contact you and will send some computer-generated film.'

'Thanks.'

'Thank you,' Hannah adds.

In the car the wipers brush away a thin white blanket of flakes. Lights picking out and reflecting those remaining. Hannah starts the hydrogen motor which purrs near silently. 'Can we take a different route back?' Jim asks. Hannah checks her dashboard and speaks to the on-board computer.

'Everything's fine,' she says, as if Jim hasn't heard the conversation. 'Where do you want to go?' she asks. 'Please turn up the heating,' she says to the computer.

'I want to surprise you,' he says. 'Are you okay using the car?' She nods. 'I mean, is there a limit to how far we can go? I guess we'll be tracked.'

'It's okay, I'll say you were driving,' she laughs. 'What could they do?'

'Just kill me in advance I guess.' They laugh.

'Are you hungry? Do you need a drink?'

'I'm fine,' he says. 'It's been intense.'

'I want to talk with you about a few things,' she says as she manoeuvers the car. 'I need to get directions,' she huffs.

'Override it,' Jim says. 'I know where to go, I think. I'll direct.'

'Not sure Clint's going to like that.'

Jim smiles. 'Give him a fist full of dollars and tell him to get out of town. Jim's in charge.'

'Well…'

Jim directed.

The city had changed somewhat. And new roads had been built. Roads for the elite who had cars and those like Hannah who had access to company cars. They had to turn around a few times but it seemed like Hannah was enjoying their adventure. Modern architecture and lighting of the inner city soon gave way to gloomy housing and empty shops. Lighting became sparse and Hannah was slightly worried about using too much fuel. Checking the gauge put her mind at rest. And the car had said nothing.

'Where are we going?'

'You'll see. I hope.' He sees Hannah's reaction. 'Joking.' Though he was having difficulty navigating from memory. 'Take that road,' he says. 'Watch out for potholes.'

There was little traffic on the roads, though where trams ran the carriages were lit up and their interiors revealed what looked like worn out travellers. The inside of the car was kept at a healthy temperature as they drove up an incline onto an out of town main road.

'This would have been full of cars when I was younger,' he says.

'Better as it is,' Hannah answers.

'Yes, maybe. But something's been lost.'

Just as they turn there is a giant poster. It's some kind of advertising for the National Government.

'There aren't any elections, are there?' he asks.

'I don't think so. Maybe. Maybe I heard something.'

'I'm not sure about our leader,' he says.

'Me neither,' Hannah says. 'But where's the opposition?'

'I don't trust him. Never trust a man with a double-barrelled surname.'

'Hughes-Kahn?'

'Exactly. Him and his bunch have been in power too long.'

'Maybe they'll get kicked out later this year, if there *are* elections.'

Jim laughs. 'The people love their Civic Duty. That is, until it gets right up close to their face. Keep going, it's a few miles.'

'You and your miles!'

'It keeps me connected with the past,' he says. Jim can't see much out of his window as they begin to leave the city. Snow falls heavier now but the wipers beat it away.

'Come on Jim, where are we going? We're getting further and further away. I'm beginning to get hungry.'

'Not far,' he says. There should be a tower, like a folly coming up on the right. It's big enough for us to see even in this weather. Slow down then and a couple more miles, kilometers, there's a turning right to a place called Lower Didford.'

'Jim?'

'I need to, Hannah. These past few days have been trying. Mentally. Dare I say it, spiritually...'

'Jim!'

'Yep. I know. You don't expect that from me. But I tell you, this future-fields stuff. It's...well it messes with your mind. Messes with everything.'

Hannah glances at him, at his profile. There is enough light for her to see his features and his reflection in the window. 'I hope this car is okay in snow,' she says.

'We'll find out.'

The tower loomed over the trees and Jim found its presence reassuring. Most of the sky was dark but there was a yellow tint to some of the clouds and occasionally a weak, waning moon winked through. The snow seemed to be growing thicker and at times a stronger wind drove it on.

'Slow down,' he says. 'This is it coming up. Turn right.'

Hannah reacts and the car slides slightly. But she sees it neatly around. The road is covered in snow and the trees on either side resemble black walls.

'Nearly there,' Jim says.

'Are you sure?' Hannah says.

'I have to,' he says. 'I have to.'

Jim points out a lane to their left. The car doesn't struggle. Hannah confirms with Clint that everything is okay. On their right is the church.

'Park up there,' he says. 'I'm hoping the hotel will be open. Maybe it's survived. There were a lot of rich folk around here. Jim gets out of the car and pulls up the lapels of his jacket. 'Have you got a torch?' he mouths, wagging his hand as if he's using one.

'Use your phone,' she says. Hannah doesn't want to get out of the warmth into the snow but she also doesn't feel entirely safe. 'I'll bring mine,' she says, 'it's bound to be more powerful.'

'Turn the engine off.'

She talks to the car and it hibernates. Jim walks to the church's small gate.

Quickly she runs to him and holds his arm. In the churchyard the ancient graves are blanketed with snow. The gravestones are like black eyes peering into the past. Opening the wooden doors, they step inside a porch.

'I hope it's open,' Jim says. 'A lot of churches got vandalised.'

'I know,' she says.

Jim tries the latch. He is reminded of the door in the wall in his created reality. He has a lot to tell her. But first. The door opens. Thankfully. It belonged to a bygone age and a time long gone in Jim's life. Long gone but still hot and urgent in his blood.

The inside of the church was lit automatically, dimly, but lit. Jim was surprised. There were unlit candles too. It was as if the previous near three decades had never existed. For a moment he stopped and smelt the musty air. This brought back the smell of the hallway in 'his' cottage. Hannah came to his side. She held his hand. Jim closed his eyes. It was in the late summer of '31. He'd been back a few times but not many after he got together with Hannah. It was a different life. As different a life as his future life promised to be. He would need a church in his future-fields, some sacred place. A haunt of ancient peace.

'So, we have to find the book,' he says. 'She wasn't buried. I couldn't do that. I couldn't put a small coffin into the earth and seal her up. I couldn't do that. I wanted her to sail up into the sky and be with the stars. I couldn't do it.'

Hannah sees a tear roll from an eye. 'I know, Jim,' she says.

'You understand?' he says. 'I had to take charge. I had to be the strong one. But I wasn't Han,' he says. Hannah flashes her device around the interior of the church and shadows dance like phantoms in the old stonework. She imagines a congregation at a birth. How it might have been. She recalls such an event. She's a lot younger than Jim but there is still a part of her tied to a different time. 'Come on,' she says.

'I know where it is,' Jim says. 'I know where the book is kept. There's a... I don't know what it's called,' he says. 'Like an old chest of drawers,' he continues. 'This way Han. I'm pretty sure it's to the side.'

Hannah smiles, it's been a long time since he's called her Han. 'Are you sure it'll still be here? Wouldn't they have taken all these records?'

'But the church is open. Someone must still be looking after the place. There's been a few revivals. During the Grey Wolves times.'

Jim leads her by the hand. 'Shine over here,' he says. 'Yes! Yes,' it's here.'

'Will it open?'

'If it doesn't open, I'll force it.'

'Jim!'

'I will,' he says.

Hannah shines on the lock. The wood is heavy oak. Jim tries opening the doors. 'Is it locked?' Hannah asks.

'Not sure,' he says, blowing on his fingers.

'Careful.'

'If I have a stroke make sure you get your money back.'

'Jim!'

The doors pull open, hitting his head slightly. Jim pulls down a lid on the inside and there behind it is a huge book. 'Yes,' he says, touching his head. Hannah imagines a growing bruise. Jim can sense her concern. 'It's nothing,' he says. 'Parochial records,' he exclaims. 'I thought the church kept them in-house, as it were.' As he says this he opens the book and throws over a clump of heavy pages so that he is close to its end. Scanning the years, he slows down as he approaches 2031. 'Come closer,' he says. 'Shine down on the page.' He turns over another leaf and finds the listing for September 31. And he stops. A shiver as cold as the walls of the church passes through his body. Hannah instinctively holds him. There is her name – shortened, as he intended, As they had agreed. The way they knew her. The way they remembered her. *Maddy*

Jim is struck by emotion, feels his legs give way. Touching Maddy's name he moves his head back as tears flow. 'I wouldn't want to smudge her name,' he says. Hannah holds him, comforts him as best she can.

'I need to sit,' Jim says.

They sit in the gloom. 'Are you okay,' Hannah asks, squeezing his hand. She turns off her phone.

'That's all that's left of her. Yes, memories of course, and some cuddly toys I let Ellie keep. I should have kept something tangible too. Something I could hold onto. I'm glad there's no grave though.'

'It's what you keep inside that's important.'

'I know. But some of the memories are beginning to fade. No matter how hard I try to hang onto them. Sometimes I lose the contours of her face and the way she would smile.' Jim's tears flow in the dim light. 'I wonder who goes to church these days,' he says. 'Did the church even try to fight what was happening? Now people are reduced to names on pages, more likely on computer records, that's if they're lucky.'

Hannah knows to let him be. Just be by his side. His fate, their fate, was cruel. It was effective in that only those nearing their civic duty truly understood. And then it was too late. Didn't it used to be three score years and ten of life, or was she imagining that?

They rested for some time in the quiet. Hannah imagined the weather outside. And occasionally the noise of the wind found its way into the stone of the ancient church. She had things she needed to talk to Jim about. She would wait.

Hannah has an idea, 'Shall I light a candle?' she says.

Jim nods.

Leaving the pew she went back towards the entrance. There were candles there and as she approached another dim light switched on. Pocketing her phone, she took a candle but realised she had no means to light it. There in front of them was a box of matches, it felt as if the box had materialised out of nowhere. She struck a match and held it over the candle's wick, until it took. Then she took two more. One for them both as well as Maddy. One of the candles she placed in a holder, the other two she carried in both hands as a particularly violent rush of wind howled through the roof's beams. The dim light and the entrance light were extinguished.

'You okay Jim?' she calls.

'Yes,' he says, in the near pitch black. As he looks around he sees two flames burning. As Hannah approaches the light of the flames seems animated, as if with a life of their own. 'Be careful,' he says.

'Keep talking, you can guide me,' she says. At one point she stumbles against the end of a pew. And then the dim lighting is back on.

'Time to go,' Jim says. 'We have to live,' he says. 'For as long as we can.'

Hannah reaches him. 'Okay?' she asks.

He nods. 'I'll close the book. It'll probably be the last time. Maybe I'll meet up with her soon.'

Hannah thinks. 'You haven't tried to recreate her Jim?'

'How could I,' he says. 'I can't really recreate anyone. I tried with Ronnie. But Maddy's too close. I'm not even sure I should have tried with Ronnie. I should have let him be.'

'But it's not him,' Hannah reassures.

Jim puts the book back, lifts the wooden flap back and shuts the doors as hard as he can. As he does so he imagines Maddy inside the great oak bureau.

'I know it's not him,' Jim says. 'But it feels like him. Feels like he's back right there with me. I didn't see him last time though,' he says. 'And I didn't see Anna.'

'Anna?'

Jim doesn't know where to begin. How to explain. 'She's like you,' he says.

'Like me? But I'm alive, Jim. Alive and will be for another eleven years.'

'She's not you,' he says. 'But I'll need company.'

'Can't you wait?'

'Wait for what? You can't enter my world, as I can't enter yours. Maybe if there's a Heaven...'

'You can replace me just like that?' she says.

'No,' he protests. 'Not now Hannah...'

'At least you got the name right.'

'Come on, you're not being fair. It's not real.'

'It's not real. You think it's not real? Then why am I paying to keep you there?'

'Then don't,' he says. Jim screws his hands into fists, his nails cutting into his palms. Hannah turns around and goes to the entrance where she plants the candles.

'Look,' Jim says, 'it wasn't my idea. It wasn't my idea, it was the doctor's.'

'The doctor's?' she says. 'Now you're lying to me!'

'What do you mean?'

'The doctor told me about you wanting to create a woman. Well he said me...'

'Do you want me to be lonely? If I have a woman that reminds me of you that keeps the link we have.'

'It won't be me.'

'It will be the next best thing,' he says. 'The next best thing to having you with me.'

Hannah says, 'Let's get out of here,' pushing open the door to the vestibule and then the heavy oak door to the outside. A swirl of snow enters. Jim follows her out. She takes her phone but its light diffuses weakly. They tread new footprints in the snow. Jim is concerned about whether they can get back okay. He grabs Hannah's coat. 'Listen,' he says.

'It's freezing,' she says. 'Let's get in the car.'

'I wanted a woman who would remind me of you. I know, not you,' he shouts above the wind. But at least reminds me of you,' he stresses. 'She isn't real.'

In the car they sit silently for some time. 'Let's get something to eat. There's a hotel close by that used to do food, maybe they still do. Be rational,' he says.

'You drive,' she says. 'Do something useful.'

Jim is angry at her reaction. They hurriedly swap seats, crossing in the darkness of the night and the whiteness of the falling snow.

The car starts easily but slips and slides as he quickly accelerates away.

Jim begins to breathe easier. 'What do you expect me to do for an eternity?' he says. 'Can I betray you with a woman who is based on you and who isn't real?'

'There you have it,' she says.

'When did you speak with the doctor about this?' he suddenly asks.

'Last night,' she says, then quickly, 'evening.'

'Where?'

Hannah wants to spite him, 'He took me out, if you must know.'

Jim bangs on the brakes and the car spins round, sliding dangerously close to the side of the road. 'You didn't tell me about this,' he shouts.

'The doctor told me not to,' she says.

'It's getting worse,' Jim says.

Hannah's voice changes in tone. 'He was worried about you and wanted to speak with me.'

'Couldn't anyone speak with *me*?' he says. 'Am I at rest already. Am I already a dead man?'

'Don't be melodramatic,' she says.

Jim eases the car forward and tentatively turns it around. 'I trust you,' he says.

'I thought I could trust you,' she answers.

'You can. Listen. I'll do away with this woman, this copy. I'll live like a monk, if you want.'

Hannah says nothing. The snow continues to fall.

'Hello Milly, this is a secure line we can talk freely.'

'Alistair,' Milly answers. 'Good to hear from you, personally.'

'Good to hear you,' he stresses, 'and not have you acting up...'

'That was your idea.'

'It works, it's working,' he says.

'It is.'

'You can keep it up?' he asks.

'Of course. I've been well trained.'

'Well trained indeed. I saw something in you. And I was right.'

'You're always right,' she says.

'I can see through that answer Milly.'

She feels his smile through the encrypted line.

'To business. I need a couple of butterflies, two cocoons and a moth. You've time. And get your bags ready for February the thirteenth.'

'Nice date,' she says.

'Better than that, it's a Friday.'

'Where are we going?' Milly asks.

'New Africa Isles.'

'Sounds gorgeous. It feels like ages since I've travelled anywhere.'

'I have connections in high places, remember. And now the isles are independent, we have more leeway, shall we say.'

'How long will we be there?'

'A week should do it. You'll be having a nervous breakdown...You'll need the break.'

'Again?'

'Again. Just a minor one. My doc will sort things out. I'll keep Jake in the know, to a degree. How's he getting on with my avatar?'

'It's coming along,' she says.

'Well I'm missing out. And I don't want to be.'

'I understand,' Milly says. 'Leave all that to me.'

'The butterflies have to work and make sure the cocoons are young but aren't too young, and make sure they're all well programmed. I've got the usual contacts. You've got time to put it all in place. And you know what to do.'

'Yes.'

'John will be coming too.'

'Hughes-Kahn?' she asks in confirmation.

'Who else.'

'Pretext?'

'There are two up and coming Nat-Gov members that might cause trouble. We can't have that with the elections coming along...'

'But they're always fixed,' she laughs.

'Yes, of course, but that could be part of the problem. These two are idealists. They believe in what they're doing. But a little dust and a wing or two and they'll be well taken care of.'

'What about the other three?'

'Two of them are business connections, party funders. We need more money and we don't want to have to ask too often.'

'Are they the cocoons?'

'No, one's a moth-lover.'

'The other?'

'An entertainer. Well known. You'll see. And you know what they're like. Once he's drunk he'll go for anything. But it's going to be an enjoyable break. We can talk freely there and have fun.'

'Sounds good,' Milly says.

'Great. I'll keep you posted and keep up the good work. Remember all this is for national cohesion and continuity. We can't be derailed now. It's been thirty years since the idea was seeded. Look at the country. We'd still be in utmost poverty were it not for our vision back then.'

'I'm lucky I was born when I was.'

'Lucky we found you. Though not sure how much luck was involved. Perhaps I should say, lucky for you.'

'Definitely lucky for me.'

'Okay. Back to normal status. Over.'

'Goodbye,' she says.

Immediately she opens up her private computer and begins organising the professor's requirements. Would she start with the butterflies or the cocoon girls...And she hasn't told him about the film either. Maybe he expected her to bug the doctor's apartment. Maybe he knew nothing about it. She'll play it cool. What he doesn't know, he doesn't need to know.

Jim found the hotel and there were lights on.

'Come on,' he says. 'I have to tell you some things. It's bigger than any problems we have. Maybe.'

They hurry to the door. It is an old, granite-built building.

Hannah's hair has snow crystals shining in it, sparkling in the outside light. Jim holds her. 'This is serious stuff, maybe,' he again qualifies. 'We have to be together. Strong. All of us. You, Henry, Joanne and me. We can't bicker. Trust me.'

She looks hard at him. It's as if the cold has been driven away by the light and the wind isn't quite as harsh. 'Get in,' she says.

Pushing the door open, they are met by an interior that could have been a stage set. It's warm and a large fireplace has logs of wood burning in it. Jim looks at Hannah, they are surprised. Pleasantly. There are only a few folk in there and a man is behind the bar. He smiles. 'Good evening,' he calls over to them. 'I'm surprised to see any travellers tonight.'

'We got lost,' Jim says.

'You're driving?'

'Yes. I am,' Hannah says.

'What is it?' the man behind the bar asks.

'A Stellar.'

'Top of the range. Nice. They handle all right in the snow?'

'Seem to,' Hannah says. She's still somewhat cold inside and out.

'Nice to see a proper fire,' Jim says.

'What other fires are there?'

'Well, you know,' Jim says, 'I thought they were banned.'

'Probably,' the man says, 'but we don't pay much attention to that. We're left alone. As you can see,' he smiles. 'Robert,' he says. 'I'm the owner. A few locals have managed to get out, wasn't as bad earlier.'

Hannah is petting a dog that has come close to her.

'That's Barney. He likes you. If he likes you, you must be okay.'

'Jim,' Jim says, walks up and proffers his hand.

'Old school,' Robert says.

'I guess.'

'Why not, no plagues recently,' he jokes. 'What will you be having? Got some genuine Scotch whisky, stored in oak barrels mind you, French wine – some good stuff, like gold these days. Beer brewed locally.'

'Hannah, if you can tear yourself away from Barney,' Jim calls.

'Is that his name, so adorable...'

'Thank you,' Robert jokes, 'on behalf of the dog of course.'

'What do you want to drink?' Jim asks her.

'Something hot,' she says, keeping close to the fire.

'Can you do that?'

'Tea, coffee, hot chocolate?'

'Hot chocolate, please,' Hannah calls over.

Jim senses she is thawing. 'I'll have a shot of scotch.'

'Good man,' Robert says. 'Oh, and if you have your phones or any devices on you, we like to keep them quiet in a special box, under the bar here. Prying eyes, ears and the radiation,' he says jovially. 'The box is effective.' Jim and Hannah comply, exchanging glances as they hand over their phones and device.

They make some small talk. It seems Robert's wife, Jim surmises, has got the hot chocolate on the go. She appears quickly and disappears nearly as quickly, stopping only to whisper something or other to Robert.

After some minutes, 'Here you go, and here's your whisky.'

Jim takes the hot chocolate over to Hannah. In his other hand he balances the large glass of whisky. They sit down tentatively on an old settee with a throw over it. There are dog hairs covering the seat cushions.

'Whisky? You hate it. I mean have you ever actually tried some?'

'It's genuine stuff,' he says.

'Says Robert.'

Barney jumps up on the settee next to Jim. Jim can see Robert looking over and smiling. He holds up a glass and Jim does likewise, they swig their drinks in unison. 'Shit,' he whispers. Hannah laughs. 'It's fuckin' fire water,' he says.

'Good stuff,' Robert calls.

'Excellent.'

Jim sees Robert cast a glance at his regulars.

'It's like stepping back in time,' Jim says. He thinks of Maddy caught in eternal time. 'But we can speak freely here, at least.'

Jim is angry with the way Hannah has reacted. Part of him wants to walk out in the snow and leave everything behind. Freeze to death and get it all over and done with. Maybe he'd be reunited with Maddy. Maybe they could do the things a father and daughter would, and should have. Then he thinks of Joanne. Their relationship has been difficult.

'So?' Hannah says.

The fire is alive and breathes out its smoke occasionally. It animates the lounge bar. Robert is talking to a customer but he also calls back to his unseen wife. Is she cooking? Jim is hungry. And he thinks Hannah is too.

'So?' he replies.

'What's the big deal?'

'The big deal is...' He stops. Looks at Barney, back at Hannah. Is this real, he wonders. 'The big deal is, there's something going on at Portway...'

'Something going on?'

'Let me finish,' he bites. 'I'm not exactly sure what's going on but I think I witnessed a woman's body being thrown into a dumpster. That's something isn't it?' Jim almost sneers.

'Where? When?'

'I went for a walk on the first night, I couldn't sleep, as usual. You know. But I lost all my memory of this. I think the doc drugged me. I don't know. But after the second experience I had, future-fields,' he explains, 'things began coming back to me. And I'd been seeing this woman's face, terrified, her mouth gagged...'

'Where did you see her?'

'I mean, I don't know. I don't know if I saw her being put in the dumpster or not. I don't know what's real. But I do know that the men who dumped someone, the way they talked wasn't right. I can't remember too much...'

'Where was this?' she asks.

'Some underground place. It was very dark.'

'It's probably where they take the bodies that have died in that Gateway place, or something. They aren't going to wheel them down the corridor are they?' Hannah says.

'I agree, thought the same, but the doc told me no-one had died there. No-one, not for a few years at least. So, no...'

Hannah takes a sip of the hot chocolate. 'That's it?'

'That's it. Except I got caught going out another time.'

'Caught?'

'It's like an open-prison. Fine in the day but you better not go walkies at night. The guards were scared of getting into trouble if I was found. Look, I tell you now, there's something strange going on. I saw a dumpster being wheeled down a path too, dead of night. I just know something's going on, I can feel it. The guards were scared. It's not normal.'

'Maybe not,' she says. 'The doctor took me out for a meal,' she blurts.

'I guess he's got class. And money,' Jim snarls.

'He wanted to talk, I told you...'

'You didn't tell me he took you out to a restaurant.'

'Well he did.'

'And you went!'

'I went.'

Jim bit his lip. 'Go on.'

'Okay. He told me you were designing a version of me. But. Honestly. I think there was more to it, this evening out.'

Jim says again, 'Go on.'

'Well, why do you think he invited me out and you none the wiser back at Portway?'

'And you went.'

'I went because I was worried about you.'

'You think he wanted to seduce you?'

'Perhaps.'

'The whole place stinks,' Jim says. 'I'm beginning to wonder if it's best if I pay a whole lot of money and get smuggled out of the country.'

'Jim, keep your voice down.'

'You think Barney's listening?' Jim tries to look under the dog's collar.

'Always joking Jim.'

'No. Not joking at all. Serious. You know I have hunches and you know I'm usually right. I was right with you wasn't I?'

Hannah almost blushes. Jim knocks back the whisky.

'You don't have to drink it,' she says.

'I've got to keep up the macho look with Robert. I think he fancies himself.'

'What do you mean?'

'Not like that. I reckon he thinks he's hard.'

'Jim, you're as soft as putty.'

'You think?'

'I think.'

'Okay, I'll put that to the test. I'm effectively as dead as a doornail, right? With an extended lease at life's half-way house. In which case what have I got to lose?'

'What are you talking about?'

'I, maybe we, have got to find out what's going on at Portway.'

'How can we?'

'I'm going back in a month. I'll befriend the guards who nabbed me. Ask questions. I don't know. And,' he pauses. 'Maybe you've got to find out a few things from the dear doc.'

'What are you asking me to do?' her voice rises and Barney shifts and moves closer to Jim.

'Find out things. You're a woman. He took you out. He fancies you, the bastard. Okay, we'll play him. You on the outside with him and me on the inside, with who or whatever. Something's going on I swear.'

Hannah looks into nothingness.

Jim continues, 'The doc seems keen on my design work. Let's get designing our own plan. If there's something to hide, we'll find it. I'll do some digging. I still have access to some banned sites. I'm good at investigating. And you can lead him on. If we've got him wrong, then the joke will be on us. You can tuck me up in a drawer and carry on living. Portway is exonerated. But if they're up to something we can expose them. Frankly, it's our civic duty,' he smiles.

Hannah gazes into the fire. It spits out an ember that smoulders on the surrounding tiles.

'A moral obligation?' she asks.

Jim nods. 'It might seem crazy, maybe I'm crazy. But something isn't right. Who knows what they're up to, could be a front for any kind of business.'

'I heard about a weird conspiracy theory,' Hannah says. 'They say that girls, girls normally, are being abducted and programmed. For the elite. They get them into deep states of consciousness and do all kinds of things to program them. They use fear and torture and threats. All sorts of stuff. They're called Butterfly Girls.'

'Are they young?' Jim asks.

Hannah nods. 'They take them from all kinds of places...even children's homes...'

'The woman I can see in my head, she's old. Must be sixty plus. Who knows? I can't see them trafficking children from Portway.'

'What would make money? Hannah asks. 'That's the clue.'

'Well they're making plenty of credit from us aren't they? Which reminds me,' he says blandly. 'I have no idea how much things cost here. I guess we'll settle up at the end. Pay by your device, or my phone.'

'Device,' she says. 'Maybe your friend's syphoning credit off as we speak...'

Ignoring her last comment, Jim says, 'What could they be a front for...drugs maybe? That would make sense,' Jim says.

'Don't get carried away,' Hannah says. 'The doctor says you've a great imagination.'

'An idea,' he sparks up. 'What if they're hiding folk there? Kidnapping them and holding them for ransom?'

'I guess it's possible. But we can't go jumping to conclusions,' she says. 'It's probably all your...'

'My?'

'Imagination,' she says.

'Maybe.'

'Are you hoping this will be your way out?' she asks.

'Way out?'

'The hero's way out. You'll discover what's going on and in full glory be pardoned Civic Duty...'

'Wait,' he says. 'No, no, of course not. But. That's interesting. I take it that the elite don't die along with the rest of us mere mortals. They're not put 'to rest', or 'resting' in a future-field. Maybe they're helped to live on...'

'What do you mean?'

'Organs. Transplants.'

'They'd have young ones wouldn't they?'

'What if young organs don't work. What if healthy organs from older bodies was the way?'

'You really have got a sick imagination,' Hannah screws up her face.

'But it's a possibility,' he says.

'Yes it is,' she answers coolly.

'I fancy another scotch,' he says.

The car pulled up outside their house. The snow was turning to sleet. The journey back had been made mostly in silence as each of them thought deeply about what might lie ahead. They'd eaten at the hotel and at least their bodies felt warmer. The food hadn't been at all bad and Barney had contentedly fallen asleep, with a scrap-full stomach, in front of the crackling fire. Just out of range of ember missiles.

Hannah opens the front door with her device as they climb out of the car. 'I'll leave it out tonight,' she says. 'Tomorrow the snow's likely to have gone. I have use of it till Friday morning. If you wanted...'

'Maybe,' Jim says. 'I've got to think things through. I've got to work on designing characters too.'

'Anna?'

He stares at her as they walk towards the front door. Inside the air is warm and they automatically relax. Jim feels a little tipsy, he'd drunk a fair amount of whisky. He'd sobered up somewhat on the way back but he heads straight to the kitchen to put some coffee on. It has been an intense and emotional day.

'I have some ideas,' he says, wondering if he should have tea instead.

'Regarding Anna?'

'Yes. But I need your help to get the doc's co-operation.'

'Tell me more.'

'No, I have to think things through properly. It has to be right.'

'Let's leave it for now. I'm exhausted,' Hannah says. 'Are you sure you want to drink coffee before bed?'

'It'll give me energy,' he laughs. 'It'll get my head straight.'

Next morning Jim lies in bed. He's had some curious dreams. And one very poignant dream he struggles to keep hold of. He'd heard Maddy's voice calling to him. He was on a mountain side, clinging to large rocks, with a biting wind and swirling snow surrounding. It felt like he couldn't go on but he also knew he couldn't let go. And that's when he heard a detached voice – talking to him. Clearly. Despite the weather, as if the voice was in his head. 'Papa, you can do it, you can do it.' Just these words but he knew they were Maddy's.

'Are you getting up?' Hannah calls.

'In a bit.'

Moving to the bedroom doorway, she says, 'It's beautiful outside. The sun is shining and there's still some snow.'

'On the road?'

'No that's clear.'

'Maybe we could take a drive. You think we can?'

'They didn't give me a limit...'

Jim wants to escape. He'd like to find a mountain to climb and talk with Maddy. Her voice hasn't yet left his head, his mind, his consciousness. He feels sure he'll meet her again one day. Will she still be eight years old? Or will she grow up in that unknown land. Will he grow up in future-fields? Maybe she'd get older and he'd get younger.

'I'm getting up...'

Putting on some clothes he looks out the window. They were just treading water on this earth. And destroying everything at the same time. Usually each other. He didn't want to live forever but he didn't want to die forever either. He didn't really want to 'rock the boat'. Part of him wanted to forget the whole Portway thing, it was probably just his imagination. Creating nonsense, where nothing existed.

'At last,' she says, as he walks from the bedroom to the kitchen.

'Been thinking about stuff,' he says.

'Not like you,' she smiles.

'You're right it's not like you.' he quips, 'but...'

'Go on...you want some tea?'

'Yes. Please. But. I've been thinking hard. Maybe we should forget this Portway business. I'm sure I have it all wrong.'

'If you want.'

'You want to?'

'I didn't say that.'

She pours him some warm tea. 'But is that what you want?'

'I don't know. All this time, since the end of last year, it's been about you. All about you. And now you're aiming to be a modern-day hero. Do I either want or need that? I'm not sure. If you bring Portway down somehow – where does that leave you and me? You'll be suicided and I'll be, well, looking at a radically different future.'

'Hang on,' he says, 'Henry's calling on the hologram. I guess he knows we're back from Portway. Did he message?'

Hannah shakes her head. 'That's going to cost him.'

'Must be important, we can refund...'

'We?'

'Don't rub it in. Come on into the living room.' Jim switches on the hologram receiver and Henry is there with his girlfriend Olivia.

'Hen,' Jim says. 'You're splashing out on your old man.'

'And his mum.' Hannah adds, 'Great to see you.'

'The link's unstable. If it goes off don't worry, I'll call conventional. But give me time to try and get it back if it does.' As he says this the two images seem to shiver and blur.

'Hang on Hen,' Jim says.

'I've got good and bad news.'

'Go ahead,' Hannah says.

'Well, they aren't going to let me travel...'

Jim's face droops. Hannah holds his hand. 'Are you sure?'

'It's tied up with the good news,' he says.

'Go on,' Jim says solemnly.

'Olivia's three months gone.'

'Oh wonderful,' Hannah says.

'Congratulations,' Jim says, his face lifting again. 'But why can't you travel? Maybe alone?'

'Jim, he'll have a newborn...'

'That's not the reason,' Henry explains. 'I'm being held back for potential military conscription. Or. I'm hoping, able to carry on working the land as we'll have a child.'

You're not Argentinian,' Jim protests. 'They can't conscript you.'

'I'm not Argentinian, no, but I live here. Their rules. There's trouble brewing. We should be okay. I know this isn't what you want to hear Pop. But I can't do anything about it. I applied well in advance.'

'I understand,' Jim says. Then, 'What about us as grandparents, could we visit you?'

'That would be great.' He looks at Olivia who has a wide beam across her face.

Hannah looks at Jim. 'Your dad can't travel out the country Henry. You know that Jim.'

'I didn't know that. Why not?'

'Because you're locked into your civic duty.'

'I'll get on a rowing boat,' Jim says.

Everyone laughs. The tension is broken.

'It's great that you're expecting,' Hannah says to Olivia.

'Thank you, señora Holden.'

'Hannah, please.'

Henry puts an arm around her. The hologram seems to buzz in and out of existence. 'I want to see you both, but obviously, especially you Pop. Given the...But there's nothing I can do. There's no way of crossing the border. I've looked into it.'

'Well we have this,' Jim says, 'it's almost as if you're here.'

'Thanks Pop. Oh. Credit's running out. I'll be back with more news as soon as I can. Mum, you look after him okay?'

Hannah nods. 'I will. You look after Olivia and the baby.'

'I will.'

And they are gone. Hannah has a tear in her eye and as she looks round she sees Jim in tears. He shakes as he holds the mug of tea. Hannah says, 'Henry has just sent a quick message and said if it's a boy he'll call him James. But he'll always be known as Jim.'

Jim smiles, feels the tears on his lips. 'One thing,' he says calmly.

'Go on,' Hannah says.

'Now there's nothing to lose. Nothing. I'll do my bit. I want to expose their lies, corruption, all of them who have fucked up this fucking world, split families, created wars, starved us to death...'

Hannah comforts him. 'You're right Jim. But we really have to think this through carefully.'

'Our son is a good man. Olivia a good woman and Joanne will be. Maddy could have been. Henry's worked hard for what he has created in Argentina. I wish he hadn't gone but it's what he felt he had to do. He's shown courage and grit and has been successful. But now they won't let him leave the country. This reminds me of my youth and the craziness of 2020 that began it all. Okay, maybe it began way, way before that. Maybe it's always been with us. I don't know. But now I will sniff out what the fuck is going on at Portway. But we have to make sure you'll be okay Hannah.'

'Roles reversed,' she says.

Jim smiles. 'Yep. Roles reversed. I have ideas. I've been thinking, like I said.'

Hannah smiles. 'Joanne's sent us a message too. Came in earlier. She wants to visit. We're popular. But they're stretched at work. She has got approval to travel and some time off at least.'

Jim says, 'Approval?' He shakes his head. 'Well let's get breakfast and then shoot off. Travel while we can. Mind you I can't afford you getting the sack.'

'It's even late for brunch,' Hannah says. She wants to comfort Jim. 'I'm safe at work,' she says.

'Is anyone safe?' Jim muses and then says brightly, 'Brunch that's a word you don't hear often. Okay, we'll eat something and then head up to the moors. Get some space. Shouldn't be too many folk around today, no public transport up there. Okay?'

'Okay,' she says.

'I'll order in some stuff. Are there any shortages at work at the moment?'

Hannah shakes her head.

'You're not needed?'

'I'm up-to-date. I put in extra while you were at Portway.'

There were some cars about and the tramway system was working. Most people were locked-tight into their homes, glued to screens. Others had travelled to work. Who were the lucky ones?

Before long they get clear of the city, heading north. Hannah's phone flashes. 'Work,' she says.

'Fuck 'em,' Jim says. 'Put your foot down.'

As they climb in height there is more snow but the main roads are clear and the sun is gradually melting the evidence of the previous night.

'I need you to cosy up to the doc,' Jim says. 'Not too cosy though.'

'He is quite charming,' she half-teases.

'Do you think he's a good or a bad man? Maybe he's nothing to do with whatever's going on. It's possible. But what happened to me on the first night? I still can't piece all that together.'

'I don't know,' Hannah answers. 'Being at the restaurant with him showed me a different side for sure. I know I've got to be careful. We could be mistakenly messing with people's lives – even their livelihoods.'

'If they're innocent, they have nothing to fear.'

'Come on Jim, life doesn't work like that.'

They have reached the moors whose bleakness is almost overwhelming. The winter season giving them formidable power – energy, like the wind that blew across them. The peaks of the surrounding hills are snow covered.

'Stop off up there,' Jim says. They have driven deep into moorland. Hannah sees a small road on the left where she brings the Stellar to a halt just off the tarmac. 'I wonder where this lane goes?' Jim says.

'Nature hasn't reclaimed it yet, so there's probably a farm down there.'

For a moment they look out across the moors in silence.

'A sheep farm maybe,' Jim muses.

'Maybe. They didn't manage to wipe out the farmers did they? Now they need them.'

'They might have got rid of the meat and dairy industries if they'd given us a truly natural alternative. Now they stuff animals in factory farms.'

'Maybe. At least some animals are still able to graze in the open. On these moors.'

'Where are the tractors? There's still lots of weeds breaking through the road's surface...' Jim looks at the lightly snow-covered road lying ahead. 'You see that hill over there. Can you drive to that? Can't be that deep if the weeds are showing.'

'I'll try, if there's a usable road all the way.'

'I wonder why they maintain these roads at all,' Jim says.

'Jobs maybe. Perhaps the state has ideas for the future.'

'Well they fucked-up the past, for sure. Are you certain we're not being tracked?'

Hannah drives on, shakes her head.

'Up there,' Jim says. 'Wow, that's beautiful. That's perfect.'

'The road's not good from here. It's too icy under the snow.'

'There's a place, there, on the right. Park it there and we can walk up.'

'I think I can get a little further. It's cold out. We'll be able to see across the moors from there.'

'Go for it.'

Hannah steers round potholes where the snow has been blown away and avoids the sides of the road which has now become a track. But she gets up closer to the summit, then stops the car.

'Plenty of power left?'

'Plenty,' she says.

'Are you coming? Come on. It'll give you a lift.'

'I'll probably be blown away...'

Jim gets out. Feels the harsh air against his face. Hannah reluctantly gets out, winding a scarf around her neck and face and pulling up the lapels of her jacket.

'You're always prepared,' Jim shouts above the wind.

'There's a jacket of yours in the back. I thought about the weather.'

Jim quickly takes his thin coat off and grabs the jacket Hannah has left for him. He grabs her hand and they walk briskly. Snow lies across the fields but the track is mostly clear, the wind picking up the flakes and creating flurries in the air.

At the top of the hill the view is magnificent. Jim turns about and looks down at the moors and a distant valley.

'This is weird,' he says.

'Bloody cold.'

'No, it's weird,' he states again.

'Not weird but windy,' Hannah says.

'Hannah,' Jim says desperately. 'No, it's like I've been here before. Not exactly. But similar. Not in the snow.'

'Well, you have been here Jim, lots of times.'

'I mean right here. This feels like a rerun.' Taking her hand, he leads her over to the other side of the summit. 'I know what I'll see,' he says.

'More moors,' she says, smiling.

Jim stands still. Hannah's hair has escaped the scarf's grip and flies wildly about her, her hands trying to manage it again.

Down in the valley Jim sees a village. It's in the distance at the edge of the moors and there are trees around it. Snow covering has finished at the outskirts of the village but the rooves of houses he can just see are still partially covered. 'It's not exactly the same,' he says. 'Not exactly.'

'What are you looking at?' Hannah asks intently.

'My future,' he says, solemnly.

Doctor Abraham arrives early at Portway. There has been a raft of new applicants for Future-Fields and he needs to process them and make headway in the case of others.

'Morning doctor,' his secretary sings, like a slightly nervous bird.

'Morning Milly, please direct calls to my office, I'll be there all morning.'

Pushing open the door to his office he feels strangely lacking in drive. Normally he likes the blinds to be closed, with the lighting low but with a daylight lamp over his desk and screens, which he can turn on when engaging in intricate, close work. All the screens have additional lighting too.

Slumping in his chair he stares vacantly into nothing – summoning the will to get started. A light flashes and he's brought back into the present.

'Yes?'

'It's Milly. I've got some coffee for you.'

The doctor lets her in. She places the tray down carefully.

'You didn't need to,' he says. 'I have coffee here.'

'I had a feeling you needed it,' she says. He smiles. 'I've sent you all the files you need.'

'Thanks.'

'Do you feel well, doctor, is there anything I can get you?'

'No,' he says sitting up. 'You know Milly, you've been here quite some time and I know next to nothing about you.'

'There's not much to know,' she says.

'Never thought about marrying?' he asks bluntly.

'No,' she half laughs.

He smiles. But warmly. 'I think we're doing a good job here Milly...'

'Yes we are Doctor Abraham. You are. An important job. Giving people a new life.'

'I think so...'

'Of course you are. We're lucky to be alive in such an age,' she says.

'You think so?'

'Yes,' she says, pouring the coffee. Black. Nothing added.

The doctor knows so little about her. Other than that she's very nervous around him, yet now she seems at ease. Picking up the mug he takes a gulp.

'Down to work,' he says.

'You need to take a holiday,' she says. 'Everyone needs a break.'

'Milly,' he smiles. 'Thank you for your concern. I'm perfectly okay though. Really. Now I must...'

'Sorry doctor,' she says, slipping into her nervous-sounding voice. 'I'll leave you be.'

The doctor flicks on his various screens and machines, takes a sip or two of the coffee and begins his work. He has to concentrate on blocking images of Vicky. 'Damn,' he says out loud. 'Discipline Jake. Discipline.'

Milly hacked into the computers of the first of the island's guests. She'd dig deep. She'd find something, she always does. Find some quirk, some sexual deviation. If not she'd get a feeling for the man and create her own deviance to suit him, then sort out a butterfly girl or whatever. Businessmen worked hard and played hard, she'd find something. You never knew what was below the surface, behind the apparently normal veneer. It was fun for her to do this work. As she was acting under orders from Professor Stone, she was protected from intrusive questions. Doctor Abraham knew not to disturb her when she looked busy. But she also knew he had no idea what kind of work she got up to.

Like many her age she'd gone without luxuries and even food at times. Her parents had done their best. When the National Government had been elected she was still only nine years old. Her mother suffered with some anxiety and her father was terrified that she'd be euthanised, following the second assisted-suicide act. Unknown to either of them Milly was developing anxiety too. But she determined, somehow, never to show this to them or in public. It was an irony that she now had to act 'nervous'. It was a cover, designed by the professor. She was paid well and given many perks. But sometimes she felt as if she were becoming like her mother. She had to keep it together.

'Yes!' she says out loud. She finds certain images on the hard-drive of the first businessman's main computer. Making notes for a bespoke butterfly, she smiles inwardly. Have they no idea they're being watched. The state keeps tabs on everyone; from the unemployed man getting close to the chop to...well...to everyone at Portway and the like.

She taps in details and is presented with an assortment of butterflies that would do the job. Such pretty creatures, though maybe not as pretty close up. A wonderful collection of butterflies pinned by their description. 'Perfect,' she says. And she smiles wryly thinking of the doctor.

The doctor was thoroughly engrossed in his work. But he was alerted to a secure call.

'Jake,' comes the voice.

'Alistair.'

'How are things?'

'Pressing on.'

'The avatar?'

'Soon be ready.'

'Good.' There is a pause. 'Just a heads-up,' Alistair says, 'you might need to pack your bags at short notice next month.'

'Okay,' Jake says. 'Any clues?' he asks.

'Not at the moment. But I wanted to give you plenty of notice.'

'Business or pleasure?'

'A bit of both.' Jake can hear the professor's silent laugh through the ether. 'I have a little news about the recent resurrection...'

'Go ahead.'

'Well the organs were in pretty good shape. We'll need a few more testimonies and then I think we can go live, as it were.'

'Meaning?'

'Meaning substituting suicides. You've got everything set up there?'

'Yes. I have. But I've kept it all hush-hush apart from those directly involved.'

'You've got dirt on them all?'

'Of course. I've been working full weeks too, as cover. There's a complete team ready to step in when the work's finished.'

'What's your cover?'

'Well, as you know there’s a genuine new creation room being constructed. The team works weekends too, and nights. Often out of the way.'

'Excellent. And very convenient. When it's up and running we can show high-level ministers, of a certain age, proudly doing their civic duty. Seemingly. Getting a new transplant in reality. There's an epidemic of rotting organs,' Alistair spits. 'I'm not sure what's happening. It's like the '20s and '30s again.'

'It should all run smoothly,' Jake assures.

'It *will* all run smoothly, as long as you have the dirt. Make sure all security knows the score too...'

'They do. Don't worry,' Jake says.

Good. I might pop over in early February to see how the avatar's coming along.'

'Yes, yes, fine.'

'Over and out,' the professor says.

'Over and out.'

The doctor isn't sure why Milly didn't direct the call through. He is sure the professor trusts her if nothing else, though for the life of him, he can't imagine what dirt they might have on her.

At lunch Jake joins Jayne and Dan who are engaged in close conversation. 'Do you mind?'

Jayne is surprised to see him. 'Not busy working?' she digs.

'I'm on thinking duty,' he says.

Dan says, 'I don't think people realise how much time we spend staring into space...thinking,' he adds hurriedly.

'It's essential,' Jake says. 'You can't create constantly and keep up the quality. You have to step back. Think. Turn ideas over. Even sleep on them.'

'Do you sleep doc?' Dan quips.

'It's been known.'

'I heard he sleeps in a velvet lined coffin,' Jayne laughs.

'Oh I do,' he laughs. 'Though there's no coffin here at Portway, not in my office bedroom at least.'

Dan's unsure if the doctor is telling the truth or not. Nothing would surprise him. 'I admire your work ethic.'

'It's easy,' he says, 'as you all say, my life is my work.'

'And talking of work,' Dan says, 'we're very close to some trials.'

'Avatar?' They both nod. 'Good. The professor might be paying us a visit next month.'

'He's not so bad, is he?' Jayne asks.

'We've got rid of a number of glitches,' Dan says, 'and we've got a formula for an initial day's outing. Though what that will mean in double F terms is a different matter.'

'You think time could be different?' Jake asks.

'Why not. There have been people in comas who have lived, say, for thirty years in three weeks. Okay, that was some time ago when patients were sedated...'

'Ah, I see,' Jake interrupts. 'You think the sedation the lifers are under might make time elastic?'

'We'll find out,' says Jayne.

'Will one of you two be...'

Before he finishes, they both nod then turn to each other and smile.

'You must feel fairly confident.'

'What's the worst that could happen?' Jayne says, turning to Dan. Then continues, 'Heart-attack, death and ill-equipped for the fields, or Double F as Dan calls them,' Jayne says quickly. 'Like a small boat drifting out to sea with one heck of a storm brewing.'

'Poetic,' Dan says.

'You have to be,' Jayne says.

'Yes, we have to be,' Jake adds. 'We're creators, after all. Designers of the future.'

'Of or for?' Dan asks.

'Whichever you prefer,' Jake retorts. 'We would have been minstrels in a bygone age, or novelists a century or two ago. And gamers recently,' he adds quickly. 'We encompass all of humanity's skills.'

Jayne and Dan look at each other quickly. It's only rarely that the doctor allows himself these moments of grandeur.

'We create life,' he states. 'A new life.'

Jayne bends her head forward and takes a fork full of food from her plate.

'Must be going,' Jake says. 'There's a lot of work to catch up on. It'll be filtering itself down to you two soon. Be prepared.' But he adds, 'I suppose you stepping into our avatars will be like stepping into a new persona?'

'We can neutralise personality beforehand,' Jayne says. 'They will be us as we use them, then when we hand over the suits to you, they become you.' They laugh.

Jayne and Dan watch as the doctor leaves. 'Never sure what to make of him,' Jayne says.

'You can't fault his commitment.'

'Well...'

'You can't,' Dan stresses.

'This place gets to me sometimes,' Jayne says.

'Sometimes?'

'Look, we both know there's stuff going on. Not sure how legal it is...'

'Jayne, ssshhh, careful...'

'Is your phone or device on?'

'Phone's on. Just for calls.'

'Turn it off.'

'Let's hope no-one heard you say that.'

'Don't get paranoid Dan. Listen. Portway offers a service. It's good and efficient. We have great jobs and plenty of money. But I have heard rumours.'

'Where, when?'

'Over the years.'

'What rumours?'

'Bodies taken out of drawers and the organs harvested...'

'O, not that one,' Dan says. 'Come on Jayne, you're a scientist.'

'And a listener. Nothing would surprise me.'

'I agree there,' Dan says. 'Not with this fucking government.'

Jayne smiles. 'Takes a lot to get you swearing, Dan.'

'Well not when it comes to Hughes-Kahn and his mob. They might have done some good stuff years back, but we might as well be living in a dictatorship.'

'We are,' Jayne says.

'Well. Regardless. No-one's going to do anything about anything. Everyone's just glad to be alive and have food to eat.'

'It's better than before.'

'Yes, but we're paying some price. Frankly, I couldn't give a hoot about what might or might not be going on at Portway. As long as I'm not part of it.'

'You are part of it. You can't escape being part of it.'

'Nor you in that case.'

'Yes, I know. But at least we're doing something positive.'

'We are?'

'Dan!'

'We extend life, for some...'

'We give, what did the doctor say?' She thinks. 'New life.'

'Some kind of life. Maybe it's a bloody nightmare. Ever taken DMT?' he asks. Jayne shakes her head. 'Well you get to see and experience some pretty weird creatures. And these creatures pop up for most folk. It's like they're there, out there somewhere...'

'In there,' Jayne says. She taps the side of her head.

'I guess,' says Dan. 'Everything is inside our heads, maybe. But how come we all experience the same reality?'

'If we do.'

'We seem to. Come on. I'm not talking about solipsism. Just that everything is probably inside our mind. Hence double F. That's what we're doing isn't it? Helping them create this new life.'

'In which case,' Jayne says, 'I wonder how similar the realities being experienced are?'

'We'll find out. I don't see why the avatars wouldn't work.'

'Let's hope they do. The professor's chomping at the bit.'

Dan says, 'Maybe we could get Hughes-Kahn to do a bit of double F-onautics and then cut his return path.' He stairs into space. 'Then again he'd probably take over that person's reality and become master of the universe.' They laugh. Dan carries on, 'But do you believe in all that conspiracy stuff?'

'Who knows,' Jayne answers. 'I guess you've got to trust Portway though, as we're an integral part.'

'Who even runs Portway? Is the prof actually the main man?'

Jayne shrugs. There's some silence. 'We have a good job,' she confirms. 'What else would people like us do?'

'Like us?'

'Well we're failed scientists and failed creatives.'

'Failed?'

'Unsuccessful,' she modifies.

'Have you played Magneto?' he asks.

'How many sales?'

'Okay. Unsuccessful. Who knows it might get discovered. I mean a game about creation turning everything we thought we knew on its head, who wouldn't want to play that?'

'No-one plays,' she says. 'You'd have to get it created as VI and VR. And you'd need to have people selling the idea on your behalf...'

'Okay. Okay. But it could happen. And if anyone did happen upon it, you know, some filthy rich business person, then...'

'Dream on...'

'You have to have dreams.'

'Or double F.'

'Breasts?'

'Dan!'

'A man can dream.'

'You're going trans?'

'I'm going out tonight to a club,' he laughs.

'I could report you for that,' she says, 'and saying it in front of a woman.'

'Yeah...guilty,' he says. 'Which reminds me. They're building VI, VR prisons.'

'I know,' Jayne says.

'That could be fun work,' Dan says. 'Imagine the punishments. You could create some horrific scenes and landscapes.'

'Dan, prison is for rehabilitation, less of your medieval fantasies.'

'What kind of fantasies do you want me to have?'

'None. Now let's get to work. We have Double Fs to create,' she says with a wry smile.

Hannah sent an audio message to Doctor Abraham: Dear doctor, sorry, Jake. I'm worried about Jim's mental state. He seems depressed and is currently unable to connect with future-fields in any meaningful way. I wonder if I might come to Portway and speak with you. If you have some spare time.
Doctor Abraham responded: Of course Hannah, I'll see you as soon as I can. I'll be honest, I have a lot of work on at the moment. Let me see. (He talked into his computer.) Monday, February the second. Can you do the morning, just before lunch?
Hannah messaged: I'm sure I'll be able to. What time exactly?
Doctor Abraham responded immediately: Come for 10:30 and we'll have some coffee together first. It will give me a break too.
Hannah: Great. Thank you doc...Jake.
Doctor Abraham: My pleasure. But please always feel free to call in direct. Out.

Hannah placed her phone down. She read the exchange of messages. She hated this kind of thing. She hated duplicity. She hated VR games where someone was framed and they were deemed guilty. She hated misrepresentation. But she'd done it. She'd become what she so hated.

Before leaving for work she went into the bedroom but Jim was obviously already up. She checked the small office. Not there. There was a room upstairs which was used as their alternate lounge and office combined. The house, though small, used its space effectively. A spiral staircase at the opposite corner from the hologram reception wound upwards. At the bottom she called up but there was no reply. She climbed the stairs.

Pushing open the handle-less door she sees Jim plugged into his computer. Sensing her presence he swivels around in his chair. 'Not gone yet?' he asks.

'Yes,' she says, 'I'm a portable hologram.'

'Well, portable hologram, what can I do for you? You know if I swish my arm through you all the scattered parts will each reflect you in your entirety?'

'Even if I'm in bits?' They laugh. 'Talking about being in bits,' she begins, 'you're depressed.'

'I am?'

'You are.'

'Okay. You've communicated at last, I presume.'

'I have.'

'Good. What's transpired?'

'I have a meeting on the second of February.'

'Good. And the reason is, I'm depressed...'

'I'm worried.'

'I'm worried,' he jokes. 'Then again I *am* depressed,' he says. 'Actually I'm less depressed, bizarrely. Concentrating on this has scattered all my worries and memories to the wind. A bit like your holographic self.'

'Maybe I should be depressed. Okay. Enough. You're depressed because...well...'

'Now I'm beginning to reconnect my worries and memories and am actually getting depressed,' he says.

'You haven't got time to be truly depressed...'

'I've got just over ten months in fact. Then it's cuckoo land.'

'Who knows.'

'Ah, hope springs eternal,' he says. 'Let's face it, were it not for being depressed, I wouldn't have taken that night walk and been haunted by a terrified apparition. It just gets better.'

'Admit it,' Hannah says, 'you feel very much alive right now.'

'Yep. It's true. How's the verse go, to see the world in a grain of sand and eternity in an hour. I might have misquoted. Maybe if eternity can be squished into an hour it'll be a doddle to crowbar it into ten months.'

'Squished...crowbar? Eternity...'

'Okay,' Jim says, 'I'm with you, I'm depressed but cogent enough to keep digging the dirt.'

'That's it.'

'I *am* slightly jealous,' he says.

'Of the doctor?

'Who else? Twenty years my junior, lots of money, great job. Obviously not as handsome as me,' he laughs.

'Have to go,' Hannah says. 'As it's me funding your excavation skills.'

'What?'

'Digging dirt,' she says and waltzes out.

Jim stared at his screen. Everything he came up with he tried and he tested. All the ideas bubbling up or flying into his consciousness like froth. Some of these ideas melted back into the vast sea of his mind. Some seemed to stick. But that was only the second stage of his creation. Maybe it was the hardest – to dredge ideas from the seabed or the sludge of myriad experiences. Maybe the ideas he received were external to him? Thoughts, for the most part, came unbidden. Those are the most genuine of thoughts because they seemed to materialise out of nothing. If he formulated a thought into an idea it could seem contrived. Equally, if he really thought things through, thoughts could be superior – more... He laughed - Thoughtful. An idea full of thoughts. But not in a contrived fashion. He leant back. Needed to keep digging, keep being occupied. Occupied thoughts. An occupied consciousness. An invaded brain. He laughed again.

Looking out of the skylight he saw a patch of blue sky and was reminded of Portway. He was going to have to factor in weather conditions too. If it was always sunshine maybe he'd get bored. If it rained all the time he'd be depressed in future-fields. He shook his head. Blue sky. Sunshine. Showers. Wind. What about snow? What about Christmas, for what it's worth these days? Christmas had been just him and Hannah this year. And the New Year celebrations had been solemn. Then he thought about entertainment in his new life. This had completely bypassed him. Was the doc going to mention entertainment? Would they have VR, VI and AI in an AI and VI world? Boxes within boxes. If they were to have that, where would he escape virtually to? But this was just being creative though, not 'digging dirt' as he had told Hannah.

Jim had already talked with the doc about dreams. Okay, it wasn't something they could know. Unless he went into a VR so tired he falls asleep, or they pump him full of sedatives and he's forced into sleep. He'd talk to Jayne and Dan about that. They were supposed to control everything through drugs, bots and computers. What if he went into his future-fields and they'd created VR. If he tried that out would it work? Or would the technology already need to exist in that future world. How might he get it in if not? Another thing to ask. Worlds within worlds within worlds. A dreamer of dreams. What if he was dreaming now? Not that old chestnut. Jim. Jim. Concentrate. You'll go mad if you think too much – keep the thoughts concentrated. Would he go mad if he didn't dream? Was he now thinking in a contrived fashion?

He wished he could talk with Jayne and Dan straight away. Open a line. Get the Portway welcome and shut the line down. He mustn't overstep the mark. He'd had a lot of time and attention, he could talk with computers about these things. But he didn't want to. Dirt. He'd carry on digging dirt like Hannah had suggested. He'd accessed files about the beginning of Portway, all tied in with the government's assisted suicide and euthanasia programs. He'd been thirty-four years old when the government had introduced their second assisted-suicide act - their most radical to date. Soon after that, centres had been opened up across the country offering euthanisation services. Centres even competed between themselves to give the best service. People could check out the methods on offer. People were recommended to their nearest centre. If they were depressed, or ill or physically compromised or deformed (he shuddered at the word which was no longer used) then their chances of leaving the centre, at least un-tagged, was remote. Once identified, one's death was honed into like a missile locking onto its target. Curiosity not only killed the cat, it killed a lot of folk who could have lived meaningful lives. At least Jim thought so. But you went in and everything became overwhelming.

Jim had seen dark-edge movies. He shouldn't have done but a work colleague had shown him stuff. They'd got drunk. Maybe the colleague took a risk. Was Jim a risk? Were these movies real or not? It had been hard for Jim to tell. But they had their effect. They *were* dark. Clever people tying up vulnerable folk, and sometimes not so vulnerable in webs of words. Glistening webs. The death spider waiting for a movement in tension to give people away. Then a quick dart. Papers signed. Computers enacted. A pathway revealed. And. Bang. Out went the lights. Were they real people or actors?

Hannah was meeting the doctor. It was becoming real. They were not play-acting. If what he thought might be true, *was* true, then he hoped they'd have qualms in taking them both out. He had responsibilities. Jim. Jim. Don't be a selfish bastard and drag Hannah into this and by default their children. He was crazy, utterly crazy. A child thinking he was an adult.

'Fuck,' he says and kicks out at the table legs. He calls Hannah.

'Hannah?'

'I'm driving.'

'Put it on automatic, I have to talk.'

'Okay.' A moment passed. 'Done. What is it, you sound worried?'

'I am. Listen, cancel the meeting with the doctor...'

'You really are jealous...'

'No. Listen Hannah. I'm getting you into something. It seems unreal, like fun, maybe...'

'Not really,' she says.

'It isn't. It wouldn't be. If we uncover something and get found out, what do you think's going to happen to us?'

'I don't know.'

'Anything might happen. Anything. I should never have said anything. I blurted it out after our argument. I should have kept silent.' Quickly he says, 'This is encrypted?'

'Yes. If it works.'

'Cancel the meeting. We're not the police. Fuck it, I'll have fun for another ten months and then walk to the gallows and drop into another world. It'll be fun. Whatever's happening – *if* anything is happening is not our business. We're customers. I was wrong. I've fucked up. At least I'll have had five free years to think...'

'I'll call you later,' she says, 'if I can, otherwise we'll discuss it all tonight. We *have* time.'

'Okay. See you later.'

'Dig the dirt regardless,' she says and then cuts the line.

Jim gets seriously depressed. Goes downstairs to the fridge and opens a beer. This is a luxury. He could only buy it because it was brewed locally. Bad credit offset by good credit. He drinks straight from the bottle.

He went upstairs after the beer and stared at the screen. What was the point? He had to get himself together and think things through seriously. A message came in from Joanne. She was a young woman. She'd adjusted to this life and was doing well. One day she'd have her own veterinarian practice, he was sure. She was shrewd and knew what she wanted. Both his children were doing well. What would happen to them if he exposed Future-Fields as a corrupt front for...for.. What if they were all up to something. What was he saying? There was absolutely no evidence that anything was going on. 'It's your imagination Jim.' Yep, it was most likely so. What was he to do? Stop the whole business that was for sure. Stop it right there and then. That was the right thing to do, the manly thing to do.

Putting on the entertainment screen he watched sit-com after sit-com all laden with their clumsy propaganda. He even dozed off. He needed to sleep. Sleep while Hannah was at work. But as he drifted off and deeper into sleep, the image of the woman with the terrified eyes and gagged mouth filled his dream vision. And then, as he looked at her in a kind of frozen fear she ripped off the gag from her face. He had never seen her arms, thought they were tied behind her back perhaps. She ripped off the gag and moved closer to him but he seemed paralysed.

'Help!' she cries out.

Opening his eyes, he quickly looked around the room. The apparition had seemed so real. He felt she was in the room. Rubbing his forehead he banged his fist down on the desk. Things jumped. His heart jumped. He went down the spiral staircase and over to the front door which he opened quickly. The air was cold and comforting. Breathing deeply he felt himself alive. A young woman pushed a toddler along in a buggy. She was one of the lucky ones. He was on the way out and the little boy or girl was entering life. He had a duty. He had a fucking duty. But who to? He decided to put his coat and shoes on and take a walk – while he could, He was free enough for the time being. Air blew out of his mouth like smoke. He thought back to when folk smoked and to the hotel, restaurant, by the church. He walked down the path and kept right on, more-or-less in a straight line towards the main entrance of their gated area. The woman and the buggy had disappeared and he was all alone. Or so it felt.

He just kept walking, only stopping to tap in a code at the controlled gates. Looking. Observing. It was cold but there was sunlight. Gradually the modern little boxes gave way to scrub land and old factories. There were walls covered in graffiti; meaningless scribble except to the initiated. Probably long dead. There was an old dark-bricked bridge that invited him to walk under. Some white paint read Grey Wolves – still visible after all this time. Political graffiti. The underneath of the tunnel smelt damp and his footfall echoed. Out the other side there were pylons, they were buzzing in energy to the city. He wasn't sure he'd ever walked so far, though they hadn't been at their new house for many years. Stopping, he gazed about. This was the hinterland. Where urbanisation gradually faded into countryside.

Following a path which seemed to circle round, he eventually reached another bridge – this time he was on top of it. There were a few abandoned cars about and streetlamps with no real street to illuminate, if they still did. From the side of the bridge he looked down and saw a canal's muddy waters cutting between a towpath and trees. As he was there, as he was bored and uninspired, he decided to scramble down the muddy bank and onto the path. There was a kind of reverence he felt, the same feeling he had in the church; a time forgotten but still ticking over. He was able to see under the bridge where the canal headed back into the city and the way he chose to go which was heading into the countryside. The canal felt used and worn out - when he got to a lock there was water pouring through cracks in the rotting wooden gates. He tried to push against the great arms of the lock. Smiling, he carried on. There was a slight sense of optimism filling him again.

In the canal, old pushchairs and buggies were coming up for air. He thought about the canals of Venice when it was an open city – how they'd drained and dredged them and found curiosities, treasures and junk. The canal he walked by felt it would only heave up black sludge. But as he continued the air felt lighter and the trees opened up to fields, a few housing estates in the distance squatting like black growths. And then, like a miracle, he saw a swan gently, or so it seemed, glide through the grimy water. The white of the swan was untarnished. Its neck was regal, curved and its head and markings seemed to Jim to be mystical. When had he last seen such a creature.

He heard some noise. Sounded like children approaching. He really didn't want to see anyone. At last he felt at peace, the swan signifying something...but what?

'Over here,' a boy's voice calls. Other voices follow. 'We got one here.'

Jim is worried but they're not looking towards him.

A crash of bodies burst onto the towpath and Jim sees the swan rise from the water, its wings flapping. Stones hail down upon it. It seems to carry an injury – hidden within its magnificent body.

'Hey,' he finds himself shouting. The youths, more like children, halt. The swan makes its way down the canal.

'Who the fuck are you?'

'What are you doing?' Jim says. 'Why are you doing this to a swan? It's protected.'

'Protected my arse,' says a girl.

'Who by?' says the boy.

Jim can't recall. He thinks the queen but she's long dead. 'By me,' he says.

They laugh. Another says, 'Shouldn't you be dead granddad?' They begin to approach him.

'Don't try anything,' he says, 'I'll take enough of you with me if necessary.'

'Hard man,' says the girl.

'Hard enough. Nothing to lose.'

A couple of the gang try and move to his rear. Jim skips up a slope away from the towpath. 'Why are you stoning that swan?'

'Fun,' says the boy.

'It's white,' says the girl staring at him.

'It's an innocent creature,' Jim says.

'Nothing's fucking innocent,' the girl says.

Jim sees the swan disappear. He needs to deescalate the situation.

'You're telling me you think it's fun to injure wildlife?'

'Why not?' says another boy. 'Who cares?'

'Who cares what we do?' says the girl.

'I do.'

They laugh.

The boy comes closer to him. 'Well we don't,' the boy says.

Jim plants his feet down square and braces himself. The boy rushes at him and pummels his fists into Jim's body. He falls back slightly. The others rush closer and cheer. Jim can't get at the boy as he's smaller, stouter, punching furiously. The gang are shouting encouragement. The boy stops for a fleeting moment and looks up, a snarl on his lips. But this movement opens him up. Jim punches him square on the face and he sees blood spatter from the boy's nose. The gang fall into silence.

'Anyone else want to try?' Jim says.

'You've had it now mister,' when we tell on yer,' the girl says.

She comforts the boy. Another girl spits at him and says, 'Think yer big hitting a child?'

But they melt away. Jim watches them disappear into the bushes, onto a hidden path then into the field. They stare at him and give him a finger or two. Jim maintains his position until they're well away and then turns and runs.

'The world's gone fuckin' mad,' he says out loud. And then, 'What have I done?'

'You did what? You hit a child. Let's hope this doesn't get out...'

'A child, a youth,' Jim says. 'I didn't have much choice.'

'Walk away?'

'There was a whole gang of them, they would have cut me off and then God only knows what would have happened. You're taking this too lightly,' he says.

'Lightly? Do I sound like that?'

'I mean lightly in terms of what might have happened to me. You know. Me. The innocent-fucking party here...'

'Not so innocent.'

'I don't feel good about this,' he says. 'I don't feel good at all. But these little monsters were stalking a swan. Come on. I think they'd already injured it, I don't know if it could fly or not. I do know I had to put myself between it and those kids. Stones hurt you know.'

'So does punching a child's nose...'

'Stop saying 'child' these were youths.'

'How old?'

'I don't know. Teenagers.'

'That's a wide age range in fact.'

'Okay. You weren't there. You have no idea how it went. Being beaten up by a gang of kids,' he spat, 'might only be in degrees better than being beaten up by adults. What if they'd knocked me unconscious and then thrown me in the canal? What if I hadn't said anything and the swan had been stoned to death. I mean, I did what I felt was right, given the speed with which it all happened. Yeah, one of them got a bloody nose but maybe that'll make them think twice about things in the future. It's about doing what's right. Isn't that why we're doing what we're doing?'

'You think you'd get away with a bloody nose if you got caught by Portway security?

'I *was* caught.'

'You know what I mean. If they think you've been spying and exposing heavy stuff, what the heck do you think would happen to you? If you're scared of a bunch of kids, get out now, before we do anything.'

'And let 'the swan' be killed. And maybe its cygnets. Is that what we do?'

'I'm saying,' she says, 'you better understand what you're getting us into...'

'Me. Into. You have free will. You seemed to be into the idea.'

'Maybe,' she says.

'You weren't there. They were full of hate, I tell you. They would have killed the swan, and hurt me. Bad.'

'And as I have said,' she tries to keep calm, 'if you get found out spying or exposing horrendous crimes, what do you think will happen to you?'

'So we have a choice. A decision. Give up because of fear of the consequences or carry on, no matter how scared we might be or how dangerous things might get.'

'Can we do that?' she asks.

'Can we not?

'I don't know. Well I didn't expect this.'

'In a sense it was nothing,' Jim says.

'Nothing unless they know where we live.'

'They can't know. I'll lie low for a while. Keep my mug out of view.'

'That'd be a good start.' Hannah stares hard at him. 'Maybe you did the right thing,' she says. 'I don't know. I wasn't there. But a chi...kid.'

'A kid nearly as tall as me,' he says, stretching the truth. 'And a whole gang behind him.'

'I thought he was small and that's why you couldn't fight him?'

'He wasn't that small,' Jim says.

Hannah flops down in a chair. 'You did right defending the swan. What happens tomorrow though? Will they stone the swan again? Will they want to do that as a kind of revenge on you?'

'Or maybe they'll forget that particular pastime,' he says. 'Perhaps they'll learn something.'

'If we expose Portway,' she says, 'if, and I mean if, they have done something bad. Do you think they'll learn? Or will you be the swan?'

Jim sits down too. 'I don't know,' he says. 'But sometimes you just have to do what you think is right.'

'And know the consequences,' she says.

'I guess.'

'This isn't some film, some book,' she says. 'Anything could happen.'

'I know. I agree. Let's take it all slowly. We can drop out any time. Fuck it, I can walk into an assisted-suicide office and be kaput in an hour or so. Fast-track me for fuck's sake, I'm being hunted by psychotic killers out for revenge.'

'It's not funny,' she says.

'I know.'

'I've ordered dinner,' Hannah says. 'Then I'm back off to the office.'

'They must love you.'

'They do, which is good for you,' she adds. Right on cue she receives a notification. 'Drone will be here in five minutes.'

'Working the graveyard shift?' he asks.

'I'll be back before midnight.'

'The witching hour.'

Hannah looks at him. 'You have some strange turns of phrase sometimes.'

'It's being so old,' he laughs.

'It's here,' she says. Jim opens the door and a rather large drone selects their dinner. 'Code please?' it asks. Hannah sends her code. The drone drops close to the ground and releases their package.

'Thanks,' Jim says.

'You're welcome,' the drone replies.

'Where am I welcome?' The drone ignores him, lifts up and flies to its next destination. Jim picks up the package. 'Remember when folk made their own meals?' he asks.

'You're welcome to,' Hannah laughs.

'Welcome to the kitchen...' Then, as he takes the parcel to the table and as Hannah gets some cutlery, he says, 'I don't like drones. They kill and they hunt...'

'That one brought you your food.'

'That one. But I'm being serious, the technology, like any technology they can use, has been turned to killing or keeping us all in order. Drones have often made warfare a war between man and machine. A man is helpless against a drone or these bloody robotic dogs they're using. I remember the riots in the early forties where the police, the government, kept the people squashed down with their use of those prototype dogs. A man's best friend eh?'

'Not like Barney,' Hannah smiles.

Jim lays out the various containers and the trays and cutlery provided. 'Why can't they make the cutlery optional? If I had a travel token for every set of cutlery I've had, and not used – I could have flown to Argentina.'

'Eat,' she says, 'it's one of your favourites.'

'I never told you this,' he says, quickly forking food into his mouth. 'When I was at school, there was this kid, small, scruffy. For some reason he had it in for me. We had schools then...'

'I went to one. Remember?'

'Hahaha, not quite as old as me though. Anyway. This kid wanted to pick a fight with me. And he had older, taller and bigger kids, shall we say as back-up.'

'You've told me,' she says.

'Listen again. It's relevant. He attacked me and was pummelling away at me, well, like the kid next to the canal. All his mates behind him. I was helpless until I caught his tie, pushed him back and socked him one. Right on the nose.'

'And?'

'Well, that was that. The fight was over. And his mates did nothing. I'm pretty sure I was subconsciously thinking about this when that kid thought he could take me on. Because he had a gang behind him. And. Well. Isn't that what we're up against now. Maybe, if it's true, the stuff going on at Portway is like a bully getting his way...'

'It's a stretch,' she says.

'It's that moral obligation we talked about before.'

'Another scenario,' Hannah says between mouthfuls, 'is the bully and his gang beat you to a pulp.'

'But he, they, didn't.'

'Children. Okay, youths, not multi-million dollar businesses Jim. As I keep saying. You really have got to think deep and hard at what you're getting into. And what I'm getting into...'

'But you are, aren't you? Something deep inside is forcing you to go against safety and logic. Because you know what's right. And wrong.'

'Maybe. But for the moment this is all speculation.'

'I've found a few 'hints' shall we say in my dirt digging.'

'Hints?'

'On-line speculation, shall we say. We're not the first to think something's not quite right.'

'Did anyone else do anything?' she asks.

'I don't know.'

'There you go. It's typical of you Jim, seeing this kind of thing and getting sucked in. Either that or you make a big joke of everything.'

'It's why you love me,' he says.

'It is?'

'Exactly,' he laughs.

Later, when Hannah had left for work Jim went back to his assortment of screens to keep digging. He could have been like any other person waiting to be delivered to Double F via a technological coffin and some drugs. But he wasn't - as far as he knew. He also needed to keep designing his future world. Maybe they'd find nothing on Portway, maybe they would and get away with it and he'd go into a new reality...He stopped. Maybe that reality wouldn't be available to him. Would they stop everything going on at Portway? What would happen to all the minds linked up to the computers? What would happen to him? No-one 'lives' after their sixtieth birthday. Well they get a few days grace, it was considered vulgar to suicide on a birthday or go into future-fields. Had to have your birthday first. A few balloons, cake and a shot or two of the hard-stuff. Then. Wait for the notification and the knock at the door.

'It's been lovely knowing you Hannah, give my love to the children, I'm stepping out now, I may be a few hours...'

'Bye Jim, see you in eternity.'

'In mine or yours?'

That was kind of how it happened. Not the party, as such...a kind of pre-wake. And then, he thought, you woke up and it was all a dream. A nightmare. And life was exactly as it had been in those halcyon days of re-imagined youth.

'Wakey, wakey, Jim. Surprise, surprise!'

Ever the joker, eh? He wanted to get out. If he had a car, if they'd let him have a car he would ride out to the moors again. He wondered what rural life was like. How tightly could they control farmers and village life? But they'd been in the gated estate for a few years now. He'd never been to the canal though. Walked out that way, or somewhere like that, a few times. He should have investigated more. Should have seen more of the world while he could. He thought of that song that went something like, *Don't it all seem so unreal, when you don't know what you've got till it's gone.* Something like that. Then again life had been some roller-coaster ride. All the shit that went down in the last forty years. He was surprised everyone wasn't insane. Then he smiled, you couldn't be insane for too long. A hint of insanity and – euthanised. Wasn't it a bit like eugenics? The government was always on about it being there for the people. A government of the people. In the early days they had filmed high-profile government ministers entering a suicide pod for their civic duty. Now he thought it was all show. But the people believed what they seemingly saw. Like astronauts they waved at the camera before entering their particular shuttle. Then out the back, into an unmarked car and a new life on an island - a 'contaminated island' prohibited to travel to.

All this got Jim thinking. He got up and walked about. The wars, the weather, the diseases...the control, the separation of the elite. Where was religion? Where had all the adherents gone? And yet there was a new religion, people who believed so vehemently it scared him. People were so afraid of life that they would sacrifice themselves to its order – or be sacrificed. That was it. They were being sacrificed. Even the lucky ones. Flopping back into his chair he stared into nothingness. Squeezed his eyes shut. And that damn woman came into full view, tearing off the tape from her face. It was as if he could hear her:

'What are you doing? You have to do something. Be a man. Do what is right.'

'What can I do? Me against all this.'

'You do what is right,' she repeats. 'You do what you need to do to be a true human being, authentic, real. Courageous. Look at me, thrown away like trash, rolled away in a dumpster, disposed of. Once of use, now no more...'

'Maybe the same fate awaits me.'

'Your fate is in your hands. For now.'

She screams. He jolts in the chair. Fuck. He'd fallen asleep. Everything was getting to him. His life, his normal life was ticking away. How did he know, really know, if there were any future-fields. Maybe it was all some concocted lie. Too late. He was walking out on the plank and the sharks were circling. But he still ate, urinated, defecated, could still smash a boy's nose and splatter blood. He still had sex – what for? He was finished. He still got drunk and phased out on tablets and he still cried. Cried for what might have been.

Where was everyone? He was alone. Well, not really. But he felt it. No man's an island. O, they were all islands all right. Locked inside. Desperate to touch and be touched. All of them. And the fanatics were the worst; they knew nothing of real love. Just slogans and empty rhetoric. But they ran the bloody place. The world had come close to destruction a number of times. Many millions had died. And their solution? Kill their own. Take out the weak and the vulnerable and do it all under a red flag. Hughes-Kahn and his cronies had made people fall in love with their love of death.

Jim thought he saw a shadow pass by close to him. He thought of his ancestors. His family. His hope for the future. Being a young man full of desire. And he thought of Hannah and his children. All of them. The world was made of thoughts, controlled by thoughts; people manipulated by words. Pacified by second-rate entertainment. He laughed. He'd been the same, he was no better. But now he had a chance to be a man. He laughed again. What was a man? A state of mind? A biology? Outdated ideas. He had conformed, to a degree. Thought he was outside the system, thought he had side-stepped it – but in the end he was well and truly caught. Yep, the sharks would be circling beneath him.

Hannah wasn't able to use a car to get to Portway so took public transport and walked. The morning was bright and razor-sharp cold. She passed a square where she recalled demonstrations being held in the old days. There didn't seem any open opposition to the government any longer but people talked in private with devices and phones switched off and moaned about life in general. There had also been many problems with people's kidneys, hearts and livers during the last ten years, it was getting worse but no-one seemed to know why. There had been some surprisingly open conversations on the state media regarding the availability of organs for transplant. Many people were demanding that young folk who chose to commit suicide, or those who were euthanised, should have their organs harvested as a matter of course. They argued it was a simple waste of resources. Others seemed to hold an old-fashioned opinion that the body was sacred even in death. Doctors had certainly been trying to modify animals' organs, pigs in particular for human transplantation. There was even research into laboratory grown complete organs and some transplants had taken place. This had been picked up from work done in the 20s and 30s.

Hannah looked at the young folk she passed. Did they look healthy? What were they doing on the streets, she wondered. She also noticed women with babies. Every baby was hope for the future. The government was promising them a future of abundance...well, just around the corner. The winter had been a cold one through January and now into the beginning of February. She pulled her scarf up and buttoned up the top of her jacket. Watched a pushchair pass with a baby wrapped up against the cold. She missed her children. But that seemed to be the way of the world. It was harder to travel, harder to find work – and yet there was always this promise of things getting better.

She passed through the biometrics of Portway and was then shown by the doctor's secretary where to sit and wait. She had arrived early. It was going to be difficult to find out anything. She wasn't sure it was in any way possible. And she had to make up a story about Jim being depressed. Maybe he was. He wasn't going to die but he was leaving her, their, life. She'd known plenty of her family, and some friends, who had died fighting or from lack of food. The country was depressed. It had been in shock and now it was...recovering? There were more young people and they brought life and energy. Despite the lower population the government still pushed euthanasia. Why would it do that? She glanced at her phone – old technology that continued to survive and evolve.

'The doctor's ready to see you,' Milly, his secretary says. Hannah grabs her coat and gets up, ready to go to his office. 'He says to stay here and he'll join you shortly.' Hannah sits back down. When Milly leaves, Hannah stands and walks round the medium-sized waiting room as if looking for clues. There is information on the walls and a screen silently extolling Portway's virtues. As she stares at this, Doctor Abraham enters.

'Hannah, good to see you.'

'Hello,' she pauses, 'Jake.'

Jake smiles. 'Okay,' he says, 'I was going to suggest we go to the restaurant as it will be empty at this time. But maybe we could just stay in my office. Or walk around. After having a coffee of course.'

'Yes, that would be good,' she says.

'Follow me,' Jake says and takes her past Milly who has her back to them and is focussed on at least two screens.

Inside the office Jake points Hannah to a chair next to his desk. The doctor takes her coat and hangs it up. 'Great to see you again,' he says. 'I've got more of that excellent coffee. We're trading with South America,' he says, adding, 'as usual. The States will be opening up soon too.'

'I have a son who lives in Argentina,' she says.

'Interesting. When did he go out there?'

'Four years ago,'

'I'd like to visit the USA, and South America,' Jake says. 'Not high enough up the ladder yet. But it's been promised. I'm talking about the USA,' he clarifies. 'I just know it from old films. Do you watch old films?' he asks.

'Sometimes. I'm usually too busy. But there are actors I like.'

'Here,' Jake passes her a delicate mug filled with the special hot coffee.

'Where's it from?' Hannah asks.

'I'm not sure,' he says, 'I could find out...'

'It doesn't matter,' Hannah replies quickly.

'Are you okay? I know we're here to speak about Mr Holden, Jim, but how are you?'

'I'm fine,' she says, 'a lot on.'

There is a pause. Jake gets up and goes to the blinds and peaks out. 'I'm glad you're here,' he says, not looking at her. 'I enjoyed our time at the restaurant.'

'It was nice,' Hannah says, half-smiling. She sips at the coffee. 'Do you think the world's getting back to normal, at last?' she asks.

'Normal? Was it ever?' Jake jokes.

'Do you think there'll be new wars?'

'I don't think so. But possibly. Are you worried?'

'I have a son, as you now know and a daughter. My son might be conscripted into the Argentinian army. A kind of civic duty,' she adds.

'Yes. I can imagine that's of concern. You have a lot on your plate,' he says. 'That's a funny expression isn't it? Though I presume it means you have too much to eat. Too much, or too much choice. Forgive me, I'm rambling.'

'It's fine,' Hannah says and relaxes. The more she senses the doctor is nervous around her, the more control she feels. Feeling bold she asks, 'Do you think the government will continue our civic duty?'

Jake is slightly taken aback. 'Yes of course,' he says. 'I hope so. And it's why Portway exists, and my job...'

'But do you agree with it morally?'

'What do you mean exactly?'

'Just that. Surely it was brought in at a time we had limited resources and food. There was a point. Is there a point now?'

Jake looks at her puzzled. 'Are these your thoughts, Hannah?'

'Or?'

'Well, Jim's.'

Hannah laughs. 'They are mine. Do you know what I do as a job?'

'I...I'm not sure of the details.' He feels frustrated, as if he should recall.

'I appraise businesses. I find out how businesses are doing and how to improve them. I use intuition and abstract thought, which AI and VI do not yet have. They're good. But they haven't got a sixth sense, a feeling...Therefore I'm quite capable of asking serious questions,' she stresses.

The doctor sits down, calmly. 'Just after I was born, wars erupted over the globe. By the time I had just become a teenager, the world looked as if it might not survive. When I was fifteen, the National Government was elected. A year after that, the idea of civic duty began. My last teenage year saw the first Civic Duty Act. It was a chance for people to show their love for their fellow humans. And to make a sacrifice for the future. It was no different to any time in the past when grandparents would sacrifice for their grandchildren or parents for their children. The old had had their day. It was selfish of them to continue eating up resources...'

'I'm aware of the history,' Hannah says. 'I was a baby when my parents and grandparents made sacrifices for me. Made sure I had enough food to live.'

'Civic Duty simply ratified that instinctual behaviour. It codified love.'

'Is it the state's right to codify love?'

'In such times, yes.'

'So you think the state had a moral duty?'

'Yes.'

'And it was okay to assist-suicide the long-term unemployed?'

'It was a hard decision. In hindsight I'm not so sure, but at the time...'

'And now it's all very clean and clinical,' she says, surprised even by her own words.

'And you are benefitting,' Jake says, sitting back in his chair.

'I'm going to lose my husband,' she says.

'But you're not.'

'I am.'

'You know Hannah, I don't have these kinds of conversations with anyone but you...well, not entirely true, I sometimes have them with the creation team leaders. And I have them with Jim. That's funny isn't it?'

'A husband and wife grow together, they can't help but think alike, if the relationship is working.'

'Therefore, I presume it is?'

Hannah smiles.

'This isn't why you're here though,' he continues.

'In part,' she answers. 'Because what happens to Jim affects me and at the moment he's depressed.'

'I presume he's depressed because of his civic duty.'

'He's depressed because his life here, on this world, effectively, is going to be terminated. And please doctor, Jake, that is what is going to happen. That depresses me double-fold. I presume you can sec that? But maybe you have to be married...'

He darts a glance at her. Stands up again. 'You know I have trouble with...with opening up to people. I have done with you. And you have with me. I appreciate that. Listen,' he sits down again. Tries to hold her gaze but looks down. 'I don't think Jim is depressed when he's here. When he's talking with his creation team, or with me. When he's here he seems really engaged and alive.'

Hannah smiles slightly. 'Maybe,' she says. 'Perhaps it's my fault,' she questions.

'No, no, not at all...'

'But you don't know.'

'You are stimulating company,' he blurts. The doctor plants his feet down on the floor firmly. 'Perhaps he could spend a week here, an intensive week.'

'Like an asylum?' she taunts.

'Like a man in need of creative immersion...'

'That he can't get from his wife.'

'Hannah. Don't play with me.'

She stares at him.

'Let's go for that walk,' he says. He takes her coat and helps her into it. He looks down at her slender neck.

Jake guided her through the building, through the first garden, through the glass building, past the creation and control rooms and on to The Gateway, where she had been before. Unknown to her she was following Jim's footsteps. They didn't enter The Gateway or The Chest, but the doctor took her into the garden. Hannah buttoned her coat and took her scarf from one of its pockets.

'I don't really feel the cold,' the doctor says.

They walk through the still garden, beneath the blue sky. A plane flies overhead and they stop to watch. Hannah wonders if it's flying to South America.

'This reminds me,' Jake says. 'Let's go over to the greenhouse,' he says. 'It's warm in there and we're safe to talk.'

'Aren't we normally?'

The doctor smiles, 'What do you think?'

They find a seat, near where Jim had sat and Hannah takes off her coat and lays it down.

'Is that better?' he asks.

'Yes. You were saying...' Hannah prompts.

'Yes,' he begins. Can feel her presence close to him. Can imagine her...He is uncomfortable in the heat as the sun's rays saturate the glass. The air smells of plant life and compost. 'In fact, I am going to fly to the New Africa Isles in just under two weeks.'

'Oh,' Hannah says, intrigued.

'I've been invited, it's some honour. The professor will be going, I mean he invited me.'

'The professor?'

'My boss. In reality. Well, I'm not sure I should mention that,' he glances at her.

'I don't know who he is,' she says, putting him at ease.

'Well, I've been invited. It should be great. I get to fly and the islands are magnificent.'

'I've not heard of them.'

'They belonged to Spain,' he says, 'until...'

'Ah, I see.' Hannah has a fairly good sense of the world's topography but, in many senses, the world had got a lot smaller during most of her life.

'It's like they're paradise islands now,' Jake enthuses. 'Sun. Freedom. Hospitality...'

She feels him hold back, 'And?'

'Just sheer luxury. It's what I've been told. Anything you want.' He looks at her. 'Anything you want.'

'Sounds great,' she says, a little flatly.

'A dream come true. They're protected islands now. Nothing like they were. Almost deserted. I think.'

'The last holiday I had was Christmas. Whatever that means,' she says. 'Jim went a bit crazy on the local alcohol. I used to be surprised the government was so lenient when it came to booze.' She laughs, recalling that old-fashioned word. 'Now I'm not surprised at all. They even encouraged us to celebrate this year. Do you think something's going on?'

'I have no idea.'

'I was joking.'

The doctor has moved slightly away from her so he can talk and sometimes look her in the face, the eyes. 'Christmas isn't much these days,' he says. 'But the New Africa Isles...'

'Hotter than this greenhouse, I imagine, even at this time of year.'

'Well. In fact.'

'Go on.'

'Well in fact. I thought...'

'Go on doctor, Jake.'

'I thought that week I'm away, Jim could have his intensive week and perhaps...'

'Perhaps?'

'Perhaps you might like a break.'

'A break?'

'Hannah, please don't make this more difficult than it is.'

'I don't wish to be presumptuous.'

'Would you like to accompany me?'

Hannah instinctively knows she has a small window of opportunity to dig...and get as deep as she can. 'That's very kind,' she says. 'So who would be coming, I mean, I have to think things through but I'd also need to know...'

The doctor stalls for a moment. No-one is listening. No-one is watching. 'The professor and a companion. That's all I know. There'll be no-one else we'd, I'd, know. I imagine it would be a small jet. I do know that on the isles we'd, I'd, be treated like a king and any woman, a queen, or princess.'

'How very old-fashioned,' she smiles.

'It would be like a thousand old-time Christmases rolled into one.'

'And what's the purpose of the visit?' she asks.

'I don't know,' he answers honestly.

'Is there normally a purpose?' she asks.

'I imagine. But I don't know what it might be. Or even why I've been invited.'

'I see.' Hannah ponders. She has found out next to nothing. She has a dilemma. This might be a very useful means to find out information. But she thinks she knows what she might expect. Jim would no doubt urge her to accept. It would be logical and, frankly, much to look forward to. Yet she finds herself saying, 'I don't think I can, unfortunately,' softening her voice.

'Oh. That's a pity. Work?'

'Yes.'

'No chance of rearranging commitments?'

'I don't know,' Hannah says. She has to be careful how she responds. Give hope, or not.

'Well, please let me know.'

'Of course,' she says.

This is between us?' Jake asks.

'Of course.' There is a pause. 'If you have anyone else you might like to invite, please let them take precedence. I doubt I can escape work at such short notice.'

'Yes. I'm sorry. I was only told recently.'

'Not to worry.'

The doctor straightens up. 'Well, let's walk through the garden once again and then we can discuss Jim and his depression. And if there's anyone else you'd like to talk to. I can arrange that.'

'Thank you, Jake,' she says, 'I appreciate your handling of this. And your professionalism.'

He gives her a quizzical look. 'Well, work must always come before pleasure.'

Hannah decided she'd like to speak with the creation team. The doctor had handled a rather tense moment quite calmly. She was impressed. As they walked through the garden in the icy cold, another plane flew overhead. Perhaps it was going to the New Africa Isles. She'd done so little travelling, apart from for work and that was always within the British Isles. Most of her work was done through screens, like anyone else. But they did like her being at Head Office. They consulted her in person when they could, she had a good reputation. And she was considered odd, and in some ways magical. She could out manouevre AI and VI – not constantly, but certainly most of the time. They said she had a gift.

'Here we are,' Jake says. 'Let me introduce you to Dan and Jayne. Wait a moment.' He came quickly back accompanied by a female. 'This is Jayne Davenport. Dan, the other leader, is busy with a client. Jayne, this is Jim Holden's wife, Hannah.'

'I think we've met,' Jayne says.

They shake hands. There is a brief pause.

'Can I help?' Jayne asks.

'I'd like to find out how Jim is doing.'

'I can't tell you much, client confidentiality.' Jayne looks at the doctor.

'It's okay,' he says. 'You're acting on my behalf.'

'Shall we go into an office?'

'Sure,' Hannah responds. To the doctor she says, 'Thank you doctor.'

'I hope we can catch up soon,' he says. 'My apologies again...' He notices Jayne's inquisitive glance. 'I'm just very busy,' he qualifies, looking between the women.

Jayne and Hannah enter one of the creation team's offices.

'Take a seat,' Jayne says. 'Would you like tea or coffee?'

'I need the...'

'The door at the end there. Then on your left.'

Hannah sits down in the cubicle and considers her next approach. Jim has told her about Jayne and she noticed a tension when the doctor was talking in front of them both.

Looking in the mirror, while washing her hands, Hannah studies her eyes. It wasn't often that her business insight spread into everyday life, but she sensed something between Jayne and Jake.

'About the tea or coffee,' Hannah says brightly as she re-enters the room.

'Tea, coffee, something stronger? Just a joke,' Jayne adds quickly.

'Well I started on coffee so wouldn't want to mix drinks.' Hannah takes off her coat and sits down. 'It's cold out.'

'Jim's doing well,' Jayne says starkly.

Hannah looks at her, 'Good.'

'Are you worried about him?'

'Not unduly. But he seems depressed.'

'We *have* talked about death,' Jayne begins. 'He told me about Japanese mummies, monks, living dead...'

'Oh yes, he likes that kind of stuff. He likes unusual things. He's got into a lot of stuff these past few years.'

'We've talked about freewill and determinism too...'

'Now you know why he's depressed,' Hannah laughs, 'and me too.'

'Are you?'

'No.'

Jayne shrugs. 'He seems quite optimistic, looking forward to his double F.'

'Double F?'

'Sorry, Future Fields.'

'That's encouraging. He's been talking about creating his FF and mentioned an Anna too.'

'Double F,' Jayne says, then, 'Oh, he told you?'

'Yes, of course.'

'Well she's based on you. But she's different,' Jayne stresses.

'Yes, he told me that too.' Hannah sips at her coffee. Maybe she's getting too much caffeine.

'You're not jealous?'

'Of course not. Why would I be? She's not real. He hasn't met her yet, has he?'

'Didn't Jim tell you about her?' Jayne pauses, dramatically.

Hannah laughs. 'Maybe the doctor did, deliberately obfuscating. Do you like working with him? The doctor?' she clarifies.

'He lets us get on with things.'

'What things?'

'Work,' Jayne says. 'He trusts us.'

'Do you trust him?'

'Yes. That's an unusual thing to say Mrs Holden, Hannah.'

'Yes, Hannah please.'

'But it is somewhat inappropriate.'

'I'm sorry.'

Jayne gets up and presses a button for coffee. 'I suppose you've noticed the similarity of names?'

'Oh, you mean Anna and Hannah. No, I hadn't really registered that.' She pauses, then, 'How long have you been working here?'

'A long time.'

'I think you're younger than me.'

'Maybe,' Jayne says. 'I can see you're much younger than Jim.'

'Yes, well eleven years. But given that we only live till sixty these days, that feels like, well, a quarter of a lifetime.'

Jayne smiles. 'We have to make the best of the years we have.'

'Not married?'

'Is this conversation about me or your husband, Hannah?'

'I'm sorry. We've got off to a bad start. I had a difficult conversation with the doctor. I apologise.'

'Accepted. Let's concentrate on Jim.'

'Yes, yes, of course,' Hannah says. 'It's just...'

'Just?'

'Well, just by chance I stumbled on a few screen-articles about Portway. I'm just a little worried. Forgive me. It's all very stressful.' Hannah dabs an eye.

'Articles about what?'

'No, I really can't say.'

'You must,' Jayne insists. 'You must have complete confidence in us.'

'Yes, yes...thank you. I imagine these ideas are absolute nonsense.'

Jayne looks at her. 'Hannah. I'm a scientist. Straightforward and logical. I think that's fair to say. If there is anything concerning you, troubling you about Portway, then I am sure I can put any worries to rest. We have a great reputation and we constantly strive to improve our service.'

'I'm sure, I know, you do a good job,' says Hannah. 'I'll talk with Jim about this and if he wants to talk with you perhaps that would be better.'

'Yes,' Jayne says, 'but I would like to hear from you too, directly.'

'I can't really say. I think Portway began during a different time. We were all in a different time. Things went on. You know. Dead bodies. Bodies used for...'

'What on earth are you insinuating?'

'Nothing,' says Hannah. 'I'm not insinuating anything. These are just rumours...'

Jayne feels stabbed by this word. Takes a sip of coffee and leans back, crossing her legs. 'Well,' she says, 'this is certainly an interesting and unexpected conversation.'

'I'm so sorry. Maybe it's me that's depressed and Jim isn't at all. I apologise. You're a busy woman and I'm talking nonsense.'

'Perhaps you could send me these articles,' Jayne says, 'and then I can put your mind at rest, as I explained. It sounds like the conspiracy theories from the twenties. I'm a scientist,' she stresses, 'I use reason, logic and tried and tested procedure.'

'If we talk about what you do with Jim, that might help,' Hannah says. 'Please don't mention this aberration to the doctor, Jayne. Can I trust you, woman to woman?'

'Yes, you can. You have client confidentiality.'

'Thank you.'

'Well, I presume you know from Jim what goes on here. And you've visited haven't you? I seem to recall having seen you, met you, previously.'

'Yes, I've been here a few times in fact. Jim is certainly getting good service, almost seems like a special service...'

'The doctor has taken to him. We all have. He is unpredictable. A loose cannon perhaps, as they say.'

'He can be. It's true. So, tell me more and tell me about Anna.'

'Firstly, there's nothing much to tell you about Anna. He hasn't met her yet in his double F – future fields. I think the doctor's created her. A template. Maybe he's been influenced by you Hannah...her character will develop as Jim interfaces with her.'

'Interfaces.'

'Interacts.'

'That sounds nicer. Let me think,' Hannah pauses. 'How will they interact?'

'They'll meet, they'll talk...'

'Touch?'

'If they want to. It would be odd if they didn't.'

'Sex?'

'They are liberated from any bodily restraint,' Jayne says.

'I don't think Jim needs 'liberating',' Hannah retorts. 'So they could have sex?'

'Yes.'

'But it would be virtual sex.'

Jayne draws in breath then lets it out quickly. 'I'm not sure if you have a full grasp of Jim's future life...'

'Enlighten me.'

'It is a life, like this life. For anyone in double F it will seem totally real. I mean, what is reality?'

'You tell me,' Hannah says.

'We have different realities, don't we? Like when we dream. Like a film, or a movie from the old days. I presume you watch the old American movies?'

Hannah nods. 'Are we film stars? Characters? The product of someone else's imagination?'

'Maybe all of that. But I have to say, double F, yes I know that sounds somewhat silly, I've picked it up from a colleague, *is* real life. That's the whole point. That's why we put so much hard work in creating a client's reality. Their thoughts, their intentions, coupled with basic programs and templates – getting inside the client's mind. Deep in. Tracking his responses and movements. It's a deep psychological experience for all of us. We're getting to know Jim. And maybe you too Hannah.'

'Well you'd have to ask Jim about me.'

'We may well do.'

'Don't believe a word,' Hannah says, trying to lighten the tone.

'It doesn't matter what we believe or not,' Jayne says. 'He will create his own world.'

'With Anna in it.'

'Yes. Okay. But he will modify her. Do you want him to have someone?'

'He has me.'

'For the moment.'

'When I have my double F,' Hannah begins, 'couldn't I join him?'

'At the moment, no.'

'In the future?'

'It might be possible.'

'And if I join him in the future and Anna is there?'

Jayne leans forward, 'We can't control these types of interaction. We're not gods or goddesses.'

'Do you want to be?'

'Too much responsibility.'

'I imagine.'

'In short Jim is an interesting man and his future-fields will be suitable for him.'

'Suitable?'

'Just right. Just what he'd want. But. There are elements of randomness sewn, stitched into his narrative. You could say sown in too, flung into the garden he's creating. It makes things less predictable. Do we want to live in a predictable life, world, existence?'

'Jim told me a little of the conversation he had about this. Didn't you argue against freewill?' Hannah asks.

'I believe in science, Hannah. Much of what we do is programmed, we are the puppets of our DNA. But there's always a little leeway. Between one extreme and the other is where life finds its way. Maybe the road is set but not every bump in that road. I think Jim would concur.'

'I'm really interested in the road Jim will be on just after his sixtieth birthday...'

'And I've answered,' Jayne says. 'He has a created world, based on his ideas, thoughts, desires. But it's not immutable. That's what I'm trying to say.'

'And the characters themselves?'

'We create them, with Jim of course, at least the main characters, wind them up and let them loose.'

'Like automatons?'

'No,' Jayne replies, 'not like automatons at all. Jim has and is putting a great deal of effort into his characters.'

'I know,' Hannah replies. 'But not into Anna.'

'No,' Jayne sighs, 'not into Anna. That is true. But as I keep trying to stress, and having talked with Jim, she will resemble you.'

'But not me.'

'Not you.'

'She couldn't be me,' Hannah says, 'there is only me.'

'Yes indeed,' Jayne says.

'You're happy with Jim's progress and you don't think he's depressed?'

'That's correct.'

'Good. That's a weight off my mind. Thank you. And sorry for all these questions, as if I'm in a law court.'

'Not a problem. We are aware of the stresses placed on family members and friends and the need for transparency.'

'Thank you.'

'And regarding transparency,' Jayne says, 'please don't forget to send me the screen-articles.'

'I'll see if I still have them. Probably just some screenwriter's imagination. You know.'

'Do screenwriters still exist?'

'Probably not.'

Jayne looks squarely at Hannah. 'Perhaps there are some posing as VI.'

'Who knows?' Hannah says. 'A nice thought. I don't watch any of the VI stuff myself. But some folks are hooked on them.'

'We agree,' Jayne smiles. 'In fact these VI films and series can be a problem for us. A lot of people want their double F to imitate the entertainment they watch. Or are being fed...'

Hannah picks up on Jayne's shift of emphasis. 'I expect it's what the government wants,' she says.

Jayne eyes her. 'Maybe. I couldn't say.'

Hannah has finished her coffee. She leans back in her chair and thinks. Again she probes, 'What do you think of the doctor?'

'He's okay,' Jayne replies.

'You said he'd had the idea for Anna, but he doesn't seem the type of man that really knows a woman.'

'He's a trained psychologist. He's a doctor. He designs characters for a living, amongst other tasks...'

'I see. Forgive my judgmental attitude, but my job is centred on intuition. And I'm a woman.'

'I'd noticed,' Jayne half-smiles. 'The doctor's a dark horse. There's more to him than you might imagine.'

'Tell me more.'

'That's not my place. That is *his* confidentiality.'

'Oh I see,' Hannah says. 'I presume you two have known each other for a long time?'

'Yes. As work colleagues. I have a lot of respect for him.'

'That's good. Important. Have you both been here from the start?'

'The doctor's been here since Portway was extended and relaunched, about twelve years ago. I've been here nearly ten years.'

'You must know each other very well.'

'We do.'

'And you must have a great working relationship.'

'We have.'

'Well,' says Hannah, 'I said it at our first visit and I'll say it again, Jim's in good hands.'

'The very best. A Magenta too.'

'Yes, Jim's a Magenta. I wonder what I'll be?'

'Who knows, Civic Duty might be completely different then.'

'You think so?'

'Who knows the future?' Jayne says.

'Who knows indeed. Does time work in the same way in double F?'

'We imagine so, but we're not totally sure. Perhaps time is dependent on each client.'

'Perhaps each client knows their future?'

'I don't think so,' says Jayne.

'But you don't know.'

The two women look at each other. They hold each other's gaze until the door is knocked and Doctor Abraham enters.

'The doctor wanted you to go and you turned him down?'

'Of course I did. I'm a married woman, married to you, Jim!'

'But that was a great chance...'

'Chance for what?'

'To discover stuff. Listen. I've been digging hard, I haven't got any further with Portway, but there's a place, another place, where it seems they were storing bodies. Like Portway. But no Future-Fields. Just keeping bodies alive. I don't know the pretext and I don't know exactly when, but early on, maybe before Civic Duty. They were keeping these bodies, these people alive, barely...so they could harvest organs. You know you have to harvest organs from a live body?'

'But brain dead,' Hannah states.

'Whatever brain death *is*! They were being stored so that their organs could be taken when needed.'

'Are you sure?' Hannah asks.

'Of course I'm not sure. Who knows, maybe they're still doing it. Maybe that's why families can't visit and interact at Portway. Maybe they could, if they wanted.'

'That's horrible, Jim. But lots of stuff went on back in the thirties. Times were different. Harsh. I saw things...'

'Well, it might explain the body I saw being dumped. Maybe they'd extracted organs.'

'Old organs.'

'Old organs for older people perhaps. It might make sense medically, I have no idea. My organs are old – but nothing wrong with me.'

'Not your body maybe. But...'

'My head.'

'Exactly,' she says. 'Anyway, I'm not going to go away with the doctor, though I haven't closed the door completely. But it's the end of next week. I can't do it Jim. You know what he wants.'

'You're presuming.'

'Come on. I'm not stupid. I'm a woman, with a woman's intuition, not so hard. We've learnt to sus out you men.'

'Maybe.'

'Certainly. I know the price I'd have to pay. What's it going to change Jim? Get real. It's all going to be so guarded – not a way in.

They'll close ranks. No-one's going to squeal, they'll incriminate themselves...'

'How did you get on with Jayne?'

'I think she has a thing for the doc.'

'You think so?'

'I think. That's all. I guess I could try and sow a little discontent. Keep you out of it. You're an easy target for revenge Jim. Pull life support, sabotage life support and it's all over.'

'It doesn't happen like that in those old American movies. I need to think of a plot.'

'It doesn't happen in movies, because it's fiction Jim. This is life. It's not predictable, well not like a movie. We have to think things through carefully.'

'You're right, Hannah. Thanks for turning the good doctor down. Let's see what happens. If you can afford it, I can go to Portway for that week and I'll be working with Jayne and Dan. I think the only thing we can do, apart from digging, is let them give themselves away...'

'If there's anything to give away. Remember that.'

'Yes. Yes, I will.'

'I have to go to work. Do what you can. But also keep creating your world.'

'You've never said that before.'

'You need to create the best world you can Jim. Who knows how long you'll be there.'

'Twenty years at the utmost,' he replies.

'Yes, maybe...'

'What is it?'

'We don't know how time will behave in double F.'

'Double F?'

'Future-Fields.'

'You're picking up the jargon Han.'

She smiles. 'I won't be too long. I have to meet with a CEO, that's all. I can do most of the other work here. But I'm going to have to work at the office most of this week.'

'Okay,' Jim says. 'Hannah?'

'Yes.'

'Take care. And thanks again for not jetting off...Not sure how I'm going to be with the doc, except he has good taste.'

'You be good or I'll change my mind,' she says.

'It's cold out. It's a bit cold in here. Wrap up.'

'I only have to get to the car,' she smiles.

Jim watches her leave. Then climbs the spiral staircase to their office above.

Jim decided on a whim to check out John Hughes-Kahn. He hadn't been the first leader of the National Government but came in soon after. In fact he hadn't been elected. He was a new broom and the people responded to his calm, authoritative style. That was before folk learnt a broom could sweep *and* beat. Trained as a lawyer and having worked for the state as a prosecutor he introduced a distanced coldness between himself and the people as soon as the honeymoon was over. For once Jim hadn't taken an instant dislike to him, feeling indifferent to both him and the government. That soon changed. There were some that championed the government's ruthlessness, explaining their actions away as 'necessity'. Jim saw the old ways kicked out of the door of the new brutalist construction of the country - both metaphorically speaking and manifest in the new utilitarian architecture and the pulling down of the old. England had taken a beating since the second world war and that had only increased as they came close to a third. There had been some hope of freedom with the 'special relationship' between the UK and the USA. But world events had quickened. The weakening and isolation of Britain had been the direct result of that relationship. At the same time the European Union began to dissolve: corruption, mismanagement, fraud and increased inward migration witnessed its implosion. But that was all just history. History had shaken up the whole world.

Thanks to Jim's latent creative talent and a few friends he'd kept in distant touch with – he was able to navigate The Onion. The dark side of the internet they couldn't shut down. He learnt quickly how to peel each thin, membranous layer from the core. If indeed there was a core at all. And he decided to peel away layers to get at John Hughes-Kahn. It was a whim – but an intuitive one. He still hadn't found much about Portway, but as it was a centre for Future-Fields it had to have had government backing or license. But he did find the speech from Hughes-Kahn, given at an early rally - when they were still allowed:

People ask me what my motivation is; what truly motivates me. Well it's to save the United Kingdom. And if that's out of my hands, it's to save Great Britain. Save us from starvation and death. Give everyone a hope for the future, for them and their children. That's my motivation.

People criticise the government for bringing in Civic Duty but it gives every man, woman and child an ideal and a means to sacrifice for the greater good. We have brought in an act recently that allows sixteen-year-olds to vote. Why? Because we believe in the future. Children of all colours, ethnicity, background. And all faiths.

We have been through a lot together and you have shown your continuing faith in us, in me, as I take the reins of this national government. Which I think of as an international government. Because we're all in this together. Some have criticised us, me in particular at times, for curtailing the lives of eighty-year-olds. But many older people have congratulated me and have told me face to face that if by their death others, children especially, get to live a better and fuller life they will end theirs. The noblest of acts. To sacrifice for the good of others is the greatest of all deeds. Others have criticised me for culling the population when our numbers have decreased so much. Culling? Many, many of your loved ones willingly suicided themselves, knowing they could not live a fulfilling life and were consuming rare resources. Again another great sacrifice. We have called on those of eighty years to lay down their lives.

Those unwilling to work, yes, unwilling, who would let children starve, those of feeble minds, those so depressed they had no function – they all sacrificed for the greater good. They knew their civic duty at the very least. They sacrificed in the way our farmers did, as we took over farms for the national good. Our food needs have, in the main, been met. We had not been self-sufficient in food since the end of the second of the great wars. Now look at us. Look at what you have done. People. Be proud. All those assisted-suicides can be proud and also their families. We are close to being able to feed everyone and we have the youngest population we have ever had. Again a mix of everything – race, ethnicity, religion. Above all, one race, the Human Race.

We call ourselves Welsh, British, Citizens of the UK – but we are a tiny island off the continent of Europe. Look at the fate of many of those nations within the once mighty European Union. We are young, we are healthy, we are beginning to trade again and restore the infrastructure of Great Britain and the UK. We do this together. Everyone. From the mother who gives her bread to her child, to the depressed person who willingly walks into one of the help-centres, to those who beg to do their duty now before they even reach eighty. Some, even healthy men and women, suiciding for the greater good. We are lean but no longer hungry like we were before. Keep your faith in this

National Government, keep your faith in the children and their future. We are all equal before this struggle. And equal in hunger and need. People of the United Kingdom, I salute you all. Thank you.

Jim watched him closely as he viewed a second time, looked at his eyes. How many of the elite were being euthanised, he wondered. And that, back then, was just the start. Hughes-Kahn had now been leader for over twenty years. How old was he? No-one knew, exactly. Surely he must be approaching sixty? Each election the party was voted in again. Computers don't lie. The opposition had collapsed. Though there were recent rumours of dissident groups coming together. Spreading misinformation about the sanctity of life; saying that all life was sacred. And that people needed their own space and protection.

Jim sat back and thought about the life he had witnessed and the horrors he had seen with his own eyes and how close he had come to being tortured or killed. But he'd never shown them any weakness. He'd used his humour. Yes, he had taken pills to sleep and he had also proved that that was not depression but grief. As he had never allowed his feelings to interrupt his work, they could never euthanise him. Despite the grief that haunted him he'd laughed and joked his way through life.

He thought deeply. In his future-fields he would need to think about law and order. Would that be necessary? He needed to think about justice. Would any characters go rogue, had they made provision for that? But his world was of his making...he had to make it good, fair, just and free. Freedom was the main thing. He really had to think it through with great care and attention, as Hannah kept telling him. If he got his future world wrong he would have messed up both his 'lives'. Sometimes he even considered being euthanised over his new life, to get it all over and done with. But what, if anything, lay beyond. Now of all times he felt a passion to live and do something. The irony. It wasn't lost on him.

They had lost continuity with the past, and he felt that loss. And yet he'd also experienced an affinity at times with the past. When they'd had weak energy supplies. When houses and towns were plunged into darkness – even without warning. When dogs howled outside for lack of scraps. When youths built up pyres in the streets. When shadows passed across walls, like lost ghosts. When medicine and drugs had been scarce and people had trusted themselves and old inclinations again. There was always bad and good. Like lives smashed into shape on a blacksmith's anvil - life went on. It always had and it always would. And there were always those who wanted to rule.

Thinking back to the swan and the youths, Jim could see in the old architecture and buildings that surrounded the canal, even the canal itself, an insight into the past. The children didn't belong either to the past or the present. The future would guide their lives in a way they could never comprehend. Life would be uncertain for them. He would be gone. Not a worry of the present, living in a parallel world of his making. Given all his thoughts, Future-Fields once again felt enticing. He had time. He had the time a woman carries a baby.

His parents were dead. So was Maddy. And his best friend. Maybe he had friends who were now dead that he didn't even realise.

'Fuck it Jim,' he says out loud. 'James. James Marshall.' He stops. Bangs on some music: *Well, I stand up next to a mountain, and I chop it down with the edge of my hand...* 'Hendrix,' he smiles. Not far off a hundred years since the Experience was formed and here he was creating his own Experience.

Again he speaks out, 'I could end it all right here, right now, Jim. James. Gone. Like all the world has gone before everyone alive now. Who gives a fuck? No one. NO, fucking one. That's the beauty of it,' he says. He's cold. Nearly shivering. Thinks of the interior of the church. Thinks of the hotel and bar. Why couldn't he go to those exotic isles. Was he going to finish his life as a prisoner in a coffin?

'Here's to all the musicians and politicians, and mothers and babies. Here's to me and Hannah. And the children I don't see. And the child long gone. Has to be more. Has. To. Be. More.'

He pulls his chair close up to the screen. 'I should have studied more, I should have remembered more. Read more. Read books!' He shouts into the cold air of the upstairs. 'I should have done something with my life. God, I'm not even drunk,' he jokes. Thinks about swallowing a whole lot of pills and helping them down with alcohol. But if he dies, they'll have won. 'You're not going to win,' he shouts. 'Concentrate Jim. Think of something funny. Wouldn't it be funny if the whole of this reality is unreal? All of it a big con. A flimsy cover for something else. Pull back the curtain and there's the Wizard. Pull back the curtain and the old cinema screen is revealed. Another world behind a world, behind a world. Step right in folks and find yourself somewhere completely new. Roll up, roll up, your future beckons.' He laughs out loud. Looks behind as if a phantom might be watching.

A message arrives. It's Henry. 'How are you Pop?' comes the lively voice.

Jim pulls himself together. Allows himself the strength of a father. 'I'm fine son,' he says. 'I'm fine.'

Doctor Abraham

The doctor took one of the old novelty electric car taxis to the airport. It was early morning and a few flakes of snow were dancing down to the ground. The party was meeting in the refurbished control centre. A once huge airport had become condensed. The flight they were taking was government approved, though private. The doctor had only flown a few times before and this would be his longest flight. He was excited to be in the company of the professor, Hughes-Kahn and government officials.

Arriving at the Hospitality Suite, Doctor Abraham was shown to the party's departure room. There were a number of people already there but they were all, like him, early birds. He introduced himself but recognised none of their faces. Jake was excited. He took a seat on a couch near the main group. An airport hospitality worker came quickly to him and offered a menu of drinks, with a full breakfast range. Jake thanked her and asked for a coffee only.

After a few sips of his coffee, Jake was relieved to see the arrival of the professor but somewhat surprised to see Milly with him.

'Professor. Milly,' Jake smiles. 'I'm surprised to see you here. I guess my instructions for you taking the helm are redundant, or perhaps you're not flying.'

'I am,' she says.

'She's my guest,' the professor explains.

'No need to worry about Portway,' Milly says. 'Jayne and Dan are having any important calls directed to them and I've cancelled any new clients. I didn't say anything doctor because...' she falters.

'Because, I wanted you along Jake and knew you'd be resistant if Milly came too. I know how conscientious you are.'

'Thank you, Professor. Alistair,' he quickly adjusts. Jake gives Milly a vaguely quizzical look. Then smiles. 'You're a dark horse Milly,' he says. She smiles back.

The professor pulls Jake to one side, 'Milly's having a few problems, on the verge of a breakdown. I'm only telling you this in case she acts, unusually.'

'I see. She did tell me she was feeling unwell for the past week. I didn't realise in what way. I did tell her to take a break,' Jake adds.

'And now she is,' the professor smiles. 'In fact both you and Milly have been able to take the place of John...Hughes-Kahn. Neither he nor his partner were able to come. Hence the last minute notification.'

'Thank you for thinking about me,' Jake says. 'And Milly of course.'

'And yes, Milly...She really needs the break.'

Before they boarded the flight there was quite a hubbub. Through the lounge's large glass windows Jake noticed a group of young folk being escorted to the airplane. Five in all. Four women, perhaps girls, and a young man. Jake was fascinated by them – each of them very attractive. Even at a distance and through the windows they exuded a strange kind of magnetic charm. One of them appeared familiar.

The jet was luxurious and there was plenty of room for the whole party, including the five young folk who quickly separated themselves as they sat at the back of the fuselage. The doctor glanced at them but Milly took his attention as she sat down and offered him the window seat next to her. In front, the professor sat with two members of parliament. Jake tried to look back but his view was now obscured and he thought nothing more of them.

Hospitality staff saw to any of their needs and the flight lasted just under six hours. Jake tried to listen to the conversation in front but couldn't hear clearly. In between Milly's conversing with him he looked out of the window and nodded off. When the plane landed on the island of Benahoare, Jake took his small holdall from the luggage section and waited patiently to disembark.

'Everything okay?' the professor asks Jake.

'Excellent. Very convenient. I didn't realise it would be this simple.'

The professor smiles. 'It wasn't always thus, Jake. Things are getting back to normal, a new normal should I say, thanks to the government.'

'Are you okay?' Jake asks Milly.

'Just a slight headache,' she answers. 'I'm not used to flying,' she explains. Jake remains silent in the surrounding noise.

As they leave the plane and walk down the steps, Jake is immediately hit by the heat. It is mid-February but the temperature, he discovers, is in the mid-20s. The effect astonishes him.

'Wonderful,' Milly says, 'it makes you feel so good, instantly...'

Jake smiles at her.

The professor has flown throughout the troubled years, knows what to expect, but he too feels the contrast of temperatures.

'Transport should be here soon. We won't go to Nouvelle Rabat but head to the south of the island. There's one of the island's dramatic beaches there and a converted holiday complex we have full use of.'

'How long will it take?' Jake asks.

'Well the main road's been resurfaced, so about thirty minutes. First time I was here it was incredibly difficult to get around, needed a jeep or a Land Rover. Had to have petrol or diesel.'

'Are you feeling okay now Milly?' Jake asks.

'I'm fine. It's good not to feel cold outside.'

'It's hot,' Jake stresses, 'too hot for me.'

'I have to sort out the party,' the professor interrupts, 'hang on here until the coach arrives.'

'Petrol or diesel?' Jake says.

'The latter.'

'That should be fun,' he says.

Jake smells the coach before it arrives. The fumes snorting out from its exhaust.

'Not the newest of vehicles,' the professor laughs, 'despite all the wealth. The island is under African jurisdiction but they could at least have updated the transport. We keep the bloody place going.'

'Who's the 'we'?' Jake asks. The professor responds only with a faint smile.

Jake is fascinated by the coach as its engine throbs and its fumes hang in the hot air. Staff load luggage into its sub-interior. Jake thinks of an ancient god being fed sacrifices. He sees his suitcase swallowed by the beast, but he keeps his holdall tight.

'On you get Jake, Milly, and save me a seat.'

'Will do Alistair.'

Milly gets on first and finds three seats about two-thirds of the way back. The five young folk follow them on and head directly to the backseats. Jake again has a seat by the coach's window. He lifts his holdall to store it. As he is turned away the young folk file pass, say nothing, not looking at either Jake or Milly. As more people get on the coach becomes full. The driver is Moroccan but introduces himself as a descendant of the Guanches. Jake can see that this pleases him enormously. The coach splutters out more fumes, lurches forward and is then remarkably smooth as it speeds over the road's shiny surface.

'It's so beautiful,' Jake says, 'but hot, stifling...'

'La Isla Bonita,' the professor says, sitting across the aisle. 'That's how it's known, the beautiful island. And it's not so hot Jake, trust me.'

They head south towards the tip of the island, although turn and drive north-westerly before reaching the sea. 'They have salt fields at the foot of the island and produce wonderfully pure salt,' the professor explains, 'you'll get to try some.'

As they continue Jake looks out of the window at the impressive scenery. Milly's eyes close and she flickers between sleep and wakefulness. The professor leaves his seat to talk with the driver, or other members of the party.

'Is this just a holiday?' Jake asks Milly as her eyes snap open.

'A reward, I think...'

'You don't know?'

She shakes her head. 'We're very lucky being here. You have to be very rich or very important.'

'We're not?'

'I'm not,' she says. 'You're head of Portway, but even you wouldn't be allowed to live on the island. I know it didn't look like it back at the airport but security is ultra-tight. But they don't want us thinking we're in a controlled environment.'

'How do you know?'

'The professor told me.'

'How long have you known him?'

'Not long,' she says, 'over the phone mainly,' closing her eyes again.

At the complex they disembark and Jake takes in the scenery. It is such a contrast.

'You look a little uncomfortable,' Milly says.

'No. It's amazing. But I'm not used to being away from Portway and my office.'

'Relax,' she says, 'we both need to relax.'

Jake smiles. Even that surprises him. He hangs around to wait for the young folk to leave the coach but the professor takes them with him to the lobby of the complex. He catches sight of one of the girls, could it be?

Jim

Hannah is working in the office above. Jim calls up to her, 'Friday the thirteenth, good job you're not flying.'

'I can't hear you.'

'If you can't hear me how do you know I said anything?'

'What? I'm working, Jim.'

He goes to the stairs and climbs up to the door. Pushing it open he says, 'I'm going for a quick walk.'

'Where are you going?'

'Just down the road, I need some air.'

'Take your device and phone.'

'See you later?'

'Bye,' she answers, distracted by her work.

Outside, Jim did his jacket's top button up. It was cold. A dry cold at least. Once out of the gated area he saw the path to the main road but took the path he had used the previous time he'd gone. He needed to get out. He was glad Hannah was at home but he wasn't sure if he'd be called into Portway or not. The doctor wouldn't be there – but did he need him?

Without thinking too much, Jim found himself leaving the modern part of the town and into the old industrial area. Again he found himself in an area he partly recalled. On a whim he decided to see if he could find the canal and get back on its towpath. Hannah had said to keep away, but he wasn't going to be put off by his previous experience. She was being paranoid. As he walked he thought about whether or not to add a little danger to his new world. Was danger, or the threat of danger, a natural component to life? He recalled the recent wars, which seemed like a lifetime away; how the first nuclear missiles since the Americans dropped *Little Boy* and *Fat Man* had been used and the world had teetered on the precipice. They'd balanced precariously, leaning forwards and eyeing the chasm of death, then pulled back. This happened a few times. It would have been some Civic Duty.

Thoughts passed time quickly, which he thought an interesting idea. He was mulling on this when he saw a path winding down from the main road. Taking this, he soon found himself on the canal's towpath. The canal's waters looked icy. Deciding to walk in the direction he'd previously gone he kept a lookout for errant teenagers. It seemed as if he'd subconsciously found himself there back by the canal. Hardly a vibration disturbed the air. It was as if there was no city. No people. Certainly no teenagers. No swan. Except.

Up ahead he saw a figure seated on the arm of a lock gate. Instinctively he looked around, the last thing he wanted was another altercation. Apart from the sudden call of a rook, there was silence. As he got closer he could see it was a girl wearing only a white dress and a cardigan. She must have been freezing. Her legs were bare and her shoes light and insubstantial. She was looking at the ground and hadn't noticed his arrival. When she saw Jim, she looked startled.

'It's okay,' Jim reassures. 'I'm just out walking.'

She looks at him, not quite blankly, but as if she belonged in another realm.

'Are you okay?' he asks. She nods. 'You must be cold,' Jim adds. Again she nods. There was something about this girl...something familiar. Without thinking Jim takes off his coat. 'Here,' he says, and holds at his arm, his hand offering her the coat. She stands and she is white cold. Her white dress barely touching the knees of her white legs. 'Please,' he says. Tentatively she moves closer. She is like a wild creature. A bird landed, resting before flying southwards. Slowly she moves towards the coat. 'It won't bite,' Jim says.

She suddenly snatches it from his loose grip. 'Thanks!'

'You can speak.'

She pulls the coat on and is smothered by its warmth. Jim feels the cold, a little. Her hands are lost inside the sleeves. The length of his coat hides her white dress. Jim's not sure what to say to her, but he is curious. 'Do you live nearby?' She nods. 'Do your parents know where you are?'

'I only have a mam,' she says.

'You should dress up warmer in this weather.'

She nods. She sits back down on the heavy wood of the lock gate's arm. 'Are you feeling warmer?' Jim asks. Again she nods. 'Do you mind if I sit?'

'Course not,' she says. Her hair is thick but bobbed, cut roughly.

'If you check one of those pockets you'll find a special bar. It's healthy. Approved,' he says.

Feeling inside, she soon takes out a white paper bag, and pulls out the bar. 'Eat,' Jim urges. She devours it. 'Are you hungry? Jim asks stupidly.

'Not so much now,' she says.

Jim has perched himself on the wooden arm, but at a reasonable distance. 'No school?' he asks.

'Internet is down,' she says.

'I see.'

That's why I'm here,' she adds.

'You like it here?'

'It's quiet and mostly no-one comes.'

'I was here not long ago and I saw a gang of children, well teenagers.'

She looks at him inquisitively. Almost interrogating him. 'I don't belong in a gang,' she says quietly.

'I'm sure you don't,' Jim smiles. They sit silently for a few moments. 'Is the coat warm?'

'Yes...thanks...'

'What are you doing out here in the cold all alone?' Jim asks.

'Oh, I'm not alone,' she says. 'No, not at all.'

'Who's with you?' Jim asks, looking around.

'The other boys and girls,' she says.

'Boys and girls? Did they run away when I came?'

'No. They. They just disappear. I dance with them,' she says.

'You dance with them?'

'Do you want me to dance?' she asks.

'Why not,' Jim says.

'I'll have to take your coat off.'

'You'll be cold.'

'Not if I dance,' she smiles. As she struggles out of the over-large coat she looks around, as if checking something. She carries the coat to Jim. 'Here.'

'Are you sure you won't be too cold?'

She shakes her head. Jim watches her poise herself. Her bare knees, the shabby white dress and her thin cardigan. But he notices a concentration in her eyes and how she carefully positions herself. As if she can hear music she moves and sways, an imitation of some ballet she has seen, perhaps. But would she ever have seen a ballet? Gliding on the concrete and the grass around the lock gate she is deeply earnest. Jim notices the seriousness in her eyes. And the beauty of her face and her roughly cut, bobbed hair. It seems as if she has rehearsed a series of moves, pivots, graceful turns and she lifts her heels in imitation of a ballerina pointing her toes. At one point she stares into nothingness and holds her arms as if she is in the embrace of another dancer. And then, abruptly, she stops. Bows. Looks at Jim and her serious face breaks into a wide smile.

Jim claps. 'Bravo,' he says.

'What does bravo mean?'

'It means well done. That was lovely. You dance beautifully.'

'Do you think so?' she asks.

'I think so. Now, put on the coat and get warm.'

She shakes her head. 'I have to go. All the children have gone.'

Jim looks at her and a tear rolls from an eye.

'Why are you crying?' she asks.

'Oh, no reason,' Jim says, trying to smile. 'You danced so beautifully.'

'And that makes you cry?'

'Yes,' he says. 'And I'm remembering things from long ago.'

'What things?'

'Someone who was very close to me. You reminded me of her.'

'Could she dance?'

'Not as well as you,' he smiles. 'But sometimes she'd dance like crazy,' and Jim tries to imitate a memory.

The girl laughs. 'She sounds funny.'

'She was funny. And beautiful...'

'Where is she? Are you married to her?'

'No, that's another funny girl,' he jokes

'So?'

'She's with God,' he says.

'God?'

'She's with the angels, teaching them to dance. You know who God is. You've heard of angels?'

She shakes her head again. 'They sound nice.'

'They are nice.'

'I'm glad she's happy,' the girl smiles.

'I'm glad you're happy,' Jim says. 'And you've made me happy.'

'Because I danced?'

'Yes. And because you brought back happy memories of...'

'What's her name?'

'Maddy.'

'It's a nice name,' the girl says. 'Maybe I can dance with Maddy one day.'

'One day,' Jim says. 'Now please, don't get cold. You need to go home and have a hot bath.'

'If we have hot water,' she says.

'What's your name?' Jim asks.

'Everyone calls me Ree,' she says.

'Is that short for something?'

She nods. 'I'm not going to tell you what though.'

'Okay Ree. You don't have to. Ree is a nice name. Mysterious.'

'Mysterious,' she coos. Jim smiles. 'Are you happy now, again?' she asks.

'Of course Ree. You said that everyone calls you Ree, but what do you call you?' Jim asks.

'I don't call myself anything,' she laughs. 'Now I must go and get back home,' she says, 'before...'

'Before?'

'Before I'm told off,' she says coldly.

'It's been nice knowing you Ree.'

'And you...'

'Jim.'

'Jim. That's a funny name.'

'It used to be popular.'

'I like it,' she says. 'Now I must get back.'

'Run as fast as you can and you'll feel warm.'

She runs off and as she does she imitates a bird flying or taking off. Jim smiles and also tears form again. He takes the inside of the jacket and brings it to his nose. It's as if he can smell Maddy again. How he misses her. He can smell her warmth. He can smell her room. Sensations and memories rush in. But he also keeps watching Ree running down the towpath.

'Be careful,' he shouts.

She lifts her arms higher. Like a graceful bird she disappears from sight. Jim smiles. Then he laughs. 'How magical,' he says out loud. 'Perhaps the canal is magical. With wicked children and graceful dancers.'

He slips on the coat and heads back the way he came. He thinks Ree might be short for Regal, like a regal swan. This thought cheers him and as he walks he holds out a hand for Maddy to hold. Of course there are invisible children.

Jayne

'While the cat's away, the mice will play.'

'But who's going to be the guinea pig?' Dan asks.

'It's usually me, isn't it?' Jayne smiles.

'You're more adventurous than me Jayne. You know that.'

'You mean I'm not adverse to taking risks.'

'Precisely.'

'Well. Will I be getting into the prof's avatar?'

'As you say, the cat's away. Now or never. If we've done our job, great, if there's a problem, we can still fix it.'

'Wouldn't it be better if you wore the suit?'

'It fits any size, you know how it works.'

'Yes. But. I don't know if you've noticed, I'm missing stuff...'

'That's true. That's going to be interesting.'

'Who for?'

'Both of us.'

'So it's me?'

'It's you and you know how much you want to do it.'

For the rest of the morning they set up what was effectively an experiment. They had time, as the doctor was not there to authorise any 'plug-ins', as they termed those entering Future-Fields.

'I can't recreate exactly,' Dan says. 'But we can definitely emulate the prof's likely experience. That's the main thing. But I'm not going to pierce your neck...'

'Or anything,' Jayne quickly adds. 'It would be incredibly interesting to be connected in a drawer,' she says. 'But the professor won't have that connection either, will he?'

'Certainly not at first. But it's going to be really interesting being an avatar. Don't underestimate the experience. Given that it works. I have replicated a plug-in drug dose and we'll be using their double F.'

'Should I know who they are?'

'If you want. Or you could go in blind.'

'Blind, I think. You'll be able to communicate with me?'

'Should be. Like we do in VR. Of course this is the real thing.'

'And if I meet them in their double F?'

'Come up with a story. They aren't going to recognise you, are they?'

Jayne nods. 'How do I get out?'

'You know as much as me,' Dan says. 'But when the drugs wear off, find a place to lie down...'

'And die?'

'And not get noticed. There should be plenty of warning. The problem will be re-mobilising your body, which shouldn’t be done too quickly. If it's done late don't panic, you might be in a waking consciousness or dreaming, or still affected by the drugs to a degree. But if you wake up and can't move, don't panic.'

'And this is why I'm the guinea pig.'

'Exactly.'

'Sounds like I might feel as if I'm in a coma.'

'Yes. But just remember, I'm here looking out for you.'

'And if you die, I'll be buried alive! Or lost in a far corner of outer space.'

'I don't think I'm ready to keel over just yet. I'll be monitoring your heart, brain and general health. You'll be connected to the client's computer too, to enter their world. Partially,' he smiles.

'Partially in their world or connected?'

'You’ll be connected to their computer, but not fully. You should have full immersion into their double F at the very least. But not exactly the same experience.'

'Okay,' she says quietly.

'It's going to be fun. Relax.'

'Will you be able to see me?'

Dan shakes his head. 'We have to replicate the prof's experience. But you trying this out will give us many answers, I hope.'

'Okay,' Jayne says. 'Where's the suit?'

'You know you're going to have to get naked?'

'Dan. Has this whole thing been fabricated so you can finally see my body?'

'Of course. But. You can get naked and into the suit privately... unless?'

'No,' she says. They laugh. 'No!' she stresses.

'Don't forget to empty your bladder and, if necessary...well you know. I *could* connect you up but hopefully we won't need that. You're not going in for too long. And everything's complicated if that has to be done. It will be the same for the prof. No drinking or eating and cleaning the body out first. But he'll be in for longer, I imagine. You took the evacuation pill?'

'Oh yes,' she says. 'Thank you for that.'

'I apologise.'

'Dodged that one too Dan, eh?'

An hour later and Jayne, in the fully covering suit, lies down on the table Dan has prepared. The only hole is for her mouth. The suit is aligned to her eyes, ears, her sex and across the whole of the rest of her body.

Dan says loudly, 'This is as much about imagination as it is about reality.'

'You mean...' she says through the breathing hole.

Dan instinctively does know what she means. 'It's possible you will look like a man, have the body of a man, and maybe the reaction of a man.'

'I guess that's where the imagination comes in?' she says.

'Indeed. That particular…thing…couldn't actually be covered.'

'As it doesn't exist.'

'Indeed so. But. Your mind, under the concoction and melded with the computer, might do all sorts of playful things.'

'This can't be the suit the professor will wear.'

'You know it is. But now you also know first-hand how it fits any body type, within reason.'

'I know. I know the principle and how the material and its sensory maps work. But it seems impossible. It's one thing planning and designing, quite another to be in it.'

'Nothing's impossible.'

'Try landing on the sun,' Jayne says.

'When it's cold.'

'And we're long dead.'

'I get kidnapped by aliens and taken into the future.'

'I can only imagine your future double F,' she says.

'You couldn't,' Dan laughs. 'Okay let's get you hooked up. Your body will be immobilised as we discussed. I'll let you know when to count down from twenty. Good luck.'

'Thanks.'

Dan re-checks all the equipment. The suit is activated and Jayne is effectively connected to the computer. Dan administers the drugs. He reads the brain and heart activity. It is some occasion and he feels as nervous as Jayne. 'Okay,' he says. 'Count down.'

'Twenty, nineteen, eighteen, seventeen, sixteen, fifteen, for-teen, thir-teen twel..'

Dan sits at the computer. Legally, and morally, he cannot intervene and see what's going on. The computer is designed to prevent access unless authorisation comes from the top. But he can communicate if necessary. Unlike during a VR, Jayne is effectively cut off.

Jayne's Experience 1

It felt like she was in a state between sleep and waking. As she said 'twelve' she could see again, though her sight was at first hazy. She was standing, which surprised her. She certainly hadn't lifted herself up. But there she was. Then a sense of her body grew. It was not her body and yet it felt natural to her. It felt heavier and stronger. But she only really sensed this. She could breathe freely. There was a light wind and in the distance a town. Jayne wondered what would have happened to her if she had materialised in front of people. Did Dan have some idea where she would wake into this new world?

She looked at her hands. They were not her hands. But she was connected to them and they moved at her will. She felt her face. It was not her face. Was she moving her real hands over her covered face? No. Her body was immobilised. But her mind was the same. She had not become anyone or anything else. It was her mind which animated the body – or thought it did. Her lungs filled with air and her body exhaled. She was still breathing on the table in the control room. The air she breathed there corresponded to the air she breathed now. All the 'plug-ins' breathed within their drawers. They were alive. She was doubly alive. She was not naked. The clothes she had on – where had they come from, was that the computer's doing and the drugs? Had they tapped into her mind in order to clothe her. Or him. What was she? She felt her hair which she had scraped back into a tight bun. It seemed the same.

The air felt warm enough. Was it the air surrounding her true body or the body she was now in? The program she was in, the professor's avatar, was her co-creator and guide. A combination of the live suit, which was specifically designed for the professor and the information he had supplied, made this a bespoke experience. Jayne was an impostor in that sense. She was being treated and partially created as the professor. In fact she felt unwanted thoughts come to her too, as if she shared some head space with him. It was somewhat confusing for her, though her personality did remain in control. The closest she could explain how she felt was as if she were in a lucid dream.

The surroundings appeared to be standard template design. Jayne didn't know the colour of the plug-in she'd been allocated. She'd presumed a Magenta. Often people were more interested in the details of their closer surroundings. There was a stone in the grass nearby. Crouching down she picked it up and threw it. She felt her, or his, strength. How was this possible? It was a mind-created world for sure and she was under a concoction, though without the nanobots. She wondered if she'd been totally connected, including to her brain stem, whether she would be another person. There was a temptation to take off her clothes, if that was possible and view her body. What was she expecting? How much would her expectation change that reality? At least the avatar was working.

'Can you hear me Dan? If you are able, I'm fine. Everything working as it should do, I think. It's weird, I'll tell you that. And it seems my voice has dropped an octave. Very strange. Not sure what else has changed. There's a town in the distance, I'm going to explore. I feel as if I'm on another planet.'

Jayne looked at the clothes on her - or his - body. It was an odd experience. Who had designed these clothes? The professor, Dan, a random computer program, a random act of that world? Maybe the person who was in double F. Were they in some way influencing the avatar she had become? She unbuttoned the shirt and was a little shocked to see her breasts had been transformed, flattened. She touched her skin. It felt like it belonged to her. As if it was her. Her chest felt stronger. Inhaling, she expanded her rib cage and then blew air out.

'I'm going to need counselling after this,' she says out loud. 'I'm a hybrid!' But she laughs too, does the buttons back up and strides out towards the town. She makes up her mind to investigate her body further, when she can be sure of being totally alone. It took some will power not to examine the obvious, but that could wait. And she was apprehensive. Besides, her reason to be there was to investigate her relationship with that world.

She reached the outskirts of the town. The last fields had a kind of miasma rising from them. The sky overhead was dark and ominous. It wasn't what she was expecting. She hesitated.

A voice came, 'Hello. Hold on a moment.'

She looks around and is at first blinded by a shaft of light which strikes through a cloud break. Almost instantly it is gone. A figure has walked close to her.

'Hello,' she says. 'Are you from the town?'

The figure nods, 'Yes.' It looks at her. 'Have you a name?'

Jayne almost replies with *her* name. She has to think quickly. She isn't going to say she's called Professor, but doesn't remember his name. 'Peter,' she says after a slight pause.

The figure holds out a hand, 'Antonio.'

Jayne smiles nervously. Sets her mind in accordance with the name Peter.

'I haven't seen you before,' he says.

'I'm visiting,' she says.

'Visiting? Where are you from?'

'From over the hills, back there.'

Antonio smiles. 'I see,' adding, 'we've never had anyone come from over the hills.'

Jayne smiles nervously again. 'Well, I was lost,' she says.

'Lost?'

'Yes, I woke up and found myself in a different place. I have walked for some time and am hungry and thirsty.'

'Very well,' Antonio says, 'follow me.'

'Is this your world?' Jayne asks.

'My world?'

Jayne hesitates, 'Did you create this world?'

Antonio laughs out loud. 'Of course not.'

Jayne realises how unusual, ridiculous even, her words, her question must have sounded. 'I think I might have been knocked out,' she says. 'I'm sorry.' She rubs her head for effect.

'No need.'

'Why is there this miasma emanating from the ground?'

'Miasma?'

'Yes this mist, this fog?'

He looks at her with a curious expression. 'Fog?'

Jayne holds back. 'No matter,' she says.

'Follow me.'

They enter the town and Jayne notices people going about their business. Sometimes they are static yet seem to come to life as she looks at them. Some of them bid her good day.

They arrive outside a tea room. 'You can eat and drink here,' he says. The room is empty. They enter to the sound of a small clinking bell. As soon as they step in it seems to Jayne that she has to focus sharply and details appear. And then she hears the bell again. 'Good day,' comes a voice. Jayne turns and smiles. A family is looking through the window outside as the lady who entered takes a seat. When Jayne looks at the counter again there is an assortment of cakes and sandwiches.

A jovial woman appears. 'Can I help you?'

Jayne looks at Antonio.

'Tea for two please and perhaps a tray of cakes,' he says.

Jayne thought how surreal and yet mundane it all was.

'Drinking tea, Antonio?' the woman asks.

'Why not?' he says, smiling.

They sit. Exchange greetings with the lady who has entered and hear a bell tinkle as the family enters too.

'Just how a tea room should be,' Antonio says.

The family is buoyant and the children playful, but not too loud. They also exchange greetings. The woman at the counter smiles. Then says to the solitary lady, 'The usual?' The lady nods.

Eventually their tea and cakes arrive. Jayne is slightly concerned about drinking and more so about its possible effects. But she's both hungry and thirsty. Is this a natural reaction to the drugs maybe? Or the suit? She sips the tea, it's lighter than she would normally take. The cake she bites into is too creamy for her taste. But not bad and she's hungry. Antonio watches her with a beneficent smile on his face. The sensation of eating and drinking feels normal. Is the inside of her apparently male body, her own female body?

Jayne stops to take in her surroundings once again. 'It's a lovely old-fashioned place,' she says.

'It's fully up-to-date Peter,' Antonio says.

'Yes, yes, of course...but it has a charming feel, which we don't have where I'm from.'

'From over the hills,' Antonio says.

'Yes,' Jayne says. Is he playing with her? 'Can we explore the town?' she asks.

'Of course. When you're ready.'

Jayne wolfs down the cakes, is surprised by both her actions and appetite. 'Ready.'

'You were hungry Peter.'

Jayne eyes him and nods. Gets up.

'Have a lovely day,' the woman seated next to them says.

'Thank you.'

The lady serving calls out, 'Yes, have a lovely day Antonio and your new friend.'

Jayne smiles, feels awkward. They pass the family, who seem to suddenly become alive. Jayne realises that their noisy enthusiasm must have abated, but now the children are laughing and giggling again. They sing a strange song, which Jayne is vaguely aware of.

'Have a lovely day,' the father sings. Jayne smiles. 'And you Antonio,' he says. Antonio smiles and sings a little playful melody that seems to delight them all.

They step out of the tea room to the percussive tinkling of the bell. Jayne stops and looks around. She thinks it's like something out of a fairy tale. And yet the sky has grown dark in the distance but with a luminous yellow-amber glow. Darting her eyes, she feels she can catch somebody out. Has the sensation that they are waiting for her to look at them.

Jayne and Antonio walk on down the road. As they pass various shops, Jayne suddenly sees herself mirrored in a window. Or rather she notices her eyes and where she inhabits space, reflected in the glass. It is not her. She is a man. A man walking next to Antonio, in a strange town. A town created by either a man or a woman in a box, in a drawer.

'How odd,' she says out loud in her manly voice.

Jayne's Experience 2

Jayne stares at her reflection for some time. Realises that this could be construed as being vain. 'Interesting,' she says and walks up to the shop window. Peering through her reflection she can see inside. There are dolls and dollhouses. Antonio has followed her. Again Jayne checks herself. She was going to say that this reminded her of a distant memory as a child, of a doll she had.

'What is it?' Antonio asks.

'The doll there,' she points through the shop window, 'looks like a doll my little sister had.'

'Do you want to go inside and take a closer look?'

Jayne shakes her head. They continue. Ahead Jayne sees two girls. They are dressed in dolls' costumes. One reminds her of Alice, a story her grandfather had told her. Jayne is captivated. They skip by and she can hear them singing.

'Everyone seems so full of song,' she says.

'Of course.'

'Why of course?'

'Doesn't everyone sing in your world?'

'Not usually,' she answers. 'And girls don't tend to wear such outfits. Is it fashion?'

'Fashion? I don't know what fashion is,' he says.

They continue along the road as it inclines. At the top there is an archway. But before they get there flakes of snow begin to fall. Little patterns of ice landing and melting upon them. Jayne thinks of the girls dressed as dolls. She turns about but everyone, everywhere seems wrapped up. 'Peculiar,' she says. And is immediately reminded of Alice's 'curiouser'.

'What is peculiar?'

'Everyone seems prepared for the snow, but a moment ago...' She tilts her face so that snowflakes dance down upon her eyelashes and cheeks. She wonders if 'Peter' or the professor would do such a thing. 'I love the snow,' she says.

'We all love the snow here,' Antonio answers.

Jayne witnesses the town transformed as the snow settles on the rooftops and roads. 'Where are the cars?' she asks.

'Cars?'

'Yes, you know...'

'I don't know.'

'Oh,' Jayne says and can't help adding, 'Curious and curiouser.' Antonio looks at her. And then he starts singing a melody. And all the people around join in. Jayne is perplexed but also entranced. It's as if the whole thing is being choreographed. The snow falls thickly, like interference on a screen. But she isn't particularly cold. It's as if as the snow melts upon her the cold melts away too. This appeals both to Jayne's aesthetic and scientific mind.

They walked up to the archway, Antonio still sang. And Jayne saw the two girls down the road too, dancing in the snow. The singing voices bounced off the stone walls of the shops and houses. And as she looked carefully, the cobbled street. Wouldn't she have felt those cobbles beneath her feet as she walked?

Antonio says, 'What are these things 'cars' that you asked about?'

'Things that people drive...'

'Drive? Like a team of horses and carriage?'

'Yes. Exactly,' Jayne says. She is tempted to describe how a car developed from a carriage and how modern fuel-cell cars operate. But she thinks better of it. 'We call them cars where I'm from.'

Antonio smiles. As he looks at her, or him in his perception, a bell sounds from above the archway. The stones of the archway echo its slow clanging. By its deep resonant sound, it must be a huge bell. The snow stops and the people slowly disappear into the buildings or turn into alleyways which Jayne must have missed.

'It's time,' Antonio says.

'Time?'

'Yes, a child is being born.'

'How do you know?'

'Because the bell has sounded. You say some unusual things Peter.'

'Well...it doesn't work like that in my world.'

'Elena will be here soon,' he announces.

'Elena?'

'Yes. She will deliver the baby and give it a name. A special name that will orientate it for life.'

'Can we go and see?'

'Oh no, we can't. We're men.'

'Yes.' Jayne bites her lip; she wants to see this birth.

'You'll be able to see Elena arrive though.'

Jayne nods her head. Antonio leads her through the archway. The snow clouds have passed and the day has become evening – as if the archway was a switch. Much of the sky has become a deep dark blue, speckled with twinkling stars. Jayne looks for a constellation she can recognise. As she does, patterns form and the stars make pictures in the sky. There is no plough, or bear, or Orion.

'Wow,' she says. Antonio looks at her confused. 'We don't have such stars...'

'Where you are from,' he finishes for her.

'No.' The patterns burst into life and interact with each other as if the sky is a huge theatre. 'Incredible.'

'This is the sky for the baby,' Antonio explains. He can see Peter does not understand. 'The stars tell the baby's story. Not all of it, of course. But we can see that this baby is truly blessed. Elena will be very pleased.'

'Who is Elena?' Jayne asks. She simply can't hold back.

Antonio laughs out loud. 'She's the queen,' he says.

'You have queens?'

'Of course.'

As he says this, the two young girls reappear and each takes one of Jayne's arms as if for comfort, but also to guide. 'Hello,' she says, remembering that she is a man in their eyes. There is a sweet aroma in the air. All of them continue to watch the patterns play out their spectacular show.

Jayne asks Antonio, 'Why did the people return to their houses?'

'They're not allowed to look.'

'But we can? And there are people looking now.'

'Yes we can. It's plain to understand, surely?' he asks, almost worried.

Jayne sees that there are many others around them looking. Wonders what distinguishes them. 'I see,' she says.

'Yes, you see,' he replies satisfactorily.

'Isn't it marvellous?' one of the girls coos.

Jayne wonders why she is able to see.

'Wait till you hear the music,' the other girl says.

'I haven't seen you before,' the first says to Jayne.

'He's a visitor,' Antonio explains. 'Leave him be.'

'What a lovely day,' the second girl says, almost swooning.

'Quiet, Elena is arriving.'

'How do you know?' Jayne asks.

'It's obvious,' he says. And as he says this, a flat-surfaced craft approaches in the distance, with a golden throne and a queen sitting majestically upon it. The craft glides down through the late evening sky and is lit up like a show in itself.

Jayne wants to say that this is crazy but she reminds herself that this is a created world. Had she and Dan helped in its creation? She has no recollection of such things. The world is interesting for sure and full of great surprises, for her at least.

They watch as the craft with Elena and her throne hovers above a house in the near distance. The road from the archway stretches out on what must be a plateau, disappearing into the distance. Jayne watches the craft disappear behind a terrace of timber-framed houses.

'Come,' Antonio says. 'We can watch the royal party disembark.'

As the craft lands, though hidden from Jayne's view, the aerial show stops, the stars are stilled and resume their twinkling. Some people come running from the scene holding handkerchiefs across their faces. As each one passes, the girls cry, 'Have a lovely day,' giggling as they do. There was also an intense glow of light forming in the sky.

There was a narrow road which intersected the terrace, which Jayne hadn't noticed because of the angle of her vision. Antonio led her and the girls down it. At its end the road stopped and their view opened up to a vast field surrounded by lights. At the far side of this field was what seemed to be a dense woodland. They hurried to the boundary in time to see Elena gracefully descend. Steps emanated from the craft and there were men to guide and help her walk down. Her dress was voluminous and hid her feet for the most part. But occasionally Jayne saw dainty shoes revealed. Jayne was a scientist, but this dress reminded her of fairy-tales told to her as a child, before such stories were frowned upon. Elena looked more like a princess than a young queen.

'She's very beautiful, isn't she?'

Jayne nods. She is a man after all. But her response is purely aesthetic; the response of a fellow female who appreciates such beauty.

'We won't be able to follow her,' Antonio explains. 'It's a custom we keep.'

Elena walks with regal dignity followed by two ladies in waiting. The men remain by the craft. After taking twenty or so steps, she looks around the great level field. Many people are watching. She raises a hand and they hush. Jayne goes to ask Antonio a question but she is quickly hushed. He whispers, 'Close your eyes and listen.'

Remaining silent, but with her eyes open, she watches Elena's face, which is both concentrated and serene. Everyone is silent. Perhaps two minutes pass with nothing said. Then, seemingly on cue, a huge cheer goes up and again everyone starts singing.

'How beautiful,' the girls say in unison. Jayne looks bemused.

Antonio smiles. 'Such a poignant speech,' he says. 'Always so touching.'

As Elena walks to a building on the right side of the field a huge procession of women follow. The girls rush and join it leaving Antonio and Jayne behind. The rest of the men move towards the craft and some talk with the crew. Jayne watches Elena enter the building and the sky overhead turns pitch black, no stars to be seen. The craft glows an intense white. In the distance a light glows and begins to grow, as if moving towards the building.

'What do you want to do?' Antonio asks.

'I'm going to find my way back. Is that okay? I feel tired,' she says.

'Very well Peter. You have been very fortunate to see what you've seen and I am sure the newborn will have been blessed by your presence.'

'Thank you. It's been a remarkable day. Well, time...Thank you so much for being my guide.'

'I thought you were my guide,' he laughs.

'Please forgive my departure...' Jayne feels her words and rhythm alien to her. She has to get back. Something urges her.

'Will you be okay crossing the hills at night?'

'Yes, yes, I'm sure,' she says.

'Then at least take this.' He hands her a box from an inside jacket pocket. 'Do this.' He moves his hand and a light comes on. 'You can ask it directions too.'

'Thank you.' Jayne takes the box. The air still seems warm enough around her. The weather was curious to say the least.

'Have a lovely day,' Antonio calls to her as she leaves. 'Ask the box anything you need to know.'

'Do I keep it?'

'When you don't need it, let it go and it will find its way back,' he says.

Jayne takes in the view one last time. Singing arises from the building where she supposes the baby has been, or is about to be, born. Then she heads back down the narrow road. She hears Antonio call to her. But she can't make out his words.

At the end of the road she turned left and headed back to the archway. She had a lot to tell Dan about this world. Taking one last look she noticed a bright light above the houses. As she passed through the archway she noticed the night was lighter. As if it were an early evening on a summer's day. There were people about again, milling around now as if completely unaware of what was happening not much more than a stone's throw away. Jayne crossed the road so that she was on the same side as the doll shop and tea room. She looked but couldn't find either of them. She did find a toy shop with some dolls in it and she found a restaurant with people eating. These people completely ignored her. Only a dog, the first animal she had seen in the town, growled as she walked by.

On leaving the town, the miasma she encountered previously had turned into a heavy ground fog. Before too long she was lost in its near viscous presence. Not quite knowing what to do she called out.

'Dan can you hear me? Can you hear me Dan, please.'

Nothing.

'Dan can you hear me?'

Instinctively she takes the box from her pocket and shakes it into action. A light comes on but it is swallowed up by the fog, in fact she can see less with the light shining. The fog feels almost sticky as it becomes thicker.

'Dan?'

She begins to panic...

The box: *Move forward.* She does. *Turn slightly to your right. STOP. Move forward.* She follows the instructions. It's as if the fog is a thick spider's web as she pushes it away from her face. *Turn slightly to your left. Stop. Keep moving in that direction.*

'Dan?'

The box: *Please don't worry.*

She continues to follow its directions and heed its warnings where the land is rocky or swampy. Jayne's nervousness is palpable.

'Dan, where the fuck are you?'

As she says this, she notices the fog clearing and very quickly it has gone. She looks back at the whiteout. Above her the night is now a thick black texture. Were there two nights in one day? The box illuminates the silhouetted countryside ahead. 'Dan!'

And she blacks out, dropping the box on the grass next to her. Her body crumpling like a doll's.

'Okay I got you. If you can hear. Everything's okay. I saw your scans but couldn't see you. I hacked in. Hands up. Shop me to the prof. Your body probably feels paralysed,' he continues, 'it's normal, we discussed this remember? I'm going to bring you round slowly, like a deep-sea diver. Remember them?' He laughs. He goes to the body and places a small mirror next to her mouth. It mists. She's breathing. 'Jayne what the heck was going on? Your brain and heart lines were doing the twist. Having a neurowave. Take it easy. Give me a few mins, okay? I'll take your silence as a 'yes'. Now, let me see...' He begins modifying the program and adding stimulants to her body.

'Dan you fucker, where were you?!'

'You're back.'

'I can't move. Get me moving. Where were you?'

'I was here.'

'You couldn't hear me shouting?'

'No.'

'That bloody fog,' she says.

'Fog?'

'I'll explain all. When I can move my body and get out of this damn suit.'

'Relax. It won't help if you react like this.'

'Listen I've been to crazy land, you know. You have no idea. Who the fuck created that world? Wait...'

'What is it?'

'I can feel tingling in my fingers and toes. That feels so good. Weird but good.'

'Hold on, you'll be back to normal soon. I cut a few corners...'

'Dan!'

'Well I couldn't reason with you. Hang on, I'm just going for a shot or two.'

'Dan!'

'I'm joking.'

'Wait. Wait. I can feel the inside of my body. Strange. I can feel I'm a female again. Thank God.'

'God?'

'It can turn you, being in that place. It was like being in a really weird dream.'

'Wait, you can tell me but first relax, let your body and mind get back to this world.'

'I'm coming back. I can still remember everything. It wasn't a dream though. It's a real place. A real bizarre place. Some amazing things too.'

'Try and lift your head. Yep. Good. A little more.'

'It's too heavy.'

'Keep trying. Bend your legs. We have you Houston.'

'Houston?'

'Yeah, before it got, you know, blasted. Space rockets and all that...'

'Beautiful, beautiful science, I say.'

Dan laughs.

Jayne continues, 'Maybe science isn't what we think it is. Weird. I feel weird. But...' she lifts herself from the elbows. 'Fuck.'

'I'd be taking advantage.'

'At least get me out of this suit. I thought being a man would be more fun.'

'It wasn't?'

'It wasn't. Take this fucking suit off, please.'

'Okay you asked, so it's consensual. Hear that you bank of robots? I'll be calling on you as witnesses.'

She was naked. Female. Stark. Dan got his jacket and handed it to her, offering some modesty. She took it and walked unsteadily to the room she had undressed in. Dan took the suit and checked it over. Ran some tests. Had her body sweated? Or more? He'd be discreet, he always was behind his brashness. The suit would have to be analysed. Theoretically it had been nowhere. But it had experiences.

'Ah the birthday girl,' he says as Jayne reappears.

'No.'

'It was the birthday suit...You know. A joke!'

'Get me a drink Dan. I need it. Some food. I drank there and ate some cakes...but...'

'No worries. Sit down here. Tell me about it. Hang on...'

Jayne rubs her forehead. 'I was called Peter,' she says.

'Peter?'

'I named myself. Antonio asked me what I was called. Jayne didn't seem appropriate. Not for a man.'

They laugh.

'Antonio? Tell me more, but wait. I'm going to record and film this conversation. But have some tea first. Take your time. You should be alert by now. Need to record what happened as soon as possible.'

'Can't we access the computer?'

'Verboten.'

'Who's going to know?'

Dan eyes the technology. 'You know.'

'Get the doc to override.'

'And disturb him on holiday? No. We'll handle this. First, I need to know what happened. But at least we know the suit worked.'

'It worked.'

The doctor went to his room. It was spacious and tastefully furnished. The room was air-conditioned, and there was a slight electrical hum. A contrapuntal hum came from a fridge which he quickly investigated. Cold beers were lined up inside with some bottles of spirits; some being better cold, others better taken out. Taking a beer he searched for a bottle opener. The beer was an African brand he hadn't heard of – Casablanca. Manipulating the opener he heard the beer inside hiss. He quickly emptied a bottle, despite its liveliness and then took a second. Moving over to the window he could see out across the countryside and down to the sea. In fact he had a suite, with a separate bedroom and ensuite bath and shower room. But he investigated cursorily as he gulped from the bottle. He wasn't a hardened drinker.

He was thinking about the trip and how things had suddenly changed which had, in fact, given him a feeling of optimism. He thought he'd miss his work already, less than a day in. But he was looking forward to getting outside and exploring. The change between there and England surprised him. The world had generally shrunk for most people.

As he is lost in his reverie he hears a knock at the door.

'Yes?' he calls. Then. 'Come in.'

'Doctor Abraham?'

'Yes.'

'Dinner will be served in the main restaurant at eight pm.'

'Thank you. What time is it now?' He pats his trouser pockets and shows the palms of his hands as if to say 'no phone'.

'You have time on the portable computer and you can use that to send messages, but it is monitored.' Jake looks around. 'Over there,' she points.

'Okay, thanks.'

'Is everything to your satisfaction?'

'Seems to be,' he says. 'I haven't really had time to check, but it seems to be great.'

The woman sees the two bottles on the table. She smiles. Her skin is dark olive. 'If there's anything else you need let me know.'

'Anything?' he says smiling.

'Anything,' she says firmly but smiling soon after.

'I'll bear that in mind,' he says.

She sees he hasn't touched the fruit arranged in a bowl on the table. 'They're serving snacks at the bar downstairs if you're hungry,' she says. 'Otherwise if you need me, just call reception,' she says. 'Through the portable.'

'I'll bear that in mind too. What's your name? If I ask for you I'll need a name.'

'I'm sorry,' she says. 'Nayra.'

'Nice name.'

'Gracias.'

Jake nods and bows slightly. Nayra leaves.

He presumed he had plenty of time to take a walk. But first he took a longer look at his suite. Perhaps all his hard work was beginning to pay off. Not that he could complain. And he never did, much. He'd never been regarded as particularly creative and yet that was what he now did: he both facilitated and co-wrote the near-dead's futures. Not near-dead. Immobilised-living. Not completely of this world, rather a world in tandem. He thought of Nayra and her soft, warm flesh, freezing.

Sitting down at a corner table next to the main window he fired up the portable. It was late afternoon already. He toyed with the idea of sending Portway a message, seeing if he could get through to Dan or Jayne. He wanted to speak with security too, but resisted. Getting up he took another bottle of beer and walked to the bedroom where there was an entertainment screen. Jumping on the bed, he ordered the screen on. Nothing happened. Old technology. But it was okay. Thought back to Hannah and the luxury he had promised her. Grabbing a box from one of the bedside tables he fired up the screen. Watched some animations, there was no 3D or hologram facility it seemed and finally decided to go for a walk.

Downstairs there were people at the bar and in the seating area outside the restaurant. He saw the professor and Milly but he slipped out the main entrance and took a gulp of warm air. He liked its warmth in fact, but it also felt like it was choking him. Without warmth there was no cold. He chuckled. The idea worked both ways. He felt pleased with himself. Wanted to ask for his phone at reception, all of their phones and devices having been handed in, for security apparently. But he'd made a quick exit. Needed to get away from all the people. He felt alone on that distant isle but unperturbed. He preferred his own company.

Wandering around the grounds, he noticed the rich foliage and trees. It was an oasis of colour even at that time of year. But beyond the grounds, he knew from his view from the window, that the land was rugged. Without a phone he had no real idea of the time. At the complex there were various objects projecting time and even some speaking it and each room would have had, like his, a portable computer. But time slipped away. He tried to remember what time his portable had said. But with a shrug of his shoulders he carried on.

There was a neat hedge that he thought was the boundary of the complex but beyond that there was neatly mown grass that suddenly stopped. From its bouncy surface he trod on hard earth and stone. The light was still full and invigorating but the sun was heading slowly towards the horizon. He strode out purposely, maybe he could find a path down to the beach and the sea. It was some place. A holiday complex turned into a rich man's playground. Even with some old technology. He smiled wryly.

'Hey,' comes a voice. Startled, he looks around. 'Be careful!' No one. He can't see anyone. 'Over here.' Following the sound of the voice he sees a figure coming from a copse of muscular trunked and branched trees.

'Vicky? Is it you?'

'Hello,' she says, approaching.

'I thought it was you… I mean I thought I'd seen you getting on the plane and off the coach. Wasn't sure. It's some surprise. Did you know I was out here?' he says looking around.

'I needed to get out of the hotel, or whatever it is. Needed some air.' Then she says, 'I saw you on the plane.' She breathes heavily.

'Are you on holiday too?'

She laughs. 'Working.'

'I see. Listen...about...'

'Don't say a word,' she says. 'In my line...well, in my particular line, I see a lot. But I'm not some common...'

'I didn't mean to imply anything. But it's so very strange seeing you here. It's nice seeing a face I recognise...'

'Even if she's a whore.'

'Upmarket...'

'Whore.'

'You offer a service,' he says weakly.

'Spare me the bullshit. I do what I'm told, when I'm told.'

He nods. 'I'm not even sure if you know my name. It's Jake. Oh dear, it's all so very impersonal. But not…'

'It's kind of weird knowing your name,' she says. 'Everything is deliberately impersonal. I was never told who you were. It works. Doesn't it?'

'It's an unusual name these days,' he replies. 'Maybe I like being impersonal,' he tags on.

'But here we are. It's kind of weird...not your name, I mean, well, meeting you here. Being here. Everything.'

'It's weird all right. But it's good being out of England. Out from the cold weather and the rain for once.' He eyes her carefully.

'I feel like I know you, or that I should know you,' she says, 'but I really don't. But you're the only person…'

'Did you follow me out here?' he interrupts. She nods. 'Thought as much. Are you here to…' She understands, nods again. He looks at her. She is as near perfect as a, well, whore could get. And it's why he chose her twice. The first time being luck, perhaps. It doesn't seem as if her spirit has been wiped out or crushed by her experiences. But she's also very young. Nineteen, twenty, maybe. He has been as intimate as any man could be with her and yet as distant too. Now it feels awkward. And exciting.

'You don't mind me being here?' she says softly.

He shakes his head. 'No, not at all, why would I mind a beautiful girl.'

She smiles. A genuine smile of a young woman.

'Listen, I know I kind of...' He wants to hold the past in a box and place it to one side.

She laughs. 'You think your needs are odd,' she says honestly, 'but let me tell you...'

'I'd rather not know.'

'I can't be seen with you,' she says. 'We're not meant to talk with the guests. Not unless they tell us to, when we're, you know.'

'I hope you're getting paid well at least?'

She laughs. 'Paid?'

'Of course.'

She laughs again. 'I'm told what to do. Told where to go. There's a man keeping an eye on us all.' They walk down to an area where they can view the sea. 'It's beautiful,' she says.

'It is.'

'Makes you want to live,' she says loudly.

'I hope you want to live.'

'Not always.'

'It's funny,' he says, 'I only seem to get honesty out of whor…' Checking himself, he says, 'Out of my clients before they get boxed.'

'Boxed?'

'Put in drawers for their future fields.'

'Oh,' she says. 'That's what you do.'

'You're disappointed.'

'Not at all, sounds interesting. But it's mostly government officials and top celebrities that come to these kinds of things.'

'I know my place.' He smiles, thinking back to his conversation with Milly.

'And me mine,' she says.

'Will you get given to one of these men?'

'I'll be lucky if it's one,' she says.

'What if I ask for you?'

'You don't get to ask.'

'I asked before.'

'You were lucky,' she laughs darkly.

'You weren't,' he says honestly.

'I'd like to go down to the sea,' she says, 'but I have to be back. We have to meet with, well someone who will tell us what we have to do tonight.'

'Tonight?'

'After everyone's eaten, and drink and drugs have been taken.'

'Like that eh?'

'They need to enjoy themselves.'

'And you?'

'We...'

'Okay, I understand. I don't mean to embarrass you. I feel quite embarrassed myself. It's as if my behaviour is out in this open air for all to see.'

'You have nothing to worry about,' she says.

He wants to ask her how she got into the work she was doing. But he has the decency not to pry. They remain looking at the view for many minutes. It feels more intimate than being in bed, with her lying naked next to him. And he bites his lip recalling how he treated her. In the open, in the daylight, she has become a human being again. He wants to take her hand.

'Jake,' she says, 'that's a nice name, I think.'

'Not weird?'

'Not too weird.' She pauses. Then says, 'Don't talk to me when we're back inside.'

'Okay,' he answers. Says no more. Maybe she didn't know it was the professor who had procured her for him. Maybe she didn't even know the professor.

She left him as quickly and as stealthily as she had arrived. He watched her disappear. Was she able to distance him from his actions? Should she do that? The doctor gets angry with himself. Being successful at a job was one thing but he felt unsuccessful when it came to life and love. He laughed. There he was fabricating future lives and he couldn't even get his own together. The perplexing thing for him was that his work entailed him building up rapport with his clients. He really needed to think about that, he'd taken it all for granted. But he had a skill he could, perhaps, switch over into his own life. He thought about Vicky. And he thought about Jim. He had a connection with Jim but he was using him. That was his main preoccupation – what he could get from him. He was using him as he had used Vicky.

Jake stood looking out to the horizon for some time. There was a warm breeze. It was only slightly less warm as the evening settled. He gave people hope and life. He did. He kept telling himself so as he turned and headed back to the complex. Looking at the trees he wondered again about Vicky. She must have trusted him to a degree, to approach him like she had. For her, wasn't he just some drugged-up man who wanted weird sex. Weird and cruel. It was what got him off. There were reasons, he knew that. Everyone had reasons. But that was no excuse.

Back at the main entrance there were people outside. He was beginning to distinguish faces, or looks, or the way they dressed. And he imagined they were beginning to distinguish him. He knew only the prof and Milly. He didn't know many people generally. Not personally. Smiling, he walked back in. He saw Nayra at reception and wanted to talk with her but she was busy. Had she noticed him? She didn't look up. People were starting to go into the restaurant. They'd cordoned off an area as the inside was vast. It might have seated a couple of hundred. They weren't much more than a couple of score.

As he hung back slightly he heard Milly call him from behind. He was glad she was there, another broken soul, like him. They walked over to their seating, gave their names and were shown over to a table. Immediately glasses were filled. Jake knocked back his drink and it was near instantly refilled by a waiter.

'Good wine,' he says.

Milly takes a sip. 'Yes.'

'Very good,' he says. 'Wasted on me though.' And he takes a couple of large gulps.

The atmosphere inside the restaurant was charged. This was in juxtaposition to post-wars Britain, England especially. Here they were, the variously successful, having fun while others in old towns and cities were starving. The doctor was mostly preoccupied with drinking and imagining Vicky's later fate. Perhaps he *was* a drinker. Milly was doing her best to be cheerful, it seemed. He looked about that part of the room and his eyes abruptly landed on a familiar face.

'Do you see him?' Jake says to Milly in an effort not to draw attention.

'Who?'

'That man there.'

'Oh yes,' she says.

'You know who he is?'

'Of course.'

'Ah, okay.'

'The professor introduced me to him.'

'He used to be on all the entertainment channels. Still very famous. But he has spoken out against the government recently hasn't he?'

'I don't know,' she says.

'Surprised he's here. Must be getting on a bit now too.'

'I think he's been very supportive of the government. Well recently...'

'I guess he wouldn't be successful if not.'

'Doctor!'

'Just having fun,' he says. 'It's not something I'm used to and I'm not always too subtle.'

'Don't worry,' she says.

'People are always telling me not to worry,' he replies.

The food arrives.

'I think it's going to be some night,' he says.

Milly looks directly at him and smiles.

Jayne settled down to tell Dan her story. He interjected and prompted at times but for the most part let her release her feelings and emotions: her experience.

After switching off the recording, temporarily filing their conversation, he turns to her and asks, 'What do you think the symbolism of the birth is?'

'Does it have to be symbolic?'

'Maybe not,' he says. 'Okay,' he thinks. 'Is the birth *real* in that reality? Has it been a natural outcome of events. Was it a natural or unnatural outcome of the design of that world?'

'I don't know. I'm not sure I know what you mean. What do *you* think?'

Dan is measured. 'Well, it's either a fiction or it's reality. If it's fiction then how does the baby develop? Does it get caught up in the various narratives of that world? Why were only women allowed at its birth? Who is Elena? Queen Elena. How is she connected to the baby?'

'Dan,' she begins, 'it's still all very close to me. I feel tired. Almost exhausted by the experience. You know. Because it was all new and yet familiar at the same time. These people live. Like us. And yet, as I said, I also got the feeling that I was creating this world as I observed it. Perhaps not with Antonio. He seemed within and without that world at the same time. So I don't know how much of me was affecting that place. Regarding the procession of women, that was odd. And odd that I couldn't join them as I was a 'man'. Maybe Elena is the creator of that world. Ruling her future-fields. Why not? Have you had folk that have had that kind of dream or expectation?'

'I need to think about that. Maybe I should go back over previous files. Let me sort out my notes and memories. Though I guess it's possible for someone to develop independently in their double F. Though to what extent can they still create and go on creating their own world? Perhaps it's boundless. Like space. If space *is* boundless.'

'I thought the basic world was set. But with randomness built into characters? The opportunity for movement. Who knows...'

'Yes, true. And how might that randomness pan out? Could the characters simply learn through observation. Could they become self-realised? Could they look into a mirror and know themselves inwardly and outwardly? We need to think about this. But going back to the baby.

Did someone, a couple, have sex in that world and their expectations and imagination create a pregnancy? I understand the main created characters can have an idea of their body. It would be odd if they couldn't see themselves naked. And the person whose future-fields they inhabit would have their own characteristics, enhanced or otherwise, from their previous life. But how detailed would that be? Maybe it's like in dreams where everything makes absolute sense and everything is possible.'

'I'm impressed,' she says. 'You've obviously been thinking deeply about this stuff Dan.'

'It's our duty isn't it? I mean we're casting them off into some great adventure and yet we don't really know where they're heading. Not just the mind of the person at rest but the characters they and we have created.'

'I guess,' she says. 'There *was* a feeling of them behaving like real characters. Characters behaving like characters,' she laughs. 'What else would they do? But that was only some of them. Others not so much. More like actors, the way they appeared at certain times and said the same phrase like: 'Have a lovely day.' But maybe that's just what people say there. Those two girls I told you about, they seemed very real.'

'This is why the professor is so keen on the avatars. And the doctor too. Imagine. And that's the key word. Imagine going into someone else's imagination.'

'I did. I did just that. I'm not so sure it feels right. Morally. Antonio knew I wasn't of that world. He knew more than he was letting on. That's what it felt like. But that would suggest a character can live and think freely. Be independent. Is that possible?'

'We can only observe. As in dreams, even lucid dreaming. We can look on. Don't we take dreams on-board, at face value. Dreaming has its own physics. Is there more to it? We've discussed DMT and other realms. For the moment it's early days. You're a pioneer Jayne, travelling into this new, unknown world,' he says.

'Or, as I said, a guinea pig.'

They laugh.

Dan carries on. 'Okay, let's say that someone can be born into a future-field.'

'I saw it.'

'You didn't see it, did you? You heard about it but you didn't witness it.'

'Because I was a man.'

'For whatever reason, it doesn't matter.'

'I guess...'

'Let's say it's all just a narrative playing out. You touched that narrative, like touching a live computer and information flew into you. You saw the spectacle unraveling. An observer and a player at the same time. But let's also just say that was all you did and needed to experience. We have to think about this aspect too. Your role. And in this case the baby itself doesn't exist.'

'Okay,' she says quietly.

'But let's also think about the baby being born in that world. If that *is* the case, then where has the baby come from?'

'From?'

'Meaning. How could two characters have sex and a baby be produced, as in our world? Produced. Created. Thought into being. Fictionalised into being! Where is the baby from?'

'Where is any baby from?' she asks. 'They just are. It's natural...It's not fiction. A baby is real.'

'But that is not a natural world is it, we can say that much.'

Jayne thinks. 'You've got me Dan. I don't really know where babies even come from in this world. I mean I understand the biology, but that's not the whole story. It's amazing. A miracle of life. Can't we apply that to all things that grow, their DNA manifesting in and through their growth.'

Dan nods his head. 'But there is no DNA in that world.'

'Who says?'

'There just isn't. These are characters in a fictitious world. Which we have brought into fruition.'

'We have DNA, the person at rest, resting, has DNA...'

'But the characters don't. Simple as that...'

'And yet they live,' Jayne says triumphantly.

'They live? Do they? I wonder.'

'I saw them Dan. I saw people. I saw a tangible world.'

'But an unstable world.'

'Yes to a degree. Okay. Antonio definitely lived. And I lived in that world too. Maybe they have fictional DNA.'

'Perhaps you should go back into that world, and see if you can get to see the baby.'

'As a man?'

'How long would it take to make a female avatar?'

'Well, let me think. I guess, I guess not so long,' she says. 'A matter of adjustment only. What makes us female or male in that world: information and drugs.'

'It seems crude,' Dan says.

'It's not crude *being* it,' she explains, 'because I *was* it. Like a hybrid though. There was a tension I could feel inside me. I wasn't at ease. But then it was only a brief time...We bring ourselves, our inner selves, into that world within the avatar. And that was what I experienced.'

'We'll create a female avatar. Do it on the side. Someone's going to want that experience. We'll be ahead of the game. Make some money.'

'We'll have to keep it a secret,' she says.

'Secrets. They're all around us. You know that. You've hinted as such. You've suggested as much.'

'Would we be as bad then?'

'No. Because what we're doing is valid exploration...'

'But can be used for what purposes? So rich people can enter the inner lives of others. Unknown to them. Spying on them. Replacing them?!'

'I don't know,' Dan says honestly.

'They'll kind of be in their heads won't they? As I was having the experience I was wondering if what I was seeing was coming out of the head and mind of the person at rest. I mean, it could have been. It was in a way. Does their double F have any tangible concrete existence?'

'You were there. You were in it,' Dan says. 'I tell you this feels really crazy at times. Double F is their mind-experience and yet there are characters within that that can seemingly, as we intended, operate independently. Plus, you've got into that world. It's mind-blowing.'

'Literally,' she responds. Thinks. 'And how long is the baby kept away from men? Who is the father? Was he there at the birth?'

'I don't know. But I do need a drink,' he says. 'I need to go out and get blitzed and hammered with the team.'

'It's just me and you Dan.'

He smiles. 'Yep. Me and you. And information. Information all around. People in computer maintained boxes, with all computers linked to all the people in huge boxes of drawers, linked to future-fields. And here we are. Living in this world. Which also might be in a giant box somewhere out there or in here. The whole thing might be a dream. Yes,' he sees Jayne's face respond, 'it's a cliché, I get it. But it could be. Look what we've done. We're part of all this craziness.'

'It's not as crazy as being an avatar in that world,' Jayne states. 'Imagine, I'm carrying my mind in the body of a man, fused to an extent with the professor, in a world created by us and whoever the experience, the double F belongs to. That's pretty mind-blowing.'

'I wonder if they have drugs in that world,' he jokes. 'I'm getting a drink anyway,' he says. 'You want one?'

'Sure,' she says.

He leaves the room briefly but soon returns with a bottle and glasses, pours a shot in each and hands her a glass. Knocking back the other himself, he has the bottle ready to recharge.

'In that brief moment you were away,' Jayne begins, 'I was thinking about the baby. If it's real, in some way, then what will be its ideas about the world it grows up in. I presume it will never know anything else. Will it be the only one? From what Antonio says, then not. If two babies grow up and have a baby themselves, then think of the abstraction that next baby would be in. Is that okay? Is that fine or a fucking nightmare?' she asks with a sudden raised voice.

Dan knocks back another shot and fills Jayne's glass. 'I don't know. Maybe we're in that kind of world now. Experience within experience, like an infinity of Russian dolls. Never getting to the core.'

'But we can die,' she says calmly.

'Maybe. Maybe we don't. Not in a real sense. Just one doll further in.'

'What about those characters we've created?' she asks. 'Will they die. Will they all live on forever. Or will they die when their host brain, mind, dies. Will that death snuff out all the created generations? A year in our time could be a thousand-fold there.'

Dan takes yet another shot, knocks it straight back. 'I hope they don't feel too much pain,' he says. He straightens himself. 'You know none of it's real,' he says, 'none of it. They're just characters in a movie. The movie ends and the characters are gone.'

'But the actor lives on,' Jayne says.

'Okay, they're characters in a book. Have you ever read a book?'

'Yes,' she says laughing.

'I don't mean an instant ebook. Or direct injected. I mean have you ever held a real book and flicked its pages, felt its weight?'

Jayne shakes her head. 'I've seen some. There are still books about, I know.'

'You have characters in books, you know that. What happens to them? They were created. They live in us but when we shut the book, at the end, or close the device, what happens to them then? Dead? Non-existent? Potential? The same life lived over and over again?' He smiles. 'It could be any of these.'

'You're too sentimental Dan. You get like this when you drink. The characters aren't real.'

'Drink? I haven't started yet. Antonio's not real? You think about that.'

'I'm tired,' she says. 'Don't forget we have Jim coming in for a few days, maybe over this weekend. Or is it Monday?'

'Monday, I think. I'll check,' he says. 'But for the moment there's just you and me Jayne in the whole wide, small, infinitesimal world. And we're the bosses of Portway. For a whole week!' he shouts out.

Jayne smiles, 'I'll drink to that.'

By the time they had eaten the four courses Jake felt quite tipsy, not yet drunk despite the alcohol he had consumed. Milly had begun to come out of herself. But that was only the prelude to the evening. The formal introduction. Now they were about to play.

Everyone was rounded up, no excuses tolerated and guided to another large room. There was music playing and the room had a series of alcoves in dimmed light with subdued light generally. He was shown to a table where he was asked his drink or drug of choice. Jake wasn't a party animal and he wanted to keep his head and mind reasonably intact. Milly was somewhere else and so was the professor, but it was hard to see and the music was loud and pounding. He ordered a drink to pacify the waitress. She was young and nervous.

Jake decided to wander around the room with its flashing lights and pulsing bass. It was then he caught sight of Vicky, or at least he thought it might be her. Following her he passed one of the alcoves he had noticed on entering. It was even darker inside and he could see a girl with what seemed like a couple of men. Carrying on he reached the back of the room. There was no-one there but there was a door. Instinctively he pushed it open and found himself in a lounge area. He heard some noises which he presumed came from within the room of a further door. There was a glass door to his left that opened into a conservatory. Tentatively he approached the door opposite. It was as if he was drawn like metal to a magnet. Listening at the door he could hear the muffled sound of a female, Vicky maybe, and a man shouting. Jake looked around but no-one was about, though he felt vulnerable where he was. A minute or two passed as long as an hour or two and then he heard a sound like something hitting a soft chair. But he also heard muffled cries. This was not his business and he turned to go – but as he did so a voice cried out clearly. Maybe it was the drink giving him courage but he quickly knocked the door and pushed it open almost simultaneously

A girl, with her face away from him, has been tied up and is hanging from a hook in the ceiling. She has been partly stripped and there are whip marks across her back.

'What the fuck,' comes a voice. 'Who the fuck are you?'

Jake initially feels embarrassed but as he stands quite still the girl manages to turn slightly, enough for him to see it is Vicky. They've acted fast, he can only have been five or so minutes behind her. Without thinking Jake goes to her and pulls the gagging cloth completely from her mouth. 'Are you okay?'

The man, who still clutches the whip repeats, 'Who the fuck are you?'

At the same time the man says this, two other men come from behind a curtain.

'Who the fuck are you?' the man with the whip shouts.

Vicky calls out, 'Jake.'

The two men look at Jake and they also chorus, 'Who the fuck are you?'

Jake ignores them, goes close to Vicky and reaches up to release her from the dangling rope. Her arms are stretchered upwards. The man with the whip watches as the two men who have appeared magically barge past him and exit the room. He moves towards Jake, holding the whip menacingly.

'Touch me and you'll be history,' Jake says. 'I deal with dead people,' he half-lies. The man falters. Vicky collapses into Jake's arms.

'Are you okay?' She smiles at him wanly. To the man, Jake says, 'Fuck off, before I break your nose. I'm trained for that.'

The man turns but before he does he mouths 'bitch' in Vicky's direction. Then, 'That was just the beginning...'

Jake rushes at him and the man quickly opens the door. Jake grabs his jacket but the man throws him off and is gone.

With her hands in front of her, Vicky twists her wrists and her fingers begin untying herself. Once free she tries to zip up her dress. Jake goes to her, 'Let me help.' He fumbles with the zip, gradually and carefully pulling it up. 'I can have a look at your back later,' he says, 'but I need to get you out of here.'

'I'm not sure...'

'Not sure? Of what?'

'I was meant to...'

'Forget that scum,' Jake spits. He holds her and goes to kiss her as the door bangs open. The professor is there and at least one of the men who had been hiding in the room.

'Jake, what on earth are you doing?'

Jake is perplexed. 'I...I...'

'This is none of your business.' The professor turns and says something to the man who entered with him. To Vicky, the professor says, 'Get out.'

'It was nothing to do with me,' she pleads.

The professor looks at Jake. 'Sit down, now!'

Jake is bewildered. Watches Vicky leave, he wants to call out to her but feels impotent.

The professor whispers into the ear of the man accompanying him. The man eyes Jake coldly. He says something to the professor, who pats his shoulder. The man goes to leave but is stopped. The professor makes a quick call, all the while keeping Jake pinned to his seat with an icy stare. With a nod from the professor, the man goes over to the curtains where a camera and stand is revealed.

'You've truly fucked up here Jake.'

'Me?'

'You!'

'How have I fucked up?'

'She's bought and sold and given out, like she was given to you. Remember? Did you have such sensitive foibles then?'

'I didn't harm her.'

'Treated her like your mum did you Jake, because that's not what I heard.'

'Heard? From who?'

'From the horse's or bitch's mouth, should I say. Indirectly of course. These girls are trained Jake. They do just fine without white knights...'

'Being whipped is fine?'

'It goes on. If it's what the customer, or guest, wants. I just hope that little bit of film we've got will do the trick. This is old-school hi-tech Jake. It's real. None of your AI stuff. But you had to come sniffing around.'

'Look, I have no idea what this film stuff is. I can tell you she wasn't consenting to being whipped...'

'How do you know?'

'I heard her.'

'Yes you heard her, she's trained. Trained to please. She knew they were filming. Everyone knew except you and the...' The prof stops. He says to the man packing the camera's tripod away. 'Why wasn't the room locked?'

'I thought it was. Besides, never had anyone barge in before.' He looks at Jake.

'Get it packed and out of here. I'm hoping we can treat our guest,' he looks at Jake, 'a little more hospitably. Stay ready for a call.' The man nods. Leaves the professor with Jake all alone in the room.

The professor checks the door and locks it. 'Old fashioned,' he says and pockets the key. Walking over to the chair with Jake seated, he shakes his head. Then he opens the curtains to reveal a further room.

'Do you know who it was?'

'Who?'

'The man entertaining your girlfriend, Jake.'

'She's not my girlfriend.'

'He's a big, big businessman. He's a big funder of the National Party, hence the National Government. We need to keep him on-board.'

'We?'

'The National Government. Needs funding.'

'You're part of the government?'

'Associated.'

'Hughes-Kahn?'

'A good friend Jake. A very good friend. Now the thing is, I need to smooth this over. Make him happy again. And I need to know you're with us Jake. Need to know where your loyalties lie. You know how keen I am on loyalty...'

Jake looks at him. The professor's eyes are cold.

'What's going to happen to her?'

'She's trained, programmed.'

Jake says, 'I see...'

'I don't want to have to do anything I don't need to do, all because of a whore, Jake. You understand?'

Jake nods his head. His mind working intensely.

'You know Jake, I invited you here to sound you out. Not got off to a good start have we? And what with that breach of security at Portway...'

'There was no breach,' Jake says, lifting his posture.

'Glad to hear it. Wait. Let's get ourselves another drink or two.'

The professor disappears through the curtain and then reappears with two bottles of beer and an opener. 'This is the proper stuff,' he says and hands Jake a bottle, flicking its cap on the floor. 'Go on, take it.'

Jake takes the bottle and takes a swig. 'Thanks. Listen,' he begins.

'No you listen,' the professor says sharply. Then softens. Takes a drink from his bottle. 'You have no idea about this girl Jake. In a way, you're an innocent. Maybe I've kept you innocent,' he says. 'You're like a younger brother to me Jake. Never had any brothers, just three sisters – one died at sea. Fighting for our freedom.'

'I'm sorry.'

'Spare me, please.'

Jake thinks about his words and attitude to Vicky. Nods.

'Vicky's a good looking girl. I can see that,' he says. 'Not my type. But I can see it. She's a butterfly girl, Jake. You know what that is?'

'I've heard...'

'You don't. You don't. I've kept you innocent. That's good,' he smiles. 'So now I'll have to rob you of that innocence. Open your eyes Jake, if you're going to keep working for me. You understand? Accidents happen in these kinds of places. I wouldn't want that. You understand?' Jake looks at him and then down to the floor. 'You've got a lot to live for Jake. Well respected. Portway is yours. Yes, yes, effectively yours, I let you get on with things. Imagine ruining all that for a whore. What a waste...Now what was I saying. Ah, yes, a butterfly girl. As I said, she's trained and programmed.' The professor takes another gulp of beer and Jake mirrors him. The professor grabs an armchair and pushes it close to where Jake is sitting. He talks softly. 'There are girls who want to end their life. Can you imagine? Pretty young girls with everything to live for. But. Well it could be for any number of reasons. Pretty young girls who have come to the end of their line, they think. Or get caught like so many others in a bureaucratic death hold. You think I'm exaggerating for effect?' The professor eyes Jake sternly.

'I'm listening,' Jake says.

'What's my name Jake?'

'Your name?'

'Yes, what's my name, tell me...'

'Alistair,' Jake says sheepishly. 'And known as the professor.'

'The professor in what? Do you know?'

Jake shakes his head. Alistair, now familiar again with his protégé, leans into him. 'Vicky was about to be euthanised. The centre where she'd walked into was known to us and dealt with by Milly. They recognised something in her, yes, of course, her youth and looks but they knew she was intelligent too. The best are. Her depression had led her into the darkest maze. Not a maze, a labyrinth.' Alistair says, then halts. Looks directly into Jake's eyes. 'They had the wherewithal to contact us, send us details. But when Vicky climbed into the pod, as far as she was concerned that was her reclining within a mummified chrysalis. A spaceship coffin, zooming her into...into where?'

Jake shakes his head. But is mesmerised by the professor.

'She wasn't killed. Evidently. She had a different kind of fate awaiting her. Programmed, trained, sucked-in to our requirements. Controlled. But not robotic. She's lost none of her mind. Perhaps it would have been better if she had. But we can say a word, flash an image and she's at our beck and call. We are her saviours. Now she is alive she understands the beauty of life again. In exchange for this new life and apparent freedom she accepts she must obey unconditionally...' Alistair notices Jake's flinch. 'You think this is bad Jake. But you know some of the things that have been happening at Portway. You're implicit. If anything should get out, you'd be thrown under the bus and there would be nothing I could do for you. You're at the heart of the deceit Jake. Soon to be plucking organs from the old and the young alike, those not as lucky as Vicky. Or those that resisted. Thus. Let's put this to bed. Drink, get stoned. I'll find you a girl if you want.' Jake shakes his head. 'You might feel differently later. But leave Vicky to do what she must do. If we can trust you, both she and you can carry on as if nothing has ever happened. I'm already sorting out our business friend. Maybe you can lie low a little Jake. I'd have you sent back but that would send alarm bells. Hughes-Kahn would get to hear everything. But I can control the narrative; always have done and always will. What do you say?'

Jake looks up. What can he say?

'Keep your nose clean and carry on the good work at Portway when you return. But I will be watching you Jake. Like an older brother. You understand?'

Jake nods.

'You understand?'

'Yes.'

'Yes...'

'Yes Alistair.'

'Good man. Now finish off the beer and clear out of this room. I have important work to do. Security work. Grab some drink or drugs and have an *early* night. Maybe. Things will go on all night here.'

Jake nods again. Takes a bottle of beer and knocks what's left back.

'Life could be so very simple. So very simple if people just did what they're meant to do. Concentrate on what's in front of them. Keep on the straight and narrow.' Alistair goes to the door, unlocks it and shows Jake the way out. As Jake passes him, he says, 'Don't think too much. Thinking too much gets men into trouble.'

Jake walks into the lounge area. Turns to see the door closing. His first instinct is to find Vicky and get her out. But how? Where to? His second instinct is to keep his mouth shut. Not ruin his life like his father had ruined his. He was something. Head of Portway. The professor was right, he was already implicated. Deciding to go into the conservatory he slid open its glass door and then carefully shut it. Sitting down on a hard, flower-patterned settee, he was able to gaze out at the night sky. He recalled the moment he compromised his integrity. The professor had brought him into his confidence, deliberately. It had been a trap. But he'd felt good and important. He could have done something way back then and spoken out. But he'd turned a blind eye. And now he was about to take a further leap. The operating suite was nearly ready. And he presumed it would be his hands that...that. They were dead. Dead, or as near enough. You couldn't take organs with them dead, not if you were to save others' lives. Prolong. Save. What did it matter? He didn't know what would happen to the organs anyway. And he could still walk away from it all now. But what for? A whore? He had no real feelings for her. She was a means to his own ends. That was all.

Looking at the night sky he saw what he thought a meteor flash dissolve into the emptiness. Make a wish Jake. What could he wish for? A clear conscience. He wished for that, at least in part. Absolved, he got up and thought about punching the businessman. He laughed. Leaving the conservatory, he looked around. There was no-one about. Clutching the handle of the door to the darkly lit room, he took a gulp of air. None of this was his fault, he reasoned and yanked the door open. The flashing lights and the pounding bass had not missed a beat. Walking in he closed the door behind him. The darkness and noise enveloping his senses. Quickly he made a timid effort to see if Vicky was seated anywhere or in one of the alcoves. But he moved swiftly to the door they had entered by. From that he entered a deserted restaurant with tables already cleared and emptied. Already he was leaving what happened behind.

At the reception it was like an entrance to a haunted house. Jake imagined it more unnerving than walking around The Chest. He was deliberating whether to go outside and maybe walk down to the beach or go to his room and finish off as much alcohol as he could. But a voice called to him. Nayra. Maybe the evening had yet another twist. Could he be that callous? He answered her.

Jim presented himself at Portway on Monday morning. He got there deliberately late. Milly wasn't at reception. He knew the doctor wasn't there. A very young woman instructed him to wait and directed him into a familiar room. Once again he felt confronted by himself. A flurry of thoughts came, vying for prominence. His life was contained in his thoughts. Yes, and he wore their effects on his face and throughout his body, across the whole of his skin. But his face told much of his story. At least he didn't have to look at himself, as others had to. He smiled. He'd been trying to remember a childhood friend while on his way into the city. He knew he knew their name but couldn't summon it. A few stops before Portway he let it go and looked out of the window at the city – how things seemed to have changed. On getting off the transport and stepping onto the slabbed pavement the name suddenly sprang into his mind.

In the waiting room with its dead air he thought about his memory, where his past, his life was stored. If he knew something, and knew he knew something but couldn't retrieve it consciously – what, or who, had presented it to him? He had not conjured the name – the name had come to him. Who, or what, was doing that? His subconscious? Working away behind the scenes tirelessly and, for the most part, unrecognised. Or was it some other part of him, a hidden part. Another entity inhabiting his mind, doing all the clerical work. Taking over when he, yes he, could not remember or recall.

The fact was his life was there inside his head. Yes, people might say, but your life is in your children or in the good and bad works you have done. But he, he himself, was in his thoughts. His thoughts seemed to be in his head but maybe they weren't. Maybe he only perceived them in that way. As he thought about this he also had to distinguish thoughts as memory and thoughts that seemed to arrive unbidden. Thoughts as memory carried his life. How accurate were they? And when he remembered things he didn't inhabit his younger self - but rather observed himself. As if he were objectively looking on. Contrary to these thoughts were the ones that came unbidden. Where did they spring from? Was it again his subconscious mind? Was he receiving thoughts from somewhere else? And, if so, who, or what, was sending them?

People used to say that you only died when the last person who knew you - and had thoughts about you - died too. But was that even true? What if you were a great artist, or writer, or musician. Do you, would you, could you, live on in your works. Thinking about this he sensed that an idea of the person could live on certainly, but not the person themselves. The only people contained in a novel, say, were the characters, not the author. Though the author could hide among them. Like a youth hiding among trees. Again he thought, *consciously* thought: then where do his thoughts come from? Was he just a character in someone else's life, being fed *their* thoughts and ideas? He smiled. Perhaps humans had been created as puppets but had then gone on to find their own voice, their own mind, their own thoughts and reality. Living alongside and having to make sense of the thoughts being delivered to them by higher minds.

'Mr Holden?'

'I think so.'

'Mr Holden?' the young woman asks again, unsure of herself.

'Yes,' he smiles. Watches her relax.

'Please follow me,' she says.

They walk down the corridor. This is now a building which has become familiar to him. As with anything in life, he has incorporated it into his life's narrative. It is here and in the past simultaneously.

'Do you ever wonder if anyone else is thinking your thoughts for you?' he asks the young woman. She looks at him with a certain disdain. Does not answer. 'I'm sorry,' he says, 'I've been thinking about such things.' She quickens her pace. As they walk and pass through doorways, he feels a great gulf between them, their sex, their age, their thoughts. Eventually they arrive at one of the creation rooms, in fact the usual one. The younger woman notifies their arrival.

Opening the door, she says, 'Here you are Mr Holden.' The look she gives him makes him smile. He nods sagely but with humour.

Inside Jayne and Dan are waiting.

'Jim, good to see you.'

Jim picks up on some kind of vibration between the two. 'Everything okay?'

'Of course Jim,' Jayne smiles. 'Let's get down to business.'

'Are you ready Jim?' He nods. This time they wire him to a computer and administer some Portway-approved drugs: Heaven's Sugar.

'Who would have thought,' Jim smiles.

'Count backwards Jim,' Dan says. 'From twenty.'

'We're hoping you're going to meet Anna,' Jayne says.

As he counts down Jayne is reminded of her recent experience.

Jim found himself in a bed in a musty smelling room, seemingly in the cottage he had 'visited' previously. The air was quiet. Feeling immediately awake, presuming he had slept, but not sure, he got out of the bed. He was fully clothed. 'I know this isn't a dream. I know there's something before this. I know.'

He went down the stairs, everything feeling familiar. In fact he felt as if he were 'home'. But he had a nagging doubt. It was as if his memory had been blocked. If it was a dream, then it had its own rules, its own reality. And yet, the nagging feeling he had, pertained to a dream. Perhaps. There was a sense of incompleteness in his being. It unnerved him somewhat. But there he was in the lobby of his cottage. Yes his cottage. He could smell smells that took him back. Took him to a childhood. His childhood. Yet something wasn't wholly right. Had he been drinking the previous night.

The kitchen was as he expected. Well, it was his kitchen. Why would he question the reality of his own kitchen. Laughing out loud, he put a kettle on the stove. The stove was hot and he could smell wood burning. He checked. What was going on? Maybe that was why he was dressed. He'd got up and dressed and got the stove going and then gone back to bed. That was it. That made sense. Rain tapped the window in front of the sink. He thought the window was crying. The tapping became louder as the rain lashed down. He was not mad. Just disorientated. The rain was familiar, brought back other thoughts, regular, to be relied upon thoughts. Then the kitchen door opened.

'Jim.'

He knows it isn't Rosie. Rosie. He recalls Rosie. First her name then the memories accompanying it. He turns and smiles. She is familiar enough with him to open his kitchen door without knocking.

'I got caught in the rain. I'm drenched.'

Jim was slightly flustered. 'Come in and get warm and dry by the stove,' he says.

'Where have you been?' she says.

Jim says, 'Here.'

'Yes I know, but what have you been doing?'

'Just sleeping,' he says.

'Jim. There's a lot to do.'

'Is there?'

'Yes, you know there is. Are you okay?'

'Sure,' he lies, intrigued. She's somewhat familiar.

'Warm me up,' she says, throwing her arms open.

Is it a dream? He goes to her and they embrace. She's wearing a perfume he recognises. She lifts herself and kisses him. 'Is it one of your strange days?' she asks.

'I think so.' He looks at her. He has the briefest sensation of another life behind this one. It's as if another life drained from him while he was asleep. Fully dressed in his bed. 'Do you want some tea?'

'That would be great.'

Filling a kettle, he watches her take off her outer garments. He has a jumper on that is now slightly wet. He notices her figure. All the while he tries to make sense of...of what? He tries to make sense of something he's not even aware of.

'Did you get the shopping?' she asks.

'I...'

'Jim,' she admonishes lightly. 'R and R are coming tonight, you haven't forgotten?'

'No,' he says. He thinks quickly. R for. Ah, okay, Rosie. Can he risk saying her name and getting it wrong? 'Rosie.'

'And your best friend,' she laughs. Images tumble back into his mind. 'Ronnie,' he says, almost triumphantly. 'Which means...?'

'Which means, you need to get the wine in at least. I got some shopping earlier. Didn't I call you?' she teases.

'I...I don't remember,' he says honestly.

'The rain's thrown me off track. I was out on the old lane, going to pick some fresh cress. Then the heaven's opened. I'd left the stove burning but thought you were out. Shopping!' she laughs. 'I needed to get the seedlings covered too; we'll have carrots, onions, leeks later...'

Jim thinks. Some of his thoughts being quite confusing. But thinking again of Rosie and Ronnie he smiles and nods to himself.

'You okay?' she asks.

'I'm fine Anna,' he says. He watches her. No reaction. He is right. It's Anna. *We're hoping you'll meet Anna* comes into his mind. 'My oh my,' he says.

'Jim, you're acting even stranger than usual.'

'Sorry, Anna. Let me look at you.'

'Jim,' she smiles.

'Beautiful.'

'What is wrong with you?'

'Just speaking my mind. A man needs to speak his mind on occasion.'

She gets close to him and they kiss. Naturally. As they part, Anna goes back to the woodburner and takes off the kettle that is rattling steam. 'Time for tea,' she says.

'I'm sorry Anna. I'll be back in a moment.'

'Where are you going?'

'Nature calling.'

Quickly he goes from the kitchen to the hallway and then climbs the stairs, which squeak at every footfall. At the landing he goes to the room he was in. Was this their bedroom? He looks in the other room. *That* was their bedroom, it was messy and with a heavy female presence, coming to life as his eyes scanned as much as possible. Trying to take in as much detail as he could, he then shut the door and quickly examined the rest of the upstairs.

What are you doing Jim?

'Who said that?' No answer. There is a bathroom and a small, third bedroom. The air is still, although raindrops can be heard outside. Anna. Who is she? Ronnie is his best friend. Yes, he thought Ronnie was dead but he isn't. No. He is with Rosie. His memory seems to be working again. And Anna is his...

The rain's stopped and the afternoon sun's coming out.

'Anna? Is that you?' Anna. The name's familiar. Is she his wife? The name feels...

Rushing down the stairs, he nearly falls.

'The sun's out,' Anna says, with a wide smile.

'Ah, it was you. Were you upstairs?'

'No,' she says.

'Oh, okay. I thought...'

'What?'

'I heard, I thought I heard a voice. Quiet. A quiet voice.'

'Wasn't me then,' she laughs. 'You could go out and get the wine. Maybe some cider for me and Rosie.'

'Cider with Rosie,' he jokes.

Anna looks blankly at him. 'Yes, I guess so,' she says tentatively.

'Should I walk or take the car?' he says. Have they got a car, his words just came out.

'Jim you joker. Or did you get lazy while I was away?'

'You know me,' he says.

'I do.'

'Okay, I'll go.' He hopes she'll give him clues. Stopping he says, 'There isn't a ghost in the cottage is there?'

'Lots,' she laughs.

Jim laughs too. Goes to the open doorway leading from the kitchen to the hallway.

'Jim?'

'Yes.'

'Have you got any money?'

He pats his pockets. 'No. Is there a card?'

'A card? Take cash.'

'Yes, of course,' he says. Cash?'

Anna looks at him curiously. 'There's a wallet in my coat hanging by the door. Get some ciggies too maybe, you and Ronnie, well Ronnie, will want to smoke later,' she laughs. 'He always forgets ciggies. Get some papers too.'

'Which ones?'

'Rizlas.'

'That's a paper? Oh, I see. Sure.' Part of him knows what she means but it is as if another part of his mind is feeding him information. He goes to a heavy coat. Too small for him. Checks the inside pockets and finds a wallet. Something isn't right. He shakes his head. Takes out some paper money.

'See you in a bit,' she calls out.

Opening the front door he recognises the path leading down to a gate. Walking down the path he then opens the gate. He has the idea of horses. Yes. It comes back to him. A sunny day. And now the sun is out but he can see dark, dramatic clouds in the distance. The air feels fresh with the rain slowly evaporating. Deciding to go right, slightly uphill, he walks briskly. He has no real idea where he is. Passing a pub on his right he notices a milk churn in its entrance. It's as if his mind is in a fog. Does he buy the wine there, it's close, or carry on and find a shop.

Deciding to carry on he meets a man sitting on a bench, smoking a pipe.

'Good afternoon,' the man says.

Jim mirrors his salutation. Then asks, 'Is there a shop close by?'

'There might be,' the man says.

'Is that a yes or a no?' Jim asks as politely as possible.

'If you think there'll be one then there'll be one,' the man smiles.

'I'm not sure it works quite like that...'

'But it does,' the man interjects.

Jim stares at him. Smiles. 'In which case, there will be one.' And walks on.

The man says goodbye and Jim raises his arm in recognition. A little farther on and there's a few houses huddled together and a shop nestling close-by. A shop and post office combined. Jim walks in.

'Jim,' beams the shopkeeper and possibly the Postmistress.

'Hello,' Jim says. He mooches around the shelves, aware the woman is watching him.

'Can I help?' she asks.

'Have you got any wine?'

'Yes down here, in the off-license area, where it usually is,' she smiles. 'I have to be watchful when children, well youths come in...'

'They try and...'

She nods. 'Always,' she says.

'I guess that's typical generally, but round here?'

'You'd be surprised.'

'I need some rolling papers too,' he says, bending down to examine the few bottles there were.

'I see,' she says.

'Healthier to roll your own,' he says.

Dan looks at Jayne. He should have been coming out of his experience by now. 'How much of the drugs did you give him?'

'The right amount,' she protests.

'Hang about,' Dan says. 'Shit!'

'What is it?"

'Look here. The computer's been adding information and disturbing the drug ratio.'

'What?! Can it do that?'

'Only if someone's been playing around with it. The team's probably sabotaging us. For fun.'

'Might not be fun for Jim.'

'I don't know.'

'Get a clean-up going, quick. Bring him down and override the bloody thing,' Jayne orders.

Dan begins typing in information. 'Try and contact him.'

'I can't with you there.'

'Use the back up and hack in.'

Jayne nods and sets to work.

As Jim and the lady talk the doorbell rings and a few youths enter the shop. Jim is reminded of something, but he's not sure. One of them comes over and stares at the two of them while the others go to different parts of the shop.

'Can I help you?' the woman asks.

'Yeah, we need some beer,' he says.

'I'm afraid you're underage.'

'It's for my dad.'

'I'm sorry I can't...'

As the woman says this, Jim notices another young man creeping into the post-office section. 'Hey,' Jim shouts.

The boy in front of them shouts, 'Fuck off!' Grabbing some beer, he barges into the woman. The girls with them have raided the cigarette packets behind the counter and are already out of the door. Jim pushes the boy with the beer back and then chases the boy from the post office section. Knocking over some cans from the shelves the boy shoots down the small space between the main shelves. Turning quickly the boy spits at him. Jim grabs his jacket but the boy yanks himself free.

'Come on,' the boy calls to the other. There's a car outside and the girls clamber in. Lights come on from the car. The sun has been covered by a deep black cloud carried in by a wind that has picked up.

While Jim loses the boy, the other boy with the beer wrestles free from the woman who is trying to hold him back.

'I know you,' she says.

'Do you fuck.'

Jim comes down the aisle breathing heavily. The boy tries to weave past him. Instinctively Jim belts him with a heavy punch. The boy kicks Jim on the leg and stamps on his foot. Jim looks at him, 'I know you,' he says. 'I know you.'

The boy kicks him again and then is out of the shop, the bell ringing in alarm. The car drives off. 'Call the police,' Jim says.

'The police?”

'Yes hurry.'

'There are no police,' she says.

Jim looks at her and then the shop seems to shudder with a heavy roll of thunder.

'What's going on?' the woman says.

Jim still can't comprehend 'no police'. Rushing to the door he opens it and the weather blasts down upon and around him. Lightning forks down and thunder follows almost immediately.

The woman remains inside. 'They've taken money,' she cries out.

Jim stands in the wind and rain and feels a surge of electricity animate his body. His heart feels in terrifying pain, his skin tingling...His face and hair are soaked as is his whole body. Collapsing on his knees, he falls to the ground.

'Got to get him back,' Dan says. 'I've got control. Man, when I see the team, I'm going to go crazy.'

Jayne goes over to Jim. 'Can I disconnect?'

Dan nods. Jayne begins the process.

'Is he okay?' Dan asks.

'I think so.'

'They're fucking crazy doing this,' Dan says.

'Jim, are you okay?'

Jim turns his head and vomits.

'They can clean that shit up too,' Dan says.

Jayne helps Jim sit up and puts his head down. 'You okay Jim?'

He looks at her. 'I knew him,' he says.

'Knew him? Who Jim?'

But before he can answer he throws up again.

'I need to piece all of this together,' Jim says. 'And I need your help.'

Dan and Jayne have made him comfortable. They look at each other meaningfully.

Jim continues, 'I'm never sure which world I'm in. It's like dreaming. When I'm in a dream *that* feels real, its physics are normal, even if I can fly. But we discuss and see this world I go into beforehand. Yet when I'm in it, it's something, well, still like a fog. And at the end, what the heck happened?'

'It was our fault,' Jayne says, taking on the responsibility. Dan looks at her.

'Explain,' Jim says, still confused and unnerved by his last experience. 'I feel like I should be soaked through, but my face and hair are dry. That's it,' he says. 'I mean I can remember some of what I've been through. I remember getting soaked. But when I go back there it will be lost, or nearly lost. Why?'

'Firstly,' Dan says, 'there was a problem with the drug dosage. Human, not technical error, I'm afraid.'

'Who made the error, and how?'

Jayne weighs in, 'We think one of the team had coded in some wrong information. It's already been fixed and won't happen again.'

'Do you think that's why I remember what happened at the end?'

'Maybe not just that,' Dan says.

'Go on.'

'It might be that as you were affected by the drug imbalance you reflected outwards into that world. In effect, you created what happened...'

'Possibly,' Jayne inserts.

'So it's my fault?'

'Of course not,' Dan says, 'at least not directly. You were the conduit and could do nothing about what was passing through you.'

'But I messed up my world, my tranquility.'

'We don't know. We can only find that out when you go back.'

'If,' he says.

'It's your world Jim,' Jayne says.

'It didn't feel like it.'

Dan says, 'It might be that what happened then has become, or is, a different world. Let me think. When you go back you might be in the shop, you might not yet have gone there. You might not even be where you were. But you *have* met Anna. Perhaps the raid on the shop happened in a different version of your world.'

'Which I created?'

'Yes, the shop incident was created through the drug imbalance, as I said. But it's not really you...well, partly you. But that experience doesn't belong in your world.'

'If it has disappeared, where has it disappeared to? Did it actually exist? If it did exist in that world when did that world, my world, stop existing and where did my world go? Are there two worlds existing simultaneously – over-lapping each other, or in tandem?'

Jayne and Dan look at each other.

'We're hoping that for the template, what you and we have created thus far, for the characters, especially the lady in the shop...that this was an aberration that hasn't been recorded. Just in your own personal perception,' Dan adds.

'But isn't that whole world my personal perception?' Jim asks.

'Not entirely,' Jayne says.

'We think there's an element of Future-Fields that is independent of you, us, the drugs...maybe,' Dan says.

'It would make sense,' Jayne adds.

'Would it? How?'

Jayne looks at Dan. Dan says, 'Because that's the nature of our life, isn't it? People argue that we create as we observe, others argue that that might be the case but there is also a tangible world existing independently of us and our consciousness. Others argue that we simply experience everything that is there, completely independent of ourselves, our inner being. We simply respond to this outside world.'

'And others think everything is inside,' Jayne says. 'Independent of us or otherwise.'

'How can something inside of us be independent of us?' Jim asks.

'We're finding this out, gradually,' Jayne says.

'Let me get this straight,' Jim begins, 'this world here, now, could affect the world of my future-fields?' They nod. 'But also in this created world, there might be a sense of it being independent of my, our, input.' They nod again. 'But *this* world's also created, at least in some form,' he says.

'We have created everything around us,' Jayne says.

'But we didn't create the world. We didn't create nature. Did we create ourselves? Are we just a product of different humanoids mixing and mating? You know, Neanderthals and Denisovans. Early humans across the globe becoming who we are. In all our different forms.'

'I don't know,' says Dan. 'But we all have the same mind, the same experience.'

'How do you know?'

'Because we're human.'

'Sure but we're different and complex and we don't even know what happens in another person's mind. Do we? Don't some people think that only *they* exist?'

Jayne and Dan look at each other.

Jim continues, 'Perhaps you two know each other's mind.' He laughs. 'But back to my problem here. I need a way of taking this life, here and now, past and present, into the next life.'

'Why?'

'So I can make sense of it all,' he says exasperated.

'Jim. Think about this,' Jayne says. 'If you take this world into the next, then the next world would be synthetic, an illusion, and you'd be conscious of that.'

'Okay, I see that. But I'm still me going into this new world. I'm still me with all my deepest desires etc. in my mind.'

'Yes,' Dan says. 'True. Look. You say that you have sensations of this world in your future-fields.'

'Yes.'

'Isn't that exactly like a dream. You know it's you. You don't question that?'

'No.'

'If you went into double F with your current thoughts and ideas then you wouldn't, maybe couldn't, accept that new world for what it is.'

'Who knows. I helped create it, it's an expression of mine, and yours of course. Would I keep on creating and affecting that world, as I actually did – okay, because of the *drug imbalance*,' he stresses. 'When I die, maybe I'll go into a tangible heaven, bringing everything I am now into that world. But I won't be dead when I'm in future fields. And where will I be in this world, other than a near-corpse in a drawer? How do you know that I won't gradually wake up into that imaginary world?'

Dan holds out the palms of his hands. Looks at Jayne.

Jayne says, 'Is it imaginary? Why do you say that? You expected your face to be wet and your hair soaked through. Correct?'

'Yes, I told you.'

'That was real.'

'It felt real at the time.'

'Yes. And you carried it through to this control room.'

'I guess. But you can have dreams like that too. You wake up but you bring part of the dream with you.'

'Do you think dreams are real or unreal?' Dan asks.

'Well, as a dream they're real.'

'And when you dream, as you've said, it's real to you as the dreamer.'

'Yes. Look, where are we going with this? As far as I can tell when I go into the new world, I will assume that that is reality. I'll be diving into a dream world where *this* world feels like a dream. Maybe I'll forget everything with the drugs and the experience will be total and all encompassing. The nanotechnology and the computer feeding me 'reality'.'

'Your reality,' Jayne says.

'My imagined reality.'

'Your imagined reality that you can touch, see, hear, feel, communicate with.'

'And lose this world,' Jim says.

'That's the price to pay,' Dan says. 'Live in this new world or die in this old world.'

'Not much of a choice,' Jim says.

'The choice,' Jayne says, 'is between knowing this new world exists or dying and taking a chance on a post-death experience.'

'Yes,' Jim says, 'I've thought that one through.' He touches his forehead. 'This is going to get harder as I get closer,' he says. 'Harder to accept. Harder to leave behind everything I know. Maybe I'll dream of this world, if I go to sleep in the other, the new.'

'Maybe you won't sleep,' Dan says.

'That would be torture.'

'Dan we know, well we assume they sleep,' Jayne says.

'Yes, true, but we don't know the quality of that sleep.'

'Dan. You aren't helping,' Jim only half jokes. Then, changing the subject, says, 'I need to integrate this last experience. I need to know what happened.'

'You know we can show you OCF, objective computer imagery and conversation,' Jayne says, 'but, like every other time, it will only show you this external view.'

'I've been thinking a lot about life, Jim begins, 'life and memory. Life contained in that memory. I mean that's where it is, isn't it? Does all of our life exist always inside of us? Why do we bring back certain memories at certain times? There's no substance to these memories is there? You can't hold them, or weigh and measure them. You can't always even bring them into being. A smell might bring the past to life. Yes. Yes, I can remember those biscuits Rosie made back at my cottage. This is not an external memory, I can recall living that, smelling those biscuits reminded me of my youth. My youth in *this* world with *its* history.'

'Do you remember Anna?'

Jim closes his eyes. 'If I try and recall Anna, I think of Hannah. Anna with a H either side.' He smiles.

'Do you want to view the whole thing now, or wait?'

'I've got nothing else on,' he jokes, 'have you?'

'No,' they chorus.

'We need to go to another control room,' Jayne says. 'You'll have the box experience,' she smiles. 'It's not like the real thing as you know. But you're in a kind of hypnopompic state. I mean there's still some drug influence in your blood.'

'That's fine,' he says. 'I still remember the first time. Things have moved on.'

'More than you can imagine,' Jayne says.

Jim watched a computer-generated version of himself act out his experience. Found it hard to see himself other than objectively. Again he thought of memories and how they came as objective reality. Memories had been lived but only the husk-experience remained. They only lived once with a filling of emotion, anticipation, senses, vital experience. Therefore, was his brain effectively like a computer linked to his box of memories?

'So that's Anna,' he says. 'She's nice.' He keeps a running commentary. 'It's not too awkward.' He thinks hard. 'I can almost get back into this dream. Sorry. This reality. Have you done any work on dreams?' he asks.

'There's been a lot of work done on them,' Jayne says. 'But keep concentrating.'

He sees himself walking down the path. 'I wasn't sure which way to go,' he remembers. 'Something happened, I met someone. Odd maybe.' Jim sees an old man on a bench. 'Oh yes,' there he is. Jim listens to the conversation. 'An odd chap. I didn't create him, did I?'

'No,' says Dan, 'but I think the computer was having a bit of fun with this character. Playfully.'

The reproduction carries on and Jim goes into the shop. He buys certain items. And the film ends.

As the box lifts, Jim is perturbed. 'Has it been erased?'

'I think it's a bit like the old man's answers,' Jayne says, 'maybe it is, was, and maybe it isn't, wasn't: maybe it has and maybe it hasn't.'

'Well it wasn't. Was it? Or the computer got rid of it. Maybe that happened.' He thinks. 'There was something about one of those boys in the shop. Can't you get it back? Get the computer to recreate it.'

'The thing is Jim, it may not exist now. Nothing to recreate.'

'I was there. You know. So did the computer. It exists.'

'It existed,' Jayne says. 'That's all we know.'

Jim shakes his head. 'If I experienced it, it existed and still exists...'

'But you can't remember it,' Dan says.

'I can, kind of,' Jim says weakly. 'Get the computer to recreate it, please. I want to see what happened.'

'We can tell you,' Jayne says.

'Not quite the same, Jayne. That's like telling someone... someone who's lost their memory, what they did. It wouldn't be real to them. I know certain things. A boy. Familiar. Thunder, lightning. Lots of rain.'

'I'll see what I can do,' Dan says.

'Listen. When you go back, maybe you'll remember things. Who knows? It's not important,' Jayne stresses, 'because that experience was an...'

'Imbalance of drugs,' he finishes. 'You have to keep the computers safe from any wrong doing,' he says passionately. 'People's lives could be messed up. Imagine an imbalance over a long period of time. The experience has to be well maintained and controlled.' Jim rubs his forehead. 'You've got to be careful. What if something like this has happened before?'

Jayne and Dan regard each other. Dan says, 'It won't happen again. I can assure you.'

'*We* can assure you,' Jayne says.

Jim sits in the chair, deep in thought.

'Are you staying over?' Jayne asks.

'As far as my wife is concerned,' he smiles. 'But which one?' he says ironically.

'Not enjoying the party doctor?'

'Jake, please. No, not enjoying the party.'

'Everyone else seems to be.'

'I'm not everyone.'

He watches her move.

'Are you retiring early?' she says, her accent lighter than he remembers.

'Maybe.' He thinks. Recalls making a mess of his conversation with Hannah. 'Unless...'

'Unless?'

'Unless you'd like to accompany me on a walk,' he blurts out. Adding quickly, 'If you have some free time.'

'Let me see,' she says. 'I can take a break in fifteen minutes. If you can wait.'

'Yes. Yes, of course. I'll go to my room and come back down for you.'

'Take this, you need to get in.'

He smiles.

Nayra also smiles as he walks towards a lift door.

Milly has been tracking Jake. Emerging from some seating in shadow, she says, 'Good. Keep him company. See what he has to say.'

'Sí señora.'

'Let me know if he has any ideas about the working girls.'

'Sure, will do'.

'Don't do anything stupid.'

'Of course not.'

Jake is punctual. 'Hola,' he says.

'You speak Spanish?'

'No. But it's a beautiful language.'

'You like languages?' she asks.

'I appreciate beauty.'

Nayra smiles, knowingly. 'So what do you want to do? Have another drink first?'

'I'm done with that,' he says. 'I just need some air.'

'Okay,' let me get my coat. Have you got a coat, a jacket?'

'No, I don't need one.'

'Okay. It still gets cold at night, this time of year.'

'I need to feel that cold air,' he says.

Nayra says something to the woman taking over, then they leave together and go outside. There are a couple of people talking in an area just outside the restaurant. One of them is smoking.

'You can smoke here?'

'We do what we want,' she says. 'As long as we don't cause a problem for the hotel. Do you smoke?'

Jake shakes his head.

'Do you mind if I do? It's an old habit. I usually have one cigarette when I finish my shift. Tonight, I'll have it now.'

'Where do you get them from?'

'The mainland. Africa, of course, not España.' She smiles at him. 'So why aren't you having fun like the others?'

'I've seen their fun,' he spits.

'The girls, the drugs, both?' She flicks a lighter and her cigarette glows in the semi-dark. She steers him towards a path heading away from any light.

'All of that,' he says.

'You don't like girls?'

'Yes, of course,' he says.

'Why of course?'

'Because that's the way I am.'

'Have you got a wife, a girlfriend?'

'No.'

'Why not?'

'I, I don't know. I'm...I don't think I'm the marrying kind.'

'Or the boyfriend kind?'

'I don't know.'

'But you see girls, right?'

'Sometimes,' he says. 'I'm not used to such questions. Not so quickly.'

'We talk like this on the island. I'm sorry.'

'Your English is excellent.'

'Gracias. I needed it to survive.'

'I imagine,' he says.

'I was lucky to get a job. To eat. You needed English. I got this job because of my language. You need to deal with rich, influential people.'

They stop. As she brings the cigarette to her lips, Jake can see her eyes and her complexion, darker with the limited light. The moon appears to move behind the clouds and then it's clear. There are some stars to be seen.

'You're a guest,' she states.

'Yes.'

'You surely could have had some female company.'

'I have.'

'It's not what I meant.'

'I know.'

'So?'

'I've seen the way those girls have been treated?'

'And you're a gentleman, I think.'

Jake thinks of Vicky. How he treated her and also how she was being treated in the room off the main area.

'I'm not really a gentleman,' he confides.

'What did you see happening?' she asks and begins walking again, into the half moonlight.

'I can't tell you. Really.'

'Okay,' she says. 'But which girls or girl?'

'Do you know them?'

'I've talked with them, and the boy.'

'I'm not sure I should say,' he thinks of the professor.

'I could look out for them,' she says.

'I'm not sure.'

'You don't trust me? But I'm trusting you by being with you alone in the dark.'

He stops. Nayra stops too. 'Vicky. She's called Vicky. You know her?'

'I'm not sure about that name. But now I can keep an eye out for her. That's what you say isn't it?'

'Yes. And thank you.'

'Gracias. It's a funny expression, keeping an eye out. Are you fond of her?'

'I know her,' he says.

'Okay,' she says.

They are silent for a while. 'It's why I'm no good with girls,' he says.

'Because you're fond of her and that's it? Or because she's a working girl?'

'I don't know. I really don't know...'

'But you care about her?'

'Yes. And I don't know why. I have no right...'

'You can be fond of anyone,' she smiles.

'Yes, but...You don't understand. Nothing seems fair, you know. The way people are treated. I'm no better.'

'You seem nice,' Nayra says.

'Thank you. Thank you for walking with me. I'm not nice though, not nice at all.'

'Is that the drink talking?' she asks.

'No, it's the drink bringing out some honesty. I've done some crazy things,' he says. 'And I kind of abandoned Vicky. She's in there, back there, right now. But I promised...well I have to keep my mouth shut.'

'Have to? Why?'

'I can't say. There are people here with influence. Not like me. I do my job. I have responsibilities. But I'm expendable. The people back there, being entertained, they have money, power and influence. It's all political. I've said too much. Let's go back in,' he says.

'You don't want to walk down to the beach?'

'It would be nice…But…' His words trail away.

She stubs out the cigarette, makes sure there's nothing burning and pockets it. 'Mustn't leave any evidence,' she says. 'Nothing incriminating.' She smiles.

'That's a good word to know,' he says.

Again she smiles. He wants to kiss her. But makes no move. They turn back.

As they re-enter the light, he stops. 'I'm going to walk a bit more.'

'Are you sure?'

He looks at her. He wants her. 'I'm sure.'

'Adiós,' she says.

It feels final. He's cut off. 'Thank you. Thanks for walking with me.'

He watches her disappear into the hotel complex. Then he heads back into the dark, in a direction he thinks will take him towards a path to the beach. Near where he was earlier, with Vicky. He feels engulfed by the blackness of the night until the moon and stars flicker back into existence. He is all alone. He thinks.

There is rustling somewhere nearby. 'Doctor. Jake.'

'Well, well. You've been stalking me again.'

'Watching you with that woman,' she says.

'Are you okay? How come you're here?'

'What's it to you? You abandoned me. They've had their fun and I escaped. I'll have to go back in. Soon. I saw you when I left the building. Well, I thought it was you. You were in shadow.'

'Did they do anything violent to you?'

'Of course.'

'And you let them?'

She laughs. 'What do you think I can do. Any of us can do? One of the girls is fourteen years old, maybe she looks a little older. They do stuff with her. They get off on that. Yes, and whipping me or whatever turns them on. You know,' she says coldly.

'I know. Listen. Come with me, stay with me. You can hide in my room.'

'I'm not done,' she says. 'It's only the start. Things will heat up when everyone is out of their head. You should join in.'

'Not my style. None of this is my style. Come with me. We could go down to the beach and run into the sea...'

'It would be cold,' she says. 'Ah, doctor, yes, nice and cold. What's your story? What is it that happened to you to make you like all of them? Not just power is it?'

'Not just power,' he says.

A voice calls out, 'Vicky?'

'Wait,' he says.

'No, I have to go. But tell me you'll see me again. I have no-one. No-one. Only the other whores.'

'I'll see you again,' he says.

Fumbling in her long jacket, she takes out a cigarette and quickly lights it up. 'My excuse,' she says. 'You better not be seen. Come in later and you can beat me up and fuck me,' she says. 'Or put me in a freezer.'

'Vicky...I...'

She laughs. 'See you around Jake. It's going to be a long few days.'

She disappears back into the shadows.

'Vicky?' Then a few moments later. 'Vicky, there you are. Get in. Put that filthy thing away. Is that my jacket? Come on, hurry.'

The voices die away.

Jake carried on walking. Maybe he'd spend the rest of the time getting absolutely drunk. No-one would mind a drunk doctor about the place. Tomorrow he'd go down to the beach and keep quiet. No Vicky, no Nayra. No Milly and no Professor. Looking up at the moon, he imagined its barren surface.

'Well Vicky,' he says to himself, 'you want to know why I like you cold? You want to know?' He looks about. 'Because the coldness is as cold as me. Locked outside. A father shouting. Distant. Me hiding. My mother unable to hide. Shivering in the cold. Finding old images left from another time. Girls. Taking images into an old outside toilet. No-one about. Sleet coming down, whipped and tossed by a biting wind. But I was safe. Safe there within the stone walls. Confined. Sex on my mind. My hands stiff. Not just my hands. Little things like this, Vicky, make a man the way he is. Taking girls into a shed on icy cold nights baring their body. Exposing them. Enjoying their discomfort and their pleasure. Growing up in disused, outside buildings. And me a doctor. A doctor now. Exonerated. Worshipped. Corrupt. But a success. I didn't want to whip you Vicky or bite into your flesh. Just have you cold and be cold – then warm beneath duvet and sheets. That's all I'll admit to.'

The moon seemed to race behind the clouds. He was alone. It was best for him. Alone in his mind. Maybe he could soon use his avatar and go into a future-field. That was the wild west. He'd be as free as an outlaw. He needed a drink. Raised his arms in the air. You couldn't judge a man on a few sentences – you'd need to be inside his mind. That was another wild west.

Milly has been waiting for Nayra. 'Well?'

'Safe.'

'Are you sure?'

'He has a thing for one of the girls...'

'Butterfly girls?'

'The what?'

'One of the whores, one of the working girls I told you to keep an eye on,' Milly modifies.

'Yes.'

'Is he likely to cause trouble?'

'I don't think so,' Nayra says. 'I think he has problems, despite being so successful.'

'Thank you. Now I need another favour, don't worry you'll be paid.'

'What is it?'

'Keep a close eye on this girl. Do you know who she is?'

'I know her name.'

'Vicky,' Milly states.

'Yes, how did you...? Ah, I see. Well, I'm not sure which one she is.'

'I'll make sure you know, don't worry.'

'Okay, señora .'

'But one thing, Nayra...'

'Yes?'

'Keep your mouth shut. And if you can't keep it shut, it will be shut permanently. Understand?'

'Si, señora.'

'Good, we understand each other?'

'Of course.'

Nayra takes off her coat and waits for Milly to disappear.

'What have you been up to I wonder, doctor,' Nayra says aloud. Then busies herself behind the counter. She thinks of her family and thinks of the money she makes. That is the payoff. She'll do whatever she has to. He has to come back and pick up his card to get into his room.

Keep an eye out. As she thinks this she puts a finger between her right eye and nose. She's tired. She's used a new phrase at least. Also she thinks of 'butterfly' girls. Was that a new saying for a whore, she wonders. She can hear noise, music and shouting coming from the main room beyond the restaurant. Shakes her head. Decides to make a call. She's alone. Thinks of the money she will be paid.

'Hola.'

Jim lay in bed. There was a lot for him to think about. He'd talked to Hannah and exchanged messages with Joanne and Henry. It had been a hard day, but constructive. But on his own in that soulless room he felt scared and detached. Scared of what? Death, of course. He would have to meet death on his own like everyone had to. At least he'd get a kind of trial run with double F. Double F? He laughed. He'd be put to sleep but he'd wake up in another world – a world of his choosing. Except his confidence in that world had taken a knock.

He was beginning to feel remorse for all his inactions in life. And for the knowledge and skills he'd gained which would – might – peter out. If he could take these skills with him then he could build on them. If this new world ends with his bodily death, he might have twenty to thirty years ahead. But what if his eyes rotted in the drawer he'd be put in. Would that affect his sight in his future-fields? He still wasn't sure of the correlation between his body and this new reality. If he had twenty years, perhaps they would encompass near eternity and he'd be able to do everything he'd ever wanted. As a child he'd wanted to play piano but wasn't allowed. Now he could summon a piano and have it put in his cottage. He'd need a piano-tuner; he'd summon one too. Could be a sexy girl. He checked himself. But if it was his world then he was the moral arbiter. Like a god. Why not? He could have anything he wanted. And there he was worrying about things that hadn't really taken place. He had not been fully immersed so he was only getting an idea of this future life. Those feral youths that tried to rob the shop, they were simply a reflection of the gang he'd had an altercation with by the canal side. It was psychological.

There was still that persistent sense of having wasted his time in this life. Of all the unnecessary worry he'd experienced. Of all the self-judgment. Of all the things he could have been and done. In that sense this was a run-through for death. Except in his future-fields perhaps he'd have no sense of death. But he *was* struck by lightning outside the post office and shop. Again he reasoned that that was psychological. They said nothing like that would happen again. Maybe he should choose death – joining the billions who had already died. Not long before he'd be born, there had been more people alive than had previously ever died. A whole teeming world of potential dead bodies – either rotting in boxes under the ground or spiralling ash and embers from a crematorium's chimney. A crematorium, where folk were cremated. From created to an inserted 'm'. Up the chimney and free again. Maybe wafted by a breeze to drift over a house where a week before they might have lived. Not that they were that delicate petal of ash. But maybe... Besides didn't the ash get collected and put in an urn, then was spread somewhere or other.

Perhaps that was the beauty of Future-Fields. It would be surreal. Why would you think of death? Everyone would be as young as he imagined, and if he did die then perhaps his created world lived on and he just slowly drifted off. A long slide into non-being. Maybe he'd have an after-death experience, well an after life after life experience. Had he thought about this before? Why was life forgotten even when we were alive? Whole pockets of life slipping through the fingers of memory. Or maybe everything was remembered and written in the book of life. Where had he heard that from? He'd heard about the Akashic Records when young. What were they, a record, a detailed account of everything we'd ever done? Or thought? Or imagined? Maybe he'd get judged based on his future-fields? Maybe death was a form of future-fields. Mental imagery, not chains, that we'd forged during life.

Rolling over in the bed he felt very alone. He wondered about folk facing a firing squad. Imagining the idea of being shot was only an abstract idea, a kind of hideous ghost that only took on true form as the morning got closer. Did anyone sleep the day before they were to be shot? Would tiredness have trumped fear? Could you eat? Would the convicted man be like him now as he lay in bed bombarded by thoughts? What thoughts would invade him? Thoughts conjured from a long distant youth. Friends, enemies. Happy times, free times. Feeling constricted. Falling in love. Being betrayed. Working. Marrying. Having a child or children. Regretting not having children. Thoughts upon thoughts, falling as thick as snow. Laughing, crying. A concentration of his own thoughts and fears. Regrets. Why was he being shot? Was he guilty or innocent and who had decided?

Then the darkest moment of night. Vague half dreams of being in a coffin. Couldn't breathe. No escape. Walled in. Pleading his innocence. Remembering God. Remembering parents and children and family and friends. And enemies. And then slowly the turning of the night into day. His cell. The slight smell of nature creeping into the dampness of his pen, his cage, his dungeon. Damp walls. Grid shut in the old door. Smells of those ghosts that had also waited there – before. Before. Light. A shaft of light. The yearning for life. To be among the living. To hold a child. To hold a spouse or a lover. To feel protected as a child. To feel hope and longing. Life, beautiful life. Dirty life. Uncaring life. BANG. Not a gun but a door banging behind echoing footsteps. Approaching. Did he have to die? And still it wouldn't seem fully real. He was alive. It was a dream, a nightmare. BANG. The grid was opened. He could see faces. Faces that were not trying to protect him. In they came. Methodically and coldly preparing him. He would give up his body. If he didn't fight maybe they would carry him out into a green field full of flowers and lay him down carefully. There he could live forever.

But he is held and taken without emotion – a puppet. Down corridors. Past doors. BANG. BANG. Through doors. Held tightly, without compassion. Out through another door into a courtyard where an open truck would be waiting idly. It hadn't fully woken up. The sun was somewhere in the sky. The day tasted both fresh and bitter. Hauled up into the back of the truck and seated between two sets of cold eyes. He was nothing. The truck wakes and he is driven out of the prison – free. Free for some moments. The sky became glorious and wide and the sun had risen. The smell of life filling his nostrils. Where was he being taken? He knew. But it wasn't real. It really wasn't real. He was an actor. A joke. There would be a pardon any minute. He was innocent – they knew that. How was he guilty? Of punching a bully, of raging at the world, of feeling empty of love for brief moments? The truck stopped. He was hauled out. Down on the ground. Almost lifted off his feet and taken to a wall. Used for firing practice. Not this time. Tied to a pole. Hands behind his back. Tied. Helpless. He looked as the soldiers readied themselves.

'Have you anything to say?' comes a voice of authority.

'Why?' he asks. And is ignored. There is a nod. A blindfold is pulled over his eyes, his head turned roughly so they can tie it tight.

He can listen. He is listening. There is a bird crying. What is it? Why didn't he learn about birds? He sees his wife and children approaching across a dark sea. Smiling. He smiles. Maddy is there. He smiles. Full of joy. He's going to be free.

BANG!

The following day it was as if the hotel complex was a morgue. Everyone seeming to take time to recover. Jake left his room late morning, saw another woman at reception and left the building to walk down to the sea. He spent most of his day watching the sea rise and fall. Sleeping on the sand. No hunger and no thirst.

When he got back there was a message waiting for him from the professor, saying they needed to meet the next day. Jake looked for Nayra but she was nowhere to be seen. He walked around the complex too, investigating the buildings – but everywhere was quiet.

Returning to his room, he lay on his bed, eating fruit from the bowl he'd brought in. He felt empty. Resigned. Nothing. Apart from the fruit he ate there was only some snacks he'd found. Didn't touch any alcohol and didn't go to the restaurant. His day and night was spent in front of the screen. It was mindless entertainment. And he was happy it was.

The portable in Jake's main room sends out its staccato call. Rolling out of bed, Jake goes to it, sits down and answers.

'Jake. Alistair here. We need to meet today.'

Jake is half-asleep. 'Okay. When?'

'An hour's time, lunch. But not at the complex. Be at reception for twelve and a driver will pick you up.'

'Okay. What time is it now?'

'Eleven.'

'Okay.'

'See you later.'

Alistair cuts communication. Jake looks out the window and sees Nayra walking towards reception. He has an hour to get showered, shaved and ready to go out. He is both hungry and thirsty, drinks some water from a tap.

At reception Jake waited for the taxi. Or a driver. No-one was manning reception and he didn't feel like speaking with Nayra – not this morning – well it was a minute or so before midday. It was hot and his thirst and hunger had increased. He was also somewhat nervous. Why did the professor want to see him? He presumed because of what had happened with Vicky. Was he going to be sent home, or sent somewhere else? Maybe the driver was going to take him to the airport. Maybe the professor was going to lay down the law again.

Eventually he watches a car arrive and a man get out. The man approaches and looks at him. 'Señor Abraham?'

'Yes.'

'I'm taking you to Professor Stone,' he says turning back to the car. Jake follows him. Looks back, still no-one about. The man holds a back door open and Jake gets in. The car smells of heat and hair lacquer, mixed with perfume and cigarette smoke. The window is down.

'Okay señor?'

'Si, gracias,' Jake says, hoping he has said the right thing.

They drive down a dusty road before meeting the main highway. The man engages Jake in conversation about the island and England, which he'd heard about and would love to visit one day. Before long they turn off the highway and onto another dusty road and within five minutes they arrive at a small village. There is a turning that climbs a hill, which they take. The car comes to rest outside a large white-walled villa with stone steps leading up to a level area with stone flagging. In a flash, the driver is out of the car and opens the door for Jake.

'Gracias. Thank you.'

The driver motions to Jake to go up the steps. Jake looks around. There is a pleasant breeze and a magnificent view across to the distant sea which sparkles as if it has submerged stars.

'Jake,' comes a voice. Jake has climbed the steps. There is a swimming pool, table and chairs, lounging chairs too and a wooden veranda. Jake notices the house's solid looking wooden door, slightly ajar. The professor smiles. There is a girl with him, very pretty. 'Have a seat,' the professor says, warmly.

'Is this your place?' Jake asks.

'For now,' he smiles.

'This is Ariadna,' he says, introducing the girl. She approaches and kisses Jake on both cheeks. It is an old-fashioned greeting which surprises him. 'Pleased to meet you señora,' he says. Jake looks at the professor.

'Ariadna is a trained nurse,' he says. Ariadna smiles. 'Take a seat,' the professor says to Jake and smiles at the girl. They sit round the table under a canopy with the sun reflecting in the pool's waters. On the slope of the volcanic hills surrounding there are flowers carpeting the rough ground.

'A drink?'

'Please,' Jake says. 'I'm very thirsty.'

'Hungry?'

'Yes, hungry too,' Jake says.

Without being summoned, a middle-aged woman pushes open the heavy wooden door and, surprising Jake, the professor engages her in Spanish. She quickly returns inside the house.

The professor looks at Jake. 'I imagine you're wondering why I asked you here?' Jake nods. 'I need a favour.' Immediately Jake relaxes, looks at the professor and the girl. Then up at the blue sky. Takes a deep breath. The professor carries on. 'I need a really big favour,' he begins. 'I have a friend on the African continent who needs a kidney transplant. He's a good and close friend of mine. Everything's being arranged at the moment. But I need, I want, someone I can trust to do the operation. I couldn't think who, given the logistics. And then it was clear and obvious. You Jake.'

'Thank you, Alistair. I appreciate that, your trust in me, especially after....'

'Don't worry about that,' Alistair says. 'It's finished with. I think you understand now why all that, the goings-on, was necessary.' Jake nods. 'Are you ready and able to do this for me, and my friend?'

'Yes, indeed. When would it be?'

'You'll fly out this afternoon. With Ariadna. She's actually a trained theatre nurse, she's done lots of this particular work.' Jake looks at her and smiles. 'Beauty and talent,' Alistair says.

The girl smiles and looks down. Then she says, 'I know what I'm doing'. Her voice is cool.

'This afternoon?' Jake queries.

'Later. You have nearly five hours. We have to be at the airport for six o'clock. Ariadna will prep you on the plane. It will be a small jet, shouldn't take too long. I'm keeping you in the dark, a little, there are tensions in the city my friend is in. But the hospital bosses know what's going on and the preparations will be ready for tomorrow.'

'Okay,' Jake smiles nervously. 'I haven't done a transplant for a while.'

'It's second nature for you Jake. And you'll be called upon for the OT at Portway. I need to talk with you about that too. Explain it all. But you know it's a government backed corporate enterprise. Independent of Portway, in fact, but paying its way. We may well need you. If all goes to plan there will be a lot of demand.' Jake throws a worried glance towards Ariadna. Alistair laughs, then says, 'Don't worry, she might be helping out at Transcorp. That's the name of the company. Who knows, you two could be working together in the future. It's going to be good to see how you are as a team.'

'Transcorp. Ah, okay. Well I must have spoken with their man in charge, Bennett. They've kept the name pretty well secret. I've talked with both our and their security.' He pauses. 'Okay, I can now tell Dan and Jayne and the teams, a name.'

'Leave it as long as possible. We don't want any snooping about yet. Need it cleared with Bennett. They'll go all corporate when the time comes.'

'But it is all above board,' Jake says.

'Well, in a manner of speaking. It's a bonafide company. Hidden within Portway. I mean it could easily be extra creation or control rooms if necessary. You get my drift?'

'Of course,' Jake says.

'Maybe you should be in charge of the first operation Jake. As a reward, and you *will be* very well rewarded.' Alistair smiles.

'One thing at a time,' Jake says. But that would be an honour.'

'Good. Tell me when was the last time you operated on anyone?'

'I did a lot the year before last in State clinics in suicide centres. Euthanasia centres,' he corrects. 'I get called on from time to time. Not in Portway time,' he adds hurriedly.

'Not to worry,' Alistair says. 'If all goes well, I'll try and expedite the opening of the OT suite. I'll have Portway people integrated into the security and technical staff looking out for Transcorp, making sure all runs smoothly. And leave it to me to tell Dan and Jayne. I think it would be better.'

The Spanish woman arrives with tapas and drinks. Smiling, she carefully puts the trays on the table. There is a jug of sangria and some fruit juice. She takes glasses and places them in front of each of them. The other tray has some ham and olives. Excusing herself, in English, she goes to fetch more food.

'It's all worked out very well in fact,' Alistair continues. 'And I won't forget this Jake. The patient is a dear friend.' There is a pause. 'Ariadna, pour yourself a drink. Señora Ortega will bring some ice. I was worried she'd drop the trays,' he whispers to them, smiling.

Jake can smell the aroma of grilled food. He begins to relax fully. 'A wonderful place, Alistair.'

'We use it for extra-curricular business,' he smiles. Ariadna pours a drink into her glass. 'Fruit juice or sangria?' he asks Jake.

'Probably best to have the juice,' he says. 'Is there any water?'

'Of course.'

Señora Ortega arrives with grilled chicken hearts and sardines. Also some cheese and a small bucket of ice. Alistair thanks her and again speaks in Spanish. She nods. 'Tuck in,' he orders.

After a while the professor excuses himself. 'I must make a call,' he says, 'explain everything is fine and going ahead.' He leaves Jake and Ariadna alone.

'Do you know which country we'll be going to?' Jake asks.

'It's all, how do you say, hush-hush.'

'Your English is perfect,' Jake says.

'I worked in London.'

'Really?' Jake was thinking she didn't look old enough to have worked long, or to have had credit to travel.

'Yes, really,' she smiles. 'Special dispensation.'

'This is all quite unexpected,' Jake says. 'Unexpected and, well, exciting.'

Ariadna smiles. 'We have to do a good job.'

'We will. I'll go through the operation mentally when I get back to my room. Are you staying at the hotel? I haven't seen you.' She shakes her head.

'I have all the medical notes, I can share those with you too. You know we'll be doing two operations,' she says.

'Two?'

'Taking the kidney out of one body, the donor, and putting it straight into Alistair's friend.'

'Oh, okay. I didn't assume that, I thought it would be there ready.'

She shakes her head. 'No.'

'Okay,' he says. 'I'll take some time this afternoon to go through everything and get it firmly in my head. I presume the theatre will be modern and hygienic?'

'I presume so,' she says.

'You do seem very young to be an OT nurse.'

'I'm older than I look.'

'I'm tempted to ask.'

'I wouldn't reply,' she says.

The professor returns with more soft drinks and mineral water.

'Glad to see you're getting along. Everything okay Jake?'

'Yes, indeed,' Jake answers.

'I've prepped Ariadna for all eventualities and have confirmed with the hospital just now that everything and everyone is set and ready to go.' There is a pause. 'I'll take you both to the airport. Pack enough for a few days, in case of complications. Which I'm sure there won't be. You can sight-see if not and be back here before we return to the UK. Ariadna, I'll see to it that you either stay here and work at the main hospital or go back to Spain. But if you two get on, there's Transcorp at Portway too.'

'Thank you. Gracias.'

'No pienses nada al respecto, es un placer.'

Jake looks at the professor. 'Is he good?' he asks Ariadna. She smiles. 'Bueno.'

'Right. Eat and drink up. We need to get ourselves together. Okay Jake?'

'Okay,' he says and finishes another glass of water.

'I'll make sure things are expedited at Portway. And don't forget my avatar.'

The driver took Jake back to the hotel. Jake thanked him. He had no idea if they used cash on the island, it was possible, but he had none to tip. He smiled and the driver turned about, got in the car and raced off, kicking up clouds of dust with the back wheels. Jake could only reflect on what a strange holiday, break, or whatever it was, it had been. He had a niggling feeling that he'd been set-up by the professor. It was all very convenient that he was there and a jet could take him to his friend in hospital. But he also thought it was a great honour, and frankly, he also felt a bit of leverage over Alistair. And less threatened. This made him feel good and important. The friend must be a VIP, he presumed – and very wealthy.

At reception there was a woman behind the desk he didn't know – she gave him his card to get in his room. Obviously knew who he was. As he waited outside the lift doors he imagined the professor's attitude towards him after operating successfully on his good friend. The lift doors opened revealing Milly inside.

'Milly,' he says, slightly surprised.

'I wondered what had happened to you,' she says.

'Been an interesting day.'

'I'm sure it has.'

'More than you could imagine,' he stresses.

'What have you been up to?'

'Nothing yet. But I will be,' he smiles.

'Tell me more,' she says as he holds back the lift doors.

'Ask the prof.'

She smiles and walks out and away.

By the pool, Alistair takes out a cigar and lights it up. Ariadna watches him. 'Well done,' he says. 'But keep an eye on him. Will you be okay, can you manage it all?'

'Of course,' she says.

'Hopefully you'll both be busy enough – but watch out for unwanted attention.'

'I can handle myself, señor Alistair.'

'I like it when you speak English. There's only a trace of an accent but it gives the language spice.'

'Gracias,' she answers playfully.

'Well you need to brush up your skills too. I'll get you a direct line to the hospital and you can familiarise yourself with everything. They can send you all the documents and details of the intended procedures. Should be fine. Let's see if it works.'

'I already have some details,' she says. 'Tell me Professor, do you really know the recipient?'

'Of course, I told you, he's a friend.'

'And the donor?'

'Unintended donor, shall we say. Yes, we can say that.' He puffs on the cigar. 'It's the way of the world. Certainly the modern world.'

'Well, are we to keep both parties alive?'

'Not sure that would be such a good idea. Lots of things can go wrong in an operating theatre, can they not?'

Ariadna smiles. 'I'm glad I'm not one of your enemies,' she says.

'I'm glad too. You're a beautiful girl, Ariadna.'

'Thank you, Alistair. King Minos.'

'I like that,' he smiles, 'and I will consider you my Spanish daughter.'

'So you will protect me?'

'Of course.'

'You won't amaze me with your tricks?'

'Clever,' he says. 'I am a fatherly figure.' The professor takes a glass and knocks back its contents. 'Watch out for any monsters,' he says, 'or unwanted approaches.'

Ariadna gets up and stretches. 'I should have been born at a different time.'

'What time?'

'In the afternoon,' she jokes.

'Get on with your work,' Alistair says, smiling. And with this she skips into the house. Señora Ortega soon comes out and begins clearing up.

'Gracias,' Alistair says. She looks at him with a measured glance but with a mix of emotions. Picks up a glass, fills it with some sangria and knocks it back. 'I like it,' she says in thick accented English.

Milly closed the conversation with Hughes-Kahn. She had sat down under the gnarled trees on a worn bench. The conversation was at high security status. Now she heard birds sing. She was content. It pleased her to think how so many people viewed her – and how none of them knew who she really was. Closing her eyes she dreamt of her childhood. She rearranged events and relationships, retold her history beneath the aging branches. She decided to call the professor.

'Alistair.'

'Milly. We're encrypted?'

'Of course.'

'How are things there? I'll be coming over to pick up Jake later.'

'All going to plan,' she states.

'Of course.'

'Good. Will you be here for dinner?'

'Depends if everything runs on time. Have to get Jake and Ariadna safely on their way.'

'I understand.'

'I'm hoping, well more than hoping, that as a result of this week I'll get a trade deal going and Jake's had his wings clipped a little. But I'm supervising his restored flight.'

'I take it John knows?'

'Not yet. Thought it would be a surprise on our return – give the National Party a bit of a lift. More money, you know. Especially for the elections.'

'Are they going ahead?' Milly asks.

'Well, I have no idea. But if they do...'

Milly can hear him smile. 'Okay,' she says. 'Maybe later.'

'Indeed.'

She looks out across the rough land to the cliffs and sea beyond. Wonders if her being there is fortuitous. But John, Hughes-Kahn, has played his part. Who else knows about her? She's happy to be used. Like they all are. Smiling knowingly, she gets up and walks back to the complex.

Dan and Jayne decided that Jim would go back into his future-fields the next day, but they also had another plan. Jayne thought they needed to test the stability of that world and Dan agreed. They had time before Doctor Abraham returned. Jim had gone into the city. He'd said it was time off for good behaviour.

Jayne's line sparked. The professor was calling. She walked into an office where no-one was there to hear.

'Professor Stone,' she says.

'Sorry for the inconvenience,' he says. 'The line's safe so you can feel reassured. Thought I'd keep you posted that there'll be a team coming in from Transcorp, that's the new company's name, today and hopefully for the rest of the week - getting the various rooms ready. They aren't to be interrupted and they need to have our full cooperation. Chap called Bennett's in charge, you might already have met him.'

'The name sounds familiar,' she says.

'Equipment will be coming in through the hangar. I'll be speaking with security and making sure all runs smoothly. With any luck, as I say, it will be finished very soon. You know this is a public-private enterprise and they'll work independently of Portway. Dealing with special clients. Everything will be taken care of in-house and there'll be no Transcorp drawers in Portway's own buildings. Has to be a little hush-hush because of who's involved. But the income for Portway will be substantial and jobs secured.'

'Okay. I understand. But will we have access?'

'No. I'm sorry,' he says. 'These are instructions from the top. Above me. I imagine it's a disappointment, it was only finalised recently. If Doctor Abraham wasn't here, where I am, I would have consulted you all.'

'I see.' There's a fairly long pause.

'I know I go on about this a little too much, perhaps, but how's my avatar getting on?'

'All going extremely well,' Jayne says in a business-like tone. 'It will be tested again soon.'

'Good. I have to come over for the opening of the Transcorp centre, so will take that opportunity to try out the avatar. If that's okay.'

'Of course. Any idea when that will be?'

'Realistically, mid-March. Before that I could well be here but I'll be tied up with discussing business with Transcorp officials. I think having Transcorp within Portway will secure all our futures. But. Please make it known to any enquiring staff, that no Portway workers will be allowed into these new rooms and that Transcorp, try not to use their name as yet, will have their own security. Well they already have them now, working with our own staff for the moment. I can't say too much, but this level of security is required for VIP clients. You get my drift?'

Jayne nods, quickly stating, 'Of course.'

'Good. Doctor Abraham will be fully briefed before returning. Security is aware of what's happening. We're just trying to keep exactly what's going on under the radar, as they say. That the new rooms are Portway's. It'll eventually become clearer. I hope the building work hasn't been too disturbing?'

'Not at all' she says. 'Because of its situation and the access they've created, we haven't been disturbed at all. There was some noise to begin with but it's been remarkably quiet over the past month or so. Now it's nearing completion.' She pauses. 'I had been under the impression that Portway would at least be sharing these facilities.'

'No. I'm afraid not. There had been some talk of that to begin with, but we have to be absolutely clear of the demarcation. Again, without being specific, there will be some very high-ranking clients. For that reason the centre will have all the equipment and also all the drawers required. Hence the size. Transcorp will use its own dedicated teams. I did speak with them about you Jayne, and Dan. Said you were the finest. But they insisted it was all to be in-house. I realise this might be somewhat disappointing.'

'I understand,' she says unconvincingly. 'I presume it will mean more income for Portway.'

'Yes. Transcorp will pay us for the site they are on and we are still in discussion regarding sharing communications and some facilities. The use of that new building will have a positive knock-on effect. And that will be of benefit to you, I can assure you of that. I'll be speaking to Doctor Abraham about all this. And the Board of course. But I think I can say candidly, you and Dan will receive pay increases.' He lets that sink in. 'Okay. Any questions?'

'No, not really, not at this stage,' Jayne says. 'Thank you for explaining.'

'Not at all. Good. Nice to speak with you Jayne, keep up the good work. Portway has a great reputation. It really is the finest. You are part of its reputation. We value you.'

'Thank you,' she says.

'Keep Transcorp's name tight for the time being, please. Over.'

It had been a while since Jayne had seen the construction of the new centre and its creation rooms. She thought that Portway owned the building, but now wasn't so sure. Seemed as if it was only the actual site Portway owned. Didn't seem like such a good deal. Land had been acquired to the right of The Gateway and the building constructed on a brownfield site next to the refurbished office complex adjacent to Portway. The building had its own entrance. The only time she'd actually entered it was when it was at an early stage of construction. At that time she'd presumed it was going to be state of the art technology for Portway's exclusive use. For her and Dan's exclusive use. The last time she and Dan had gone there, there had been security guards who had stopped them. She hadn't thought too much about that, even if she and Dan's position in the company was well known – well known to Portway security, of course. In fact she hadn't recognised the guards that last time.

She'd been fairly content letting things be completed, imagining that the rooms would be for Portway exclusively. There *had* been rumours. Gradually it had become clear that the new rooms were to be shared with a new company. The name Transcorp had been mentioned, or so she thought. And finally, it seemed, they were to be exclusive to this new company. Transcorp only. The professor having confirmed as such. There had been talk – you couldn't stop that. And the talk was correct.

'Dan,' she says.

'What is it? You look out of sorts.'

'I'm fuming,' she says, 'fucking fuming.'

Dan takes note of her language. 'Okay, okay, what is it?'

'The new creation rooms,' she begins, 'they're for the new company's use only. And they *are* called Transcorp.'

'What? How do you know?'

'The professor told me. I don't know why he didn't come and tell us together...'

'I do,' Dan says. 'Because I would have let him have it!'

'No you wouldn't Dan. You'd be fired and lose everything. He knows what he's doing. Now we can be sure of the hierarchy, but he's not top. One thing...'

'Go on.'

'He says we'll have a pay rise.'

'I should hope so. Keep us happy. Make no waves.'

'How could we make waves?' she says.

'Tell BMC.'

'You think they'd be interested? In what exactly. Besides, they're controlled by the government.'

'Shady corporation works going on inside government run civic duty company.'

She laughs. 'It's all above board,' she says. 'VIP treatment in top facilities. It *will* make the news and all be positive. Or do you think they'll transmit: two Portway creation team managers miss out on using top technology to Transcorp. It's a non-story. I will do a bit of research on Transcorp though, now we know for sure.'

'Do we know *anything*?'

'Hang on. Wait. Here we go. Quick search. Impressive site. Not much detail. Their advertising says they, *Transform Lives*.'

'We always get a raw deal,' Dan says, despondently.

'No we don't,' Jayne says. 'That's the problem. We're okay.'

Jim arrived back in the late afternoon. He'd had no news from Jayne or Dan so presumed they weren't ready for him in any fashion. Sauntering into the building having passed through security, he was greeted by another young woman. She was pleasant, told him to wait and she'd find out what was happening.

'Would you mind going to the restaurant?' she asks. 'One of the team will meet you there.'

'Sure.'

'Do you need directions?'

'I'll find it,' he smiles.

In the restaurant he checked his phone to see how much he'd spent. It had been fun and interesting in the city. Top-end shops were prolific as people did not want to buy the new luxury items on-line. He walked into these shops as if they were palaces. In his mind he compared the life of Ree and the children from the forgotten estates to these new rich folk. He'd also eaten at a bio-restaurant and visited the Museum of Contemporary War. He smiled to himself. Well, it *had* been raining.

Portway's restaurant was almost empty. He felt sleepy and reasonably content. He had a green tea which tasted vile but which reminded him he was still alive. He *was* still alive. He'd been expecting more moments of the mundane transforming into the magical. But being at Portway felt like an eternal state. It was as if he belonged there - eternally. With or without the green tea.

He sees Jayne and Dan enter.

'Jim,' they chorus.

'Last time I looked,' he quips. But he can sense they're not in the best of moods. They sit down at his table.

'Sorry we didn't contact you earlier,' Jayne says, 'we could have sent a message out. But...'

'But, we had things to do,' Dan says.

'Things?'

'Yes,' Dan says firmly.

'Well, we'll grab a drink while we're here. I take it you've eaten?' Jayne asks. Jim nods. 'Good.' As she says this she sees a couple of security guards enter. 'Probably Transcorp,' she says coldly.

'Transcorp?' Jim queries.

'Yep. I can tell. They're security for the brand new control and creation rooms that have been built. Are being built.'

Dan sensing Jayne's ire, says, 'Nothing to do with us though.'

'Why aren't they Portway's creation rooms?' Jim asks.

'Good question,' Jayne says.

'I guess they have the money and influence,' Dan says. 'More money and more influence.'

'But they're using our facilities,' Jayne says.

'Paying for them at least,' Dan says, looking at Jayne.

'I've never heard of Transcorp,' Jim says.

'Used to be 'Transforming Humans' in the past. Now they 'Transform Lives'. Whatever that means.' Jayne looks at them. 'You can find that information easily enough. Otherwise not too much else from a brief search.' She eyes Dan.

'Maybe the trans movement of the twenties,' Jim says.

'Maybe.'

'Well, they'll be transforming human lives in the control rooms now won't they,' Dan says.

'With better equipment than we have,' Jayne says.

Jim feels slightly embarrassed. 'I'm sure Portway's technology is top.'

'Until now,' Jayne huffs.

'You don't know,' Dan says. 'None of us know anything other than they'll be dealing with the elite. And that's only what you've told me.'

'That's what the professor said.'

'Ah, I see,' Jim says. 'I was wondering what happened to those at the top and their civic duty. Now I know. They'll be hidden away inside Portway. Possibly,' he adds.

'I imagine they're hidden away all over the place,' Jayne says.

'Did you say it was government funded?' Dan asks.

'Yep,' Jayne says, 'at least partly.'

Jim asks, 'Who's the professor?'

'Part of the management,' Dan answers.

There is a hesitant silence.

'I wonder if Doctor Abraham knows?' Dan says.

'I don't think so Dan. I think the professor says he's going to brief him,' Jayne answers.

'While their living it up on the isles.'

'Yes. It's all right for some,' Jayne says.

Jim listens attentively. 'What's it like there?' he asks. 'On the isles.'

'Like a collection of jewels,' Dan says.

Jayne laughs. 'It has a reputation.'

'It's supposed be a wonderful collection of islands.'

'That we'll never visit,' Jayne says.

Jim reflects. Senses Jayne's mood.

'Right,' Dan says, 'back to work. Let's make your new world a wonderful place Jim.'

'We're falling behind the other teams,' Jayne says.

'Quality not quantity,' Dan replies.

'Like Transcorp,' Jayne says.

'Thing is,' Jim says, 'I've been thinking about, well, Anna in particular, but also Rosie and Ronnie. I mean, what happens to them when I'm not there?'

'What do you mean exactly?' Dan says.

'I mean, do they continue their various lives, doing whatever they do. Or do they become animate only when I'm around. And if they do nothing shouldn't they be frozen in time and space, exactly as I left them?'

'Hang on,' Dan says. 'I'll get Jayne here. She might have a take on this.'

They are in the normal creation room. There are some other teams in other rooms. But Jim has mainly only been aware of Jayne and Dan. The 'guardian angels', as the doctor sometimes describes the teams, are usually absorbed in their work – but friendly enough.

Jayne arrives.

'Go on, explain,' Dan says to Jim. Jim repeats what he has said to Dan.

'Interesting,' Jayne says. 'Very interesting. Two things,' she falters. 'Okay. We don't know for certain. How can we? We aren't there. We see through your experience as you also do. I'm still thinking about what happened to you in the shop. What you experienced and what you subsequently viewed. A disparity. Two versions of the same event. Were there actually two versions, we have to ask that. But also, something I experienced.' She looks at Dan. Dan nods. 'I entered future-fields through an avatar. Please keep this to yourself, Jim. I'm telling you because what I experienced is relevant. Can we trust you?'

'Of course,' Jim says. He is very curious. And after all, his life will be in their hands. 'Thank you for your trust. I knew you'd been working on an avatar, you did tell me.'

'I did,' she looks at Dan. 'But we've taken it to another level. Okay.' Jayne takes a deep breath. 'We're working hard on this avatar technology.' Dan looks at her. 'It's kind of a secret...But you know, or have an idea of it.'

'It *is* a secret,' Dan interjects.

'We have Jim's word,' Jayne says. Jim nods. 'We know him. We can trust him. Anyway, we have an avatar that I tried out,' she looks at

Dan. 'And I entered a future-field. We had permission.' Dan eyes her carefully. 'I was hooked up to the computer and had some HS.'

'HS?' Jim asks.

'Heavenly Sugar. A concoction, like you've experienced. Like you will experience. But no nanobots. No direct connection to the brain stem – obviously. So how authentic was my experience? I don't know. Like those people who have NDEs.'

'Near Death Experiences,' Jim spells out.

'Yes. Did they really die, or was it a 'close to death experience'? Regardless of this. I had the distinct impression that I was co-creating my reality. That there was a reality there, the default program, but I was bringing people and events to life,' she says looking at Dan. 'You talked about the characters in your double F Jim, would they do things when you're not there...you know like if a tree falls in a wood and no-one's there to see it, did it happen?'

'Just on that one,' Jim chirps up, 'how do we know the tree has fallen unless we have that knowledge? Someone has to tell us 'a tree has fallen'. That bugs me...'

'Quite,' says Jayne. Carries on, 'Well it seems as if characters *were* frozen unless I observed them. I brought them, melted them, into life.'

'Without the drug discrepancy,' Jim quips.

'Yes, indeed. But this bringing to life didn't happen with all the characters.' Dan looks at her again as if willing her to stop. Jayne senses this and says, 'So there you have it. Some of the characters might be dependent on us being there.'

'But what about the others. If we have a book, yes, I know, very old-fashioned of me. But. If we have a book filled full of characters, that we can turn to at any time and at any time and place within the book, they come to life as we read the words. Words about them and words out of their mouths. It's as if they're waiting for our eyes. Waiting for our eyes to bring them alive.'

'What are they though,' Dan says, 'what are these double F characters really? They're products of AI and VI. Of drugs, consciousness, creativity. They don't have volition...'

'Don't they?' Jayne speaks up.

'What do you think Jim?' Dan says.

'It feels as if they're real. They act as if they're real. They look real, everything they do seems real.'

'Exactly,' Dan says.

'I agree Jim,' Jayne says. 'I agree, but they obviously can't be. They have no substance. There isn't a place to go to find them...'

'In my mind,' Jim says, 'and if you've been in a future-field too, you know it *is* real. How does it differ from this life?'

Jayne says, 'Well the only thing I can say is that I felt some of the characters were simply responding to me – responding to digital instructions.'

'But in the real double F, I think it would be *totally* real,' Jim says.

'You're a convert Jim,' Dan says.

'I'm a realist,' he jokes.

Jayne looks at Dan. 'Jim, we have to trust you. Don't mention any of this...not even to the doctor. Okay?'

'Okay. Surely the doctor knows?'

'Maybe yes, maybe no,' Dan says.

'Maybe it is, maybe it isn't,' Jim says, part quoting from the old man he met inside his double F.

'Maybe there'll be more to this than meets the eye,' Jayne says, smiling.

Dan looks at her. 'I have to do some work on the main computer,' he says. 'It's been a fuck of a day.'

'And it isn't over,' Jayne says. 'We'll do more work with you tomorrow. Are you staying over Jim?'

'Am I invited?'

They laugh.

'Have a drink,' Jayne says. 'We have quite a lot of work to catch up on. You could talk to some of the guardians, if you wanted. They'd appreciate a new face with something to say.'

'Maybe,' he says. 'One thing,' Jim continues, 'I've been into my created world. But could I go into *any* created world in the same fashion?'

'That's what the avatar does,' Jayne explains. It syncs with the computer, yes with the addition of some drugs, but it's easy. Maybe you don't need the drugs with the suit, we'll be trying that out. Soon.'

'Why do you even need avatars?' Jim asks.

'All sorts of reasons,' Dan says. 'But we are doing this for...'

'For those higher up. Listen,' Jayne says, 'when you go into your double F, you're half-way there because it all resonates deep within you. With an avatar you can plunge into any world...'

'We think,' Dan says.

'We think,' Jayne continues, 'and be totally immersed. Like I was. I was totally in it, but I was also observing. We're trying to get these avatars so that they're easy and quick to use.'

'But what for?' Jim asks.

Dan says, 'We don't know exactly.' He looks at Jayne. 'Well we don't. Maybe just to do checks. If there are problems.'

'But the doctor says there are no problems.'

Jayne says quickly, 'If we see unusual brain patterns, are alerted by a computer, instead of un-branching, we could send someone in. See what's happening.'

'Hmmm. I don't know. Doesn't sit right with me. What if someone came into my world?'

'Well, it would be interesting,' Dan says. 'Think of it that way. And maybe…'

'Maybe?'

'I don't know,' he says flatly.

'So my experience is different from an avatar's, at the moment?' Jim asks. They nod. 'But I could use an avatar to access my own future-fields?'

'Yes. But there would be no point,' Jayne says. 'You don't want to be an observer. It is *your* world. Your world, inside and out.'

'I can really see why the doctor has taken to you,' Dan says.

'Are you sure?'

'Of course,' Jayne says.

Jim thought about the avatar. About its ethics. If anyone could use it, did it change to fit the person, or did the person change to fit it? He felt uneasy about possible privacy violations. Jim decided to visit the Forgetmenot. He'd walked past it, but hadn't yet gone in, as Doctor Abraham had stressed it wasn't for clients. Clients were to be forgotten. He also thought about both his time for entering double F and the time he would eventually die. There was no rescuing. He'd be a limp doll if they took him out after a few years. Resurfacing into what would then be an alien world. A living ghost. But he thought about what people would be doing – even those close to him. Yes, they'd think about him but they couldn't keep thinking about him. Trivia would balance their concerned thoughts. Cooking. Eating. Watching some mindless stream. Typing in data. Answering a call. Reflecting. Scratching. Remembering something completely at odds with the situation. Disconnected thoughts, as he was disconnecting from life. They'd be getting on with their lives. And soon he'd be forgotten by most.

Jim thought of Jimi and his music. That music, those vibrations kept beaming out. Someone, somewhere was keeping his memory, his work alive.

The Forgetmenot was close by, he'd passed the AI and VI pods and then carried on down a corridor. He walked up to the door. He had to look in an eye scanner. The door did not open. Looking inside he saw some people in the gym section. There were open plan retail areas he could make out. Again he looked into the scanner. Had they forgotten about him already? No entry. No entry to this world of fun. Another door led into the inner garden and Jim opened it and stepped through. The sky was dark and ominous. Fat rain drops fell intermittently. Closing his eyes, he could hear as the drops splatted on the stone path or where they hit the trees branches. A drop landed on his upturned face. He felt its spray on an eyelash. The drops were cold. They came faster. The dark clouds had rolled closer and denser and a crack of thunder made him flinch. He ran as the rain wet his clothes. Ran down the main path to the glass doors. Even Nature herself seemed to want to keep him penned in. Reaching the doors, he bent over and took in deep breaths. He was alive. And maybe for the first time this really hit home. He was alive. Breath, blood, skin. Alive. Mind working. Wonderful life all around - and the sound of rain lashing down.

As Dan began preparing Jim's next experience of his new world, Jim looked around the room, especially at the bright white technology.

'Where's Jayne?' Jim asks.

'She's working with another client.'

'Is that why we're in a different creation room?'

'Yes.'

'But everything works the same?'

'Yes. The technology is linked. The only difference is, I'll have to do a little more work.'

Jim smiles. 'I've had some other thoughts,' he says. 'I had ideas popping in my head all night and even this morning.'

'Go on,' Dan says, still busying himself.

'In my double F, I'll need to keep learning, keep my mind stimulated. Not just talking to characters, or walking across the hills.' Dan nods. Jim continues, 'I'd like a piano. I'd like a piano and therefore a piano tuner. It would have to be kept in tune, I suppose. Presumably once I'm in my double F it will be too late to add new things...'

Dan looks at him. Nods again, but only slightly. 'There may be developments there,' he says, enigmatically. 'Carry on.'

'Well a piano teacher would be good too and lots of music – all the music from the past, so I can choose whatever I want and the piano teacher could play me pieces to see what I think. See if I like them and if I want to learn them.'

'Start off with something really easy,' Dan says.

'Of course.'

'Twinkle, twinkle little star,' Dan says.

Jim's mouth falls open. 'Are you joking?'

'No,' Dan says, smiling. 'You've got to start somewhere. You know the tune, I presume. You can start with that and gradually move on to complicated and great works. You'll have all the time you need.'

'Okay,' Jim says. 'I'll start with that. On your recommendation.' They both laugh. He thinks further. 'I'll need books. All the great books. I don't want to read on a screen. There could be a huge bookshelf in the living room, where the piano would go too. Shelves stuffed with books. Can we do that?'

'As long as the computer has the texts which it should have, we can certainly do that. You 'll need to do some research.'

'Well, I'll have all the well-known writers,' Jim says, 'but I also want books on physics and life after death,' he smiles, 'and... yes, that's another thing. I would want books on poetry and art. And if I decide to paint, I'll need painting material.'

'Where has all this come from?' Dan asks. 'Were you waiting for Jayne's absence so you could show your sensitive side?' he smiles.

'It struck me in the night, or early morning,' Jim says. 'I suddenly thought: what am I going to do? I might have what could feel like an eternity there. I need to keep my mind sharp. Because everything will stem from my mind, won't it?'

Dan nods. 'We would have suggested ideas for pastimes.'

'I want to learn. Not, pass time. I wanted to learn the piano as a child. And I want to create something...'

'You're creating a whole new world, Jim.'

'I mean, create, create. You know. Something that's never existed before.'

'Your world has never existed, it's unique.'

'Yes, but it's like this world. I've never really created in *this* world. Not really...'

'Okay,' Dan says. 'We can do all that. You have plenty of time to get all the music and books you need. And painting material.'

'What about transport? I was thinking about that too.'

'Do you need that? Think back to your previous experiences, you went from one place to another in a blink of an eye.'

'Not always. I walked down the hill and I walked to the shop, remember.'

'Because you wanted to.' Dan smiles. 'But you can have any transport you wish. It would be interesting to see if it works.'

'Could be dangerous, I suppose,' Jim says.

'Well...' Dan falters, not sure exactly what Jim means.

Jim changes tack, says enthusiastically, 'I'd like to play football, too. In a stadium. Can we do that?'

Dan nods. 'How good are you?'

'At my age? Rubbish.'

'But as you know, Jim. You won't *be* at your age.' Dan pauses. 'Have you ever felt tired in your world?'

Jim thinks. Recalls walking down from the hill. 'I don't think so. But I did go to bed and sleep in the cottage. So, perhaps sometimes.'

'True. I think we prompted that idea though. Anyway, we'll make sure you have some template footballers, who are happy to play with you,' Dan laughs. 'Pass you the ball at least. You'll have energy enough to pass it back,' he jokes.

'I'll invite all the people from my double F to watch us play.' Jim sees himself strolling out onto the pitch, with the crowd cheering. Would there be a crowd?

Dan says, 'Excuse me a moment. Get comfortable, I'll put you under shortly. A good submersion.'

Jim watches Dan leave the room, then sits back and imagines himself scoring a great goal. And then sees himself saving a penalty.

Outside their usual creation and control rooms, Dan opened a door tentatively. He stepped in. Jayne was not there. She was probably still getting ready. As he waited for her, he began connecting one of the computers to Jim's future-fields. He smiled thinking about Jim's desire to learn. Not everyone was like that. Most people weren't like that. But they'd had some very creative folk over the years. He'd also talked with Jayne about how useful the avatars might be for future experiences. It was just a shame her suit wasn't quite ready.

A door opens at the end of the room. 'Dan. Thought I heard you.'

'Jayne. Come on over, lie down and I'll fix the suit to your face and get you connected. Everything okay?'

'Yes. And Jim?'

'All fine. He's come up with some new ideas. I'll tell you later. Okay. Stay here. I'll get the HS connected for you and then get Jim on his way. Lie down, get comfortable. Okay. There you go. I won't be long.'

'I need to prepare and concentrate myself,' she says.

'Yes, indeed. Shame we couldn't have switched to the doc's avatar. But it would be a bit of a giveaway,' he laughs.

'And mine's nowhere near ready,' she grumbles.

'No rush,' he says. 'At least the prof's going to be happy.'

Dan finally got them both ready, it was awkward, but necessary that they were in separate rooms. At least he could monitor both computers simultaneously. He wondered about the hi-tech equipment Transcorp was meant to have and how that would affect experiences. But he could only speculate. With Jim on his way into his future-fields, Dan turned his attention to Jayne.

'You're ready for this? It's going to be different from last time at least.'

'Yes. If this works, then that's me done until we get our own avatars. The prof's attention will be off us then and it will all be legitimate expenses.'

'I might have to try the doc's avatar.' Dan continues to busy himself. 'Okay, all's ready. One moment...'

'Yes, yes…'

'Okay, count down again.' Dan hears her get gradually quieter – then she is out. 'Good,' he says. 'I just hope she understands what she has to do.'

Jim was on the bridge by the river. The sun was setting and there was a fresh smell to the air. There was also a drowsiness about the air, and the animals he could see, seemed languid. The river ran, like it always ran beneath the wooden bridge, coming from somewhere and going to somewhere else. He felt content. There were echoing bird cries. He walked from the bridge down the path to the wall, along it and then pushed open the wooden door and found himself back in his garden. Though in someways it felt as if he just appeared there. As if there was information missing from his consciousness. There was the familiar smell of wood smoke drifting over. A sheep bleated from a distance. But he could also hear the sound of a guitar.

There sitting on the bank of the garden, before it dropped down in front of the kitchen window, was Ronnie. Ronnie was bent over his guitar and facing towards the cottage. Jim crept up behind him. Ronnie was chording strings but also managing to play a melody and bass line at the same time. It was *Little Wing*.

As Jim gets closer, he sings: *moonbeams and fairytales that's all she ever wanted...*

Ronnie looks about but more-or-less manages to keep the tune intact. 'Jim. How you doin' man?'

'Good to see you Ronnie. It always seems so long.'

'Just the other day,' Ronnie laughs. 'You always catch me playing Jimi,' he smiles. Finishes a flourish of notes and then plays a slow blues ending. Stops. Holds his guitar and slides down the bank, placing it carefully in its case, lying there. 'Anna and Rosie are inside.'

'Cool,' Jim says. Seems he's going to meet Anna again. There's something curious about her name. Ronnie walks past the kitchen window, case in hand, and peers in. Jim walks along the bank and down some steps as the sun flickers behind tree branches, backlighting their leaves. It feels like an eternal summer's day. And with this thought Jim hears the chimes of a solitary bell. Maybe it was counting out time.

They enter the kitchen and Ronnie props his guitar against a corner. Jim can hear voices from the living room. Goes to investigate.

'Fancy a brew?' Ronnie calls out.

'Please.'

'Ask them if they want one too.'

Jim hovers outside the slightly ajar living room door.

'Jim.' He doesn't move. 'Come in,' Anna says. Rosie smiles as he tentatively steps in. 'Join us,' Anna says, patting the settee beside her. Jim looks around, there's no stacked bookcase and no piano. Mentally he places them in his vision – but nothing materialises. There isn't instant magic. What is he expecting? Jim stops and thinks about this. Two worlds colliding.

'Jim,' Anna says, a little more authoritatively. 'Sit down.'

Jim comes to his senses. 'Tea,' he says. 'Do you both want tea? Ronnie's putting the kettle on.' They both say 'yes'.

'I'll be back,' Jim says. He doesn't feel entirely in this dream, or reality, or whatever it is in this world. But it *is* his world. Goes back to the kitchen. 'Yeah,' he says. 'All up for tea.'

'I'll bring it through,' Ronnie says, 'and some cakes, they're bound to want cakes. Well I do,' he laughs.

Jim re-enters the living room. Sits next to Anna tentatively. She puts her arm around him. But excusing himself he gets up and leaves the room again.

In the kitchen, Ronnie goes to the oven and takes out a tray of cakes which are warm. Picks one up and takes a bite. 'Excellent. These are going to blow their fucking minds!' Laughing, he puts his thumb and first finger together against his lips. 'Magnifique,' he says in a mock French accent. 'Cordon right-on blue.' Sees Jim in the doorway looking at him. 'Jim, you're like a ghost,' he laughs. Ronnie enters the living room balancing a tray precariously. Feels some kind of tension, which he brushes off. 'Tea and cakes m'lord and ladies.'

Jim quickly sits down by Anna. He laughs. Jim can smell Anna's perfume...it reminds him...

'Jim. Here you go, tea and rather a tasty cake I made earlier.'

'You'll have to eat it Jim or Ronnie'll be upset,' Rosie laughs.

'More than one apiece,' Ronnie says.

Jim feels his body close to Anna's. Puts his mug of tea on the arm of the settee. 'Careful,' Anna says.

He takes a bite of the cake. 'Nice. An unusual taste.' With this Rosie laughs. Jim hungrily eats the whole of the cake. Settles back on the settee and begins to relax. As Ronnie entertains them all, and with laughter reverberating around the old room, Jim begins to feel detached. He starts thinking about...well, he doesn't know what about, just that he is thinking deeply. He can hear the clock ticking – it becomes louder than any other sound. And it's as if his body is sinking into the cushions of the settee. The light through the window almost imperceptibly dimming. He feels as if he is dreaming, yet fully awake. The sound of them talking and laughing becomes disjointed from reality. For the first time he really looks consciously at the furniture, at the paintings hanging on the walls. At the walls themselves. The wood of the door and jamb. Then really tastes the tea as he brings the mug to his lips. It is as if he is retreating into himself but at the same time becoming more aware of his surroundings. His thoughts swirl round and then seem to spiral down in ever decreasing circles, like a soft vortex. And then he is gone. But he doesn't know he is gone. And then he's back. Back into his mind. Snapping into consciousness.

'Have another cake,' Ronnie says.

'Put some music on, Rosie,' Anna says. 'Something cool.'

Jim looks at Ronnie, says nothing. Ronnie's laugh jumps about the air. The light is changing. Nobody seems to notice. Jim feels its subtlety. Feels the nature of that room – is it old, is it new? It is an old room but it's also as if it belongs in a dream. The music kicks in with a bass drum and a rolling bass guitar. Percussion clacks and jabbers, pushing itself into the mix. The congas are raw and beautiful. Then there's some strange sounds and a guitar chopping the rhythm. Jim is surprised by the complexity. Where is he?

Anna smiles, 'Good cakes.'

Rosie laughs. 'I feel like dancing, gets up and moves around the room. Ronnie watches her, transfixed. Anna holds Jim's hand and he feels her essence through the touch of their skin. It can't be a dream. Because he can feel. And he knows he can feel. Maybe a lucid dream. Maybe this is what a lucid dream feels like. A guitar solo dances in the air, weaves and spreads its sound, then takes a bow. Jim begins to feel his thoughts eddy again and it is as if his consciousness is sucked down into a vortex once again. The music becomes texture. And he is gone. Gone. Nothing. For how long? Then with a laugh from Rosie, he is again brought back into that reality. Coming up for air.

There is a knock at the front door. Like cannon fire. Instinctively Jim gets up. Walks to the door and concentrates on stepping through the doorway out into the corridor. Shutting the door behind him he senses the atmosphere change. The door is knocked again. There is light from a small window above the doorway. Its light illuminating the air around him and he sees dust motes dancing. Tentatively he turns the knob and opens the heavy wooden door. A man is standing there. Not too old, but not young.

'Mr Holden? Jim Holden?'

'Yes.'

'I have a message for you,' the man says.

'A message? A message, who from?' Jim finds himself saying. A cold sweep of reality passing through him.

'Things are not all they appear to be,' the man says. 'Remember me.'

Jim does not know what to say. The man smiles, looks at him, then turns and walks away down the path. Jim stands in the doorframe. Again he notices the falling light. Smells the air, rich with fragrance from the flowers in the small, but long, front garden. At the gate the man turns and waves to him. Jim has the words, *things are not all they appear to be* playing in his mind. He watches as the man walks away. How long does he stand there? He doesn't know.

The music has stopped. Jim walks back to the living room. Where they live. Where they relax. He can hear the clock ticking remorselessly. Pushing the door open he sees Anna asleep on the settee. Rosie and Ronnie are gone. And then he too is gone.

He is at the top of the hill, the closest to the village. Ronnie is there, playing guitar. There is a light wind. And he can see the sun setting, layering its colours, like spilt paint over a hazy carpet. Jim feels totally relaxed and lies back on the grass. The air is still warm. The air is still warm...the air is still warm...

Jim comes round slowly.

'Jim, it's Dan. Breathe easily. If you can, try and remember your experience, like holding onto a dream.'

Dan worked hard at bringing them both back into everyday consciousness; switching between the rooms. It was much easier with Jim but he needed Jayne ready in the room with them both. He decided to maintain a slight amount of drugs in Jim's system, figuring that could well help him recall events. Plus, that would make his return to full consciousness that bit longer.

'Jim, keep hold of your thoughts, whatever you experienced, try and remember.' Jim nods. 'Close your eyes and let yourself drift back if you can. Jayne will be with us soon.'

Dan leaves the room, leans back on the corridor wall then moves down to where Jayne is.

'Are you okay Jayne?' he asks as she opens a door from the control room. She has changed from the avatar suit.

'I feel a little...well my head feels like it's full of cotton wool. I feel a bit sick.' As she says this she heaves and vomits. 'Sorry.'

'Don't worry, I'll have it cleaned up. Come with me, I'll get you a coffee. We'll go in with Jim. Do you feel a bit better? Wait here a minute.' He fetches her a box of tissues from Jim's room. 'Old technology,' he jokes. 'I'm not going to give you any recovery drugs. I know...But ideally, I need both you and Jim as clean as possible. Jim's still slightly under.' She nods. 'Will you be okay?'

'I don't feel like being sick again,' she says. 'I do feel like a diver who's come up too quickly though. It's what you always relate it to.'

'Yes. Maybe I did bring you out too quick. Take some deep breaths. Let me know when you're ready.'

She finishes wiping her mouth. 'Ready.'

Jim holds onto fast fading imagery. Dan and Jayne enter. Dan gets Jayne a coffee and sits her down near Jim. 'Okay,' he says. 'Just a quick break down.'

'So soon?' Jim asks.

'Yes Jim. I'm sorry. Has to be now. Do you remember anything unusual about your experience?'

'A lot of weird feelings. Losing myself...'

'Who were you with?'

'I think. I *think*,' he emphasises, 'it was Rosie, Ronnie and Anna.'

'You're getting better at this,' Dan says. 'Anyone else?'

'No. No I don't think so...'

Dan looks at Jayne. 'Did you open the door to the cottage at any time?'

Jim thinks. 'No. Ummm. I'm not sure.' He feels sleepy but something fights to get back into his mind. 'Maybe. Maybe. There was a knock at the door. Yes, a knock at the door. Like a cannon. Then...'

'Go on,' Jayne says.

'There was a man. Yes. A man standing there. This is weird,' he says.

'Did the man say anything,' Dan says, looking at Jayne.

'Did he say anything?' Jayne urges, energy revitalising her.

Jim is silent. Then. 'Something about not forgetting something. Remember this conversation or something. It was a message.' He pauses. 'Not everything is like it is.' Again he pauses. 'Not quite that.' He thinks hard. 'Things are not always as they appear to be,' he says slowly. 'Yes, yes. That was it. And: remember me. He wanted me to remember him. I have. I can,' he says excitedly. 'I can.' Jim lifts himself up.

Jayne looks at Dan. 'Shall we tell him?' Dan nods. 'That was me Jim, that man was me!'

'What?' He lies back down, resting his head on the thin pillow.

'In the avatar suit. I visited your world Jim and I got a message to you and you remember it. We've done it!'

'Done what?' Jim asks, gazing at the ceiling.

Dan says, 'We've connected the two worlds. We can do it. Not just visit but communicate.' Then suddenly, 'Not a word Jim, you understand?'

'Sure.' Jim lifts himself again. Dan gets a large pillow to prop him up.

'I feel like a discoverer of a new world,' Jayne says.

'Of my world,' Jim says.

'Indeed,' Jayne says.

Jayne and Dan look at each other knowingly.

Jim rests his head back. Other thoughts come to him.

It was all getting stranger and stranger.

'Thank you, John,' Milly says. 'We can meet up whenever you want. Shame you couldn't have ditched Veronica and come out...Alistair told Jake that we had replaced you.' She laughs. 'Sure...the isles are great. Everything's gone to plan. You know Jake got sent off to Africa by Alistair...' She smiles. 'Yes...Obviously. We've now well and truly got him...Quite...About us? No. No-one suspects. No-one questions a nervous, crazy woman.' She laughs. She listens intently. 'The new OT will be ready very soon, there have been a few logistical problems. We have everything almost ready. I've been busy while I'm here. Don't worry. We have a donor lined up and we have our first recipient. Bennett is aware. Trust me...Yes, as you suggested. Almost like the old days,' she smiles. 'Thursday the eleventh. It'll give Jake more time, he did a great job on the continent. Ariadna kept an eye on him…yes. And the prof. She's good...Yes, John. I watched you on the broadcast, was that your excuse? It was really good. Thank you for wearing the watch. Did Veronica ask any questions? Good. Okay...and me too...love you.'

Milly briefly thinks of her mother.

Jake hadn't seen Vicky after returning from the continent. By the time he and Ariadna got back to the isles everyone's energy seemed spent. The holiday felt over. The professor had debriefed him and had had confirmation of the successful operation from his contact at the hospital. He'd been able to have a short conversation with his friend too. Everything had gone excellently. He also went through Portway's business, the opening of the new Transcorp centre and explained the nature of the business at hand. The operating theatre suite was to be kept as secret as possible – but if word got out it could easily be explained away as being necessary for post-mortem use. The clientele were going to be rich, so there was even the possibility of operations and transplants *pre*-future-fields. The healthier someone was, the longer their survival. Of course, such explanations would simply be used as cover. Transcorp being in Portway helped its covert nature. Their main offices would continue 'transforming people's lives'.

Bennett was Jake's contact at the Transcorp centre. But the professor also had a surprise for Jake.

On the eve of their return Jake had again searched for Vicky but she was nowhere to be seen. He'd tried to talk with Nayra too but was told it was not her shift and she wouldn't be back before they'd all left. That last evening had been mostly taken up with him speaking with Milly and Alistair over dinner. Just general Portway business, and when Milly had excused herself, Alistair had asked Jake about the avatars. But he also told him he needed to talk about something in particular, in private. And arranged to meet outside, in front of the reception at ten o'clock.

'Jake,' thanks for coming,' the professor says. Jake smiles. 'Let's sit down over there.'

'Alistair,' Jake says, 'not too cold for you?'

'It's the coldest night we've had but it's not bad.' Alistair looks at Jake, pauses, then taking a chair sits down. 'I wanted to thank you again. As you know, I've spoken with my friend. Just very briefly. But I owe you a great debt. You will be paid, of course. But I owe you more than money.' Jake says nothing. 'You did an excellent job, and Ariadna too. I told you about Transcorp – well you probably knew most of it anyway as Bennett was in contact.'

'Yes, I got to know early on, ish. But I didn't tell Dan or Jayne or any of the teams. Bennett said that was to come from you. I should have talked with you, perhaps.'

'Yes, that was my instruction. I was going to come over to Portway and talk specifically with you and the teams. But I know Bennett discussed security with you and that you briefed Portway's security.'

'Nothing escapes you Alistair.'

'I hope not. I trust not,' he looks at Jake. 'Well, I want to keep Transcorp's involvement as hush-hush as possible, as you know. Info will probably get out at some point but at which time I'll hope it'll all be normalised – especially with the cover stories. There shouldn't be any logos on the building or on their security.'

'No, but their security is obviously not ours.'

'Which you've dealt with as best you can.'

'I think so.'

'Know so,' Alistair says. 'Do you mind?' Alistair asks, taking out a cigar.

Jake smiles, 'Of course not.'

'All the rage on the isles, apparently,' Alistair says. Lights up. 'Anyway, where were we...'

'Transcorp.'

'Yes. Their first operation. I'm arranging for you to be in charge. It will be something special.'

'Special?'

'Yes. Very special. Quite an inauguration.'

'Go ahead,' Jake urges.

'Well. A heart transplant.'

'Oh. I see.' Jake pauses. 'Professor, Alistair, you know I have never done one before?'

'I do. But you'll have nearly a month, at least three weeks I imagine to swat up. I assume you have a simulator?'

'Yes, at my place.'

'I'll have a state-of-the-art package sent to Portway. All being well you'll get a number of practices in.'

Jake takes in a deep breath. 'Okay,' he says.

'You're good. You're intelligent. You're adaptable. And you'll have full back up. But...'

'But?'

'You can't let me down Jake. It's a matter of face. You know. You'll be representing Portway.'

Jake nods solemnly.

'You can do it?'

'I can do it,' Jake says.

'Good man. It'll be a piece of cake,' Alistair smiles.

Jake went to say goodbye to Ariadna but she told him she was flying to the UK first. They sat together on the plane. He didn't see Vicky or any of the girls or the boy. He wanted to talk with Alistair about Vicky but Ariadna took his attention. They seemed to get on well.

At the airport, back in the UK, they all went their various ways, to spend the weekend as they wanted. Ariadna had a plush government hotel booked, usually reserved for visiting dignitaries. The professor had sorted this out for her. Jake said goodbye and took her hand. As he watched her leave, she turned and waved. Jake then booked transport from the airport back to his house. He imagined they'd all have expected him to go straight to Portway. But he didn't want to be predictable. He wanted to do nothing and see no-one. Not quite nothing in fact. He would set up the simulator in his home office, which he rarely used, download various programs and go over and over the operation he was expected to conduct. It had been one heck of a week. There was no time for him to relax from work – but he could relax from company.

Wednesday, March 10th – the day before the operation

Jake had been liaising with Bennett, who was courteous and efficient, but somewhat controlling. There would be an opening ceremony for invited guests that very afternoon and then the inaugural operation the following day. Jake was ready. As ready as he possibly could be given the amount of days he'd had. The new simulator had been installed in one of the creation rooms - it could also be used to simulate future-fields and other scenarios. Jake was able to immerse himself totally in the technology – it was, he imagined, the next best thing to an avatar suit. It felt incredibly real when he practised surgery. Almost shockingly real and he could only imagine the money it must have cost. It seemed Portway or Transcorp, or both, could afford it.

At the opening, security was tight. Cars entered Portway through the vehicle access and down into the hangar. Automatic barriers had been installed and everyone checked at entry. John Hughes-Kahn had been invited and he arrived with his wife and Professor Stone and Milly. His motor was top of the range.

At the Transcorp centre, all visitors congregated in the reception area. It was beautifully laid out and very stylish. Jake had been the only one from Portway before the professor and Milly arrived. There was food and drink for the guests – perhaps would-be customers – while Transcorp's staff went about their business. Visitors were invited to look around and to talk freely with the staff and ask any questions they might have.

Jake took the opportunity to visit the operating theatre suite. It was a work of art. Apparently the staff there knew who he was and he was addressed as Mr Abraham. One of the cardiothoracic junior doctors was there. And a fellow surgeon. They showed him the laser technology which would be used and the computer technology controlling all aspects of any assigned operation. Both operating theatres almost sparkled with cleanliness and Jake wore feet coverings, gloves and a mask. He imagined himself operating in OT A the following day. It was a great honour.

His fellow surgeon gave him a guided tour of the instruments at his disposal and Jake also talked with the main computer. It was explained that the computer would be, in effect, a fellow surgeon. Also keeping an eye on procedure, the patients and staff. It had a miniature silent drone connected to it that could be used to see what was happening from above and close-up. Both OTs had the same equipment, which communicated.

Bennett arrives. 'Impressive isn't it?' he says through his mask.

'Very much so,' Jake says. 'I couldn't have wished for more. And with the specialist computer too.'

'Both are linked up to our main frame but yes, in here, it's certainly a specialist. Has direct links to its twin in OT B and the records of all the best surgeons' minds and experiences.'

'Best operating theatre I've ever seen,' Jake says, looking around. 'Thank you. I'll check out OT B too.'

'The staff are also top notch,' Bennett says. 'You'll be well supported.'

Jake inspected OT B, which was equally impressive. They then left the OT suite after disposing of their blues. Bennett accompanied Jake to the reception area where the professor, Milly, John Hughes-Kahn and Veronica were mingling. Alistair caught sight of Jake and called him over.

'Jake. Have you met John?'

'I haven't.'

'John, this is our surgeon tomorrow. I told you about him.'

John and Jake shake hands.

'Good luck,' John says. 'This is my wife, Veronica,' calling over to her as she speaks with another couple.

'Pleased to meet you,' Veronica says as she joins her husband. 'Are you nervous?' she asks quietly.

'Should I be?' Jake smiles.

'Of course not,' Milly interjects. Jake notices Veronica's reaction.

'You've met some of the team?' John asks.

'Yes. The OT suite is very impressive. And the computers.'

'Ah, the computers Bennett is always raving about, or so I've heard,' he laughs. 'Where has he got to?'

Jake shrugs. 'They're good. Very good. I think I'll be on autopilot.'

'Well, as long as the heart is taken out and transplanted successfully. Then we'll all be happy. And the recipient's life will be saved. You're privileged, Jake. A Portway man conducting Transcorp's inaugural operation.' John looks around regally.

Jake smiles nervously.

Alistair offers Jake a drink. 'Oh no,' Jake says, 'I'll need to be clean as a whistle, cleaner than the operating theatre and sharper minded than the computer.' They laugh.

'Dedication,' John says. 'Even on the day before.'

Jake called in on Dan and Jayne after leaving Transcorp. They were busy but he was able to ask about his own avatar. It was still waiting for completion. But perhaps he could try it out very soon. He then headed for his office where he sat down in his chair and closed his eyes. He was ready.

Jake arrived early at Portway, smiled at Milly but immediately went into his office. Today was the day. The operation was scheduled for eleven that morning. Later than they had originally planned but the earliest time possible. He would take the donor's heart out while OT B would take out the recipient's. His task was simpler so he could focus on the transplant itself. In the meantime he would do necessary admin, go over some cases and then prepare himself mentally, and eat. The time he spent both on the Isles of Africa and, indeed, Africa itself had almost blurred in his mind. Yes, there were moments he recalled with great accuracy but it was as if there had been a tumult of mixed emotions. Though he could draw from the narrative that ran through the experiences, especially the concentrated peak moments. His time in Africa had heightened not just his emotions but also his expectations and skills. Generally, he sensed a world that was beginning to open up. He had tasted it. And he would weave some of what he'd experienced into his future-fields – even though his civic duty was far off. Practically, he was also becoming impatient to try his avatar. Perhaps it was ready.

Half an hour before the operation he walked to the Transcorp centre. The guards knew who he was but they still insisted he show identification. He smiled at them. Inside, he was asked to wait but almost immediately a young man came to take him to the operating suite. Jake looked about the place as they walked, it appeared even more clinically aesthetic than it had done previously with all the VIP guests.

In the operating suite he was introduced to his fellow surgeon, Mr Devi Trehan and Marcus Kerry, a trained perfusionist. They did an initial scrub-up, got changed into their blues and scrubbed up again. They walked into Theatre A. Jake had yet to meet his fellow team. There would be time for that.

As he enters the OT, Jake sees Ariadna. 'Ah, a surprise, I see,' Jake says, smiling, his mask briefly pulled down.

Ariadna's eyes twinkle, 'The professor's idea.'

'Well I'm glad. The best scrub nurse there is.'

'Thank you Mr Abraham.'

'So formal?'

'We're in the OT,' she smiles beneath her mask.

'I take it the anaesthetist is monitoring and preparing the patient?'

'Yes,' Ariadna replies.

'Good.'

There is a team consisting of Jake, his fellow surgeon, the perfusionist, a junior doctor, the anaesthetist, Ariadna and another nurse.

The anaesthetist arrives. 'Good morning Mr Abraham.' They bump hands. 'Jenkins,' he says. There is a slight pause. 'The donor is being prepped for anaesthetic and has been given a sedative. We will intubate them in the OT once we have administered the muscle relaxant and analgesia.'

'Of course,' Jake says, wondering if they trust him and his expertise. 'Thank you, it's good to have a reputable gasman,' he says in the vernacular. The anaesthetist smiles. The donor-patient is duly trundled into the operating theatre and slotted beneath the laser equipment. A drape has been placed over their head leaving enough space to allow a tube to be inserted and for the anaesthetist to monitor. The donor's body is duly attached to the computer. Jake cannot see the patient's identity but can see she is female. Her bare chest is washed with iodine leaving a dirty yellow hue across her skin. Apart from her chest, the rest of her body is covered in drapes. He briefly wonders who she is. Kept alive so someone else can live.

Ariadna attends to the body.

'Let us proceed,' Jake says to the team. 'You all know who I am and to be referred to as Mr Abraham,' he smiles beneath his mask. Cannulas have been inserted into the neck and groin of the donor-patient. Ariadna hands Jake a scalpel. 'Let us commence.'

Mr Trehan watches him closely. Jake makes an incision above the sternum and begins cutting the skin. Ariadna mops the blood, the other nurse watching her. 'Get the retractors ready please nurse.' Jake keeps cutting. Trehan offers to prepare the laser machine. Jake nods. They will have to cut right down through the middle of the breastbone.

The laser does its work and the retractors hold back the rib cage and the blood to the heart is diverted to the bypass machine. The heart has to be stopped. Kerry, the perfusionist takes control of the heart's function and the patient's oxygenation. The heart, which is now effectively severed from the body is stopped and injected with a drug to paralyse it. Time passes quickly in the intensity of the theatre. The micro-drone from the computer flies silently above them, feeding back information. All goes to plan.

Eventually and very carefully, Jake takes out the heart. He lifts it into the air admiringly; Trehan looking at him disapprovingly. The junior doctor with the team has a box ready and the heart is quickly but carefully put in and packed with ice. The box is insulated and closed. The junior doctor then looks around at the team. Jake says, 'Hurry man, take it to OT B and inform them myself *and* Ariadna will be with them shortly. And let us know if they have removed the heart and are ready or not.'

Trehan asks, 'Are *you* ready?'

Jake looks at him, their eyes connecting. Says nothing.

Jake says to his team, 'Right, that's my work done here. We've done well and it's gone fairly quickly. Mr Trehan will take over and supervise the removal of the kidneys and anything else we can salvage. Switch off the machine when all organs have been removed,' he says to Kerry. The patient is dead.

Trehan says to the other nurse, 'Contact the eye surgeon and ask him to come in please.'

The anaesthetist removes the drape over the cadaver's head, ready for the eye surgeon to remove the retinas and then take out the eyes. As he does this and as Jake is ready to leave the theatre, the cadaver's face is revealed. Jake freezes. Ariadna watches him intently, she picks up on this abrupt change of emotion. Jake cannot move. He looks at his bloodied, gloved hands. Looks about. Looks at Trehan and Kerry and then at Ariadna. Then finally at the corpse. At the face, white, still beautiful. But quite dead. To this moment the body had been anonymous - just a body. Nothing more. It could have been the engine of a car they'd been working on. Not even human. A machine to be dissembled. A beautiful machine. But she was very, very human.

'Vicky,' he mouths.

On the Same Day

Dan and Jayne explained to the professor how he must prepare for his experience. Alistair readily took the opportunity to get into his avatar while Jake was performing the heart operation. He knew who the donor was and presumed Jake would not discover her identity. Though he didn't give this much thought, it seemed fitting and poetic in a macabre way.

He wanted to be the first to try out the avatar properly, even if according to Dan, Jake's was now ready. It was simply perfect timing. Jayne decided the professor should go into the double F she had previously gone into - as his avatar. It made sense. Maybe Antonio would be there to greet him. Again.

Professor Stone was duly prepared, and as much as possible, mentally prepared.

'Count down,' Dan says. Jayne looks on, smiling. The professor is soon gone.

'We've done it,' Jayne says.

'Yes. Seems so. He's on his own. A full immersion for an avatar.'

'It's what he wanted,' Jayne says.

'It's what *we* wanted,' Dan says triumphantly.

Jake storms out of the operating theatre, tearing off his gloves, Ariadna following him.

'Do you know anything about this?' he asks.

'You mean, did I know this patient was a donor?'

'You think I'm stupid?! No, do you know who the girl is? Was?'

Ariadna shakes her head. 'No.'

Jake scrutinises her. 'Maybe you don't. But the professor must have known or Bennett. I'll find him.'

'Don't do anything stupid Jake,' she says as he tears off all his blues. Jake scowls at the eye surgeon who has arrived, then dressing quickly leaves the suite and strides down the corridor. He finds his way back to the reception area.

'Do you know where Bennett is?' he barks at the receptionist.

She is visibly nervous, 'No. Doc... Mr Abraham.'

'Doctor,' he spits.

As he says this Bennett enters the building, the inner door swishing open before him. 'Ah, Doctor Abraham,' Bennett says. 'Or should I address you as Mr Abraham?' he smiles. Jake stares at him. 'Everything okay?' Bennett asks. 'Was the initial operation a success? I was hoping to catch you...'

'Operation a success,' Jake repeats. 'Who for?'

'Well, for us,' Bennett says, unsure of Jake's reaction.

Jake strides right over to him, he is taller than Bennett. 'Did *you* choose the donor for this operation?'

Bennett shakes his head. 'No, why? Because she's female? You know very well that there's absolutely no problem with that these days...'

Jake stares at him. 'Tell me truthfully, did you choose the girl?'

'No I didn't. That was arranged by the professor. He explicitly helped Transcorp out. What's the problem? The heart's for...well, for someone important. Has he been prepared yet? Shouldn't you be…I mean is the recipient ready for his heart? Aren't you transplanting it?'

'You got your heart,' Jake spits. 'You say the professor chose her?'

'Yes. We'll be using Portway for this kind of thing. That's the whole point. I think you know, well I thought you knew about this. There's money in it. For all of us. You have the facilities, contacts...Your skills...'

'Shut. Up.' Jake says the words slowly. 'Shut the fuck up.'

'Really!' Bennett says. Goes to tap his chest.

'Call security and I'll knock you into the next world, understand?'

Bennett's hand pauses. Jake pushes past him, straight out the swishing inner doors then through the main doors. A security guard turns to him.

'Keep out of this,' Jake says. The guard looks bewildered. Flustered. Jake hurries on. As he walks, he pulls out his phone and calls Milly.

'Jake?'

'Where's Stone?' he asks.

'Stone?' she says, unused to hearing Jake refer to the professor in that manner. 'He was here earlier,' she says. 'He was hoping to talk with you...'

'Good. I want to talk with him. Where is he?'

'He...he went to the creation rooms...' Milly, like the guard, is flustered by Jake's tone. Wonders what's happening. For the first time she seems unsure of what is going on. Why is he acting like that? 'Was the preliminary operation a success?' she asks. 'I heard it was. Now for the…'

'Who told you?'

'Ariadna.'

'When?' More to himself he says, 'Right now I imagine she'll be after me with Trehan.' Then, 'She didn't tell you I was on my way out? But she let you know straight away about the op, why? You must know her,' he stresses. 'Yes, of course you do. Some kind of connection.'

Milly says nothing as another internal line flashes repeatedly.

'You know her,' he repeats slowly. 'I think you might know a whole lot more about everything, Milly. You and the professor. You and Ariadna. Who knows who…'

'I...I...'

Jake cuts the call, turns and heads for the creation rooms. Determined. Blood pulsing through his veins. Already hyped-up from the intensity of the operation and discovering Vicky. Nothing or no-one is going to stop him.

Trehan, Ariadna and a security guard arrive at Transcorp's reception. 'Where is he?' Trehan asks loudly. The receptionist cannot speak. Then, 'Where's Bennett?' She points to a room.

Ariadna says to Trehan, 'You need to get back. You'll have to take over or supervise the transplant. Who took the heart out in OT B?'

Trehan falters. Ignores her question. 'Get Bennett,' he says. 'What's he playing at? He's got to sort this out and quick.' To the guard he shouts, 'Have you alerted security? Where are they all?' Just as he says this a team arrives. Trehan nods at them and returns quickly towards the operating suite.

Ariadna addresses the team, 'Find Doctor Abraham, hold him if you can. Be respectful. Nothing too rough but I need to speak with him. If he won't cooperate then keep with him and keep me posted and I'll be with you as soon as I can.'

Ariadna and the guard stride over to the room where Bennett is.

At the creation and control rooms Jake goes directly to where Dan and Jayne usually operate from. Without knocking, he enters. Dan and Jayne turn to him and he sees someone in an avatar suit lying on a raised platform, connected to a computer.

'Doctor Abraham!' Jayne says.

Ignoring her, he says, 'Is that the professor?'

Dan nods.

Jake goes to the computer, sits down and bangs in a code.

'What are you doing doc?' Dan asks, alarmed, cutting off an incoming call.

'Putting things right.'

'But...but...we have everything in hand,' Jayne says.

'Not quite,' Jake says, overruling the computer's defences. 'There you go,' he says, and manually pulls out the connections from the professor's suit. 'Bon voyage,' Jake says sneeringly.

'Jayne, call security,' Dan says.

'Wait,' Jake barks. 'Wait,' he says more measured. 'Let me explain a thing or two, then call security if you still feel that's what should be done. I'm going nowhere. At least not yet. Don't call anyone. Turn off your phones. Listen.'

'Doctor?' Jayne says.

'Let me explain, but can you seal these rooms?'

'Why?' Dan asks.

'Transcorp security, I imagine, are right on my heels.'

Dan, nods to Jayne. Jayne sits at the computer. 'Done,' she says, adding, 'I don't want Transcorp anywhere near us.'

'What about the professor?' Dan asks.

'He'll have to wait,' Jake says. 'Gone to pastures new.'

'Can we get him back later?' Jayne says nervously to Dan.

'I don't know,' Dan says. 'I really don't know. We can try when the drugs have worn off…'

'Maybe you won't want to,' Jake says. 'Listen to me, carefully.' Dan takes a chair and sits close to Jayne. Jake continues, 'I've just completed an operation at Transcorp.' They look at him. 'I presume you know, maybe not. A heart removal – took a few hours. Took some expertise before the tricky job of putting it in someone else. Thing is, did I know I was taking the heart from a live body? Yes, of course. It had to be alive. But I didn't know it was a healthy body. I'm not talking about a brain-dead, living body. No. Worse. Much worse. A young healthy body, a girl. A girl I know. Knew. Beautiful, but an expendable girl, it seems. And you know what?' They look at him aghast. 'This is what Transcorp does. It's in the name. This is what Portway has set up. Allowed. Do you know why? Because they're in the game.'

'Game?' Jayne asks.

'The transplant game. Trans-corp. In it with the government too. Portway offers an extra layer of security. I know about this. I'm compromised. Have been for a while,' he says thinking of Vicky.

'You mean...?' Dan begins.

'I mean they have access to the suicide hubs; they have access to the young people ending their lives. They have access to the drawers and who or what goes in them. They control young men and women. Children. And they program them. And if someone steps out of line, they jump the queue for organ harvesting. And you know what? The professor knew I knew this girl. He was counting on me not discovering her identity. Her head was covered in drapes. But he was greedy and wanted everything she had to offer, not just her heart. Not just her kidneys. They were going to take her eyes too. Her eyes! And that's...' he stops, angry and emotional. 'And that's when I discovered who she was. It had probably given him some kind of a kick to know I didn't know. Or would he have told me when he wanted to. When he wanted to really hurt me. And I guess he crept down here, while I was occupied doing his dirty work and got into his avatar suit. Yes?'

Dan nods. Jayne looks to the floor.

'You are working for a corrupt organisation. Linked with the National Government and the State. Making money out of people's bodies. Their civic duty. Transcorp hiding their operating theatres under the guise of creation and control rooms. It's all a front.' He walks about the room. 'Now the question is, what do you want to do with me? Now that you know. Now you know that I knew what was going on. Sure, I was compromised. Funny thing is, compromised by my relationship, if you can call it that, with Vicky.'

'Vicky?' Dan asks. Jayne looks up.

'The young girl murdered by me and the Transcorp team.'

'But you didn't know,' Jayne blurts.

'I did before, with others,' Jake says. 'I am just as guilty. I was happy to have the glory,' he spits, 'of conducting Transcorp's first operation. The big man. Portway's man, doing the work for Transcorp. I was proving a point for the professor, showing Transcorp that he was the boss…That he has connections above them. Top government connections.'

Jayne and Dan look at each other. Dan says, 'What can we do?'

'Well,' Jake thinks. 'You can hand me over to Transcorp security and I'll no doubt disappear pretty quickly. Or you could put me in my avatar suit and send me off into Jim's world. I helped create it. I know I'd be safe. What to expect.'

'But you'll be discovered,' Dan says.

'Not if we say it's the professor in the suit,' Jayne says quickly. Dan looks at her with surprise. Jayne continues, 'We can do this. We hide the professor's body. Get the doctor into Jim's future-fields. Say we haven't seen him...Say we secured the rooms because the professor is here and it was all to be secret, until he found out if the avatar works or not.'

'But it'll be me in the suit,' Jake confirms.

Jayne nods. 'Then we get you in a drawer and wipe out your identity.'

'My civic duty coming sooner than I expected,' he says coldly.

'Yes, but you'll be alive. We can make it so they'll never find you.'

'Jayne!' Dan says. 'We'll be accomplices. He's done wrong.'

'We are already,' she says. 'We're part of all this. But we'll carry on, even if they shut Portway down they can't abandon the bodies at rest. The government would know that. We'll be safe. And in charge.'

'I'm impressed Jayne,' Jake says. 'But I *have* done wrong.'

'Thank you,' she smiles. 'You'll be in a kind of limbo. It's your price.'

'I'm kind of, but only kind of shocked,' Dan says, shaking his head.

'We have to do the best in these rotten circumstances,' Jayne says. 'We need to carry on here and protect everyone in their double Fs. I knew something was going on. I can't judge you too harshly doc.'

'Right,' says Dan. 'Let's get on with it. We have time, but I don't know how long.'

'We can do this, Dan,' Jayne says again. 'And we have to.'

'What happens to the professor?' Dan asks.

'Give him a shot or two to prolong the drug effects. As far as security's concerned he's fine in the suit and not to be disturbed. We just need to keep him out of the way for a while. I have no idea what will be happening in his mind. Where will that be, here or still in future-fields?'

'Okay,' Dan says. 'We'll get the doc in his own suit, switch the computer to its settings and Jim's future-fields and administer his HS. Why not make it as full an immersion as we possibly can.'

'We'll have to buy some time,' Jayne says.

'You're in charge, Jayne.'

'One further thing,' Jake says, then pauses. 'Do *not* trust Milly.' He pauses again. Contemplates. Then says, 'Maybe you can bring me back from the dead at some point.'

Dan and Jayne look at each other. Dan nods his head. Smiles slightly, says, 'If it's safe.'

'*When* it's safe,' Jayne says calmly.

On the Same Day

Jim was at home with Hannah working upstairs in the office. He was due to go into Portway the following Monday but nothing had yet been settled, and it was already Thursday.

'Hannah,' he calls up. 'HANNAH!'

Pushing the door open, she calls down, 'What?'

'Come down for some tea, take a break.'

After a few minutes she walks down the stairs.

'You need a break,' he says softly, passing her a mug of tea.

'Thanks.'

'Have you tried the doctor again?' he asks.

'I left a message yesterday and his secretary got back to me. Sorry, I forgot to tell you. He's performing a big operation today but will let me know, or you, before the weekend what's happening.'

'Leaving it late.'

'Do you need to go in so often?'

'I guess not.'

'So don't worry.' She sips her tea.

'Don't worry,' he says. 'I don't worry too much. I'm resigned to my fate.'

'Don't be so...'

'Melodramatic?' Jim laughs. 'It's all a question of time. Time and experience of that time.'

She holds out her hand and touches his. 'We'll see Joanne soon and Henry and Olivia are so happy. Obviously concerned about you.'

'None of it needs be like this,' Jim says quietly.

'I know.'

'At least I've been lucky with my health. Haven't really suffered. That's one good thing about civic duty, isn't it? I mean all the problems that come with old age. I know there are people who do still suffer, if they're lucky,' he says cynically. 'But. But a lot of things that we used to experience, we're now saved from. A lot of old age disease is a thing of the past. That's what they're always telling us. Banging on about. How lucky we are. A bit like Joanne putting an old dog down. It's done out of kindness. You wouldn't want the dog to suffer now, would you?'

'I don't want you to suffer,' Hannah says gently. 'But I want you with me for as long as possible.'

They both pause. Light streams in through the window.

'Do you want to know something funny?' Jim asks.

'Go on. Surprise me,' Hannah smiles. They seem to have come back to normal life.

'Well, it's the eleventh of March, right?'

'Yes.'

'That means it's nine months and a day to my birthday. So this is my conception.'

'Without the sex,' Hannah laughs.

'Yes. Just my conception. The moment I come into being. Right now. Today. It's not an exact science. But in nine months I'll be born into my future-fields.'

'Nine months and a few days,' Hannah says softly.

Jim looks at her. 'I'm conceived,' he says enigmatically, 'and I'm beginning to experience.'

'This is our experience,' Hannah says, a tear rolling down her cheek. 'Our experience.'

Printed in Dunstable, United Kingdom

80623116R10179